THE COMING OF
ARMAGEDDON
HISTORY'S LONGEST NIGHT

H. Richard Austin

Disclaimer: The book is based on extensive research utilizing sources around the world that are considered reliable; ongoing discussions and interviews; and the author's personal experience. Because of the difficulty of obtaining accurate information regarding China, a totalitarian state where information is carefully managed, what can be considered reasonable estimates are occasionally employed. Among various objectives, the book (a novel) attempts to "dramatize" the future implications of recent events and trends in the worldwide, economic and political scene. As a result fictional characters and situations are often used. Any similarity to actual persons is accidental and unintended.

The image on the cover is a declassified, U.S. Defense Department photograph from a series of nuclear tests known as "Castle Bravo" (1954).

ISBN 978-0-692-45238-7

Readers are invited to visit the book's website where related information of importance regarding the subject matter will be posted by the author on a regular basis - "**TheComingofArmageddon.Com.**"

The name "**Armageddon**" originates in the *Book of Revelations* and appears only once in the entire Bible. For nearly 2000 years this cryptic term shrouded in legend haunted humanity, and during all that time scholars were unable to agree about its meaning. What was never in doubt is that this troubling admonition at the end of Scripture embodies a stark warning that a disaster beyond imagining would one day befall the human race. In the early 21st century the world entered a time of prolonged crisis. Widespread signs of impending calamity appeared as if chaos itself was stalking the globe. These include an environment in turmoil; the world economy and its resources corrupted by speculation on a grand scale; and most ominous of all, the spread of incessant violence. In the Middle East ("along the great river Euphrates"), criminals and fanatics were triumphant beneath the dark banner of perdition raised into the sunlight; and "to the east" weapons that embody the power at the heart of creation in the hands of the vengeful reveling in the ability to destroy. Soon it became apparent that humanity had entered a period that would change history forever. And then many realized that what was happening around the world was remarkably similar to the fateful events leading to "Armageddon" that are described in the Biblical text and later in the predictions disclosed at "*Fatima*" in 1917 ("The Three Secrets") that finally explained what had been foretold almost two millennia ago.

BOOK OF REVELATIONS

"Saying to the **sixth** angel, *Loose the four angels [of violence] which are bounded in the great river of Euphrates* (Middle East). And the four angels were loosed [in Iraq, Syria, Kuwait, Iran]." (Chapter 9: 14-15)

"And the **sixth** angel poured out his vial upon the great river *Euphrates*; and the water thereof was dried up [by warfare], *that the way of the kings of the east (Russia and China) might be prepared...* " (Chapter 1**6**:12 [**6**+**6**] = **666**). "And [then] he gathered them together into the place called in the Hebrew tongue *"Armageddon"* ('*Har*'-mountain)...and there was *a great earthquake*, such as was not since men were upon the earth..." Chapter 1**6**:1**6**-18).

"And I beheld when he had opened the **sixth** seal and lo, there was a *great earthquake*, and *the sun* (high altitude, nuclear explosion) *became black as sackcloth of hair, and the moon became as blood* (reflecting red afterglow). (Chapter **6**:12 = **6**+**6**) = "**666**."

"And the stars of heaven fell unto the earth, even as a fig tree casteth her untimely figs, when she is shaken of a mighty wind. And *the heaven departed as a scroll when it is rolled together...* and the great men, and the rich men, and the chief captains, and the mighty men...and every free man hid themselves in the...the rocks of the mountains." (Chapter **6**: 13-15). ...."tormented five months...third part of men killed, by the fire, and by the smoke, and by the brimstone."(Chapter 9:5,18 = **6**+**6**+**6** = **666**).

"The army of the horsemen (invaders) were two hundred thousand thousand (200,000,0000); and I heard the number." (Chapter 9:1**6**). "Power was given unto them over *the fourth part of the earth (China) to kill with sword,...and with death and with the beasts of the earth.* " (Chapter **6**:8)

"Here is wisdom. Let him that hath understanding [of these events] count the number of the beast; for it is the number of a man; and his number is *Six hundred three score and six."* (666) (Chapter 13:18 = **6**+**6**+**6** = **666**)

FATIMA

On July 13, 1917 (time of the Russian Revolution), a lady described as "*brighter than the sun*, shedding rays of light clearer and stronger than a crystal goblet filled with the most sparkling water and pierced by the burning rays of the sun" appeared for the third time near Fatima, Portugal. At that time she made certain, dire predictions regarding the future of the world that have become known as "*The Three Secrets*" To confirm the validity of what she stated, a miraculous event involving the sun occurred on October 13, 1917 that was witnessed by an estimated 100,000 people. This large assemblage included representatives of Portugal's most important news organizations, who verified what took place in the sky. This event cannot be explained by any recognized, scientific criteria. The mysterious lady is believed to be Mary, the mother of Jesus Christ.

According to the *Second* and most important secret: "The war (World War 1) is going to end, but if people do not cease [from a course] offending God, a worse one will break out during the Pontificate of Pope Pius XI (World War 2)...If... *Russia* will be converted (turn away from communism), there will be peace; if not, she *will spread her errors throughout the world, causing* **wars** *(plural) and persecutions....* The good will be martyred *...and various nations will be* ***ANNIHILATED...***"

Definition: Annihilation (noun) "**reduced to nothing.**"

During the Second World War a number of nations were badly damaged. However, **at only two locations did true "annihilation" occur** – **Hiroshima** and **Nagasaki** after they were obliterated by atomic bombs.

PREFACE

The manuscript handwritten on weathered paper records the fateful period when **humanity headed inexorably toward history's greatest catastrophe**. Later a few people were identified who might be the author of this troubling account, although probably it will never be known who he really is. Referred to only as "Lawrence," this unknown espionage agent for years worked deep undercover in the Far East. Now some regard him as one of history's most ingenious spies and even compare him to the legendary British super-agent, Sidney Reilly. Similar to Reilly, his ultimate fate remains in doubt and probably always will.

Initially Lawrence set out to seek his fortune in international finance. At few times in the past has there been such conspicuous wealth and excess as the early 21st century, the pursuit of money becoming an all-consuming ideal. While unfettered commerce was thought to be a panacea for the world's ills, Lawrence soon encountered a different reality - one where corruption and greed flourished on a grand scale and the weak were often preyed upon. Turning to espionage, he undertook the difficult task of trying to influence the fateful course of world events. His long years working as a spy exacted a heavy price, and eventually he came to regret a role that exposed him to so much danger and heartbreak. While surviving with difficulty in such a duplicitous realm, this unheralded agent became an important witness to what took place during an era that would change forever the course of human history. It will always be disputed what effect he might have produced on the events that followed.

His personal account was written on a remote island where he took refuge. In essence, it details one man's journey into the dark heart of the modern era, when the human race supposedly reached the apex of civilization but instead declined repeatedly into barbarism, including mass murder. The manuscript was discovered by a British businessman, who liked to bargain-hunt while traveling and found it in a non-descript, antique shop on a back street of Tokyo. Although he had been in the area many times, he never noticed the tiny shop that didn't have a sign on the front. What attracted his attention was the jewelry displayed in the window. Among the various items were some unusual, silver rings.

He went inside but was soon distracted by a box of leather-bound books left on a table. Although he wasn't much of a reader, he purchased the box sight-unseen, thinking the fine, leather bindings would add a nice touch to a flat he was decorating. A few days later he remembered the rings and returning to the shop, was disappointed to learn that they had been sold only hours before. The fancy rings were the type usually bestowed by a lover on his lady's fair hand, and he suspected that like many, intriguing objects that turned up in antique shops, they had a history filled with poignant secrets. Had the rings brought joy and good fortune to those who possessed them, or sorrow and even the ruin of dreams?

Eventually he got around to examining the contents of the box that contained a variety of items including photographs of a tall, athletic-looking man. Among the books there were various classics such as *War and Peace*, Homer's *Iliad*, George Orwell's *1984* and others about those perplexing subjects that throughout history have remained unresolved – war and tyranny. Each volume had extensive notes written in the margins, and it was apparent the person who once owned them had devoted considerable time trying to understand their meaning. In addition, there was a curious item that didn't go with the rest, a small, hand-size diary stained by rain and dust that once belonged to a British soldier during the colonial wars. It was wrapped in plastic to protect it from further damage, and inside the front cover was a Union Jack made of tattered silk. Beneath the books was a stack of papers the businessman thought was the draft of a novel. Some pages appeared to be missing, and quickly losing interest in the rambling account, he passed it along to an acquaintance at a publishing house in Singapore. Eventually a limited edition of the book was produced that attracted fleeting interest. One can only speculate how the anonymous author's account of his quest during that fateful era along with some of his possessions ended up in a shop filled with discarded things. In spite of the fact he participated in such transforming events, all he left behind that evidenced his perilous journey was contained in a medium-sized cardboard box sold to a complete stranger for a mere one dollar and 20 American cents.

1

Amid the seclusion of this tiny island far at sea, I await the tragic events that lie ahead and will attempt to create a written record of what I know about this tragic period in history. I wish that my tale could be more grand like the heroic exploits of ancient Jason searching for the prized fleece or wandering Odysseus, who contended with the fearsome Cyclops and the sea god himself. Instead this is a tale about the modern world, where myth is diminished and a man on his quest must journey through lands where the dark and perverse lurk and even incarnate evil .

Since I lack a devoted chronicler, I will record my own deeds during the long and troubled years when I lived in a realm inhabited by opportunists, the greedy and cruel. At times many of these individuals could seem quite charming, and some I regarded as friends and out of necessity depended on them. With no allegiance except to themselves, they proved to be invariably corrupt, and always I knew that at any moment I might be killed - and probably in the worst, possible way.

During all that time my true identity was known to hardly anyone, and I existed only as a hollow invention of my own making. To achieve objectives I considered noble, I assumed a role very different from the person I really am, repeatedly compromising myself while acting in a manner similar to those I now condemn. Ultimately I even harmed grievously the few I loved. And always there will be the troubling question of whether the many risks I took accomplished anything at all. A terrible war on a global scale seems inevitable, and I suspect that at a certain point the world's fate was already sealed. Perhaps I was a fool to believe that a lone man could affect such momentous events. Hopefully I can preserve at least some of the dark reality I experienced, and one day my account will be read by those who can appreciate what I record on these pages.

Every day I listen to the news reports on the BBC, wondering when the great war will begin and countless, innocent lives sacrificed. For years there was speculation about whether another, global conflict was possible. Sadly it appears that such a disaster is about to happen and humanity will risk annihilation by misusing in the worst way the extraordinary power at the heart of creation. The terrible consequences will likely exceed anything that can be imagined, although I continue to hope that at the last moment something will intervene to prevent such madness. In spite of the many secrets I stole from the innermost recesses of that diabolical regime, I never guessed what they really intended to do. And then I saw the documents that disclosed the details of the monstrous scheme that for decades they implemented with such care while deceiving the rest of the world. Also I finally learned the truth about the place referred to cryptically as "X" in many of their top secret documents, a mystery that bedeviled me for years. Who could have guessed what they had been doing there?

This tiny island in the South China Sea isn't shown on a nautical chart, and hopefully I will be able to survive here. Now I can only wait for these tragic events to run their course and each day write a few, more pages of my troubled saga. For better or worse, my brief role on history's stage is finished, and I am left to ponder what I might have done differently. Often I think of beautiful Lily with her long, black hair and porcelain-white skin. Without her, I wouldn't be alive to write this account. She was considered little more than a vain, Hong Kong party girl, the embodiment of expensive chic. Instead she turned out to be completely different from what everyone thought. Even I, her lover, didn't fully appreciate her. Perhaps it was inevitable that tragedy would overtake the two of us, although I wanted so much to believe otherwise. She is the real hero of this tale - the person most worthy of being remembered.

I picture her at the beach on our little sanctuary of Cheung Chau, making chalk sketches of the seascape or searching along the water's edge for the exquisite shells that echo with the eternal life of the sea. The idyllic days we shared there ended so quickly as if snatched away by a cruel, unseen hand. How sad that what is so magical and difficult to find should have happened to two people when it was already too late. Now she too is gone, lost forever along with the others I cared about.

The ocean scene around the island is enthralling, the blue-green sea stretching away to the distant horizon where it merges with the cloudless sky as if one is an extension of the other. Occasionally a freighter passes far offshore, the only indication of a distant, troubled world on the brink of war. Amid all of this exquisite, natural beauty, who would think that such a catastrophe might soon erupt. How fortunate I am to have found my tiny refuge, although I wonder if I will ever leave this speck of land in the midst of the vast ocean.

Today before the sun goes down, I will explore more of the reef just offshore that I discovered recently. It is a magnificent, underwater garden filled with diaphanous sea plants stories high that undulate gracefully in the gentle current; endless varieties of multi-colored fish, and coral ablaze in the sunlight filtered through the clear, pale green water. It took millions of years to create such intricate beauty, and probably I am the only human who has ever seen it. I am left with the extraordinary thought that it was created over eons so one day a fortunate person like myself would happen upon it and experience such awe. Perhaps none of this will be here much longer. Because of human folly on a monumental scale, this island and countess others scattered like little jewels across the peaceful sea will soon be obliterated by a giant tidal wave sweeping through a dust-filled, nuclear twilight.

2

Could the great conflict that looms ahead be the horrific event predicted long ago in the Biblical *Book of Revelations* - mythical "Armageddon," the mysterious name shrouded in ancient lore that throughout the centuries has haunted humanity? **All along did we humans possess a cryptic but highly accurate insight into our own perilous future that we chose to ignore?** A few years ago I learned much about this transforming event described ominously in the final book of the Bible. It was at a meeting with a prominent scholar at Cambridge University, Professor Robert Chesley, whom I met while studying at the London School of Economics. During my last trip to England I went to see him again. A small, slightly built man, his inconspicuous appearance belied his stature as a noted, international scholar, who has written extensively about the defining role of "belief" in human history. He died only a few months later, having left me with some of the profound insights it had taken him a lifetime to discover. Unfortunately I didn't appreciate fully what he told me.

Our meeting took place late on a spring afternoon, his small office filled with the aroma of the countless books that covered the walls. I'm sure there are few ideas of significance that weren't contained in his private library, and no doubt he carefully read every volume. I can still hear his prophetic, softly spoken words as if they were uttered only days ago.

"The *Book of Revelations* is one of the world's most extraordinary documents. In fact, in all of literature - sacred or otherwise, there is nothing quite like it. At the same time *Revelations* remains to this day among the least understood," he said as the sun set outside and the light in the small room dimmed slowly until I could barely see him. It seemed as if that brilliant man soon to die was gradually fading away right before my eyes. And before departing from this earth, he made me the reluctant custodian of his understanding of that transforming, world event often referred to as the "Apocalypse."

"In barely a dozen pages," he continued, "*Revelations* explains some of the most profound truths of our existence. In fact, without *Revelations* there are some things we wouldn't know, especially about the historical process - a remarkable tale that over time is gradually playing itself out through a series of "ages" like the chapters of a great book. While it is recognized that the physical universe functions in a cyclical fashion and is governed by an evolving, underlying order, few recognize that this is also true of human history. In other words there is a profound rationale to the process that on the surface appears to be random, even fortuitous. As a result each generation participates in events far grander and more complex than is realized, our much-heralded philosophies falling far short of comprehending what is really taking place.

"Typically each historical age begins in aspiration, moves through distinct stages or "eras" and concludes in excess, decay and often widespread turmoil. At such times objective truth fades; opportunism and selfishness predominate; and humans even come to believe their own fantasies. Of late, we have entered such a climactic period as the world order gradually unravels and forces assert themselves that defy control. It is out of such a period that great tragedy can arise. What is particularly noteworthy about the current era is not only the incessant violence that continues to spread but also the perversion of "belief" itself, especially religious, along with deceitfulness on a grand scale. *The present era represents nothing less than the dramatic conclusion of one the most important ages in all of history, one that began in the mid-to-late 19th century. In essence, we are witnessing the climactic resolution of the forces that shaped the modern world. This era is so important because it will bring about a seismic shift in the course of recorded history extending back at least 5000 years.*

"Because of the lack of a formal narrative and unusual imagery, the message expressed in *Revelations* is often difficult to understand, confounding those who try to interpret the document. What we know for certain is that this final book of the Bible is the faithful record of the mystical visions of an unknown and reclusive holy man named "John." Unfortunately we have no specific information about him, except that when *The Book of Revelations* was written, he lived on the tiny island of Patmos in the eastern Mediterranean. It appears that he had some sort of leadership or teaching role in early Christianity. Many mistake him for the Apostle John, who authored one of the four books of the New Testament. However, they are different people. Because of the importance of his message, John of Patmos is regarded now as one of history's greatest mystics.

"In overall form *Revelations* is the pastoral letter of instruction that he composed for the "seven" congregations of early Christians established at the time in Asia Minor - a period of much tribulation for believers. Thus they are exhorted to persevere in their convictions because the Almighty will reward them with great gifts symbolized by that rare and precious gem of the heavens - "I will give him the *"morning star."* (2:28)

In his letter John explains in detail what he experienced when allowed to visit the celestial realm. He states that having departed from his physical body, he briefly "was in the spirit" and "a door was opened in heaven." (4:1-2). And then "I John saw these things and heard them." (22:8). He describes for us one of the extraordinary creatures that he encountered there: "the angel was] clothed with a *cloud*, and a *rainbow* was upon his head, and his *face was as it were the sun...*" (10:1). Some compare this passage to one written by the prophet Daniel that is thought to refer to Gabriel (one of only two angels identified by name in the Old Testament): "he was ...girded with fine gold... and *his face as the appearance of lightening...* and his eyes as lamps of fire..." *Daniel* (10:6)

9

"We are also informed by John that much of what he learned came directly out of the Book held in "the right hand of him that sat on the throne" [and that was] sealed with *seven* seals." (5:1) - the great Book that summarizes all others ever written. As a result the seals that keep this Book of all books closed were loosened briefly so what lies within could be revealed. In this way John, a human being like us, became the means through which many of life's most profound truths could be disclosed.

"Loosening the first four seals reveals the legendary "Four Horsemen," one of the most frightening images ever portrayed in the written word. These terrible creatures are given emphasis early on (Chapter **Six**), because war has played such a dominant role throughout recorded history. The horsemen always ride together, inseparable in their violent mission. The first rides a ghostly, white horse, and as the text states: "he that sat on him, had a bow; and a crown was given to him; and he went forth conquering and to conquer." The second rides a red horse, and "power was given to him that sat thereon to take peace from the earth, and that they should kill one another." On a black horse rides famine, and finally the most frightening of all - the horseman astride the *pale* horse (devoid of all color). *"…his name that sat on him was death, and Hell followed with him and power was given unto him to kill with sword and with hunger and with death and with the beasts of the earth…"* (**6**:2-8).

"Thus the dreaded Four Horsemen introduce John's account of humanity's tragic journey that through the centuries has often been dominated by war and cruelty and one day will culminate in an event of unimaginable violence - the great battle of "Armageddon." It is this catastrophic occurrence that will dramatically bring to completion the long and tyrannical reign of the Horsemen. When the **sixth** seal of the Book is loosened in Chapter **Six** at verse 12 (**6+6**) (a most significant section - the numbers adding up to the mythical "**666**"), we are provided with a frightening *description of the terrible weapon that will be unleashed during*

Armageddon: "And lo there was a great earthquake; and the sun became black as a sackcloth of hair; and the moon became as blood. [And later] the stars of heaven fell unto the earth, even as a fig tree casteth her untimely figs, when she is shaken of a mighty wind. And the heaven departed as a scroll when it is rolled together, and every mountain and island were moved out of their places." 6:13-16)

"Because of such devastation, many through the ages have concluded that John was describing the end of the world. How else could something so horrific take place, the name "Armageddon" becoming synonymous in most peoples' minds with this interpretation. However, the text doesn't specifically say that, an important point that is overlooked. Instead Armageddon is likely quite different - a violent, pivotal event that will alter the course of history and usher in a new period unlike anything that has occurred before. Afterwards worldwide peace will hopefully prevail - at least for a very long period. It is for that reason this extraordinary event is referred to in the text as the "great day of God Almighty" - (serving his purposes). (1_6_:14)

"_In order to grasp the complex message contained in Revelations, it is necessary to understand the pivotal role played by numerology - a literary device often used at the time the Bible was written. Thus two, key numbers appear repeatedly - six and seven, both of which serve a specific purpose._ The emphasis on these numbers is not mere artifice. Instead they are integral to the text and a highly effective way of expressing its profound meaning .

"While the number "Six" (including the infamous "666") refers to evil, **the number "Seven" represents God**, who is composed of "seven" spirits. As stated: "And out of the throne proceeded lightnings and thunderings and voices and there were seven lamps of fire burning before the throne, which are the _Seven Spirits of God_. And before the throne there was a sea of glass like unto *crystal...*" (4:5-6) (The number "seven" is mathematically indivisible - cannot be separated evenly into its component parts. Similarly the essential qualities of the Almighty embody a perfect unity.) Thus the "book [of life] written within and on the backside, [is] sealed with <u>seven</u> seals." (5:1). And "<u>seven</u> angels stood before God; and to them were given <u>seven</u> trumpets" (8:2)... the <u>seven</u> angels which had the <u>seven</u> trumpets prepared themselves to sound." (8:6). Also, "<u>seven</u> angels having the <u>seven</u> last plagues (15:1)...<u>seven</u> angels [and their] <u>seven</u>, golden vials full of the wrath of God, who liveth forever and ever. And the temple was filled with smoke from the glory of God and from his power; and no man was able to enter into the temple, till the <u>seven</u> plagues of the <u>seven</u> angels were fulfilled." (15:7-8). This emphasis on the number "seven" in connection with God occurs not only in Christianity but in many, other, major religions as well. In the ancient *Mundaka-Upanishad* of the Hindus, we find the following: "That heavenly person... the seven senses also spring from him; the seven lights...these seven worlds in which the senses move, which rest in the heart and are placed there seven and seven (repeated to an infinite degree)..." And later in the Old Testament: "Thus the heavens and the earth were finished, and all their multitude. And on the seventh day God finished his work that he had done, and he rested on the seventh day...blessed the seventh day and hallowed it..." (*Genesis* 1:1-2)

"In *Revelations*, each of the seven "seals," "trumpets" and the "vials of the last plagues" relates to one of the life-giving spirits or essential qualities of God. According to theologians these spirits are opposed by the transgressions categorized as the seven, deadly or "cardinal sins," that comprise evil in human terms. In turn, each of these major sins emanates from one of the seven, great, fallen angles or demonic spirits, who led the rebellion against God before there was time. We can conclude that the "sixth" transgression is "pride" or the obsessive preoccupation with self to the exclusion

12

of all else. The counter-quality in God is humility or selflessness, which might seem a contradiction since God is all-powerful. According to the Bible the fateful quality of pride is embodied to its fullest in the former angel of light - Lucifer, the fallen Satan, who originally was the most magnificent creature God ever created. In *Isaiah*, he is referred to as the "*son of the morning*" (14:12). "In Eden, the garden of God, *every precious gem* was thy covering, (adorned by) the sardius, topaz, and the diamond...the sapphire, the emerald... [you were] the anointed cherub...in the midst of the *stones of fire.*" *Ezekiel (*28:13-14).

But soon Lucifer was possessed by a limitless pride - the greatest sin of all and the basis of every other, which precipitated his tragic downfall. "How are thou fallen from heaven...cut down to the ground... For thou hast said in thine heart,.. I will exalt my throne above the stars of God (all the other angels)." *Isaiah* 14:12-13). In essence, the battle of Armageddon, the most terrible of all human wars, will represent the ultimate expression of pride and cruelty in the temporal realm. In this way the prince of *darkness* will briefly bring to our world the perpetual night and terror that possesses his tortured realm from which all radiance is banished forever.

"In a theological sense history can be viewed as embodying the ongoing conflict between the "seven spirits" of God and the opposing qualities that came into existence during the original war in heaven. As John tells us, "I stood upon the sands of the sea, and saw a *beast* rise up out of the sea, having <u>seven</u> heads and ten horns, and upon his heads the name of *blasphemy* (opposition to God)..."(13:1) And elsewhere: "behold a great red dragon having <u>seven</u> heads and ten horns." (12:3). This terrifying image recalls the multi-headed monster of Greek mythology, the serpent-like Hydra that was known and feared by the ancients, especially those that went to sea. As the mighty Hercules discovered, the Hydra was impossible to kill. When one of its many heads was cut off, it was replaced immediately by two - in effect, like evil endlessly perpetuating itself. The reference to this grotesque creature in *Revelations* harkens back to *Book of Psalms* 74:13-14 ("the heads of leviathan...") and ultimately all the way to the <u>seven</u>-headed monster in early Mesopotamian legend, when the first literature was created. Already at that time this terrifying, mythic image representing evil was embedded in the human consciousness.

"John further states: "And they worshipped the dragon which gave power unto the beast; and they worshipped the beast saying, Who is like unto the beast? Who is able to make war with him?" (13:4). While each of the "seven" heads of this symbolic beast represents one of the seven, demonic spirits linked in opposition to God, "the ten horns which thou sawest are ten kings, which have received no kingdom as yet, but receive power as kings one hour with the beast. These *have one mind*, and shall give their power and strength unto the beast." (17:12-13) On this basis we can conclude that during the long span of history there will arise ten, great kingdoms, or nations, that will be controlled by leaders, who will act in an important way on behalf of "the dragon which gave power unto the beast."

"One of these nations will lead humanity to the horror of Armageddon, when evil will achieve one of its greatest triumphs in the desolation of history's most destructive war. In the past there have been many, tyrannical regimes, every one of which ultimately fell in ignominy. During the current era, the most powerful of all have risen in perverse glory - the modern, totalitarian state that has attempted repeatedly to dominate the world. Not surprising, these monstrous states are virulently atheistic while employing false belief to mislead the masses, even perverting religion itself for the purposes of furthering a violent agenda. At no time in history has the process of human belief been distorted to such a degree; atheism asserted on such a widespread scale; and the concept of a benevolent deity undermined so aggressively.

14

"In addition, at their essence all of the totalitarian states of the modern era are fascist-type regimes run by a privileged minority that employ a cruel agenda to achieve their objectives. This has led to the atrocities committed in Nazi Germany, Imperial Japan, the Soviet Union, the killing fields of Southeast Asia, and more recently in North Korea and the vast system of jails and psychiatric hospitals of Communist China. In fact, mass murder (along with deceitful ideology) can be regarded as some of the defining characteristics of modern history. While humanity supposedly reached the apex of civilization, the most barbaric crimes have been perpetrated repeatedly in the name of the common man. *In essence, the battle of "Armageddon" will be the greatest act of mass murder of all as well as the most vivid embodiment in recorded history of evil itself*.

"Just as "seven" is representative of God, **the number Six**, which also appears repeatedly throughout *Revelations* (including nine - the inverted six), **relates to the legions of the demonic** allied to the serpent from the "bottomless pit." Thus it is stated the total number of the great, fallen angels, that led the primordial rebellion, "is the number of a man: and his number is Six hundred threescore and six" - **666**. (13:18) "There was a war in heaven...and the great dragon was cast out, that old serpent, called the Devil, and Satan was cast out into the earth *and his angels were cast out with him*." (12: 7-9) "And his tail drew the third part of the stars (angels) of heaven, and did cast them to the earth..." (12:4) As stated in Luke (10:18): "I beheld Satan as *lightning* fall from heaven." In essence, all wars on earth throughout the ages have been an ongoing expression of this violent, seminal event that resulted ultimately in the creation of the physical realm we know. And soon this enduring struggle between good and evil through warfare will be played out to its violent conclusion for all to witness on the ruinous battlefield of Armageddon.

"We are provided with many specifics about this event,

the key references in the text identified by the symbolic number "six," including in pivotal Chapter Six. There are additional references such as when the "sixth angel" sounds a trumpet (9:14-21), and we are told about the huge number of people who will be involved in this great struggle - "two hundred thousand thousand," (9:16) or 200 million people. Furthermore, this protracted event will commence in the Middle East, when the "sixth vial" of God's wrath is poured on the earth - specifically *"upon the great river Euphrates... [so] the way of the kings of the east might be prepared."* (16:12) In this way John informs us that the conflict will have its beginnings in the vicinity of the Euphrates River, which, of course, includes Kuwait, Iraq, Iran, and Syria - the *four* countries where recently so much strife has occurred.

"Thus John speaks of the *"four* angels which are bound in the great river Euphrates... And the angels were loosed, which were *prepared"* (made ready to foment warfare). (9:14). In both the celestial and earthly worlds, important angels often hold sway over an assigned realm. To John, the four, demonic spirits inspiring these events appeared literally to rise out of the river, each of them influencing one of these temporal nations while setting the stage for the monumental conflict that will take place elsewhere.

"In that regard John also states that the water "of the great river Euphrates... was dried up." (16:12) – an unusual description, although it is actually quite appropriate. Traditionally the Euphrates valley was one of the most verdant regions on the globe. Recently large portions of this area have taken on an arid, dusty appearance resulting from so much warfare. Therefore John assumed that the river had literally evaporated, leaving only the barren landscape seen in his vision. Since the former Mesopotamia, or the valley of the Euphrates River, is the cradle where civilization, as we know it, began, it is perhaps fitting the climactic events that will bring to an end the violent reign of the Four Horsemen should be initiated there.

16

"What occurs in the Middle East, however, will be only the prelude to the much larger conflict that will occur in the "east," which is Asia or specifically Russia and China. Based on John's account, we can conclude that this terrible war will dwarf what happened in World War I or II. The various descriptions in the text suggest the type of devastation that can only result from the use of nuclear weapons - the ultimate tool of war and its preoccupation with violence. Because these weapons weren't developed until recently, it was assumed that destruction on such a scale could only occur when the world came to an end. Now we know differently. With the development of modern, atomic physics, human beings have been privileged to gain access to the most powerful forces at the heart of creation that make possible life itself and all its beauty. And one day this great gift will be misused in the worst way - in effect, nature's exquisite design perverted and turned against itself to serve the interests of the prideful and cruel.

"The conflict that John foresaw will ultimately involve many nations, and therefore he tells us that the "kings of the earth" will participate (**16**:14). In his time political leaders were kings while today they are secular in nature, and, as I said, he states specifically that "the number of the army of the *horsemen* (invaders) will be 200 thousand-thousand" - far more than all of the world's armies put together. He adds that "I <u>heard</u> the number of them" (was actually told) (**9**:16) so it was not a guess on his part. Therefore, those participating in the conflict (on the side of the aggressor) will include large numbers of civilians along with military personnel. Only China, which, of course, is synonymous with the "east" and at various times has comprised one-fourth of the world's population, could be the source of so many people. ("And Power was given unto them [the Four Horsemen] over the *fourth* part of the earth...") (**6**:8) It is perhaps no accident that a benign version of the "dragon" has traditionally been the dominant symbol of China. It is there the legions allied to rebellious "serpent" will make

17

their last stand in the effort to dominate the world through organized violence and conquest on a grand scale.

"But **where could "Armageddon" be located**, the focus of this monumental conflict? This unusual name is actually the Greek transliteration of the Hebrew term "*Har* Megiddo," which means literally the "*mountain of Megiddo*" - in essence, a unique linguistic construction that embodies the idea John was trying to express. In Biblical times Megiddo was a minor town or administrative center on the plain of Esdraelon in northern Israel. Currently its ruins sit atop a hill about 100 feet high and not a mountain. Probably John wasn't widely traveled, although it is likely that he spent some time in Israel, which isn't far from Patmos. Therefore, he would have been acquainted with Megiddo, which to him appeared similar to the unknown place seen in his vision. Apparently for that reason he assumed it was Megiddo. The plain of Esdraelon is a relatively small place (only about ten by twenty-five miles) and could never accommodate 200 million people, especially if most are soldiers with equipment. Furthermore, because there would be an opposing army as well, far more than 200 million will be involved. For such a large number of people to be present at one time in this limited area, it would be necessary to pile them on top of one another to a depth of many feet, in effect completely immobilizing them. Obviously such an enormous conflict could never occur at that location.

"Nonetheless, as the text states, the war will be focused at the place "called in the Hebrew tongue Armageddon." (16:16) Since "*Har* Megiddo" literally means the "*mountain* of Megiddo," the location in question must be considerably larger than the Biblical site that is only a small hill. Somewhere "in the east" (China) there is a mountain vaguely resembling ancient Megiddo that will be the focal point of this greatest of all wars. Why this unknown location will play such a significant role is one of the biggest mysteries of all. During the time of Mao Zedong, the Chinese created hundreds of miles of enormous, underground tunnels in the mountainous, northern part of the country. The purpose was protection for their military against bombing as well as aerial surveillance. To this day, they continue to conceal in this vast tunnel system large amounts of military equipment and materials. I suspect this unknown mountain contains a cavern holding something that will play a pivotal role in the monumental conflict that will change history forever. It is ironic and sad that violence on such a horrific scale will emanate from the great, ancient culture of China that brought us the lofty principles of the *I Ching*, Lao Tze and Confucius - in essence, some of the earliest forms of humanity's most important, religious beliefs.

"The Biblical text also provides revealing clues regarding the **circumstances** when Armageddon will occur. While introducing the Four Horsemen, John notes that "I heard a voice *in the midst of the four beasts* say, a measure of wheat for a penny, and three measures of barley for a penny; and see thou *hurt not* the oil and the wine." (**6:6**) Note the unusual language employed here. Material goods that represent wealth are spoken of in a manner normally employed in connection to a precious, living creature such as a child. That is exactly the way the greedy feel about the wealth they covet with all their hearts. To such people money and its substitutes are truly precious. In this way John tells us that "war" bears an intrinsic connection to the obsessive quest for treasure. In fact, greed on a grand scale (the desire of one society to seize the land and wealth of another) is the fundamental cause of war. Thus in the Russian language, the term for "war" is virtually synonymous with thievery.

"In Chapter 13 we learn about a second beast that "exercised all the power of the first beast (the multi-headed Hydra) before him ... [and] he causeth all, both small and great, rich and

19

poor, free and bond to receive a mark in their right hand, or to their foreheads: *And that no man might buy or sell, save that he had the mark,* or the name of the beast [blasphemy] or the number of his name...." (13:12-18). Being "in spirit" during his vision, John saw the people revealed to him only in their spiritual essence or their actual souls - the tableau on which the story of each person's life is vividly and permanently etched like a distinctive portrait. Shaped by our own hand, this portrait in its final form constitutes for all time what we ultimately become. As for all humans, the souls seen by John were marked or shaped in this way. Since so many of those involved in commerce bore the distinctive mark associated with evil, we can conclude that at the time of Armageddon commerce will be dominated to a significant degree by those who conduct themselves in an evil or rapacious manner. In that regard it is appropriate to note that in many of the world's myths, the "dragon" always possesses and jealously guards in his lair a hoard of treasure, especially gold.

"Thus it is apparent that the *greatest of all wars will arise out of a period of unprecedented wealth and materialism. Currently we are living in such an era,* one dominated by speculative excess and greed on a truly extraordinary scale. Around the world central banks have created a limitless amount of paper money that has become a potent force unto itself, especially in the hands of the unscrupulous and reckless. Giant trading funds, mysterious speculators, power-hungry oligarchs, and enormous, global, financial institutions regularly manipulate international commerce. At times even national governments have ventured into this dubious realm in order to implement their partisan objectives. Recently we witnessed the consequences of this destabilizing behavior during the catastrophic events of 2008 that almost brought down the entire, global economy. Sadly the pawns of this poisonous competition are often the vital resources that sustain life on the planet. At times these essentials to human existence are effectively manipulated solely for profit by artificial paper instruments that give extraordinary prerogatives to those who control them. The power of money and its surrogates have crept insidiously into all aspects of society, even art and culture, becoming the ultimate arbiter of almost everything taking place during the current era.

"If World War I was caused by excess competition among nations (nationalism), World War II added the poisonous element of perverse ideology to the volatile mix. While both nationalism and distorted belief are still potent, driving forces in the turmoil of the current international, political scene, the upcoming global conflict (World War III) will be rooted to a significant extent in garden-variety human greed on a grand scale. Ultimately the seductive illusion of great wealth will be employed to strengthen the violent, undermine the world order and help to precipitate the most destructive of all wars. Among the various insights given to us in *Revelations*, this is one of the most troubling of all.

"Through the ages scholars have tried to determine the **timeframe** when the catastrophe of Armageddon will occur. Based on current events as well as information in the text, we can now make a reasonably informed guess. In this regard John emphasized repeatedly the collective "number of the beast; *that is [also] the number of a man... 666.*" Thus he makes clear that this pivotal number has both a temporal (earthly) significance as well as a spiritual one. As a result it has occurred repeatedly at key points throughout history as the beast and his cohorts periodically asserted their malevolent influence over humanity. At these times important leaders arising from obscurity have appeared unexpectedly and initiated events favorable to the cause of evil - such an occurrence often involving in some way the symbolic "666."

"Recently this has happened once again in an emphatic way, providing further evidence that the calamity of Armageddon could be drawing near. In fact, many of the parallels are so vivid it is difficult to dismiss them as mere coincidence. Look back exactly 666 years, and you come to the ruinous 14th century, a disastrous period that to date has no equal in human history. Even during the great wars of the modern era the forces of chaos never gained enough strength to imperil the human race to such a degree. At that earlier time many areas of Asia and Europe were depopulated completely, and in some locations the destruction was so extensive a recovery never took place. It's not surprising that many believed the end of the world had arrived.

"Study those earlier events and their relationship to the present, and you will note some extraordinary similarities. These include the destabilizing role of widespread, institutional greed that during the 14th century (*"Black* Guelph" banks) undermined world society, greatly magnifying the catastrophic effects of genocidal warfare. During the present era it is likely that greed on a grand scale will magnify considerably the war-related destruction while also being one of the reasons that it occurs. Consequently we can expect that this disaster will result in the loss of much of the excessive wealth created during this era of grand acquisitiveness - in essence, such greed bringing about its own demise.

"In *Revelations,* the aftermath of Armageddon is compared to the downfall of the most opulent city of ancient times - mighty Babylon, the Biblical symbol of materialism itself. Thus John states prophetically: "and [at the time of Armageddon] the cities of the nations fell, and *great Babylon came in remembrance ....*" (16:19).

"Babylon the great is fallen, is fallen, and is become the habitation of devils, and the hole of every foul spirit, and the cage of every unclean and hateful bird...And the kings of the earth, who have...lived deliciously with her, shall bewail her and lament for her...Alas, alas that great city, Babylon, the mighty city! And the merchants of the earth shall weep and mourn over her, for no man

22

buyeth their merchandise anymore. The merchandise of gold, and silver, and precious stones, and of pearls, and fine linen, and purple, and silk, and scarlet, and all thyme wood...and odors, anointments and frankincense, and wine and oil, and chariots, and slaves, and *souls of men.*" (Chapter 18 = **6+6+6**): 2-13)

Since my meeting with Professor Chesley, I have given much thought to what I was told by that brilliant scholar regarding the vital information disclosed in *Revelations.* How ironic I later thought that the diabolical scheme seeking world domination, that was devised by such a virulently atheistic regime, should have been disclosed many centuries ago in a book inspired by a God that supposedly doesn't exist. In addition, I have come to appreciate the corrosive effect of the materialism that has become such a destabilizing force during the modern era. Of late, a significant amount of the world's excessive supply of wealth continues to be devoted to manipulation on a grand scale as well as criminal activity, much of this money stolen in some way from the vulnerable, including the helpless citizens of many nations. I know a great deal about this shadowy realm that spans the globe. As you read this account, you will see that at times I played my own role in this corrupting process, especially regards the enormous sums that disappeared out of China and Russia. And as the perverse genie of money was freed from restraint and along with other factors destabilized the world order, I watched as events gradually spun out of control.

Before all of that took place, however, I finally uncovered the details of their grandiose and cruel plan to wage what I believe will be World War III. The mysterious mountain location that resembles ancient Megiddo is in fact the place referred to cryptically as "X" in many of the top secret documents that I stole from the innermost recesses of that paranoid regime - their most terrible secret of all. Hidden in the distant mountain seen in John of Patmos' prophetic vision is the most destructive weapon ever devised by the human mind, one so monstrous that in seconds it can inflict death on an unimaginable scale. Even now I don't want to believe that anyone could be foolish enough to unleash such a terrible force, although apparently that is what is going to happen. This chilling realization leaves me little peace as images of the destruction caused by this ultimate violence and its aftermath often crowd into my mind.

WAR – a madman's tale seared into
the human brain with fiery iron --
the last act of this cruel drama
played out one, long and fateful night
at a remote mountain glimpsed centuries ago
by a lone prophet but known only by the name
Armageddon *- when all in this enlightened age*
will be summoned there
by the siren's call of the treacherous,
who speak with the seductive voice
of a murderous maiden luring a fool to his doom,
history's tragic legacy made complete
with a terror none could imagine,
when the light of a hundred suns
will sear the flesh of millions,
and through the vapor of death
evil's gaunt face will finally be glimpsed
in all its hideous splendor before
blinded eyes turned white as chalk.

3

Now I will provide you with some information about the man telling you this fateful tale, an unknown, American espionage agent who out of necessity will remain anonymous. Along the way you will learn many of the details of my failed struggle, information that previously I disclosed to no one. Until recently exotic Hong Kong was my adopted home and base of operations, an amazing place that in my mind has assumed the qualities of a dazzling mirage. For several, long and dangerous years I outwitted many of the best in that grand, Oriental emporium of uninhibited wealth and tireless deal-making, its harbor bustling with quaint junks, elegant ocean liners and giant cargo ships that brought rich commerce like tribute from all over the globe. Truly no city embodied so completely the splendors and excesses of the modern era as well as all the great cities throughout the long expanse of human history, including magnificent Babylon of ancient times.

Although the global economy eventually experienced an inevitable and ruinous decline, the privileged life in Hong Kong continued for the most part as before. Finally near the end it reached a crescendo of frenzied activity as if somehow everyone realized the grand time of plenty and pleasure was rapidly drawing to a close. At night, beneath a moon that often was the color of pure gold, the great metropolis was incandescent in all its artificial glory, living on borrowed time as humanity hurtled towards doom – the giant buildings of Kowloon ablaze with countless lights as if suddenly the city would burn itself out like an enormous flare exploding in space.

No one epitomized Hong Kong's extravagant, moneyed existence more than Lily Chan, (Of course, like nearly everyone in this account that isn't her real name.) One of the most beautiful women in a city known for the exquisite, Lily was always being copied by her countless admirers, who could never unlock completely the secret of her extraordinary looks. Slender and tall, she was the epitome of the elegant Chinese woman, who at the same time is both refined and provocative. Her waist-long hair was like fine, black silk that she often adorned with flowers and little, sparkling gems. But most of all, it was her lovely face that was so bewitching. No one doubted that Lily could make any man fall in love with her if she wanted to bother, which she rarely did.

Dear Lily, who could have guessed that you were doomed like the rest of China. For months I admired that remarkable lady in the city's top nightspots, where she often went with her devoted entourage of chic friends. The cream of Hong Kong's privileged youth, many were the children of "princelings," some of the richest and highest-ranking communist party officials. The "princelettes" - as some like to call them - had at their fingertips every luxury one could desire, and at times I couldn't help being envious. Over the years I became close friends with many of them. Although self-centered and spoiled, they were smart and attractive, and I have to admit that I enjoyed being around them. They knew how to have fun on a grand scale, and if I wanted, my life could have been nothing but an endless succession of glittering social events given by the princelettes to whom money was no object.

Now, to relieve the boredom, I recall trips to spirited horse races on the Mongolian steppes, lavish hunting parties with yaks piled high with expensive food and supplies, and all-night, fire-lit drinking parties under the stars in the summer fields of Tibet. Also there were the many luxurious cruises along the coast on magnificent yachts. One of them was more than 300 feet long and belonged to a princelette whose father was a member of the commission that investigates the excesses of party officials, or is supposed to. Toward the end Lily and I stayed out every night till dawn, wandering hand in hand among the city's top clubs while in between putting in a quick appearance at one, extravagant party after another in palatial apartments and country houses. In my mind all that frenzied activity has become a tantalizing blur of fast music, champagne and handsome, young faces, and at times I wish that grand celebration never had to end.

It was unusual for a Westerner like me to be accepted in such a rarefied level of the "new" Chinese society. Although for a time the princelettes and their friends treated me with caution, all of that eventually changed, and bits and pieces of overheard conversation became some of the most valuable secrets I stole right under the noses of the regime's ever-vigilant secret police. It was a task that of late was made easier by the fact I was Lily's boyfriend. At first, I didn't think I had a chance with her because she was pursued constantly by the city's most eligible men. But one night she was briefly alone, and on a lark I asked her to dance, not expecting that she would accept. Fortunately she did, and I soon realized she was interested in me too. As we moved swiftly around the dance floor, I looked into her lovely, dark eyes and knew immediately that I was bewitched. At the time I never imagined how deeply we would fall in love or the sorrow it would cause both of us.

Appropriately Lily lived in a private realm befitting a true princess - a lavish penthouse atop one of the tallest buildings in the exclusive heights of Hong Kong Island, the view on a clear day extending almost a hundred miles across the South China Sea. I can't even guess what such a place would cost in a market that has some of the highest priced real estate on the planet. It was truly Lily's garden in the sky. In every room there were always lots of fresh, fragrant flowers transported regularly from the mainland, and on the outdoor terrace little trees and lush shrubs in irrigated, copper boxes flourished like a miniature, tropical forest. Often the apartment was enveloped in a cool sea mist luminous with sunlight that came in low over the island, and at such times I could almost believe that Lily and I had floated away on an enormous, fluffy

27

cloud, escaping to some magical Shangri-La where time stood still and forever we could forget the troubled world seething with contradiction and conflict.

Throughout the apartment there were lots of oversize, flat-panel TVs on the walls. Even late at night they were rarely turned off, displaying a non-stop panorama of flashy dance videos, fashion shows and programs about the refined, Oriental painting of which Lily was so fond. Like many others in Hong Kong, she rarely missed an episode of the charming Kim family - China's version of American reality TV. Beautiful sister Kim, her brother and their patriarchal, communist father for a time became the country's darlings. Although the series was never shown in the inland provinces where there is so much poverty and misery, it was constantly on everyone's television screen in the prosperous coastal cities like Shanghai, Shenzhen, Guangzhou and Hong Kong, providing vivid proof of the communist party's seductive vision of a limitlessly prosperous future. Many spoke of the Kims as if they were real people, and I suspect that for a time nearly everyone in Hong Kong convinced themselves that the Kims did exist and were just like they were portrayed on TV. To me, the similarity between Lily and Sister Kim was obvious.

On a balmy night Lily gave a party to which only the members of her privileged, inner circle were invited. Although none of us could have known at the time, it was the final, indulgent gesture of the princess to her adoring court - that night marking the beginning of the end of Hong Kong's long time of limitless plenty. The party was held on her spacious, outdoor terrace suspended under the stars high above the brightly-lit city, the breeze fragrant with the rich aroma of frankincense emitted by the Oriental lanterns glowing among the shrubs. While a band played softly, overly polite waiters in white coats kept circulating with trays that contained Lily's favorite drink, a champagne cocktail in a fancy, Venetian goblet with a large cube of sugar so it was sweet as

28

possible. Nothing else was served at her parties, and I never heard anyone complain and ask for something else.

As usual, she was fashionably late, and I'm sure that everyone would have been surprised if Lily was ever on time, even for one of her own parties. That night she was later than usual. For hours she had been trying on expensive dresses brought there from the city's best stores that were always at her beck and call. When she finally made her appearance, no one was disappointed, a pleased gasp followed by silence spreading through the adoring crowd. Her choice was perfect - a long, turquoise silk gown that clung to every curve of her slender, statuesque figure. Her black hair arranged on top of her head sparkled with tiny rubies, although before the night was over, many of those expensive gems would be lost.

She hurried over to greet me with a kiss, always with genteel formality calling me "Lawrence." As our lips met, she gently touched my cheek. On her hand were the silver rings that for a long time she wouldn't wear, although I knew that from now on she would never take them off. And then she went around greeting her guests as if suddenly realizing all those people were there. I knew that most of the men were jealous of the fact I was Lily's boyfriend. Initially I assumed our relationship wouldn't last long because her whims often changed with a sudden turn of her pretty head. But after several months we were inseparable while at the same time I became increasingly troubled by the contradictions implicit in our relationship.

Soon after we met, I discovered that Lily was the daughter of a prominent, retired general of the People's Liberation Army (PLA). A distinguished member of the inner circle of China's huge, military establishment, the general has been given much of the credit for modernizing the country's army. Years ago, the US Pentagon got a big surprise when it became aware of China's rapidly growing arsenal of advanced weapons that include top-level missiles and fighter planes. In addition, this growing technological sophistication includes the ability to blind with lasers or shoot down America's invaluable, communication satellites, including those on which the military depends. As a result the predictions it would take years for China to become a significant, military threat were quietly scrapped. I knew that being seen around town with the daughter of such a prominent, military official would greatly facilitate my work as a spy. In fact, it's difficult to imagine anything more useful. In essence, the daughter of one of the most violently anti-American figures in the entire country had fallen in love with a man whom China's counter-intelligence operatives had been trying for years to track down. At the same time it meant that our relationship was built on deception, and I could never tell the woman I loved what I was really doing in her country.

Understandably I wasn't popular with Lily's family. From the outset her relationship with an American angered her father, who considered it a scandal. Her older brother, who was in the navy and a strong nationalist hostile to the United States, was also opposed. However, her younger brother, Gao, was intrigued that she had a boyfriend so different from everyone else she dated. In spite of her father's opposition, Lily occasionally took me to lunch at an exclusive club frequented by Hong Kong's communist big shots. I knew the choice on her part was deliberate, and no doubt suitable notice was taken of my presence there. Lily could be very strong-willed, and it was apparent she was making a statement no one could miss, especially her father.

As we drew closer, I became aware of things about her that I never suspected, including the side of her personality she hid from everyone. Underneath she was actually quite shy and in spite of her wide popularity had few close friends, only an endless supply of admiring hangers-on. The fact there were always so many people around her was misleading. Most were just there for the ride, eager to share in the electric excitement she generated and have some of

30

it rub off on them. Also I realized that Lily kept up such a dizzying social pace with hardly a minute to spare in order to distract herself from the many things she didn't want to think about. Whenever the news came on the TV, she quickly switched channels to some innocuous program lacking controversy. It was apparent that she was trying to create a wall of distraction between herself and everything that was unpleasant and difficult to explain, especially the cruel struggle being waged for the soul of her nation.

The people in her circle paid little attention to politics and couldn't have cared less. Her girlfriends thought only of clothes, men and parties, and usually in that order. Naturally everyone assumed that Lily was the same although eventually I realized the opposite was true. She was too kind to ignore completely what was happening in her country. Aware of how terribly wrong things were, she was trapped in a dilemma from which there was no escape. Her prominent father had spent his life defending militarily a regime that was the greatest mass murderer in history. In fact, the deaths of its own people caused by the regime were so astronomical (more than 80 million), the actual number long ago became academic. At the same time Lily owed to the communist system everything that made her life so desirable. I'm sure it was the reason she rarely dated anyone who was an important communist official. Her father constantly received overtures from party bigwigs eager to date her. But she always refused which annoyed him even more, especially since of late she was seen constantly with a well-known American.

Early in the morning, Lily and I left the party with Gao and his latest girlfriend, Annie, departing by a backdoor so no one would notice and want to come along. Gao just acquired a new, high-speed boat that he kept at the yacht club. It had been manufactured in Japan, cost two million yuan and had a powerful aircraft engine. The warm night was perfect for a fast run on the ocean. After leaving the club's mooring, we sped briefly around a huge, cruise ship that loomed above us like an enormous, brightly lit wedding cake afloat on the becalmed harbor. And then we raced down the eastern shore to Resolute Bay. After swimming off the boat, we headed to Lantau Island. I had never seen the ocean completely becalmed, Gao driving the boat so fast we seemed to be flying. The sleek hull barely touched the water that was like a vast sheet of black glass streaked with moonlight.

Anchoring near the northern end of Lantau, we drank champagne straight from the bottle and watched the jets taking off from the ultra-modern airport that is such a remarkable, engineering achievement. The silver planes roaring away into the sky every few minutes were a thrilling spectacle, the sound of their engines echoing like thunder across the water. Lily and I sat close on a big, fluffy cushion, and I felt the exquisite touch of her damp skin. Gao offered me the boat whenever I wanted. He had access to a limitless supply of high octane gasoline and insisted that I use the boat as if it was my own. It wasn't the first time that he or his sister made some sort of overly generous gesture, indicating how much they trusted me. They had no idea there was any reason not to do so - that in reality I was a traitor in their midst, who for years had been spying on their government and passing along many of its top secrets to American intelligence. In essence, I had been trying to undermine everything that made possible their perfect, carefree life. Without their numerous privileges, I can't imagine how Lily or Gao could survive for long. If I was unmasked as a spy, Lily would be disgraced. The regime didn't appreciate anyone viewed as a collaborator, and none of the people so eager to be her friends would ever associate with her again. Only her father's exalted position might keep her out of prison, and perhaps even he wouldn't succeed. It was one of many things that of late I tried not to think about, including the fact I was deeply in love with a woman whose family was at the heart of the genocidal regime that I had been trying for years to expose.

"To Larry, our wonderful friend," Gao said warmly, raising a freshly opened bottle.

I looked at Lily and saw the tenderness in her lovely eyes. She started to say something but hesitated, although I knew what it was. Something I never expected had happened: Lily had fallen as deeply in love with me as I was with her. That night on the boat I should have realized the situation could only lead to heartbreak for both of us. The last thing I wanted was to harm my fine lady, and at that moment I decided that soon I had to end my espionage work and take her away to a new life abroad. It had become apparent that all my years in China had accomplished little. Most of the revealing information that I obtained, especially about the cruelties being inflicted on the Chinese people, had been largely ignored in Washington. Also I could no longer disregard the fact my situation was becoming increasingly precarious, and as never before, I was in danger of ending my days in one of the bleak, penal camps hidden far from the eyes of the outside world. What I couldn't be sure of was whether Lily would be willing to flee with me to the West, and if she wasn't, could I leave without her? Based on the information I acquired recently, it appeared that time was running out faster than I expected. Soon everyone in China would be in grave danger and no longer in control of their destiny. Instead that would be in the hands of the tiny, hidden group of party fanatics at the top of the regime, who with their hawkish allies in the military, were about to unleash history's most terrible war, one utilizing the most destructive weapon ever created.

4

As best I can, I will explain how this tragic situation developed and also what I tried to do about it. To appreciate the perilous nature of my long years in China, it's important you grasp the fact that a spy can only survive by adapting constantly to changing circumstances, in effect performing what amounts to a perpetual, juggling act. To avoid detection in such a hazardous environment, I cultivated the persona of an American businessman eager to further economic cooperation between China and the US. In essence, that became my convenient excuse for being in the country while I constantly snooped around. Fortunately no one suspected otherwise. Years earlier, I came to China with the goal of exposing to the world what's really happening in that vast, troubled land encompassing nearly a quarter of the human race. However, my real motivation was an old and festering grudge against the regime that I was determined to settle even if it cost my life. At the time I had no idea that my stay would last so long, involve so many, unexpected twists and turns and ultimately turn so dark.

Initially I doubted that I would have much success spying on such a secretive dictatorship that on an ongoing basis keeps legions of the helpless confined in brutal jails (many appropriately referred to as "*black*") and also countless, so-called psychiatric hospitals. To understand how I accomplished this difficult task, it is necessary that you appreciate the nature of what passes for an economy in China, one dominated by dishonesty and corruption on a monumental scale - what I call the "money game." This bizarre situation provided me with a highly effective way of penetrating the veil of secrecy that shrouds the government. In China, the economy is riddled with such extraordinary corruption that few on the outside can comprehend what it is really like. Under the so-called "communists," China has been transformed into a state dominated completely by the deviousness and dishonesty of those in power. At the same time all of this corruption developed in the service of a sinister, long-term objective. Probably nothing similar has occurred in all of human history. This bizarre situation resulted from the attempt to fuse western-style capitalism with a harsh, totalitarian regime run by a privileged minority. This was done with a specific purpose: to modernize the nation's industrial base and also the military so one day China would become the dominant, global power. Ultimately these objectives would be focused almost entirely on waging a monumental, war of conquest. Meanwhile this long-term program, that was overlooked almost completely by outsiders, also prevented the regime from collapsing from within. Thus China skillfully escaped the fate of the communist government in the Soviet Union that eventually was undermined by the economic inefficiency endemic to all totalitarian states, especially those espousing the fanciful principles of Karl Marx. Instead under the communists China evolved rapidly into a world power, the loyalty and dedication of party functionaries purchased by the opportunity to acquire wealth and privilege on an extraordinary scale.

In order to accomplish all of this in a limited amount of time, the so-called communists looked around for a creative way to achieve their objectives and found a willing ally in the outside business community with its own, singular focus on self-interest. Thus the capitalists were seduced by prospects of exploiting the supposedly unlimited Chinese market and eagerly rushed into the country with all their valuable technology and deep pockets full of money. Ultimately much of this money was employed by the Chinese to build up the military, while at the same time a not-insignificant portion was stolen by the regime's own functionaries. Unfortunately along the way some of America's prominent corporations ended up being corrupted (and hence compromised) to a significant degree. It took me a long time to comprehend the scope of this ingenious plan in all its ramifications, that only the Oriental mind at its best could have conceived. One of the most conspicuous results was that a large portion of America's industrial base with much of its advanced technology was transferred to the most dangerous regime on earth - the same resources that enabled the United States to win two world wars. Furthermore, this grand strategy was augmented by infiltrating western economies with so-called research scientists as well as thousands of phony "front companies." In this way additional relationships were formed with the naïve in order to steal additional, highly sensitive technology.

No doubt, some will claim that I'm misrepresenting the situation because what I say about China is so different from the laudatory information that for years appeared in the western media. This includes the claim that hundreds of millions of hapless souls were being lifted compassionately out of poverty as capitalism and a fledgling democracy supposedly took root in the country. Unfortunately that proved to be little more than a cynical fantasy, much of it spread around by the outside business community that saw China as the greatest profit opportunity of all time. The truth is that the vast majority of ordinary Chinese citizens only sank deeper into poverty and helplessness so they could be exploited more effectively. (To do otherwise would have invited the regime's demise.) As a result many in China had their small parcels of land seized for development projects sponsored by the politically well-connected. Meanwhile an ever-growing, displaced mass of itinerant workers wandered around the country living hand-to-mouth on a pittance. Also all the rapid industrialization gradually destroyed the environment to an unprecedented degree, ruining the health of countless millions. In essence, the great Chinese market of more than a billion eager consumers never came to fruition and wasn't intended to be anything more than an enticing illusion that the gullible capitalists bent on self-delusion couldn't resist.

Because the economy in China remained at all times under the strict control of the party and its close associates in the PLA (People's Liberation Army), several of America's most prominent corporations soon found themselves working closely with entities connected to the virulently, anti-western Chinese military. From the perspective of those on the outside, that, of course, made absolutely no sense. Nonetheless, many in the U.S. government and corporate community managed to convince themselves that eventually trade would bring democracy to China. Instead, history's most repressive dictatorship only grew more dangerous. *Through the eager participation of foreigners, who should have known better, a situation of unparalleled danger gradually developed, and a brutal regime strengthened until one day it could unleash history's greatest war. In effect, the nations of the west, especially America, systematically created a monster that ultimately would embody their worst nightmare.*

While I explain what I experienced inside China, it will also be apparent that over the years I developed a cynical turn of mind regarding the devoted "communists" and those so eager to profit handsomely by associating with them. Of necessity, however, cynicism became the indispensable ally that helped me to survive in such a dangerous realm. After arriving in China, I soon discovered how much the devious game the communists were playing had corrupted its own members. In fact, the black arts of financial corruption have been perfected to an unprecedented degree by high-ranking party members, becoming an indispensable part of the enormous wealth and privilege they enjoy. At the same time all this corruption spawned a seductive glamour enjoyed by a privileged few in which I was more than willing to participate. And often I found it hard to believe that what at times seemed so splendid and had flowered in the beautiful woman I loved, was rooted in so much deceitful behavior and heartlessness.

The bizarre "money game" played by China's influential

37

communists has many components, all of them intended to provide maximum advantage to key party members. One of the most important is the generous gift to the helpful friend in whatever "network" one is privileged to belong. In the West such a gift is referred to crudely as a bribe or kickback, terminology that understandably would offend my communist friends. At every level of government and business there is always a hand eagerly reaching out, and little is done unless that hand is liberally greased. In essence, what I found in China was a land of unparalleled corruption that even eclipsed what I experienced in Russia after the collapse of the Soviet Union - something I didn't think was possible. At the same time I soon realized this perverse situation provided fertile ground for espionage. Therefore, to achieve my objectives, I set about learning to play as skillfully as possible China's corrupt version of real-life monopoly.

I found my special niche in another key aspect of the all-pervasive "money game" - the ongoing siphoning off of the public's monies, a significant portion of this illicit horde quickly disappearing into the murky depths of the international financial system. In essence, a key component of the system so often praised in the West was nothing more than garden-variety theft perpetrated on a vast scale. After realizing all that money accumulating in such a small number of pockets needed a safe haven far from prying eyes, I placed my extensive knowledge of international finance at the disposal of well-connected party members. Over the years I discreetly helped many of them, their families and, of course, the girlfriends, to move their ill-gotten gains out of the country. As I've often said to my high-ranking communist pals, no one should be faulted for playing it safe and providing prudently for the inevitable rainy day. In fact, I can state with confidence that eventually I became one of the most effective money launderers in China. At all times I was willing and eager to serve the venal self-interests of corrupt officials, especially those about to join the many, other faithful believers in Karl Marx who had already disappeared over the horizon.

While not wanting to appear overly boastful, I would add that I managed to develop some of the most innovative techniques that cause large amounts of money to evaporate into thin air, or at least appear to do so. The corollary, of course, is that this same money soon reappears in a safe and very remote location. In the international banking system with so many, murky offshore havens peopled by greedy functionaries eager for their piece of the action, the task was relatively easy to accomplish. This was especially true for someone like me who approached the problem in an appropriately cynical frame of mind.

No doubt, China's apologists in the West will always deny the extent to which large "undocumented losses of funds" occurred on an ongoing basis throughout that huge country. In fact, such losses became an accepted fact of life, and it would have been a miracle if this devious game ever came to an end. To put the matter in perspective: in just one decade an estimated $3 *trillion (US)* mysteriously disappeared out of China. Even by today's inflated standards, that's a lot of money. This figure reflects the actions of a variety of greedy culprits across the spectrum of Chinese society. Of significance are the businessmen involved in foreign commerce, who are so fond of altering trade invoices. The amount pilfered by the party's dedicated members is probably about one-half of the overall $3 trillion, much of it stolen from state-owned enterprises. Often upwards of $20 billion disappeared per month, and in one year more than $50 billion was laundered just through the city of Shenzhen. I must admit that over the years I did my best to facilitate the process.

These remarkable sums, however, reflect only a portion of the shameless greed of party officials, who control key industries as well as vast amounts of real estate and natural resources. The wealthiest 50 members of the party are conservatively estimated to be worth at least $100 billion and probably a lot more. According to a prestigious Chinese academy, a little over a million high-ranking party members control at least 80 percent of all wealth in a country of about 1.5 billion people. In contrast, the average Chinese citizen (who are mostly farmers) subsist with difficulty on only a few dollars per day - that is, if their tiny plot of land hasn't been stolen by the politically influential. Additionally the rampant greed of CCP members also includes generous allotments for lavish travel, vacations and officially sanctioned self-indulgence of various sorts, a corrupt process that annually is estimated to consume upwards of one-half of all the national tax receipts.

As you might expect, little or no official notice is usually taken of any lost or misappropriated funds - that is, unless the people involved lose all self-control and go out of their way to embarrass their equally corrupt associates. Nonetheless, the veil of secrecy regarding the loss of the public's money was occasionally lifted, and like all information released by the regime, it was probably altered in order to further some partisan agenda. Under the circumstances it's understandable that personnel in China's banking institutions are such skilled practitioners in the black arts of financial deviousness. Although at times my competitors, I have to admit that they developed some highly inventive methods of their own that make sizeable amounts of money disappear quickly.

I will give you an interesting example. People in China, who are knowledgeable about the subject, still speak with amusement about an episode that involved no less than 42 provincial branch governors from the country's four, most "respected" banks, including the Bank of China. Suddenly one bright and sunny day this distinguished group simply vanished along with their family members and more than a few, very attractive mistresses. Shortly thereafter, it was discovered that a total of about $10 billion (US) was unaccounted for in various fake accounts, including over $2 billion in lost foreign exchange.

Whether the branch governors were responsible for the losses or as loyal, self-sacrificing communists merely ran away because they were embarrassed by this huge shortage has never been officially determined. Nonetheless, the situation was over the top even by the party's corrupt standards, and briefly the central government's ire was aroused by such inventive excess. On the side many commented that the government officials who launched the probe were merely jealous.

While the investigation into the lost funds was conducted officially by a Task Force of the Central Commission for Political and Legal Affairs, little money was recovered, and it is doubtful that was the real objective. The problem was made more difficult by the fact that more than 70 provincial bank branches had failed to submit auditing reports of any kind. Virtually all branches in 85 cities had numerous false accounts that didn't belong to anyone, and some branches had from 2 to 8 different sets of books in order to deal with the inconvenient problem of some brazen individual trying to snoop around. With that many, inscrutable accounting ledgers to decipher, it wasn't surprising the entire matter was eventually swept under the rug, and those in charge of the investigation decided to take a prolonged and lavish vacation.

With so much stealing taking place in the country's most prominent financial institutions, it became obvious to those in power that there was a significant problem. Fortunately the communists always had at their disposal a most convenient way of dealing with adverse developments caused by their own venal members. Once again they turned to their ever-helpful friends in the outside business community, especially the ever-astute Americans, who were always eager to rush in and pick up the tab. That was, of course, one of the main reasons for allowing all those greedy capitalists into the country in the first place. Therefore, the problem of the massive loss of funds from the country's largest banks was promptly dealt with by permitting the compliant capitalists the dubious honor of paying for the losses. A few years after the branch governors and their mistresses faded into the sunset, investors from the outside were allowed to buy small positions in the banks, thereby covering the known losses as well as any that might turn up in the near future. As expected, the foreigners eagerly purchased all the stock that was offered on the basis of sketchy information at inflated prices. Ironically the illusion of the great China profit opportunity once again became self-fulfilling, and the stocks actually went up, at least for a while.

Over the years I worked closely with officials in China's top, financial institutions, all of whom I found to be both helpful and amazingly dishonest. When I needed quick access to a foreign exchange market, they always went out of their way to facilitate matters as long as the price was right. If on occasion they weren't cooperative, there were many other avenues at my disposal. These included obscure, corrupt banks in Japan, Thailand and India. However, my tried and true favorites - the "old reliables" as I like to call them - are in Russia, where so many financial institutions are still connected to the former KGB. For the right price, the "old reliables" always demonstrated their corruption that as far as I can determine knows no bounds.

It might be assumed that someone who facilitated flight capital out of a police state was living on borrowed time, and I am not suggesting that a high degree of prudence on my part wasn't in order. On numerous occasions, I was interviewed by some harassed and poorly dressed investigator from an obscure government bureau trying to trace funds that disappeared along with the conscientious people entrusted with their care. Unless the object of the exercise was embarrassing or displacing a political opponent, however, such a meeting was usually brief. I knew the real objective was to put the matter to rest as quickly as possible and avoid embarrassment to other party members, all of whom had probably stolen even more money. As many an investigator commented to me, bookkeeping errors happen all the time in China and have a way of creating the unfortunate appearance of funds being diverted. Consequently, it was the usual result of any investigation that the true status of the lost monies was never determined and the conclusion reached that another unfortunate error had occurred in a country whose imaginative accounting methods are so complex that no one has ever been able to understand them.

It should also be emphasized that I only plied my craft on behalf of people whom I knew were well-connected and came to me highly recommended. In addition, I always required that they have access to the type of confidential information at the highest levels that made my efforts worthwhile. What I preferred were documents discreetly copied from the files of top government bureaus. Usually this generous sharing of inside information was my only compensation, although occasionally I couldn't resist taking a small cut of any money when it reached its final destination. Most of the time, however, I asked for little or nothing in return, preferring to keep the high-ranking official indebted to me. When to my surprise, I kept hearing rumors that soon the regime might initiate some sort of military adventure, I decided to call in some of those markers in order to find out what was going on. However, that turned out to be more difficult than I expected, and the answers that eventually I obtained were very different from anything I expected or thought possible.

Over the years I was often pleasantly surprised by the type of secrets I managed to steal, that invariably contradicted the information coming from party mouthpieces and the highly paid lobbyists of big business in Washington. For example, a report I found particularly informative - as well as amusing - appeared not long after the disappearance of the 42 provincial branch governors and all that stock was issued to underwrite their huge, private retirement fund. I suspect that few in the West appreciated the obvious irony exhibited by the memo that came from the prestigious Central Financial and Economic Leading Group, another bastion of unquestioned financial integrity. Of significance is the following:

"It is regrettable that such a large percentage of the loans in the banks in which stock was floated is non-performing. Needless to say, it would have been inconvenient and counter-productive to discuss such information in detail. This is especially true because most of the bad loans were made to state-owned enterprises run by people connected to the party. Therefore, it might be concluded by petty critics that the communist state lost the money from the banks it controls by lending the money to itself and its own officials.

"The problem of bad loans, however, goes beyond our four, most respected banks. As is well known, the country has one of the highest savings rates in the world, the diligent Chinese people often putting aside a large portion of their meager income. The reason, of course, is the country's need to grow rapidly has prevented us from having a proper retirement or health-care insurance system. Unfortunately, at this time much of this vast pool of unregulated funds is tied up almost entirely in non-performing loans that could exceed $1 trillion (US).

"In recent years it has not been unusual for as much as $20 billion to leave China in only one month. Fortunately for the regime the negative impact of such a constant outflow has been largely neutralized by generous foreign investors and also the American trade deficit that is caused by the fact that we successfully peg our currency (yuan) at an artificial level favorable to our interests. This very large surplus of funds has enabled us to obscure the true condition of the nation's financial system, including the banks in which stock was floated. On top of that, the surplus has also provided the means to help modernize the military, provide aid to countries hostile to the United States and also potentially to manipulate the American currency during a time of crisis."

The memo also pointed out that most people in the western business community could be counted on to contradict any information that didn't substantiate the enormous success supposedly prevailing in the Chinese economy. After all, the statistics issued by the regime's own bureaus proved that the economy was doing superbly, and certainly there was no reason to believe these numbers weren't completely accurate. According to those brave enough to study such bizarre goings on, dubious loans are thought to involve at least three-quarters of all Chinese enterprises. Because of the ongoing problem of falsified statements and lost documentation, however, it is unlikely that anyone will ever be able to determine the exact amount of the enormous sums that over the years were creatively stolen or misappropriated.

Certain naïve people at an outside rating agency along with a prominent Chinese university once attempted the impossible task of evaluating the performance of China's state-owned enterprises run so diligently by party members - the positions that enable them to live in luxury while constantly diverting as much money as possible into their own pockets. As I and many others expected, the project was quickly abandoned after much wasted effort because none of the financial statements were found to be "believable." In other words almost everything was made up. Anyone in China, who was familiar with the situation, could have saved them a lot of trouble.

After acquiring the confidential report regarding the true condition of China's banks, I promptly sent it to Washington assuming it would produce a strong reaction, including a healthy dose of indignation from those who trustingly brought all that bank stock backed to a significant extent by non-performing loans. To this day it is not known what ultimately happened to all those worthless loans. As far as I know, most, along with many others, were conveniently swept under the same, very large, collective rug and quickly forgotten. The response on the outside, however, was quite different from what I expected. Hardly anyone was willing to consider the possibility that such flagrant dishonesty could really exist, especially since many, supposedly smart Americans were eagerly investing in China's financial institutions, some even risking their futures to be a player there. In a rare moment of candor, a US accounting firm had the audacity to release detailed information regarding the obvious problems of the banking system. But when a highly negative reaction occurred in both China and the US, the figures were promptly retracted as if someone had used some very bad language and told never to do that again. According to the estimates by this accounting firm, the amount of bad loans in China's banking system could be nearly one trillion American dollars, most of these so-called loans no doubt connected to the thievery and incompetence prevailing in state-owned enterprises. No one seemed to grasp the interesting fact that at the time one trillion was nearly equal to the entire amount of the vast savings that had been set aside by the frugal Chinese people for their retirement. In other words almost all of their savings had probably been wasted or stolen. Ultimately, however, this substantial sum would prove to be a pittance, as the mountain of dubious credit essential to keeping the leaky ship afloat continued to escalate. Of course, most of this money came from the West as investment funds of various sorts kept pouring into the country. Not surprising, much of this money would eventually be lost. Before that happened, however, it would be put to good use serving the regime's carefully thought-out, long-term expansionist objectives.

The following is an excerpt from another informative memorandum issued by the prestigious Central Financial Working Group that criticized some of the cruder methods employed by venal party officials to send their ill-gotten gains out of the country.

As far as I was concerned, it provided a good example of why the services of a skilled money launderer such as myself should always be employed for the purpose of discretely creating a tidy nest egg abroad:

"The issue of excessively large amounts of money fleeing the country continues to be a matter of concern, one discussed recently in both the Politburo Standing Committee and the Central Discipline and Inspection Commission. Of particular concern are bulk shipments in cash of foreign exchange, which are exported without official permission, causing shortages in local banking systems of Euros, British Pounds, Swiss francs, Canadian and Australian dollars. In some instances large amounts of these currencies and Renminbi have been withdrawn from reserve accounts by using false numbers. As a result, there has often been an acute shortage, requiring these currencies to be brought in by plane to several cities including Shenzhen, Guangdong and Shanghai.

"At various times substantial amounts of missing foreign exchange have turned up in shipping containers, cargo boxes and even military trucks that were altered to accommodate packages filled with money. Recently two, large speedboats driving too fast across the Bohai Sea from Beijing were apprehended after sideswiping boats fishing in the badly polluted water. Each of the speed boats carried more than 10 million (Euros) neatly arranged in stacks of candy boxes located in their cabins. Various shipping containers that have been seized were addressed to locations in New York, San Francisco, Vancouver, Toronto, Tokyo, Rome and other cities. This activity remains a serious problem and warrants vigilance by the appropriate authorities. It is to be expected that a certain amount of unavoidable "leakage" of foreign exchange will occur during the normal course of conducting business. Furthermore, party officials frequently move private funds abroad for investment in the international economy, an important effort to support the globalization of commerce, which is highly favorable to our interests. Aside from this, we are currently investigating suspicious, foreign exchange transactions involving billions of yuan that continue to be executed through the nation's banking system. However, the spectacle of such large amounts of hard currency being stuffed in shipping containers and sometimes falling out on docks in plain view is an embarrassment to the party and its good name among the local populace and must be stopped."

5

At the beginning of each quarter, the "East/West Friendship Society," the prestigious, Hong Kong business association of which I am a founding member, gathered in one of the opulent conference rooms of the Grand Hyatt Hotel. The group's stated purpose was to encourage outside businessmen to buy into the great, Chinese illusion of unlimited profits. Of course, they didn't need my help to deceive themselves, and I was always surprised by the large turnout, the upbeat mood fueled by the limitless supply of gourmet food and strong liquor that after a few hours completely stupefied everyone who was there.

It was considered quite an honor to receive one of our gaudy invitations printed on expensive paper that provided most of the recipients with little more than an opportunity to give away their money. As far as I know, the only big winners from the outside were a small group of large American, European and Japanese corporations with lots of political clout in their own countries. For the average, small foreign company it was not unlike rolling dice in a rigged casino, less than 10% of them ever making any significant profits. Eventually more than half of these determined losers simply threw up their hands and abandoned what they brought to China, including their valuable, intellectual property. Thus they left with nothing but a very big hole in their pockets. Nonetheless, that was no concern of mine, even if I did encourage them to come aboard and royally screw themselves. Unfortunately that was an essential part of the devious game that I was playing, and I couldn't allow such fine distinctions to get in the way.

A couple of weeks after Lily's final party, the last of the Society's meetings took place. Political as well as economic conditions around the world continued to worsen, causing many to voice concern about where such a perilous situation might ultimately lead. This was especially true in the Middle East where, as John of Patmos predicted, violence continued to rage "along the great river Euphrates." Unknown to many, China had for decades played a key role abetting instability in the area with transfers of money and weapons. Meanwhile greed and speculation on a grand scale continued to undermine the global order. This included the manipulative activities pursued by many of the world's most prestigious financial institutions that constantly destabilized commerce, especially regarding the cost and availability of essential commodities.

Also China was disintegrating rapidly from within while building up a massive military machine focused on the most lethal weaponry. The true situation regarding the propped-up Chinese economy had for years been obscured by a giant, credit bubble that eventually rose to the unimaginable sum of more than $20 *trillion* dollars. Many warehouses supposedly filled with valuable commodities used as loan collateral were found to be empty, once again leaving the outsiders holding a very large and empty bag. In addition, loan grantors across the country kept shutting their doors, while many, prominent municipalities were known to be insolvent. The defaults in the bond market for small to medium-sized firms continued to rise ominously and could only go higher. Many of these supposedly secure bonds had been acquired by foreigners, who had eagerly invested for the "long term" in the most corrupt and manipulated, large economy on earth. In fact, I was shocked to learn that this market had grown to the obscenely large sum of at least $15 trillion. As a result it eclipsed even the U.S. corporate bond market that served a much larger economy. *I realized that when it came to the fantasy goldmine of easy profits in China, the propensity for self-delusion in the West was truly limitless.*

To the end, this cynical illusion kept growing even more outrageous. Eventually the average American was provided with the irresistible opportunity to participate in all sorts of worthless, so-called investments in China, especially those where reasonable accounting standards were virtually non-existent. Not surprising, various funds and Wall Street firms went out of their way to facilitate this corrupt process, demonstrating once again an eagerness to please at any cost their new-found communist associates.

With the international market for debt nearly exhausted, the ways employed to raise additional funds to prop up the regime took a variety of creative forms. For a while Chinese companies were listed on U.S. exchanges by employing a legal slight of hand involving a merger with an American "shell" corporation (reverse takeover). Through this "backdoor" strategy, the Chinese company was sold to the investing public while eluding initial scrutiny. Eventually many had to be "de-listed" but only after the significant sums invested in them were long gone.

Another method employed to milk naïve, outside investors is an ingenious device known as the "variable interest entity" (VIE). The best example is the much heralded "Alibaba" IPO (initial public offering of stock) that took place with much fanfare on the venerable New York Stock Exchange. With this one, the clever, Chinese strategists really outdid themselves. Often compared to western companies such as Amazon.com, Alibaba is likely nothing more than a front company concocted by communist officials to monitor in real time all e-commerce in China. In this way the party knows exactly what everyone is buying and selling and also how much disposable income they have - an extraordinarily effective tool of internal surveillance. In effect, with the IPO the West was given the honor of subsidizing the entire, devious operation, while pumping even more money into the regime's bottomless coffers. Not surprising, Wall Street also eagerly pawned this dubious concoction off on their fellow Americans, many of whom "invested" their retirement funds in what is essentially a shell, holding company in the Cayman Islands. Unfortunately this entity has only a vague contractual relationship with what exists in China. In other words no meaningful control or auditing can occur, the shareholders owning next to nothing but a largely unenforceable promise. (To make matters worse, in China the VIE concept has only limited legal standing.) Furthermore, without telling anyone, Alibaba's management quietly sold off the valuable payment system (the company's main asset), hiding permanently the project's underlying purpose as well as what passes for profitability. Nonetheless, after all the hype Alibaba soon became one of the most valuable, listed companies on U.S. exchanges, acquiring a market cap (value) greater than Walmart, the world's largest retailer. Equally significant, based on this grand ruse, more than $25 billion of badly needed funds headed for China never to be seen again along with several, additional billions raised by a subsequent bond issue.

No doubt, the communists couldn't believe their success with this ingenious ruse. Knowing the VIE vehicle had to be used sparingly, however, the regime decided it was time to grant overseas investors the ultimate opportunity to rip themselves off while supporting the most dangerous regime in history. Thus the Hong Kong IPO market and Shanghai Stock Exchange were opened up to the foreigners so they could fill their portfolios with abysmally corrupt, small to medium-sized Chinese companies. Many are the remnants of failed, state-owned enterprises that already had been milked almost to death after floating absurd amounts of loans or bonds that could never be repaid. Not surprising, the outside investment community eagerly supported this irresistible idea as well, realizing that another, lucrative gold mine of commissions and consulting fees had been discovered. Thus in the space of less than two decades, Wall Street had progressed from floating stock in countless, highly speculative tech and internet ventures, most of which eventually collapsed. Next they moved on to mortgage-backed securities secured by mountains of sub-prime loans that hardly anyone believed could ever be repaid; and now they were pushing the true carrion of the investment world - common stock in corrupt companies in a totalitarian state that couldn't be scrutinized. Eventually I heard that some on Wall Street were emphasizing the importance of such "investments" for the truly balanced, international portfolio. Presumably this applied to the average worker's 401k retirement plan that of late had been evaporating rapidly. How can anyone outdo all of that for sheer audacity?

While the communists continued happily to best the capitalists at their own greedy game, there was, of course, a finite limit to how much longer the regime's corrupt, leaky ship could be kept afloat even with so much eager assistance from the outside. After hearing the rumors about a possible war, I began to notice that large numbers of ordinary Chinese businessmen were trying to leave the country. This included a large portion of those with assets of at least $2 million. What I couldn't understand was why such a mass exodus was being tolerated with all the negative consequences for Chinese society. Eventually I realized that the regime didn't care because they no longer found these individuals useful and at this perilous time considered them a potential burden because of questionable loyalty.

Also of late, the social unrest throughout China continued to escalate. There has always been lots of internal turmoil, much of it caused by endemic corruption and the on-going, illegal seizure of land for speculative, real estate ventures. Invariably this left many subsistence farmers totally impoverished because few were ever compensated. To aggravate the situation even further, the environmental degradation caused by uncontrolled industrialization had reached such a destructive level that the drinking water available to nearly one-half of the entire populace was polluted.

In a typical year the protest demonstrations in China often numbered 100,000 or more, many turning into pitched battles. Local police around the country, along with the vicious, internal troops known as the People's Armed Police, often employed the most uncompromising methods to suppress dissent. With exports falling and loan defaults rising ominously, unemployment reached dangerous levels. This ignited additional protests. At times the regime was encountering so much difficulty preserving order that *local police were being trained to employ bayonets* in the most lethal fashion - in other words summarily kill their fellow countrymen who had been legitimately wronged. I suspect that for some of the protestors, such a fate would be preferable to being carted off to one of the countless, aptly named *"black* jails" that kept proliferating across the country.

Other evidence that something significant was being planned by the military was provided by the fact that many party officials, who had grown too powerful, were being purged for conveniently uncovered corruption. Obviously the ranks of those with influence were being streamlined. Many, foreign companies suddenly found their prerogatives curtailed and of late had been subject to less than subtle harassment. And finally to everyone's surprise, there was a renewed emphasis in schools on Maoist principles and the strict discipline required.

At first, I assumed that if there was going to be a war, it would amount to only a limited engagement in order to divert attention from the country's mounting problems. Later this would prove to be a major miscalculation on my part. The fact the regime was amassing huge amounts of gold should have tipped me off. When planning a major war, totalitarian governments (such as Nazi Germany and Imperial Japan) invariably acquire key commodities, especially those representing an easily disposed of storehouse of value. One of the excuses for stockpiling so much gold was that the yuan was supposedly being groomed as an international currency to replace the US dollar. However, contrary to what was believed by many commentators in the West, it was unlikely that would ever happen. Then the situation grew even more interesting. The regime sought to make Shanghai with its massive, newly constructed "underground" storage facilities the center of international gold trading. A large, so-called gold "fund" for investing in mines around the world was added. Thus a significant portion of global precious metals (the ultimate storehouse of value) would soon be controlled by a regime about to unleash history's greatest war.

In spite of the rapidly worsening situation within and outside China, the turn-out for the Friendship Society's final meeting was surprisingly large and as usual included many government officials. In addition to providing an opportunity for them to get completely drunk, the meetings afforded me with an easy way to monitor how the various factions in the regime were getting along. While most outsiders view the Chinese government as a rigid monolith, in fact it has always been plagued by incessant infighting over all the easy money and power that at times could turn deadly. For anyone seeking influence, information or their own chunk of the pie, it was important to be up-to-date on the subject of who was in favor and who was rapidly going down the drain. When it pleased those above, some unfortunates no longer in favor simply disappeared. Therefore, in order to ensure my own survival, I was always careful to play both sides of any fence and have at least a few friends in every camp. After all, I supposedly had little interest in such internal squabbling and was there merely to make a nice, quick buck like all the other starry-eyed capitalists - an idea that party members regardless of their faction could easily relate to.

In order to impress everyone at the meeting, I brought along Lily, who was her usual, gorgeous self. Not surprising, many in the room couldn't take their eyes off of her, and probably she inspired at least a few of the gullible foreigners to make an even larger, losing commitment in China. For a while everyone's attention was distracted by the enormous, 10 foot-high television screen at the end of the room, which showed a recent episode of the Kim family, the darlings of Chinese reality TV. Sister Kim was driving a sleek, new car that was a present from her overly generous father, a prominent communist official. As the television series emphasized repeatedly, this "loveable" individual constantly spoiled his charming family and was a soft touch for nearly everybody. Supposedly his generosity was only one of the qualities that made the old man so likable, and often the point was stressed that it was his extraordinary kindness as a communist official that led to the wide respect that undoubtedly he commanded throughout the country.

No one in the room could fail to notice the similarity between Lily and Sister Kim. Like Lily, Sister Kim was tall and had luxurious, long hair that blew seductively in the wind as she drove too fast through the scenic countryside in her flashy, new car. Not surprising, it was a brand new model manufactured with technology obtained from a helpful, foreign company that also provided 100% of the investment required to start a joint venture. Unfortunately, most of that technology along with the personnel patiently trained by the outsiders was diverted to a rival car company by the friendly Chinese business "partner." Soon thereafter, Sister Kim was given her fancy, new set of wheels to tool in style around Hong Kong.

While everyone's attention was focused on the TV screen, I briefly caught the eye of Liao Dan, a top official in the General Secretary's Office, who over the years had been one of my best, ongoing sources of information. In return, I helped Dan and his relatives discreetly dispatch more than a $50 million (US) of embezzled funds out of the country and then a few weeks ago an additional, sizeable sum to Australia. This meant, of course, that I had every right to ask him for something in return, especially since I knew where every dime of his illegal funds was located.

The previous week we met for dinner, and I inquired about the rumor of an impending military action, still wondering if it was true. Of course, it wouldn't be the first time that war became the means of propping up a corrupt regime and dealing with the enormous problems caused by its own venality. I continued to be skeptical, although one of my sources was a "princelette," who had an appealing habit of saying more than he should after drinking too much. In general, I rarely ignored information emanating from a princelette, especially one so well-connected. When I uttered the word "war," Dan's face went pale suggesting that whatever was involved could be more serious than I thought. Nonetheless, he denied knowing anything about such a development. As we looked at each other across the room, he discreetly shook his head indicating that as yet he didn't have any information on the subject, or at least that's what he wanted me to think.

With Lily on my arm, I went around squeezing as many fat, little hands as possible. Most of the Chinese in attendance represented either a supposed entrepreneur or someone from a state-owned enterprise, both of whom were probably connected in some way to the military. Essentially the state-owned enterprises served a multiple purpose: build up the nation's industrial base, acquire technology, especially for the military, and also provide a very large piggy bank for party functionaries. Regardless of their particular objectives, however, the Chinese were always eager to do business with the generous, naïve outsiders and grab their own piece of all that precious capital and technology. As expected, the conversations I overheard concerned various, fanciful deals that supposedly were going to generate the enormous profits that at our meetings everyone always fantasized about, especially after they were obviously drunk.

In the Hong Kong business community, I was on a first-name basis with nearly everyone of consequence, and many at the meeting made a point of coming over to greet me. Fortunately not a single person in the opulent conference room had the slightest suspicion that I was anything but the pleasant glad-hander they all knew and liked, one always eager to pass along a bribe or do something else appropriately corrupt - that is, of course, for the right price. In fact, over the years I came to exemplify enlightened "engagement" between China and the US and was often referred to euphemistically as one of Hong Kong's top "facilitators of mutual interests." In other words I had become a poster boy for *one of the most cynical fictions of all times - namely, that so-called engagement through commerce was somehow going to make a brutal, totalitarian regime evaporate magically while everyone developed instant amnesia about the horrific crimes that for decades had been perpetrated on its helpless citizenry.*

As expected, several representatives from the security services were also thoughtful enough to show up. Whenever there was a get-together of consequence in China, the undercover agents were always there trying to blend in and appear harmless while doing their best to snoop into everyone's affairs. Over the years I made a point of getting to know as many of them as possible, and at times we developed a real rapport. Although I couldn't be sure, I suspected that the person who lately had been following me was probably at the meeting. I have to admit this unexpected snoop had considerable expertise, and recently I was lucky to spot him. It was a long time since anyone had shown so much interest in my activities. Whoever it was had probably been doing so for quite a while, which raised the question of what they might have learned. It bothered me that I hadn't noticed sooner and realized that I was getting careless, something that can be fatal in my line of work. For too long I had been rolling the dice and getting away with it, but hopefully my luck would hold a little while longer until I could complete my mission and get out of China with Lily - that, is if she would flee with me to the West.

If the time ever came that I was found out, it would come as a big surprise to party officials, many of whom considered me a friend, or at least as much as any American could be viewed that way. In the event my cover was blown, I had a plan to quickly leave the country. Unfortunately, in such a situation nothing is guaranteed, and if I didn't get away, I knew only too well that I would experience the harsh realities of the country's brutal, penal system, a portion of which is a carefully designed refinement of Soviet Russia's legendary Gulag. Over the years the stories I heard about that bleak realm made my blood run cold.

What can be seen by the outside world, however, is only the most visible part of a vast, detention system that also includes slave labor and death camps along with an extensive network of psychiatric hospitals conveniently named the Ankang ("peace and health"). It is there that the more uncooperative citizens are sent for reformation because of such alleged crimes as "political monomania" and "litigation mania." In other words, for communist officials these dim, covert locations were the convenient place where anyone viewed with disfavor could be quickly put out of commission, especially members of the peace-loving Falun Gong. As you might expect, the few who managed to come out alive were usually incapable of functioning in a rational manner.

A few days before Lily's party, I received a letter that emphasized how precarious my situation in China had become. It came from the only person in the CIA who knows my true identity. I will call him Ben. His letters always went to a mail drop in Taiwan that I visited once a month. All communications I considered sensitive were sent there so they couldn't be intercepted. Ben is one of the most astute agents in the CIA, and without him it is unlikely that I would have gotten into espionage. Over the years he skillfully handled agents all around the world before being transferred to the Operations Center in Washington. Nonetheless, we regularly kept in touch, and it was always reassuring to know he was there. He's a straight-shooter who looks at things the way I do. After he left Hong Kong, I worked with a replacement, Larry Kress - actually his real name. It doesn't matter that I tell you since he managed to get himself shot to death while trying to set me up. When meeting with Kress, I always wore a disguise, and to the end he thought I was a Russian named "Sergei." Fortunately I could still mimic a convincing accent acquired during my Moscow days.

Once again Ben warned me of the effort being made in Washington to learn my identity. We both knew how politics, self-interest and espionage get mixed up in the nation's capital, where opportunistic leaks of confidential information are an ever-present problem. If my situation with the CIA hadn't been arranged so I was completely anonymous, I'm sure that my cover would have been blown years ago, and I would have already died in a very unpleasant way.

It was indeed unfortunate that I couldn't allow my own countrymen to know who "Sergei," one of their top agents, really is, some of whom out of irresistible expediency would have willingly betrayed such a valuable intelligence source. In essence, all those years Ben remained my sole lifeline, and except for him I was completely alone, surrounded by people who could have killed me in the blink of an eye.

As usual, Ben's letter went right to the point:

"Your recent info hit some big nerves, especially the latest details about China's growing military sophistication, a lot of it derived from the high tech obtained from western corporations. We both know that the stakes keep getting higher, and money has a way of obscuring other concerns. For good reason, many, big multinationals are being allowed to make large profits while the Chinese use their influential lobbyists to quiet criticism. The sad truth is that some of this country's top corporations are literally in bed with the so-called "commies." And now you've sent all this embarrassing information about the fate of political dissenters and Falun Gong practitioners. Needless to say, it's rather unsettling to contemplate how the Falun Gong are being warehoused so their organs can be harvested for sale in the country's military hospitals. Apparently the world's memories of Auschwitz and other recent places of horror have faded very quickly. Of course, the State Department doesn't want to hear about such things.

"Some keep pressuring me to disclose more about you. Of course, I tell them that I only know that you're a Russian – a somewhat implausible explanation although I keep to the story. Apparently they're feeling the heat from some very important people. I'm convinced that you're in danger as never before. It would be worth a lot for someone to find out how you're getting away with so much information right under the noses of China's security services. If you're not careful, you could end up like some of the Falun Gong. I'm sure that Chinese counter-intelligence would enjoy having the last laugh and consider that a suitable retribution for all the embarrassment you've caused them."

The prospect of sharing the tragic fate of the Falun Gong was another unsettling possibility that for years I had to live with. While fraternizing with the spoiled youth of the country's communist big shots, that gruesome thought always lurked ominously in the back of my mind. Most people on the outside know little about the Falun Gong. When I mentioned the name to an acquaintance from New York, he thought I was talking about a Tokyo baseball team. It is a discipline that emphasizes peace, tolerance and compassion, qualities that understandably the virulently atheistic regime in China views with much disfavor. In fact, the harsh treatment accorded the Falun Gong is a prime example of the deep hostility of all modern, totalitarian states toward anything with spiritual overtones.

61

As a result the notorious **6**10 office came into existence for the specific purpose of eradicating the Falun Gong by various punitive means, including the ominously sounding objective of "physically destroying" its adherents. A ministerial level operation connected to the all-powerful Central Committee, the 610 office has branches throughout the country, its authority super-ceding even that of the internal police. Although specific numbers were always difficult to come by, it was known that at least a quarter-million, hapless Falun Gong were usually incarcerated in an estimated 36 special camps. Supposedly the notorious 672-S camp could hold as many as 50 to 100 thousand.

The central feature of the persecution of the Falun Gong is the "harvesting" of the valuable, internal organs of healthy, young practitioners in order to help subsidize China's hospital system. Since the Falun Gong were to be "physically destroyed," it was apparently decided that the government might as well make a few bucks in the process or, I should say, a lot of bucks. The regime already had a well-known practice of utilizing for profit the organs of condemned prisoners, most of whom were conveniently dispatched just when their organs were needed. Thus, with the establishment of the **6**10 office, imprisoned Falun Gong became what amounts to an invaluable, living bank of healthy and very useful hearts, kidneys, livers, skin, corneas and whatever else could be stolen from these helpless victims. In addition, it was well-known that the primitive operations to remove the organs were usually performed without anesthetics. The reason was that this additional cruelty saved money, although a very small amount. Furthermore, it guaranteed that the organ was fresh as possible.

I knew that espionage agents always got the worst treatment and was sure that I would be a prime candidate for the organ bank. After all, over the years I've taken very good care of myself, and probably camp personnel would develop an immediate fondness for my heart, liver and probably most of my other body parts as well. Such a gruesome specter caused me more than a few, sleepless nights, although in the Grand Hyatt's plush, air-conditioned conference room I tried to avoid thinking about that depressing subject for at least a few hours.

As the meeting was about to end, I spotted a familiar face across the room but couldn't recall where I'd seen him. I rarely forget people, and it troubled me that I couldn't remember. Having arrived late, the tall, handsome, blond man was talking with an official from the Bank of China, and I assumed he was an American or European banker. And then I remembered and was surprised how little he had changed over the years. His name was Robert Verrelin, and I last encountered him in Moscow when the old "gang wars" were at their peak.

In those days Moscow was quite a spectacle in a very bizarre way. While the gang wars raged on, the assassinations and bombings made headlines every day on the front pages of Moscow's newspapers. One of the most impressive photographs showed "Sylvester's" fancy Mercedes limousine with tinted windows blown up not far from the city's top shopping area. Everyone agreed that Sylvester went out in style. He considered himself a real "big shot," and on that day he certainly proved it. Sylvester was his name in the underworld because he looked so much like the American actor, Sylvester Stallone. Rolfe, my boss, was very fond of Sylvester, who was an excellent poker player and added a lot to our late-night games. Unfortunately, while huge amounts of money were tossed around like confetti at our table, many continued to starve in the frigid streets outside.

For a while a particular day or week in Moscow was identified with whoever had been shot at least a dozen times or blown up. Supposedly the gang wars began when "Rambo," the enforcer for the old Bauman crime gang, was ambushed in a particularly sneaky way. Then a few years later Sylvester was blown up, and after that the gang wars gradually fizzled out. In the public mind that unique era of Moscow's troubled history lasted officially from "Rambo" to "Sylvester." Around the city that briefly was the big joke.

The man across the room showed up at our parties just before someone late one night crudely eliminated everyone, including Rolfe, with a machine gun. That was a couple of weeks before Sylvester evaporated into a cloud of smoke. Fortunately I wasn't at either location, or I wouldn't be telling you this story of unbelievable greed and folly that will culminate in what is likely the greatest war of all times. I never learned who was responsible for killing Rolf. A rubout is supposed to have a certain, perverse logic. Since no one really benefited from his death, it appeared to make no sense. Our company did business with all sorts of corrupt officials, especially former KGB operatives and their pals in the underworld, and we always gave them excellent service. Because of the nasty way Rolf was eliminated, I concluded that someone must have thought we double-crossed them. After spreading around lots of money, I learned to my surprise that the killer came from the west - something unheard of in Moscow where there's a limitless supply of hit-men eager to ply their trade. Usually for enough money you could find out anything, even if it involves the perpetrator of a major hit. But not this time, which deepened the mystery. For years, outside trading companies and financial institutions reaped a bountiful harvest in Russia. It appeared that some disgruntled person connected to one of them didn't appreciate the fact that so much information was leaking out about how the Russian people were being systematically ripped off by former, communist fat cats and their foreign business pals. Fortunately, whoever it was didn't put two and two together and figure out it was me.

For some reason Robert Verrelin always stood out at our parties. I soon learned that he worked now for an American financial group planning to make a big commitment in China. The following day I sent a letter to Ben Cramer asking him to find out everything he could about Verrelin. Through the CIA Ben has access to excellent sources, and I was sure he could come up with something useful. The next time I visited the mail drop in Taiwan, there was a lengthy letter that didn't disappoint me. A lot of information about Verrelin was floating around, including a sizable Interpol file, and none of it was favorable. Originally a South African, he carried a French passport and at one time was connected to some large, diamond interests, including a prominent exporter of "blood diamonds." At various times he used different aliases, and supposedly his real name was Zellkovin. Recently he was connected to various shady but highly profitable financial deals, although his actual role was never clear. In a couple of them some of the top people died suddenly under mysterious circumstances.

6

It should not be assumed that overnight I became a highly skilled money launderer, one available twenty-four hours a day to assist corrupt, Chinese officials so they could be milked for information before retiring abroad to a life of even greater decadence and self-indulgence. Instead it took many years of effort in the obscure vineyards of international finance to perfect my most creative techniques. I found the perfect training ground in which to serve my apprenticeship in this dubious but highly useful field when the recently liberated Russian nation was looted so skillfully by patriotic insiders - an experience that prepared me at least in part for the even more grotesque spectacle of exploitation taking place in China.

After the collapse of the Soviet state, departing KGB and ex-party officials along with their allies in the underworld demonstrated their patriotism by systematically stealing as much of the country's enormous wealth as they could quickly grab. This included vast quantities of petroleum, minerals and even valuable military hardware. Eventually, as if by magic the country's gold reserves suddenly disappeared, a skillful sleight of hand that would have intrigued even Houdini.

At the time the company I worked for functioned as a middle-man facilitating the transactions with the foreign business interests eagerly buying up the spoils for resale in the west. It was my rude introduction to the corrupt underside of international, "free market" commerce that in recent years has had such a large impact on the world economy. Eventually I passed on to the CIA details of the transactions that enriched so many foreign corporations while despoiling Russia's wealth and causing millions to sink further into poverty. A key part of the company's role was to channel the money paid for the bonanza through a chain of compliant banks into overseas investments on behalf of our well-connected Russian "clients." These investments included expensive real estate on the Cote d'Azur, the coasts of Florida and posh sections of London and mid-Manhattan. It was obvious that the KGB people and their former party apparatchik pals knew a good neighborhood when they saw one. In addition, these enormous, stolen funds later became an important element in the large scale speculative activities that constantly destabilized financial markets around the world.

A key aspect of the return to power of the KGB's old boy's network under Vladimir Putin - the *sloviki* - was the tendency of critical journalists, political opponents or those merely uncooperative to meet a quick and untimely end. This included being shot in the back of the head, poisoned with some exotic, difficult-to-trace substance, or suddenly developing an irresistible urge late at night to jump out of a window on a very high floor. Understandably the amount of criticism of the new government dominated by the less than subtle *sloviki* lessened considerably. The imaginative KGB folks even had the audacity to attribute the destructive effects of their own larceny to others and use it as an excuse to regain power. In that way the world got another object-lesson in how dictatorial regimes operate.

While studying market theory at the London School of Economics, I had no idea of what I would eventually experience in the real world where economics and the perversities of human nature often morph into a fatal, witches brew. After graduation I worked initially as a currency analyst for various New York firms, finally landing a job at a prestigious hedge fund group - Crenbar Capital. As most people know, hedge funds are the prima donnas of the investment world, and invariably the name conjures up in the public mind exotic images of financial brilliance. In general, these secretive pools of wealth operate largely free of regulation and have become a key component of the huge, international supply of restless, speculative money that's always on the prowl seeking a quick, financial kill. Of significance is the impact on the commodity markets, which has influenced significantly the cost of sustaining human life on the planet. Unfortunately a large portion of this enormous pool of illusive wealth comes from sources impossible to identify, including both flight capital and the fruits of large-scale criminal activity.

According to one of the few, non-politicized studies produced by the United Nations, at least one-quarter of all of the capital floating around the world comes from a grey or "black" source. In other words it was probably stolen or cleverly embezzled. However, this impressive total eventually proved to be quite conservative. After being "parked" in some innocuous location, much of this questionable wealth, loosely identified as belonging to the so-called "super-rich," eventually finds its way into legitimate, financial markets. Thus over time it has come to play a significant role in the increasingly perverse way these markets perform.

After nearly a year at Crenbar, I was sent on a tour of the overseas offices and learned that except for one, small fund, all of the firm's money was located abroad in various tax havens. These included locations known for their scenic appeal as the Isle of Jersey, Nauru, the Cayman Islands and, of course, good, old Vanuatu. It was also interesting to note that none of the firm's offices had any identification on the outside - only a small, bronze plaque containing a street number. In addition, a sumptuous apartment was usually maintained at each location in the type of luxurious building where everything is done through security cameras, remote-controlled doors and computer cards so the people who live there for years don't even know who occupies the apartment next door.

Although the firm was regarded as a New York-based operation, the secretive Cayman office was really the headquarters

68

and operational center, all the records kept there behind a protective wall of indulgent, local laws. It isn't surprising that thousands of financial firms from around the world are located in such places, although for many what amounts to their main office is merely a mail drop and a phone answering service.

The son of the managing director, Rolfe, a middle-aged man with a crew cut who was doing his best to look about half his age, soon joined me in Georgetown, the capital of the Caymans. The two of us spent a lot of time discussing the firm's operations, although it was obvious that I was being told only part of the truth. Nonetheless, I knew that he was working his way up to making some sort of proposal. One evening we had dinner on the firm's palatial, private yacht that had just come into port. From a distance I thought at first it was a small, cruise ship. After we went on board, it moored in the middle of the harbor, the lights along the shore sparkling around us on the placid water. Briefly a balmy, salt breeze, that was like a refreshing tonic, stirred and died away again. Served by waiters in tuxedos, we ate at a candlelit table on the back deck, the dinner featuring succulent filet mignon and the best champagne I've ever tasted.

While savoring the champagne and looking around at all the fancy, oversize yachts in the harbor, I suddenly remembered a chill, rainy autumn night many years before when I was a boy. My mother, Karen, and I had been turned away from the door of a cheap hotel because we were a couple of dollars short of the amount needed to rent one of their crummy rooms for a few hours. It was somewhere in western Pennsylvania, and we'd gone there to attend a conference about feeding starving people in an obscure African republic. You must understand that I had a most unconventional or, some might say, bizarre childhood. I was raised by a mother who devoted her entire life to an endless series of pie-in-the-sky causes that were supposed to improve society, and to this unique upbringing can be traced my own attraction to the

69

downtrodden and miserable.

Unfortunately most of the projects that aroused my mother's selfless devotion failed completely or never made any sense in the first place. To attend the conference, she was paid a small fee by a magazine to write an article, although the money wasn't enough to cover our meager expenses to go there. After suffering the ignominy of being rejected by such a fleabag hotel, she and I had to walk a couple of miles through the cold rain with our one piece of beat-up, water-logged luggage. Along the way I insisted on carrying the bag for a while that was so heavy I had difficulty not dragging it on the ground.

"You're always such a big help, my little man," Karen said in recognition of my valiant effort with the suitcase and gave me a hug. I always liked it when she called me her "little man." At that moment I looked up at her face that was ashen with fatigue wanting so much to protect her, although there was little I could do. When we finally reached the bus station, my sneakers were filled with water and squeaked loudly with each step I took. Briefly I was so cold I couldn't stop shaking in my thin jacket made of worn corduroy - the only one I had. We spent the night on a rock-hard bench until an aging bus that smelled of years of stale, tobacco smoke finally showed up and took us back to New York. After arriving, we stopped at a street corner outside the bus station and shared a single hot dog smothered in mustard that was purchased from a vendor with a cart. It was the first food that either of us had in more than a day.

"Are you interested in becoming rich?" Rolfe suddenly asked, motioning to the waiter to refill our glasses with the champagne that probably cost hundreds per bottle or perhaps even more, and for a moment I thought I hadn't heard him correctly. "Unfortunately most people don't appreciate what it can be like having really big money."

"I understand what it means to have or, should I say, not

to have it," I answered, although he couldn't have known what I was referring to, and kept thinking about the odd, squeaking sound made by my wet sneakers.

"Is it important enough to do almost anything?"

"I guess that would involve the circumstances," I responded, curious what he was getting at.

"To own a yacht like this, you can't be squeamish. I don't want you to get in over your head."

"Neither do I."

"Frankly, you impress me as our type of man," he said, and I wondered if I should take that as a complement or not. "You're about to be offered an opportunity to make more money than you ever dreamed was possible and, of course, that means everything that goes with it: exquisite possessions and homes, traveling whenever you want to the most fashionable places, and, of course, hot women. I'm sure that's of interest to you."

"Well, sure," I said trying to visualize all those beautiful women who suddenly were going to find me so irresistible.

"It means doing what's necessary to achieve such money. The type of women we're talking about like the big bucks and what they buy. Let's be frank. The firm plays the financial game very hard and sometimes with people we don't like very much. It's a tough league, although we wouldn't consider playing for lesser stakes. I'm speaking to you this way because there's still time to stay at the New York office. You can make a nice living there analyzing currencies for the firm. From what I'm told, you have a real knack for that sort of thing. But my impression is that you're a guy who wants to be a 'player.' Otherwise I wouldn't make you this proposal. The firm has opened an office in Moscow that we don't talk about. It's all very hush-hush. I'm running the show, and I'd like you to join me there. I need the help of someone with your expertise in the international financial markets, including arbitraging currencies. As you know, moving money into the

71

wrong currency can negate everything else that's done right. You'll find the job a real challenge and, as I say, very rewarding. At the moment Moscow is the site of one of the greatest bonanzas of all times. That's the only way to describe what's happening there. The country's most valuable assets, that haven't already been stolen, are being purchased for a few pennies on the dollar through a process of privatization that's really just a corrupt giveaway, especially to the politically well-connected. In all my years in finance, I've never seen anything like it. Everything is up for grabs: oil, precious metals, the country's military hardware and supposedly even nuclear material," he said, his eyes suddenly getting large.

"You mean bombs?" I asked almost getting up to leave, although that wouldn't have accomplished much since we were in the middle of the harbor.

"Of course, we don't get involved in that sort of thing. After all, we do have our scruples," he quickly added as if to reassure me that there was at least some degree of responsibility to what they were doing. "And all those riches are going for practically nothing. Are you interested in a tank with the latest armor to drive around late at night - leisurely, of course, so you don't crush too many cars?" he joked.

"It might be a little difficult finding a parking space for something like that on the streets of Manhattan," I answered, although at least that's one vehicle that wouldn't be stolen.

"Or perhaps a high-tech submarine. Who needs a fancy yacht when you can cruise the Mediterranean in your own, high-powered sub. Imagine how that would impress the fat cats in Monaco when they see you rolling into the harbor. Heck, you could even have a personal flag like you own your own country. You must admit that a sub would be a great place to hold a cocktail party. Maybe you think that I'm joking. I can pick up the phone and in less than an hour get you a quote. Or perhaps, you're into entire factories or even research institutes," Rolfe said with growing enthusiasm as if we were discussing fancy, used cars for sale in a newspaper. "When select members of the Communist Party and the KGB realized the old order was collapsing, they decided not to spend the rest of their lives in poverty and set about concealing as much money as possible or even better moving it to the West. Essentially the KGB people are running the show. While poor Gorbachev was knocking himself out trying to keep the sinking ship afloat, everyone else was running for the exits with everything they could grab.

"The KGB?" I said intrigued by the comment.

"They're the ones that mostly we deal with. The whole thing started when Colonel Veselovsky of the KGB's First Chief Directorate had a frank talk with Nikolai Kruchina, who was in charge of the party's property at the Central Committee. Apparently Kruchina objected to what they planned to do. Not long after that, he couldn't resist jumping out a very high window with the inevitable result. Then it didn't matter what Kruchina knew. At this time it's not necessary to go into a lot of details about how such things are handled. Eventually you'll learn some of that."

"You must be talking about a lot of money. It's not easy moving around such huge sums without someone noticing."

"True, but at the moment you can get away with almost anything in Moscow as long as you have the hard, western currency everyone wants. Unfortunately the city has become a very dangerous place so you need *krysha*. In Russian, that means "roof" or more specifically "protection." The Russians have a quaint way of expressing things. However, a roof can occasionally spring a leak, and a couple of times it's been necessary to have ours repaired. But you're a good-size guy, and I understand that you like to play rugby. You'll do alright and soon experience the rarefied feeling of being really rich. And wait till you see the women in Moscow. Hot, very hot," he added, his eyes getting large again.

The following week we arrived in Moscow on a flight from

73

Geneva, and my education about life in the new Russia began immediately. We drove in style from the airport in an enormous, Mercedes limousine complete with tinted windows. At the moment that was the mandatory mode of transportation around town for anyone who wanted to be taken seriously. Along with the limousine came a burly chauffeur and bodyguard, both of them former army commandos. When we were bogged down in traffic near the center of the city, the driver expedited matters by taking a quick detour onto the sidewalk. To clear the way, he kept blasting the loud, irritating horn at the frightened pedestrians, who desperately jumped aside to avoid being mowed down. For a couple of blocks we continued on the sidewalk, narrowly missing terrified office workers and little, old ladies with shopping parcels. At one corner we passed a police officer, who made a point of looking the other way as if we weren't there. I assumed that of late Moscow's shoppers had been getting a lot of practice avoiding the shiny, new limousines that brazenly went wherever they wanted.

Executing such a maneuver with a large car isn't easy, and I had to admire the driver's perverse skill. Glancing out the rear window, I noticed another limousine follow our example, the beleaguered pedestrians once again having to jump out of the way to save their skin. Probably many other cars came along after that, temporarily transforming that section of Moscow's crowed sidewalks into a private road for the arrogant *nouveau riche*. The quick detour onto the sidewalk accomplished the desired result, and soon we pulled up in front of an enormous building that looked like a hotel a short distance from Red Square.

"Anatole's perfect driving record is still in tact. To date, he hasn't mowed down anyone, or at least I don't think he has. Anyway, it wouldn't matter. No one would do anything about it. If they tried, we'd just pay a few bribes. Behold home, sweet home," Rolfe said proudly. "Originally it belonged to Grand Duke Oransky. He was a cousin or something like that of Czar Nicky

Romanov. That was before the Bolsheviks dragged the Duke into the street one afternoon and beat him to death with axes. Apparently, in those days the populace derived considerable satisfaction from that sort of gruesome activity," he added nonchalantly, and I suspected that some of the pedestrians we almost ran over might feel the same way. "While it lasted, the old-time aristocrats had a great life. After the Duke's untimely demise, the house belonged to assorted communist bigwigs. The last owner was a KGB Major General. I'm not sure what happened to him. Lately it's a fact of life in Moscow that one day someone is here and the next they're gone, and you don't give the matter a great deal of thought. After all, what's the difference?"

"Does everyone drive like Anatole?" I asked.

"The gangsters started it. They're very impatient. After all the years trying to survive in the gloomy gulag, they're making up for lost time," Rolfe answered and opened the huge front door that was made of cast bronze and at least 10 feet high. We entered a cavernous, two-story foyer with a polished marble floor that was like a large echo chamber. In history books I'd read about places like this but never imagined that I'd see one in person, much less live there.

"How many rooms?" I inquired.

"A hundred or so. We got the place for a song. At the moment everyone wants dollars so you can easily buy anything, even a palace like this."

That evening Rolfe and I ate dinner in the palatial dining room, the elaborately decorated ceiling high above barely visible in the dim candlelight. We sat at either end of a table so long we almost had to shout to hear each other, the meals served by servants in fancy green uniforms. From the way Rolfe ordered them around, I think he really believed he was a latter-day grand duke or the equivalent. Afterwards we adjourned to the library where the bookcases covering the walls were filled with priceless, leather books. I leafed through a few of them, noticing that none had ever been opened.

"The old prince wasn't much of a reader, and I suppose that goes for the KGB people too," I commented.

"I do think the books give the room a certain class. Make sure you put them back just the way they were. I want the place to look exactly like it did when the old duke was here. You have to admit he had taste," Rolfe said with satisfaction and poured us a couple of glasses of cognac. "This stuff is at least a hundred years old. There's a lot of it in the cellars. In one room I even found a skeleton."

While we polished off the cognac, he provided me with more details of how the Russian nation was being looted so effectively. A few years before, the ruble was deliberately manipulated to only a fraction of its former value by a shadowy group of foreigners that included assorted traders, opportunists, criminals and supposedly even a few CIA people. It was a scandal of major proportions overlooked in the West, and the key, first step in victimizing an entire country. As a currency expert I was aware of the non-convertible ruble's precipitous and unexplained drop in value but never imagined it was the object of an ingenious scheme to undermine its value. In that way the purchasing power of foreign currencies was greatly increased for everything in Russia that wasn't nailed down.

"Did you ever think a major currency could be successfully manipulated - especially on such a large scale?" Rolf asked proudly and grinned. "Nonetheless we pulled it off and, when I say we, I mean the "consortium.""

"Consortium?" I asked with interest because in financial circles the term is often used as a convenient grab-bag to cloak in anonymity virtually anything and then some.

"It's in some records I'll show you later. You'll see how the ruble was systematically pounded down by a blizzard of sham

76

transactions. For a while we were able to take complete control of the float. It surprised me how easy it was and certainly worth the effort. Now everything is being sucked out of Russia for a song. There's nothing like market forces when they're working for you. A word of caution. Nothing in any of the records that I show you should ever be discussed on the outside. To say the least, it would be embarrassing. And one other thing: you might be interested to know that along the way the Soviet Union's gold supply disappeared - that is, with a little help from those on the inside. Amazing, don't you think? Perhaps as much as 3000 tons with hardly a trace left behind. Those KGB boys really know how to do things with style. Can you imagine the underlings at the central bank opening the vault door one morning and discovering the place was empty except for a couple of mice running around the floor?"

"One thing's for certain - the mice didn't steal all that gold," I answered and downed another large, crystal glass full of one-hundred year old cognac that we were polishing off as if it was tap water. Like many others in the West, I heard rumors about the apparent theft of Russia's gold and always wondered if they were true. Now I knew.

"Let me give you an idea about the type of volume we're handling in some of these deals. You can easily guess how much money all of this will bring in outside markets," he said and handed me a piece of paper taken from a desk drawer. It listed huge amounts of invaluable raw materials apparently pilfered from the nation's mines, smelters and refineries. Among others, they included benzene, cobalt, calcium carbide, copper, an valuable rare earth metals.

"Wow!" I exclaimed with amazement.

"This isn't unusual," he bragged as if to put the matter in perspective.

"How do you get hold of such quantities?"

77

"The people who control the state enterprises like refineries and smelters are eagerly selling whatever they can grab so it can be turned promptly into western cash. Of course, lots of bribes have to be paid to government officials for the invaluable licenses to export all of this stuff without paying any duty. Often the licenses come along with bulk purchase of deflated rubles. Any government official or businessman, who doesn't want to play ball, soon finds himself with a serious health problem. One episode in particular received wide attention and served as an object lesson for all concerned not to cause problems. It involved Ivan Kiveldi, who used to be one of Russia's most respected businessmen. He was a major industrialist and founder of the sanctimonious Russian Business Roundtable. What a bunch of stuff shirts they were. Apparently Kiveldi considered himself too big and important to cooperate and offended a lot of the wrong people, which is something you don't want to do. In the middle of a phone conversation one afternoon, Kiveldi collapsed on the floor frothing at the mouth and died. It was later determined that an invisible nerve toxin had been smeared on his telephone. His demise sent an unmistakable message to the rest of the Roundtable, which suddenly didn't have many members," he added with a smile, and I realized that for a while at least we wouldn't be hearing much from the Business Roundtable.

The following night I was introduced to Moscow's wild and gaudy night life, which was like nothing I'd ever seen. With the demise of communism, fancy clubs and casinos had been springing up everywhere fueled by the huge amounts of black-market money flowing like an underground river through the city. Like everyone else, we didn't stay anywhere for long unless there was lots of action, and later while the limousine sped past the looming walls of the Kremlin, Rolfe pointed to the nearby Rossiya Hotel.

"That's where the Chechens hang out. Supposedly they have around 400 fighters living there in expensive rooms with no lease. Because of the hotel's central location, they can quickly get to any part of the city to do battle with a rival gang that's foolish enough to confront them. Obviously the Rossiya isn't a place where we'll be going for dinner anytime soon," he observed with the bemused tone that was in his voice when talking about the bizarre goings on in Moscow. "Of late, there are two main coalitions of gangsters. I've heard that in all there could be as many as 5000 individual gangs across the country combined into these two, powerful federations. In essence, since the fall of communism, Russia has become a huge, criminal state of unimaginable proportions. Of course, that's to our advantage."

"Where did all of these criminals come from?"

"A traditional underworld always existed in Russia, especially during the days of the Czars. It was called the *Vorovsk Mir* or "thieves world." With the collapse of communism, most of the convicts, including many, underworld big shots, were released from prison. Others, who had been in the shadows, suddenly surfaced. You see, the KGB often worked closely with the country's criminal element that at times took care of difficult matters for them. Now with the state in disarray the gangs are demanding and getting their share of the spoils. In addition to the rackets, their old KGB pals are helping them take over legitimate businesses. Everyone is paying for protection and using the gangs to deal with unwanted competition. It's the ultimate Darwinian world where only the strongest and most aggressive survive. However, it also offers an enormous opportunity for people from the West who want to share in the spoils. Actually I like many of the gangsters. They're very amusing guys and usually are quite helpful. You'll meet some of them. They often come to the house for drinks. Also they're able to find us things that are difficult to locate for export to the west. One gang just located a huge supply of aluminum and cobalt we're shipping out in a few days. This year, our firm will be a big player in the international spot market for

79

aluminum. I could end up handling as much as 20% of the world's entire trade. Not bad, huh? What do I know about aluminum? Nothing, although what does that matter? And our share of the spot nickel market could be almost as large," he rambled on as the luxurious limousine sped on through Moscow's dim, grimy streets.

Next we stopped at the fashionable Cherry Casino on the Novy Arbat. The casinos were the places to be seen, all of them owned by one of the gangster groups, and at the moment the Cherry was the in-place. When we drove up, both sides of the street were packed with expensive western cars, the casino humming with activity. What I saw that night was quite a revelation. The pervasive drabness of Soviet communism had suddenly been replaced by an outlandish extravaganza fed by limitless amounts of crooked money. Inside the crowd was dressed expensively, especially the women, all of whom were very good-looking. The men were an assortment of business types and thugs, many with scarred faces left over from their prison days. Also the bulges under their coats made clear that they were carrying guns. At the gaming tables the wagers were obscenely large, and it wasn't unusual for someone to bet several thousand American dollars on a single spin of the roulette wheel. In fact, it was obvious that the players were really interested in showing how much money they could throw around. Rolfe seemed to know everyone and introduced me as a prominent businessman and "sportsmen" from the West with emphasis on the latter term. Presumably he was referring to the fact that in London I had been a rugby player while studying at the School of Economics. It was a description that seemed to produce for me instant credibility.

Rolfe spent most of his time at the roulette table where he made some big wagers to attract attention. He even won a few of them, and it appeared that he could do nothing wrong when it came to money. Soon he had a beautiful woman on each arm and was obviously having a ball. He fit right in along with all the hustlers and gangsters. Although the Cherry had a gaudy appeal, I immediately hated the place that represented everything I detest. Returning to the bar, I had another stiff drink and stared at myself in the mirror behind the bar, wondering if I should leave the next day and return to the States. On Wall Street there would always be a demand for someone with my skills. But I couldn't just walk away from an opportunity to make really big money. After all, isn't that the dream of most Americans, and since I was young, it was something to which I always aspired. By the end of the night and several drinks later, I knew that flashy, dangerous world had gotten a fateful hold on me as if I just imbibed a highly addictive narcotic.

In later years I often looked back at that first night at the Cherry Casino, realizing how much easier my life would have been if I just walked out and the following morning took the next available plane to the West. In New York I could have quickly found a good-paying job, had a family and joined the legion of prosperous executives commuting from their comfortable homes in Connecticut or Westchester. But the ordinary life wasn't for me, and at the moment I was intent on nothing less than joining the exalted ranks of the super-rich. And now that the door to that privileged inner sanctum had swung wide open, I wasn't about to turn my back on an opportunity I never thought would be mine.

In the coming months I learned more about the devious methods that were being employed to rapidly drain Russia of the wealth that had taken centuries to develop. Of course, such wholesale larceny could never take place if insiders weren't eagerly participating in the corrupt process. One night over dinner Rolfe explained a scheme that had looted a significant part of the cash reserves belonging to the central bank, the country's main financial institution. It was larceny on a stupendous scale made possible by the fact that most of the nation's financial institutions were dominated by corrupt officials, who could easily be bought. In essence, what amounted to a fortune supposedly belonging to the people was stolen through a simple stratagem, and as Rolfe went over the details, I had difficulty believing that it actually worked. Key officials were bribed in order to obtain the invaluable transfer codes used to move money among the various payment centers around the country. Typically one fake bank would send a wire transfer to a second, fake bank, and the latter would use the transfer code to obtain the proceeds in cash at a payment center. By the time the central bank's auditors discovered the fraud, both banks that never existed had disappeared without a trace. In this simple but effective way, hundreds of millions were stolen from Russia's meager coffers out of which pensions for the elderly and the salaries of ordinary Russians working dutifully for the state had to be paid. No doubt, much of this money soon went abroad, joining the vast stream of wealth disappearing every day into the murky depths of the international financial system.

"Unfortunately, the Chechens took the whole thing over," Rolfe commented indifferently and lit another high-priced cigar.

Every night we put in an appearance at whatever club was briefly fashionable and shunned those that quickly fell out of favor. For a while Rolfe's favorite was the Casino Royale (its real, not very original name) that briefly rivaled the Cherry among the city's high rollers. Wherever we went, there was always a table for us even if it was necessary to evict several people in order to provide one. Rolfe reveled in the feeling of being important, and it didn't hurt that he casually dispensed fresh $100 bills as tips. He had his cash sent directly from New York so the bills were always crisp and new. According to him, it was poor form to hand out a large bill as a tip that had been touched by too many, grubby hands. Sometimes he would tip a hundred if someone merely lit his expensive Havana cigar. Considering the exchange rate it was an enormous windfall for the average Russian who could live well for weeks on just one of his lavish tips.

Most of the women who turned up at the discoes were

from the provinces, having been drawn to Moscow by all the glitz and flashy money, and at times it seemed as if Russia had an inexhaustible supply of gorgeous, compliant women. They hung around the city's nightspots hoping to meet a rich, well-connected man. Barely able to pay the rent with whatever miniscule salary they earned at a menial day-job, they dreamed of being rescued from their limited circumstances. It must have been an intoxicating experience for them to see so much money being thrown around like confetti. They tried to make themselves attractive as possible, which included wearing an alluring dress that probably cost every cent they could spare.

Eventually I learned that many had the misfortune to simply disappear never to be seen again. Those who were alone and sufficiently vulnerable were frequently kidnapped on their way home and sold into the thriving white, slave trade that preyed incessantly on Russia's women, a brutal fate that supposedly was endured by thousands. Even in Moscow's cruel, Darwinian world, such a number seemed overly gruesome - that is, until Vera disappeared, and I spent more than a year trying to find her. I followed a long and crooked path through a world of unbelievable degradation across Russia and down into the Caucuses until it finally ran cold. Sometimes late at night I still think about her beautiful hair glistening in the sun as we walked through the fields near the little, provincial village where she grew up. And always I wonder if she could be alive, and if so, does she ever think of me.

For a couple of years I became a recognized part of Moscow's nightclub scene, acquiring a closet of expensive silk suits along with a series of flashy girlfriends for whom I felt nothing. I even bought an expensive, diamond-encrusted, French watch that was almost as ostentatious as the one Rolfe wore. Since this was my big chance to join the super-rich, I was determined to make full use of it. Like most of those who came to the late-night parties at the old palace, I wasn't interested in becoming merely prosperous or comfortably well-off. Instead I wanted to experience the exhilaration that only big money used recklessly can afford. Soon, however, I realized that I was becoming Rolf's clone. In many respects the two of us could barely be distinguished from one another, especially when we were out at the clubs throwing around big tips and encouraging those we viewed as underlings to fawn all over us.

Meanwhile I did my best to ignore the cruel fate befalling Moscow's ordinary people as the so-called "gold rush" grew increasingly outlandish and even more carpetbaggers descended on the city. After all, what concern was that of mine? I didn't create the situation but was merely "maximizing the value" that could be wrung out of it like all the other opportunists clever enough to appreciate what was there for the taking. Eventually, however, I couldn't continue ignoring reality. Wherever I went in the streets, I encountered the unmistakable evidence of the misery spreading like a plague through Moscow. Within its confines two, extreme worlds existed in close proximity, and although inhabiting the same geographical location, they had little to do with each other. On the one hand, there was the gaudy, meretricious realm of corrupt government officials, gangsters, emerging oligarchs and the western opportunists with whom they collaborated. This world, that subsisted off exploitation on a grand scale, came into its own late at night under the pulsing lights of the flashy clubs, its excesses far outdoing anything that took place under the old aristocrats. In stark contrast was the shabby, crimped realm of Moscow's ordinary folk. As more and more money poured into the pockets of gangsters and speculators, they found it increasingly difficult just to survive. Soon many couldn't even do that, although before succumbing to their fate, they displayed remarkable ingenuity.

With the old, Soviet-style supermarkets almost empty, a migration took place during the warmer months into the countryside where desperate Muscovites returned to their roots trying to make ends meet. With a few handfuls of seeds, they planted pitiful, little plots of ground broken open with hand tools, much of the harvest brought back and sold in makeshift bazaars that appeared overnight all over the city. They were in empty lots along the boulevards, near train stations and anywhere some unused ground could be found. Often complaints from anonymous landlords making no use of the space caused them to be evicted, and the pathetic bazaar would move on to another location like a caravan of gypsies dragging their awnings, carts and baskets of withering produce.

On Stoleshnikov Lane near the Bolshoi Theatre, I came across one of the most pathetic sights that represented for me a turning point. Because of the prestigious location, the street attracted an odd assortment of unemployed and the elderly, who gathered there each day to hawk to annoyed passersby anything that might bring a few cents. These were not typical beggars but instead the frightened remnants of Russia's ruined middle class struggling to survive a little while longer. I saw a lady in shabby but neat clothes trying to sell a set of fine, crystal glasses that had probably been the pride of her family for generations. Beside her an old man with flowing white hair kept waving one of the beautiful, leather books that stood in a pile at his feet. In desperation, he was giving away his priceless library for pennies. I suspected he was a scientist from one of the prestigious research institutes that had been grabbed by some greedy speculator, who promptly fired everyone and liquidated piecemeal its valuable equipment. Others on the street were selling fancy clothing, knitted sweaters, little pieces of hand-made pottery and anything else that might attract some attention. Few of the sellers shouted or were aggressive. In spite of their sad lot, they were determined above all else to keep their dignity. At day's end they would wander off, their thin, undernourished forms fading into the chilly dusk descending rapidly into Moscow's cold streets. Having spent the day with little or nothing to eat, most still had their meager offerings that no one wanted to buy, even for pennies.

Almost everywhere in the city one encountered these impromptu flea markets, and for a time an item of particular interest was the heroic war decorations of Russia's aging veterans. For practically nothing the symbols of the nation's highest valor and suffering on the battlefield could be purchased. Briefly it was considered fashionable to wear them on your lapel so everyone would be impressed. At the discoes the medals turned up on bodyguards and assorted thugs. I even heard them discussing the impressive decorations about which they knew nothing, some even making the ridiculous claim the medals had been handed down from heroic fathers or uncles who supposedly gave their all for the motherland.

And then with the return of winter, the Darwinian process crushing the weak hardened its grip on the city, soon reaching a crescendo of brutality. After the frigid weather arrived in all its harshness, the hopeless and failed emerged in increasing numbers from the shadows where they tried to conceal their misery. They could be seen frozen to death in filthy gutters or in a doorway that offered no shelter from the bitter wind. While out jogging, I would suddenly come upon one of them rigid as a statue, positioned in an odd, twisted pose that emphasized the pointlessness of the death they experienced in the frigid darkness. Many pedestrians stopped going out early in the morning because of the appalling human refuse on display that within a few hours was carted off and quickly disposed of. I never found out where all the corpses ended up. Probably they were taken in dump trucks to a mass grave far out of the city that wouldn't be noticed. I'm sure that no effort was expended trying to notify a relative or friend - that is, if anyone actually cared.

Late on a bitterly cold afternoon near the Moscow Art Theater, I saw a gaunt man in a threadbare coat run up to one of the shiny limousines with tinted windows that to my surprise had actually stopped for a traffic light. It had just been washed and looked like a shiny, bloated whale on wheels. Unable to see who was inside, the man rapped at the window and tried to pull the door open. As the car started up again, he held on desperately as if to a lifeline and was dragged around the corner. Finally he couldn't hold on any longer and rolled under the wheels of a passing truck that lurched heavily as it passed over his outstretched body and sped down the street not bothering to stop. I tried to reach the man, but the traffic was too dense. No one paid any attention to the fact a helpless human being was lying there. Other cars kept driving over him, each time making a loud, thumping sound until all that was left of him was a bloody mass on the pavement. I was headed to the Bolshoi Theater to buy a ticket but instead turned around and hurried back to the house, suddenly feeling ill.

By now I had long since grown to detest the opulent palace where I lived, the clubs where the city's newly rich flaunted their tainted money and the endless rounds of racy parties attended by desperate women everyone took advantage of. I had arrived in Moscow filled with optimism, believing I would soon become the type of important, wealthy person that as a young man I always admired. Instead I found myself sinking ever deeper into what was nothing more than a quagmire of human exploitation.

I began to send confidential information about the looting of Russia to my friend Ben at the CIA. We met while playing rugby in New York. During an important game at Randall's Island, Ben scored the winning touchdown on my pass that broke him loose. That night we celebrated till early morning at a little bar on Second Avenue and soon realized we both found a friend. Ben was eager for me to join the service. I declined but decided to become the CIA's information source in Russia, hoping that eventually something might be done about such a scandalous situation.

I assumed that no one on the outside appreciated the full

dimensions of what was taking place there, including the involvement of many prominent, western trading companies. In essence, I considered myself in some small way to be alleviating all the suffering I witnessed by alerting the outside world that supposedly would soon come to the rescue. However, that assumption proved to be naïve in the extreme, and eventually I realized that no one paid a bit of attention or even cared, including the fact that criminal elements were usually involved. The looting of Russia was highly beneficial to western economies, bringing in unprecedented amounts of valuable raw materials at cheap prices that helped fuel the expansion and hold down inflation. The fact my efforts to expose all that economic exploitation accomplished nothing was a failed lesson I was never able to learn. Only later did western governments finally take passing notice of what was happening when so much of the money loaned or invested in the "new" Russia also evaporated. By that time the politically well-connected oligarchs, former government officials and gangsters had stolen a sizeable portion of Russia's entire GDP. Even the prestigious Russian Central Bank got into the act, utilizing offshore accounts to deceive the International Monetary Fund so larger "emergency" assistance could be obtained. Not surprising, in 1998 the entire economy finally collapsed from the cumulative effects of so much well-organized theft and corruption.

The information I provided to the CIA included the names of many of the outside companies that were indispensable to this grotesque process of systematically ripping off the vulnerable, Russian populace. Having purchased the loot at bargain-basement prices, they disguised what they actually paid, reselling everything at a huge profit. After a raw material such as petroleum entered the world's trading system, it moved along from one shell company to another so it became impossible to prove much of anything. Also I learned what I could about the many, financial institutions that along the way functioned as a giant, money laundering machine.

The trail of all of this tainted money was murky at best, and in Russia most of the records simply disappeared. Eventually some of the world's most respected banks would be implicated in this ongoing flood of illicit funds. For the most part, this shadowy realm through which so much money and materials moves on a regular basis is understood by only a small coterie of the well-connected. In China, I would make good use of what I learned in Russia and to my surprise encountered venal behavior there that dwarfed what I had already witnessed in Moscow.

Initially the huge sums of illicit money emanating from Russia and China were diverted to various, overseas financial centers known for their opaqueness and only later ended up in legitimate investments around the world. Among others, these include the pools of mortgages, that helped to escalate worldwide property values, and also the proceeds of America's countless, maxed-out credit cards. Ultimately this enormous, monetary surplus helped to create a general explosion of asset values, contributing to a series of destructive, financial bubbles that inevitably collapsed with far-reaching, negative consequences. All of this tainted, flight capital is one of the least appreciated aspects of international economics in the latter part of the 20th century. In this way much-heralded globalization and supply side theory praised by many academics was fueled to a significant extent by nothing more than out of control, garden-variety thievery. Not surprising, along the way both Russia and China acquired an obscene number of the super-rich. Counting oligarchs, devious government officials and assorted cronies, Moscow would have one of the greatest concentrations of billionaires in the world.

Meanwhile the economies of both countries were captured by the corrupt posturing under various guises. Russia became a giant mafia state controlled by arrogant, former KGB officials, who had far more power than during the Soviet era. At the same time China evolved into a hopelessly corrupt Kleptocracy serving the interests of the cruel, long-term objectives defined by party fanatics. To complicate matters, both of these unstable societies were dominated at the top by ultra-nationalists who shared an uncompromising hatred of the United States - the one nation that constituted a barrier to Russia and China carving up the world.

No doubt, many will always deny the facts of this painfully true story that demonstrates vividly the fateful alchemy of economics and human nature at its worst. With the world on the doorstep of World War III (and perhaps Biblical Armageddon), I realized that as Professor Chesley had predicted, this looming tragedy would be rooted to a large extent in nothing more than old-fashioned greed and scheming on a monumental scale.

One night I returned late to the palace and found the front door ajar. Rolfe always had a very large servant stationed there in the event some desperate person freezing in the streets outside tried to sneak in and steal something like a bottle of expensive liquor that could be sold for food. No one was attending the door, and right away I knew something was wrong. I walked cautiously down the long hallway towards the blaring music at the other hand, suddenly detecting a pungent aroma that I realized was blood. In the library the floor was littered with dead bodies that lay in a tight group in the center. Someone had shot the room up with an automatic weapon, hundreds of bullets shredding the old prince's beautiful, leather books that hung in tatters on the walls. The enormous pool of red liquid surrounding the bodies was slowly congealing, and in the middle lay Rolfe with an expensive cigar still in his mouth. Even in death and shot full of holes he seemed to be smiling about all the clever deals he pulled off. In a rare moment of candor while drunk, he told me a little about his mysterious father, Dragar, a gaunt man who spoke with a thick, Romanian accent. Behind his back the firm's junior executives jokingly referred to him as Dracula. According to Rolfe, he was part gypsy and during his early years in Budapest once killed a man to acquire

90

the seed money that jumpstarted his career that led eventually to Wall Street. I wasn't looking forward to "Dracula's" reaction when he found out that his only son was dead. Fortunately he didn't blame me for Rolfe's untimely demise.

The next day I set about spreading around lots of money trying to get a lead on the person who shot up the prince's library along with everyone in it. Eventually I heard a rumor that the hit man came from Switzerland or New York. Apparently the only tangible result of all the information I had been sending to Washington was to arouse the ire of some big-time, fat cat, who wasn't satisfied with the huge sums that he already made. After learning about the leaks concerning the obscene, financial bonanza in Russia, whoever it was did some homework and concluded that our firm had to be the source. After that, they took the steps considered necessary to end promptly such a serious threat to their oversize wallet.

Following Rolfe's demise, I remained for several months in Moscow, and while still representing the firm, learned as much as I could about the sale of Russia's valuable military hardware on the black market. Cautiously I provided this information as well to the CIA. Aware that soon I might be next on the hit list, I had no intention of hanging around much longer. I even learned about the sale of some nuclear material swiped from one of the provincial sites guarded with little more than a padlock. Under the circumstances it would have been a miracle if some of that coveted material didn't disappear. In addition, there were several acquisitions of important, military items by the Chinese, who appeared to have a carefully thought-out shopping list. Obviously they knew what they wanted and had a long-term plan. Of course, this was augmented over the years with all the technology pilfered so easily from American corporations and research facilities. What took place in the former Soviet Union merely jumpstarted the lethal process that eventually would have such dire consequences.

7

The road I followed that eventually took me to China was long and circuitous. It involved detours to Europe and the States, and I even spent a year surfing in the South Pacific. However, a quiet life on the beach wasn't for me, and in time I headed for China summoned by insistent ghosts from my past. I had unfinished business there, although I had no idea how to even what I considered a long-unsettled score. In China I already had some contacts and gradually made more, soon discovering a world even more corrupt than the one I left behind in Russia.

On occasion, I returned to Moscow finding a city that had gotten quite tame. My former Moscow "friends" were pleased to learn that I hadn't been assassinated or blown up like so many others. To my surprise, none of the flashy nightclubs, that once attracted so much attention, were still in business. One by one they disappeared without a trace, and a lot of the big shot gangsters were back in prison, double-crossed by their KGB cronies who no longer found them useful For now, they would have to content themselves with memories of those few, insane years when their every whim was gratified. An "authority" in the notorious Solntsevo Brotherhood, who often came to our late-night poker parties, landed in one of the more inhospitable prisons. Supposedly he was still collecting war medals and had amassed an impressive collection, including some prized Stars of Lenin that he wore on his prison uniform. At a pawn shop I found a couple of shiny medals that I thought would make a nice addition to his collection and sent them along with a brief note and a box of expensive, Swiss chocolates.

I also stopped by the location where one of the gaudiest of the old clubs once drew big crowds and discovered it had been turned into an enormous pizza parlor resembling a factory. On the sidewalk by the front door stood an enormous, plastic statue of Mickey Mouse. No one I asked could explain what Mickey had to do with pizza, although I assumed that someone had discovered an obscure relationship that escaped the rest of us. Several times I went there for a quick meal, and while eating the greasy pizza that had too many spices tried to picture what it was like years ago with all those beautiful women from the provinces dancing wildly under the flashing lights. To my surprise, I realized that I missed the gaudy show that briefly was such an important part of my life.

In China, I took up residence on Hong Kong Island and to occupy some extra time organized a fledging, rugby club. Although over the years I have begun to slow down, I still enjoy this rough and tumble sport. While getting my degree at the London School of Economics, I was a player in demand and at one point given a substantial offer to turn professional. It was one more, intriguing opportunity that I passed up along the way, believing there were more important ways to spend my life. I still wonder what might have happened if I took advantage of the offer instead of ending up in the dark world of espionage, where I was never be sure if I'd survive another day. In Hong Kong there weren't many accomplished rugby players. Almost every morning our little group of Englishmen and Americans would practice on the Happy Valley sports field. Unfortunately the games were usually slow and amateurish, although I still enjoyed being on the sunlit field, especially after a long night in the clubs. As my relationship with Lily grew closer and monopolized most of my time, I neglected the team that eventually folded leaving behind lots of debts that I helped to pay off.

The morning after the final meeting of the East/West Friendship Society, I went to the Happy Valley field, wondering if anyone would be there to toss the ball around for a few hours. Unfortunately it was nearly deserted, and after jogging a few laps, I headed to the racquet club. Following a quick shower I went to the bar for some of the refreshing punch that's the club's specialty. While sitting there, I watched the people on the outdoor courts and spotted Robert Verrelin, who had turned up at the Society's recent meeting. He was playing a Frenchman, Claude Ducasse, whom I know quite well. Although Ducasse was one of the club's better players, Verrelin was giving him a real beating, and it was apparent he was quite the athlete. Wondering if he had become a member of the club, I called over Emile, the manager who was always a good source of information.

"Mr. Verrelin is a fine looking fellow, don't you think?" Emile said. "No doubt, he'll be quite popular with the ladies, who are already taking an interest. We haven't had a new member like him in quite a while. I've heard that he's connected to a prominent US investment group that wants to become established in China. By the way, Mr. Nicolai was here a few hours ago. He stopped by on his way from the airport and asked for you."

"I was wondering when he'd be back," I said, referring to the person I considered my best friend. It was nice to know he was back in town. André Nicolai represented one of Russia's big oil companies in the Far East and before that, spent much of his life as a decorated espionage agent, rising to the level of colonel in the exalted GRU. While we often discussed his years as a spy, he had no idea why I was really in China, something I had no intention of talking about.

Soon Ducasse and Verrelin entered the bar and came over to speak with me.

"Larry, let me introduce our newest member, Bob Verrelin. He just thrashed me on the court so it's up to you to recover the club's honor," Ducasse joked as we shook hands. Up close, Verrelin looked like a fashion model and not at all like the questionable person described in the information I obtained from the CIA. Also he had an excellent sense of humor. If the information about him hadn't come from Ben Cramer, I would have doubted that it was correct. "Robert is here on behalf of a large group of American investors, who like everyone these days want to put some money into China and get on board the bandwagon. Perhaps you can be of service."

"Gladly," I commented.

"Larry is one of the people in Hong Kong it's important to know if you're an outsider. Very well-versed about all the ins and outs, if you understand what I mean," Ducasse said to Verrelin, who was looking me over carefully.

"Who do you represent?" I asked, curious if he was really acting on behalf of anyone important.

"Sometime we'll discuss all of that. I understand it's difficult breaking into the Chinese market in any significant way," he said with a pleasant smile.

"It can take a while. You need patience and capital, and, of course, there are no guarantees."

"In polite terms you have to be generous," Ducasse said and laughed.

"I've heard that."

"It's the price of doing business here, and you should only "invest" with the right people, if you understand what I mean. Otherwise the money is wasted."

"Of course."

"That's where Larry can be such a big help. He makes sure your money ends up in a place where it will produce maximum results," Ducasse added and slapped me on the back. "Isn't that the way you explained the situation?"

"More or less," I answered.

"Sometime we'll have to play a few sets and talk further. Sounds like you're the person who can help us," Verrelin commented.

"Glad to be of assistance."

"Larry will definitely steer you in the right direction. He

even dates the most beautiful woman in Hong Kong. Frankly I'm jealous. I've been here for years and never found anyone like her," Ducasse mused.

"What's your secret?" Verrrelin asked.

"In Hong Kong it's all about connections," I commented, thinking that I detected a slight recognition in his eyes, and wondered if he remembered me from the old Moscow days.

After leaving the club, I headed to Lily's for lunch. When I arrived, she, Gao and Li, another of his many girlfriends, were on the sunlit terrace where lush, new shrubs had just been planted in the shiny copper boxes. Earlier on the sports field I worked up an appetite and quickly finished a couple servings of delicious, grilled salmon carefully prepared by the caterer, who provided all of Lily's meals. Afterwards we lingered on the plush lounges, enjoying the sea breeze along with some excellent Rhine wine. The caterer was always there personally to make sure that Lily was pleased, and before leaving with his waiters, he gave her a large box of sweets that just arrived from Europe.

During lunch Lily seemed on edge. She had arranged for me to meet her mother, and I was sure she was worried how things would go. With her father out of town, I assumed that Mrs. Chan only agreed to the meeting in order to avoid disappointing Lily. Gao and Li went on to the club, and Lily and I drove through the tunnel to Kowloon, where her parents lived in one of the city's finest, residential buildings. A servant opened the door, and we entered the large, beautifully decorated apartment. Sitting on a couch in the enormous living room, I leafed through a magazine while Lily fidgeted with little things she kept picking up. I had never seen her act like this before and realized how important it was to her that her mother and I liked each other.

Mrs. Chan was downstairs visiting a neighbor, and Lily went to get her. After she left, I walked down the hall looking for a bathroom and passed a large room where there were pictures of soldiers on the walls along with assorted military artifacts, including swords and battle flags. Realizing it must be General Chan's study, I hurried in there, wondering if I could find something of interest. On the other side by the window was an elaborately carved, teakwood desk. Fortunately the drawers weren't locked, and in one of them there was a leather folder with the official seal of the Chinese government on the cover. As I sat down and opened the folder, I noticed the general's photograph on one side of the desk. Although I had already seen his picture in Lily's apartment, it immediately arrested my attention, especially the hard stare in his eyes that seemed to look right through me. A squat, powerful man, he reminded me of the tough Japanese soldiers who during World War II always fought to the last man. According to Lily, her father came from one of the country's most prominent military families. After graduating from a premier academy, he rose quickly through the ranks. As I continued to look at his unyielding expression, I knew that no one should doubt the resolve of the Chinese military, especially in the service of the cruel regime of which it is an indispensable component.

In the folder there were several papers, including some stamped "Top Secret." Amazed at my good luck, I quickly scanned each page, soon realizing the rumors about a war weren't idle speculation. Apparently something of considerable scope was involved, although unfortunately there was no map or anything else that would give me the exact details. Nonetheless, what little I was able to read confirmed that the Chinese military had for years been planning a war of major proportions. Like many others, I always assumed that any conflict would center on Taiwan. Intermittently the island made threats to declare its independence, something mainland China would never tolerate. But what I saw in the dossier was very different from a limited engagement. The number of forces involved were too large and mostly were those of the army. Also I noticed the frequent mention of a place referred to as "X."

Over the years I occasionally came across that cryptic symbol in various high-level documents and suspected it concerned one of the regime's most closely guarded secrets. Unfortunately there wasn't enough time to examine all the documents in the desk. Knowing that I couldn't remove anything, I reluctantly put the dossier in the drawer and hurried back to the living room.

I was there less than a minute when Lily returned with her elegant mother, and immediately I noticed the resemblance between them. Also it was obvious where Lily got her sense of style. Mrs. Chan was from a prominent family in Beijing that included a number of top, party officials. Years ago, the Chan's extravagant wedding took place amid much fanfare in Zhongnanhai, the party headquarters. According to Lily it was a major social event and almost everyone of importance in communist circles was there. Not surprising, many were appalled that the beautiful Lily was involved now with a foreign businessman, especially an American. It had always been thought that she was destined to marry into the highest realm of the rich and influential princelings. For the first time I realized what a sacrifice Lily was making for the two of us to be together.

I assumed the meeting with her mother would be difficult at best and expected all sorts of probing questions. Instead, to my surprise Mrs. Chan was quite friendly and went out of her way to put me at ease. It was apparent that she was only concerned with her daughter's happiness and regardless of anyone's opinion, was prepared to overlook who I was. The similarities between Lily and her mother were far more than skin deep. Right away, I liked Mrs. Chan, and it appeared the feeling was mutual. With the meeting going smoothly, I could see Lily relax. We stayed about an hour and then left to meet Gao at the club. As we drove there, she held my arm and kept talking excitedly. I could tell how pleased she was with her mother's reaction. It was obvious how close the two of them were. However, the general would never change his mind, and I expected that soon he might resort to something unpleasant to get rid of me. Probably he hadn't tried anything like that out of concern for how Lily might react, although that could change at any moment.

After what I just saw in his desk, I realized that I wasn't the only person in China with a lot to worry about. It was a bad break that I didn't have the tiny camera that I usually carried with me. Out of carelessness I had squandered an invaluable opportunity, and it wasn't likely that I would get another chance to see those priceless papers. And then it occurred to me that even if I was able to copy some of the documents, there would be a problem sending the information to Washington. Almost immediately everything might be leaked right back to China. Confidential documents circulated constantly to various congressional committees and were seen by all sorts of staffers. Of late, it seemed as if little - no matter how sensitive - was immune from being leaked to someone, especially influential journalists. For those allied to corporations with big interests in the Far East, the problem was particularly serious. Obviously the ultra-secret documents describing China's military strategy, could have originated from only a few sources at the top of the regime. If it became known that they had been stolen, China's counter-espionage agents wouldn't have much difficulty figuring out where they came from. The consequences would have been disastrous for me as well as Lily, and I was glad now that I forgot the camera.

When we arrived at the club, Gao and Li were waiting on the terrace by the tennis courts. A large, afternoon crowd was there, making a valiant effort to occupy itself until cocktail time - the focus of life for so many of the members. The attractive players on the courts were a cosmopolitan assortment of Europeans, Americans and their Chinese friends. The city's top, private clubs remained the last bastion of the era regarded with much nostalgia when the city was a privileged enclave of the British Empire. Many still did their best to ignore the fact that the communists now controlled prized Hong Kong.

After a large lunch, I wasn't in the mood for much tennis. However, Gao wanted to play, and when a court opened up, we went out there. In spite of years of expensive lessons, he was a mediocre player. Nonetheless he always played with determination, and occasionally I made a point of letting him win, aware how much it meant to him. At the same time I had to give a convincing performance in defeat, not wanting him to know I was doing it on purpose. Sometimes his game was so far off, it was impossible to lose. Fortunately, on this day his service was quite accurate so I was able to lose quickly. On the way back to the terrace, I complimented him profusely and suggested that sometime he give me a few tips regarding my own service, a comment that pleased him immensely.

Both Lily and Li had on charming, tennis outfits with little, pleated skirts. They took the court we just vacated, and I watched them with interest. Although Lily wasn't strong, she was very graceful and had excellent reflexes. If she applied herself to the game, I was sure she could have been an excellent player. But like everything else she viewed tennis as just another amusement and never spent much time on it.

The afternoon had turned hot, and Gao ordered iced gin and tonics. The drink made with the best British gin is a tradition in Hong Kong, and in the summer there is nothing more refreshing. While sipping the drink, I continued to watch Lily run back and forth on the court. Her every move captivated my attention, and briefly I forgot that Gao was there.

"You're very fond of Lily," he suddenly said.

"I guess it shows," I answered.

"I've noticed how you look at her."

"You can't blame me for that. At the moment a large portion of the men in Hong Kong are in love with her."

"It may surprise you to know that Lily doesn't like all the attention she gets. Everyone thinks otherwise, but I know better. She and I have always been on the same wavelength. I'm very different from my brother, although he just needs to lighten up," Gao said, who prided himself on his grasp of American slang that he inserted liberally in any conversation. "Do you love Lily?" he added, and I almost choked on my drink. Usually Gao only wanted to talk about himself, which meant his adventures at the nightclubs, and at time I had to force myself to listen politely. But now it was apparent that something very different was on his mind.

"It's hard to explain," I said evasively because at the moment I wasn't in the mood to discuss my personal feelings.

"I've watched you with her. There's something special about the way a man speaks to a woman he really cares about," he said, and I noticed how much his face resembled his father's, although the expression in their eyes was very different. According to the superficial standards that prevailed in the city's flashy, nightclub world, Gao was considered a bore and not very attractive. He was too short and as a result often wore special shoes in order to appear taller. Through her mother Lily had gotten most of the looks in the family. If Gao didn't have so much money to throw around, he wouldn't have had a chance with the type of women he liked to pursue.

"I guess you found me out," I finally answered.

"Lily loves you. I know that because she's told me several times. But she's afraid you're not serious and just view her as a challenge like most of the men who chase her around. At the nightclubs they're like a plague of locusts that won't leave her alone. They just want to tell their friends they've had a date with the beautiful Lily and supposedly gotten some sex. Probably there are a couple of hundred men in Hong Kong who would swear on a holy book they've had sex with her," he said, and we both laughed.

101

"Always the big talk at the bars."

"The other night on the boat, while we watched the planes take off from Lantau,   she wanted to tell you. The next morning she phoned, and we talked about it."

"I thought she had something on her mind."

"The night was exquisite. I've never seen the ocean so calm. Briefly it was like poetry. Have you ever wished that somehow your life could be only the perfect moments when everything is the way it should be and there's no boredom and disappointment? Although the best moments always slip away too quickly, they're necessary because they disclose to us what's possible," he said, and it occurred to me that I underestimated Gao. In spite of his superficial manner and foppish clothes, there was more to him than the average, vain Hong Kong playboy.

"Did Lily ask you to say something?"

"No, although she wants you to be aware of how she feels. She doesn't know how to tell you. You're the first man she's really cared about. It's a new experience for her, and she's not sure how to handle the situation."

"Your father will never accept me."

"He's a man of very strong convictions. I guess that's what made him an outstanding military man. He's considered brilliant even in the West. He showed me a report from one of our spies in Washington that mentions how much credit the Americans give him for modernizing the Chinese army. On the other hand I don't think there will be a problem with mother."

"Our meeting went well."

"Probably she thinks you have good manners. That's very important to her. She's always scolding me that my manners have to be improved," he said and signaled to the waiter for refills. "What is your family like? Who is your father? Lily is curious because you never talk about them. Do they live in the States?"

"I don't know anything about my father. We never met," I

102

said reluctantly, not wanting to go into a subject I always avoided.

"How is that possible?"

"My mother never said much about him. I have no idea who he is."

"Is she ashamed of him?"

"I'm not sure. You see, she's deceased," I answered and wished we could talk about something else. For a while, Gao didn't say any more realizing he hit a nerve. Probably he expected me to tell him that my father was an important businessman or perhaps a diplomat of consequence. I'm sure he never expected the answer he got.

"How long ago did your mother die?"

"Several years. Now there's only me. I have no brothers or sisters. You would have liked my mother. She was very intelligent and greatly admired Chinese culture."

"How did she die?"

"An unfortunate…. accident," I answered and put down my drink not wanting any more of it. I couldn't tell him that my mother was killed by Chinese soldiers who shot her during the Tiananmen Square massacre. At that moment I hated every Chinese who ever lived, although at the same time many of them were also killed.

"I'm sorry. If I had known," he quickly answered.

"That's OK," I said trying to appear casual about the matter.

Finally Lily and Li came up from the court. She sat on my lap touching my hair lightly with her hand. Smelling her delicate perfume, I wondered if she knew we had been talking about her. For a fleeting moment I saw in her eyes the same poignant expression that was there the night on the boat. But I couldn't stop thinking about my mother and wished that Gao hadn't brought up the subject. Suddenly I wanted to be by myself.

"I need to go. I have a headache," I said for lack of

anything better to tell them.

"Larry, I didn't mean to pry. It wasn't polite," Gao said apologetically.

"I just don't feel well. I'll call later," I said to Lily and hurriedly left the clubhouse, knowing that I acted poorly. However, I couldn't help it.

To this day I try to forget the way my poor mother died. While I drove back to my apartment, images of Tiananmen Square on that distant, murderous night were still so vivid in my mind as if that terrible tragedy happened only a few days ago. And then the realization struck me that I had no business wanting to marry someone whose father was a leader of the Chinese military that murdered my own mother. Although it wasn't Lily's fault or mine, the situation made no sense. At the same time I knew I couldn't stop seeing the woman I loved so deeply. I wanted to believe that somehow things would work out, although of late, I couldn't shake the feeling the two of us were doomed - an ominous thought that eventually proved to be true.

8

Even after all these years I still awake unexpectedly, recalling that terrible, long-ago night, my ears filled with the chaotic sounds emanating from the desperate millions crowding Beijing's labyrinthine streets - their collective voices an unceasing roar the likes of which I never heard before or since. In the distance sirens wailed ominously. Sporadic gunfire erupted again and again. Realizing that soon many would die, I felt death's cold, unforgiving presence approach through the stifling, summer heat. For the first time I would experience directly the true reality of life under China's "benevolent" socialist government, that over the years continued to receive such lenient, even laudatory treatment by the American media. Regardless of how brutal the regime's behavior became, few people in the West ever wised up.

At the airport it was obvious that things weren't right. The customs agents, who are known for their petty, irritating ways, paid me no heed. Even the cab drivers, who normally descend on a new arrival like locusts, remained aloof. None of them wanted to go into the city center that for days was filled with the huge crowds supporting the students who were demonstrating for democracy. Already troops were present in large numbers, and supposedly many more were on their way from Nanyuan Airport and the Shabe Airbase to the north. For several times the usual fare, I found a driver willing to take me downtown, and he could even speak some broken English. Everything seemed alright until we passed a column of armored vehicles and then large groups of sullen-looking, fully armed troops waiting alongside the road. Suddenly the driver, who had been chattering incessantly, grew silent, and I knew we were both thinking the same thing. The news reports reaching the States made the demonstrations sound like a celebration of youthful bravado. But after seeing the soldiers, I knew that I was heading into a situation very different from what I had come halfway around the world expecting to witness. Proceeding further into the city, we were suddenly immersed in a sea of people and barely avoided being trapped in one, narrow street after another. At many intersections the green and red public buses had been parked at odd angles to create barriers, and on top of them student activists wearing their distinctive headbands were defiantly exhorting the crowd through megaphones.

The crush of human bodies grew denser, and I didn't need a translator to interpret the angry sound of the crowd's collective voice. It was apparent the citizens of Beijing were determined to do anything to keep the soldiers away from their beloved students, many of the army's vehicles surrounded completely so they couldn't move. Some people were even risking their lives by lying in front of them. Others tried to slash tires or pile in the way anything they could find, which included dismantling nearby market stalls to create flimsy barriers. The soldiers seemed bewildered by the spectacle of old people and shabbily dressed workers screaming at them and waving their arms. Who could have imagined a scene like this in the world's largest, communist country, where a few decades before 30 million anonymous people stoically starved to death in the pursuit of Chairman Mao's grandiose failure known euphemistically as the "Great Leap Forward."

Finally the crowd grew so dense it was impossible for the cab to go anywhere. The driver was in a state of panic and insisted that I leave. Although we hadn't reached the hotel, I paid him the agreed sum. Grabbing my bag, I wiggled out of the window and set out on my own. For a while I was completely lost in the mass of hot, sweaty bodies that surged in one direction and then another, carrying me inexorably into the heart of what was about to become a life and death struggle. Realizing that efforts to hold back the troops were failing, the crowd grew more desperate. Some of the army vehicles were set ablaze igniting tree limbs overhead, the violent, orange flames imparting to the scene the garish quality of a nightmare.

I was dismayed that Karen had gotten me involved in such a dangerous situation. A few weeks before she came to Beijing with friends to witness the remarkable student movement that was attempting to bring democracy to a country dominated for so long by autocratic regimes. Phoning me in New York, she urged me to come over as soon as possible, the familiar urgency in her voice that I knew only too well. While I grew up, we often on the spur of the moment had to pack our one piece of shabby luggage and hurry off to be part of some demonstration or event that supposedly was going to change the world for the better. With a sense of expectation second only to hers, I trailed along, a tall, thin lad with dark hair too long, always wearing the same worn, corduroy jacket with frayed elbows she covered more than once with sewn-on, leather patches. Sometimes we ran out of money and ended up having to spend the night in a rundown railway or bus station before somehow managing to get back to whatever place at the moment we called home. Once we even slept for a few hours in the back of a church and were almost arrested. I always felt the petty humiliations we experienced more than she did and marveled how she shrugged them off. But regardless of how many times we went on another of the wild-goose chases she couldn't resist, I never lost my admiration for her unshakable belief that somehow a brighter, more humane future lay ahead for the world.

When she phoned, I debated whether to drop everything and go all the way to Beijing, finally deciding that I couldn't let her down. Surrounded now by this huge, swarm of desperate people, I realized that her persistent disregard for the practical had finally gotten the two of us into a situation that was truly dangerous. Somehow I reached the diplomatic quarter, and with relief hurried down Jianguomen Street to Goldfish Lane where the giant Palace

107

Hotel with its distinctive, green tiled roof is located. The entrance to the grounds was blocked off to keep out the crowd. Holding up my bag to indicate that I was a guest, I entered the beige marble lobby that was an oasis of tranquility in comparison to the chaotic scene outside.

As I feared, Karen wasn't there, and feeling exhausted after traveling halfway around the world, I collapsed briefly in a chair. Although I hadn't eaten since morning, I had little appetite and looked nervously at my watch, realizing that more than an hour had passed since we were supposed to meet. After registering at the desk, I continued to wait, aware that if she already left, I might never find her. I was about to go to my room when she hurried through the door followed by two men, who were doing their best to keep up. Delighted to see her, I jumped to my feet and waved eagerly. Returning my wave, she hurried over, and it occurred to me how much of my life and who I am is connected to this tall, stunning woman with long, red hair. At the same time I have to admit that on occasion I've been ashamed of her. She and her friends had the unmistakably shabby look of aging hippies living in a past they could never let go of. Not surprising, several in the lobby paused to stare at her. The fact I was ashamed of my own mother was something I didn't like to admit. Nonetheless, I was always careful that she never met anyone important I knew on Wall Street.

Although in her 50s, she moved with the energy of someone much younger and still radiated the unmistakable vitality I was always aware of as a child. Her outfit included faded, blue jeans, a worn, brown suede jacket and the battered, wide-brimmed orange hat that she had worn as long as I could remember. While the shabby-chic style was still considered fashionable for someone much younger, she continued nonetheless to cultivate it. To the end Karen would continue to consider herself a child of the counterculture and dressed the role so no one could fail to realize that she faithfully kept her commitment to it. Although most people had long since dismissed the whole thing as *passe* and gone on to other things, to the end she and her small group of friends remained loyal as ever to what the counterculture supposedly embodied, including an uncompromising opposition to war.

While hugging me, she talked fast as if running on limitless energy. But I could see how tired she was and suspected she hadn't gotten much sleep in days. I started to say something about taking better care of herself but knew it wouldn't do any good. We sat briefly on a nearby couch, and she tried to explain what happened since her arrival in Beijing almost a week ago. I knew how important it was to her that I appreciate the situation the way she did and tried to give her my complete attention. For me there would always be something contagious about her enthusiasm, and suddenly I no longer regretted the long trip from New York.

And then in her eyes I saw something that was never there before - a hint of confusion or something stronger that belied what she was telling me. I realized that she was trying to reassure herself. No doubt, she knew about the troops and could feel the fear spreading like a contagion through the city. Suddenly without warning she began to sob, something I had witnessed only a couple of times in my entire life. As she leaned forward putting her face in her hands, I noticed the prominent gray streaks in her beautiful, red hair that always embodied the vitality that drew so many men to her. But now that exquisite color was fading rapidly. The sobbing seemed to well up out of the depths of her being, and then just as quickly she sat up and forcing a laugh, dried her eyes.

"I'm just tired. That's all. Don't pay any attention. It's not like me; you know that. The excitement and all. Years ago, staying up for long periods was never a problem," she said, dismissing the episode with a quick wave of her pretty hand.

"I'll get some coffee. We both need a lift. It will take a only a minute," I said and hurried off to the restaurant, realizing how close she had come to breaking down. Suddenly the invulnerability I always associated with my mother had vanished forever. While I was growing up, nothing discouraged her - not the lagging lack of money that forced on us so many demeaning compromises; the lovers who claimed briefly to share her aspirations but always deserted her, including the father I never knew; and all the shabby places with hardly any furniture where we were forced to live. Somehow she always remained proud and indifferent to the type of things that weigh others down and deter them from pursuing their dreams.

Most of the time we lived like gypsies always on the move so I was rarely in one school for long. Whenever necessary, she managed to find a job at a radical publication or art magazine or just worked as a waitress to supplement her meager share of a family trust fund that was never enough for us to survive. Fortunately there was an inexhaustible supply of friends who were such a consolation to her, although over the years most dropped by the wayside until now only a few remained. It was as if all those people simply vanished, and even Karen didn't know what happened to most of them. One day when I was a teenager, it suddenly occurred to me that my mother seemed lost as if she never had a real destination in life. And now, after seeing her break down briefly, I knew that those long years had finally taken their toll. What I detected in her eyes was nothing less than the dawning realization that all that searching had led nowhere.

Along with the coffee, I brought some cookies powdered with sugar, knowing she couldn't resist a sweet. After a few sips of the strong coffee, she seemed to recover and smoothing back her hair, smiled as if to reassure me that everything was alright.

"My goodness, I forgot to introduce David. How impolite of me. Of course, you know Ralph," she said glancing at the nondescript, little man wearing worn denim, who like a barely noticed shadow had followed her around for years. "David, didn't

I tell you how impressive my son is. All the women in New York are fainting at his feet. Come now, admit it," she said proudly and briefly squeezed my hand.

"Maybe a few," I answered to please her.

"Of course they are. Don't be so modest. And he has a big office on Wall Street, although I've never seen it. But he's not like us - much too practical. I can't imagine where he got that. Even as a child he never threw anything away, even worn out clothes. He would fold them up neatly and keep them in a little box tucked away in the closet so no one would find them, as if they might actually take something like that. If he didn't finish an apple, he would save what was left for later, even the smallest part," she went on, the pride evident in her voice, and I offered to get more coffee. "We don't have time and must get back to the Square. I told our student friends we'd be gone only an hour or so. They know you came all the way from America and can't wait to meet you. You'll be amazed. They're so remarkable. I'm sure the news reports in the States haven't done them justice. I don't understand where their commitment to democracy comes from. It's like an exquisite flower has somehow blossomed in an arid desert. No doubt, they realize what all of this could mean for China's future. If I hadn't witnessed it firsthand, I never could have appreciated what they're trying to do."

"I guess you know about the soldiers. There are a lot of them, and it appears they mean business. Are you sure it's wise to go back to the Square?" I asked and noticed the animation leave her face.

"We've heard about all of that," Ralph said sternly. "But they can't stop the momentum of what's happening across the country. You can't put something like this back in a bottle and just screw on the cap."

"Did the "Review" send you over here?" I asked.

"They'll want to see what I write, and I'm sure they'll

publish something. They usually do," he answered matter-of-factly, although I knew how proud he was of his connection to one of America's leading, progressive journals that after all these years was still published in a Greenwich Village loft.

"They never liked my things," Karen observed.

"I just write in a way that fits their format. That's all."

"The people are doing everything to block the soldiers, although I don't think it's going to work," I persisted.

"Late this afternoon there was a brief skirmish near the Square, although it didn't amount to much. Probably just a face-saving gesture by the government so the students will show some moderation," Ralph added and looked at Karen as if to confirm that she approved of what he said.

"Let's not worry about all of that. Please, this is a time to be optimistic. How often do you have the privilege of witnessing the birth of a new democracy," she said and stood up as if to end the discussion. "I promised the students we'd be right back, and I don't want to disappoint them. You'll see what a wonderful group they are - just like we were those many years ago when we were demonstrating against Vietnam. God, that seems such a long time ago, like we were different people," she said with a sigh.

As soon as we were outside, it was apparent how rapidly the situation was deteriorating, the sirens in the distance wailing incessantly as if an air raid was imminent. Beneath her orange hat, Karen's expression turned grim, and I knew there was no point suggesting that we return to the safety of the hotel. We hurried down Wang Fu Jing, where the city's best stores are located, and then on to Chan An Avenue passing the massive Beijing Hotel. Suddenly it seemed that everyone in the city was running around frantically as if not knowing where to go, and a couple of times Karen was almost knocked off her feet.

Finally we reached the Square, the enormous, open space in the heart of the city that has no equal anywhere on the globe.

Paved with gigantic flagstones, it covers over a hundred acres and can hold more than a million people. Supposedly in recent weeks it had been filled to capacity a number of times. On that fateful night it had been transformed into an unreal scene, a smoky haze enveloping the huge, restless crowd milling about on the vast, stone surface littered with debris from days of demonstrations. On a wall at the north end near the Tiananmen (the gate of heavenly peace) was a large, colored picture of Chairman Mao's fat, unappealing face. In spite of its size, the picture looked almost real as Mao sneered at this remarkable spectacle that belied everything he stood for.

At the other end of the Square was a sight that almost moved me to tears, one that was both inspiring and pathetic. It was a crude, hastily built, 10-meter high, white Styrofoam and plaster statue constructed by students from the Central Arts Academy. Supposedly it represented the Guanyin, the Chinese goddess of mercy and compassion, although it bore an unmistakable resemblance to New York's famous Statue of Liberty. For the ruling communist government, I couldn't imagine a more provocative act, especially since the statute had been erected in the place regarded as the nation's symbolic heart. According to Karen, the students built it in only a few days, their work accompanied by the music of Handel's Messiah played on an improvised public address system. It seemed such a poignant gesture, and I took several pictures hoping they captured how it looked so I could show them around New York.

Suddenly several military helicopters flew over the Square and then came back. The sound of their engines was deafening, although the crowd acted as if they weren't there. Perhaps everyone was convinced the Guanyin or something else would protect them. Soon Karen found several of the student leaders and proudly introduced me. I was surprised how young they were, some looking almost like children, their tired, sweaty faces animated in the dim light. They shook my hand with an intensity I will never forget them, some even hugging me. They seemed deeply grateful that I had come all the way from America as if my meager support actually meant something. While gathering around us, they all kept trying to speak at the same time, and one of them eagerly described the fireworks display that would be launched in a few hours from in front of the Goddess. Suddenly I was no longer a mere spectator but instead felt like I was an integral part of the momentous events taking place there.

As Karen and I continued around the Square, strangers speaking broken English kept stopping us to find out what was being written in the foreign press. It was apparent how important it was to the average Chinese that the world community appreciate what was happening in their country. Wishing I bought more film, I used up the remaining frames, even taking a picture of Chairman Mao's bloated face. Once again the helicopters swept loudly over the Square. But this time they came in so low it appeared they would crash right into the crowd, causing many to run to the sides for protection.

When we returned to the street, I immediately spotted the troops. They were walking in single file and trying to stay low so no one would notice them. I knew right away that something awful was about to happen. In the Square one of the students was still exhorting the crowd through an improvised public address system, his disembodied voice echoing eerily among the massive buildings brooding silently over the chaotic scene.

As the phalanx of troops continued forward, they raised their guns, and the people closest to them moved back grudgingly. Suddenly without warning, those cruel guns exploded into a deafening roar and screams erupted everywhere, scores of people falling as if their legs had been cut from beneath them. Others ran as fast as they could trying to get away, the roar of the guns dominating everything. The soldiers were firing point-blank into the crowd, and it was obvious they intended to cause as many casualties as possible. Soon hundreds of helpless people were writhing on the pavement. A few went back trying to help them and were also shot as the soldiers continued forward, relentlessly murdering their fellow, unarmed citizens.

I knew that I was witnessing a crime of historic significance - the government of the world's largest, socialist country murdering in cold blood its own people, who had done nothing except express the desire for a little freedom. Suddenly a regime that claimed to be motivated by benevolent principles was stripped bare of all pretense, and after that fateful night I thought naïvely the outside world would see the Chinese government for what it really was: a brutal regime without conscience or scruples. As I would soon learn, however, that was nothing but wishful thinking, and instead I had a big surprise coming.

The acrid cloud of gun smoke drifted over to where Karen and I stood staring in disbelief at the nightmarish spectacle as the people rushing by frantically urged us to flee.

"They'll kill us, all of us," an old woman yelled, briefly grabbing my arm with her hand that felt like ice.

A terrible fear was on everyone's face, having replaced the poignant hope that was there only minutes before. Volley after volley of gunshots continued to erupt, the tide of desperate people carrying the two of us to one side. With difficulty I managed to stay on my feet holding my arm tightly around Karen so she wouldn't fall. Suddenly the student speaking through the public address system in the Square screamed as if his throat had been cut. It seemed an eternity before the gunshots finally stopped, and briefly I thought the attack was over.

"I saw Winnie fall. Probably they'll trample her if she isn't already dead," Karen said referring to one of the students, her voice quivering with rage.

Grabbing my hand, she pushed her way back through the

115

crowd, and finally we reached the injured people, many of them crying out pitifully for help. But most were already dead. I had never seen people shot with military ordnance and could barely look at the terrible damage done to their bodies. It was obvious the soldiers had been instructed to inflict maximum damage. Somehow we found Winnie, who was lying on her back near a heap of motionless, twisted bodies that had fallen partly on top of each other. Karen knelt down and placed the girl's bleeding head in her lap. With her shirt she wiped away the blood from her pretty, young face pleading with her to be alive. But there was no answer, and leaning over, she reverently kissed her forehead.

"Such a beautiful, little person with so much promise," she sobbed as if speaking of a lost child. I knelt beside her but had to look away when I saw the hard stare of death in the girl's eyes.

"Some of the students will know who her family is," I said, and finally Karen put her down.

Suddenly the gunfire erupted again, sounding even louder and more deadly than before, and I realized how close the soldiers were to us. Repeatedly I heard the dull, sickening smack of bullets slamming into human flesh. Around us people kept toppling over like dominoes, many emitting an unearthly scream that sent a chill down my spine. As Karen and I started to run, she jerked violently as if someone pulled hard on her other arm. I caught a glimpse of a gaping hole in her side as she let go and fell face down on the pavement. I tried to stop and help her. But the crowd kept pushing me away, and looking back, I briefly saw her hand desperately reaching out to me. The sight of her slender, white hand with silver rings on the fingers was the last I ever saw of my dear mother. The rings were the gifts from various men she once loved, that she still clung to long after the person involved was no more than a phantom. With all my strength I kept trying to go back to her although it was no use. The tide of terrified people carried me further and further away, and I gave up trying to resist. Finally reaching the steps of a nearby building, I waited for the gunfire to stop, trembling with anger because there was nothing I could do.

To this day the pathetic image of my mother's hand reaching out so desperately is still riveted in my memory. I wanted to believe she was only wounded but knew there was little chance she survived such a horrific injury. Suddenly amid all that chaos, everything the two of us shared since the day I was born had come to a cruel, irrevocable end. The situation was an obscenity. After the many years she championed humanitarian causes hoping in her small way to improve the world, her life had been snuffed out so pointlessly - all her bright aspirations no match for the brute force she despised, that in a brief, terrible moment made a mockery of everything she stood for.

I thought the gunfire would never stop, that awful sound blurring my consciousness until finally I put my hands over my ears. Again and again the helicopters swept in low, the dank, humid air pervaded with the smell of gun powder mixed with the sickening odor emitted by the terrified mob, their eyes swollen with terror. Finally I tried to go back to where Karen had fallen, spotting on the pavement her orange hat that had been crushed almost beyond recognition. As I picked it up, a bullet grazed my shoulder feeling like a piece of the skin was torn off, and reluctantly I retreated to where I had been standing.

"Is your mother alright?" asked a student named Yang to whom we spoke only minutes before.

"She's been shot. As soon as I can, I'll go back to her," I said holding up the pathetic remnant of her hat.

"They won't let you. Trucks will arrive soon to remove the bodies, and then they'll wash the pavement so there's no sign of the massacre," he said, the import of his words barely registering in my mind. "The authorities don't want anyone to know how many have been killed. In the coming weeks they'll say only a few died. Of course, they'll blame what happened on so-called "class

117

enemies" who are supposedly a threat to law and order. In other words, those who were killed in cold blood were acting against the party's interests and had to be dealt with accordingly. But after what happened here tonight, I can tell you there's no hope for China. Things will only grow more violent and cruel. My nation is run by a small clique that rules in the most ruthless way to preserve its power. And whatever conflicts with their dominance will be eliminated by whatever means is considered necessary," he said grimly, and I saw the tears blurring his eyes.

"What will happen to those who have been shot? I'm sure that some are still alive and need help."

"The injured... will be...," he answered and paused, realizing what he was about to say. "They will be quickly disposed of. The regime is very good at that sort of thing. They have operatives trained to take care of embarrassing situations so the truth can always be denied."

"But Karen might still be alive," I insisted, my voice breaking with emotion.

"Don't you understand? The fact that human beings are involved is irrelevant. The authority of the party elite has been challenged, and they will do whatever is considered necessary no matter how violent," he continued, and briefly I couldn't hear him because of the huge helicopter hovering about a hundred feet above, its blinding searchlight like a giant, animated finger probing the helpless crowd that like a flock of frightened birds darted in one direction and then another.

"Come over here. It's safer in case they open fire from the helicopter," Yang said, leading the way to a doorway in the side of a nearby building.

"I can't leave without finding out if she's still alive. I might be able to help her."

"Try to understand that those who have been shot are now an embarrassment to the regime and must be gotten rid of. You have to come with me. A foreigner like you is an undesirable and represents an unwanted problem. Any low-level functionary can make you disappear into some prison hell-hole, and no one will ever know what happened."

"But I can't just leave," I repeated feeling sick to my stomach.

"If you go back there, they'll immediately shoot you. As you can see, the area is surrounded now by soldiers who are ready to fire at the slightest provocation. You must save your own life. Your mother would want it that way. There is no point letting them destroy both of you. For one thing you can return to America and tell everyone about the atrocity you just witnessed. That's what the party officials don't want. They work very hard cultivating a sanitized image so no one realizes what they're really like. But you can help the outside world to know the truth so the democratic nations make them pay a big price for such cruelty," he said. Of course, that didn't happen, and to this day I still recall his naïve words. Down the street an ambulance suddenly arrived from one of the hospitals, and as we watched, the medical personnel trying to reach the wounded were also shot.

"Where are you staying?"

"The Palace Hotel."

"You can't go back there now. Plainclothesmen will be at all the hotels checking foreigners and trying to determine if any represent a problem. It's possible they will ignore you. On the other hand something about you might bother them, especially since you may have been seen in the Square. Don't forget that in a situation where the interests of the regime are threatened, it can be something trivial that makes the difference whether a person lives or dies. In a police state suspicion at all times reigns supreme. That's why everyone is so compliant. The process of determining whether you will be left alone is totally arbitrary. Perhaps the detective questioning you doesn't like the expression on your face

119

or something about your clothes. It doesn't matter. If it suits him, you will be taken into custody. Later if all your answers aren't correct, you will be sent to one of the camps far out in the provinces. There are hundreds of them in remote locations, some in underground installations once used by the military. Then you will be quickly forgotten - that is, if you aren't murdered right away. Years can pass during which you are forced into brutally hard labor while getting little to eat. Most people in the camps are soon worked to death, and there will be no record of your existence because your documents were destroyed long ago. In the eyes of the government you were merely one of thousands upon thousands of undesirables who were disposed of in the appropriate manner. Even if you manage to survive, eventually you will be gotten rid of so the space can be used to house another wretched undesirable," he continued, still speaking very fast. But my mind was completely numb, and I had trouble comprehending what he was telling me. "To westerners, the situation in China is totally removed from their frame of reference so they think the reports of concentration camps and arbitrary executions are an exaggeration. But I can assure you they aren't. In fact, hardly any of the true facts ever reach the outside world. I know what I'm talking about. Even in a country where the media is completely controlled, we hear rumors about what's going on.

"In a few days you can return to the hotel. By then, things will have calmed down. You'll be surprised how quickly the authorities re-establish what they consider a normal state of things. And in the weeks to come, everyone will appear to forget. That way they can live with themselves, and if necessary, you even learn to lie to yourself. In a country like China a person who thinks too much can lose their sanity. But after what happened today, I can tell you there's no hope," he went on, and I wished he would stop talking.

We headed down the street away from the Square, staying

120

close to the buildings so we wouldn't be noticed. And then it occurred to me that I was doing nothing less than abandoning my dear mother, who had always done the best she could for me. When we had little food, she made sure I was the first to eat. And now in her moment of true need, I had failed her. We walked several blocks, finally reaching a car where two students were waiting.

"We were worried you didn't make it," said one of them, who had blood on his shirt and kept looking at me. He started to say something but paused. "Where is your mother?" he finally asked.

"They shot her."

"How terrible! She was such a nice woman. We loved her. She really cared... about us and wanted to help."

"Liu was shot. Also, Zhang. When the soldiers started to fire, Liu charged at them waving his arms in order to make them stop. It was like he believed the whole thing was some sort of a mistake, although he should have known better. All of us should have. We are well-acquainted with the party's methods, and what happened tonight is no mistake. Something like this is always done according to the phony protocol that supposedly legitimizes even the worst atrocity. A decision is made high up in the bureaucracy, and then a directive is sent down to a functionary at a desk, who stamps the necessary pieces of paper that officially authorize imprisonment or murder. A small, rubber stamp from a drawer is pressed on each piece of paper, and for the people involved the application of that little stamp is no less final than if they were hit by a bolt of lightning," he went on, although I had stopped listening, unable to think any more about such awful things.

An hour later we reached a small house several miles outside Beijing. I stayed there for two days and during that time met many of the students connected to the demonstrations, all of them on their way to locations in the provinces where they could hide out until things settled down. They were all in shock after seeing so many of their friends murdered along with innumerable members of the public. I was surprised how easily I was accepted into their midst. The mere fact I was an American gave me legitimacy because for them America represented everything they hoped for.

According to the information brought to the house, the killing continued the next day and sporadically into the night, some of the students preferring to die rather than surrender to the force used against them. Finally late in the morning I was driven back to the city and left several blocks from the Palace Hotel. As I had been told, all signs of the massacre had been quickly erased as if a giant hand swept the place completely clean. Everything seemed normal again except there were hardly any people in the streets. The only reminder of the violent, chaotic struggle that took place a few nights before was a couple of burned-out trucks that hadn't been taken away. But everything else had been removed down to the smallest bits and pieces. What I remembered of that horrible night seemed now like a mad dream.

At the hotel I was greeted politely, and my luggage retrieved from a storage room. I decided to stay on for a few days and find out what I could about those who had been shot. While there was little chance my mother was alive, perhaps I could learn where her remains had been taken. Although the horror of that cruel night festered inside every resident of Beijing, no one would talk about the massacre and its pathetic victims. It didn't help that plainclothesmen were everywhere. For almost a week I wandered around the city, being careful not to attract attention and eventually found a few who would speak to me in a hushed whisper. It helped that I was a westerner and had an American accent. As expected, I learned that the dead were promptly carted away and disposed of in an unknown, mass grave. An old man who owned a flower shop informed me that the soldiers stole valuables from the lifeless bodies before they were thrown like refuse into the back of trucks.

I spent two, additional days visiting pawn shops all over the city growing more weary by the hour. I was about to give up when by chance I found two of Karen's rings in a little shop near Ritan Park. The price to retrieve them was little more than the value of the metal. I felt like I discovered one of the greatest treasures in the entire world. At least I now had something tangible to remember my poor mother. And yet, as I held her rings in my hand, they seemed so pathetic - the embodiment of her many dreams that started so brightly but ended only in sorrow like her radiant red hair turning inevitably to the sad color of ashes.

The next day I shared transportation to the airport with some Korean businessmen and then got a flight to Singapore. From there I flew to London. As the plane lifted off from airport, I looked down on sprawling Beijing and felt my heart sink. When I arrived there almost a week ago, I never could have imagined the cruel spectacle that awaited me. And with my mother suddenly gone, I felt completely alone for the first time in my entire life.

I promised myself never to set foot in China again and was determined to tell everyone what I witnessed so the outside world could respond in kind. One day, however, I would be back and viewed as a great friend of the regime. Many would even believe that for years I worked diligently to further the party's corrupt interests while making many friends among its obsequious, deceitful functionaries. Perhaps one of them issued the order that caused all the pointless deaths in Tiananmen Square, including my mother's. And in time many in the party would even regard me as one of their very own.

9

During the long flight to London, I slept intermittently and tried to decide how to break the news of Karen's death to her mother. I couldn't find the right words because there weren't any and wished there was some way to avoid telling her the truth. After reaching Heathrow, I rented a car and drove to the little village in the West Country where my mother grew up. While studying at the London School of Economics, I lived there most of the time, and it is the only home of any permanence I have ever known. When I was young, Karen and I rarely went there, and eventually I realized that for some unknown reason she wanted to stay away.

When I arrived at the village, night was descending rapidly, the warm breeze smelling of the fresh grass in the nearby fields. Leaving the car, I briefly heard the appealing sounds coming from a flock of sheep. And then the evening was silent again, and it occurred to me that it would be difficult to find a place more remote from the brutal spectacle I witnessed only days before. Along the narrow street, lights were going on in the little, stone houses that looked so inviting, most of the families probably sitting down to their evening meal. How glad I was to be back there, and always I will consider that charming, English village an invaluable part of whom I am.

Our family has lived there for generations, and although the house appears little different from all the others, it is unique nonetheless because it is the house where true heroes have lived - men who distinguished themselves in the bitter crucible of war. My great-great grandfather fought in the colonial campaigns beside the legendary George Gordon, and my great grandfather was a highly decorated soldier in World War I. At Verdun and the Somme, he received numerous decorations for his bravery, which included saving countless British lives. However, he returned from the war with his body shattered and spent the rest of his days an invalid who couldn't walk. Over the years the house became a place of pilgrimage for his regiment that revered a man who embodied everything the nation believed about its soldiers. His picture in a full-dress uniform hangs in the living room alongside a map of the Somme campaign, where Britain lost almost an entire generation of its promising youth in a few, terrible days. For many, that infamous battle initiated modern warfare with its mass cruelty, the final chapter of which would one day be written far to the east.

Instead of going inside, I walked down the road to the little stream that ran beside the village. An elderly couple out for an evening stroll greeted me as they passed, and I wondered if they knew about the massacre in distant China. While in Beijing, I consoled myself with the thought that a great revulsion would sweep through the outside world causing the communist regime to pay a severe price for such a blatant atrocity. For the first time, however, it occurred to me that for many the episode would seem remote and perhaps irrelevant. Eventually I saw to my disgust that the world at large had no intention of responding in any meaningful way to the Tiananmen Square slaughter. Instead, in the interest of easy profits, a course was pursued that was directly opposite to what I hoped for. In fact, in the aftermath of Tiananmen the western world, and especially many of its most prominent businessmen, would act in a manner that continually rewarded the Chinese regime for its worst behavior. By some perverse logic such indulgence was supposedly going to improve the situation. Of course, it never did.

At the moment, however, I had other things on my mind, and sitting on a bench by the stream, I kept thinking about my grandmother. I knew how much Karen's tragic death would trouble her and wondered if for now it would be better not to tell her much. I remained there until dark delaying the inevitable as long as possible. And then on the way back to the house, I realized

125

how lucky I was to be alive. Nearly everyone near me in the Square had been killed, and I will always wonder if it was mere luck or something else that spared me.

Removing my suitcase from the car, I opened the little, iron gate and entered the small garden where grandmother Lee grew herb plants and roses, the pleasant scent of basil and thyme lingering in the warm air. I rang the bell, and soon she came to the door. Although I hadn't said much on the telephone, her expression told me she already knew something serious was wrong. Briefly her eyes filled with doubt searched mine, and then she burst into that marvelous, warm smile of which I'm so fond.

"My dear grandson, give me a hug. It's so wonderful to see you. I hope you didn't eat much on the plane because I've made your favorite dinner," she said as we went into the living room.

The house was decorated with traditional, English furniture that had been in the family for generations, and although not opulent, conveyed an impression of substance and comfort. It appeared that hardly anything had been changed since the last time I was there more than a year ago, and once again I thought how glad I was to be back in that peaceful place of which I have only fond memories.

Lee had on a tailored, gray dress with a black belt and as always looked impeccably neat, not a strand of her white hair out of place. I always marveled how she kept up appearances. Although in her late-70s, she was still a handsome woman, her serene face having few wrinkles. I owed so much to her, more than I could ever repay. Out of her limited income from an army widow's pension and the proceeds from the small trust which her children share, she helped to pay for my education at a fine New England college and later at the London School of Economics. After getting a good-paying job on Wall Street, I tried to return the money, but she wouldn't accept a dime.

"How's the village?" I inquired and sat beside her on the

126

blue, velvet couch.

"Occasionally someone still asks about you," she said and looked at me again with the same inquiring expression. "Something happened. I could tell from your voice on the phone. I know you too well to hide anything from me. Is it Karen?"

"Yes...she's dead," I said, almost choking on those awful words, and wished there was something I could add that would soften their impact.

"Oh God! For years I've been expecting this. I guess I'm only surprised it didn't happen sooner," she said and began to sob. I took her hand wanting to comfort her but knew that there was nothing I could do. "Grandson, I have to be alone. When I come back, you must tell me everything, no matter how bad it is," she added and hurriedly left the room.

I paced around nervously and then tried to distract myself by looking at the map of the Somme. Decades before, millions of anonymous men fought and died there so bravely, many never returning to their homes. Now that monumental, life and death struggle had been reduced to nothing more than little, red and black markers on a pale green sheet of framed paper. In spite of the enormity of the sacrifices on that remote battlefield, most people today have never heard of the Somme.

The shelves on either side of the fireplace were filled with books. While living at the house, I read many of them, and now they seemed like old friends who once afforded me a certain comfort. I glanced through a collection of Thomas Hardy's stories. But nothing on the pages registered in my mind, and I could have been looking at something written in an unknown language. I'm not sure how much time passed before Lee returned to the room looking composed again, although I could tell she had been crying.

"Where did you call from?" she asked and sat again on the couch.

"Beijing."

"Oh, no."

"You've heard."

"It was on television. But I never imagined the two of you were there."

"It was terrible. The troops fired into the crowd at point blank range murdering thousands. We were trying to run away when Karen was hit. I don't know how they didn't get me too."

"The pictures on the TV were awful. But why were you there?"

"Karen went to China to support the movement for democracy. You know how she was always adopting some cause. By the time I arrived, she was already friends with many of the students. They seemed genuinely fond of her. I think they realized how much she appreciated what they were trying to do. But in retrospect, the whole thing was so futile. Those poor kids never had a chance. They really believed they could stand up to that horrible regime and change their country for the better."

"Didn't the two of you realize how dangerous the situation was?"

"When Karen phoned asking me to come over, I didn't want to let her down. Ironically it made no difference that I was there."

"I can't believe she's really gone and I'll never see her again coming through the door," Lee said her face softening briefly, and I wondered what fond memory she briefly recalled.

"Do you want to have a funeral?"

"Of course, there's room in the family plot."

"The casket will have to be empty. I wasn't able to recover her remains," I added but didn't go on.

"What do you mean?"

"The soldiers blocked access to the bodies. No doubt, the regime doesn't want the outside world to know how many died or how brutally they were murdered," I answered and decided not to

128

show her the rings.

"I always wished that Karen's life could have been different - I mean, much easier for her as well as you. While you were growing up, there was always so much turmoil."

"We had many happy times. She tried to be a good mother, and I knew that she loved me. That's the most important thing."

"Yes, it is."

"Did she ever say much about her father?"

"A few things, although I got the impression she didn't want to talk about him. I know, of course, that he was killed in World War II. I forget which battle."

"There's something I've always wanted to tell you, although you must never repeat it. No one else knows, not even Ned or Dorothy," she said referring to her other children. "But it's important that you know. Perhaps it will explain a lot about Karen. I loved my husband very much. Russell was a very decent man, and the years we were together were happy. But I have only one picture of him that I keep in a drawer upstairs. For years, I wasn't able to look at it, and then a few weeks ago I took it out and kept it all day on my vanity. I had almost forgotten what a fine face he had. That's what I noticed about him when we first met. There were several times I almost threw the picture away, but now I'm glad that I didn't," she continued, and I realized it never occurred to me there was no visible sign of him anywhere in the house. "When he died in the war, everyone considered him a hero. Afterwards there was a lengthy article in the local newspaper. My father was proud that like him his son-in-law was a dedicated soldier. But it isn't true. I suppose that some would call him a coward."

"A coward!" I answered startled by the term. "What do you mean?"

"I wish it was all a mistake. I would be willing to accept anything that proved it was. Because of the unusual circumstances of his death, the army held an inquiry. You see, he was shot in the back behind British lines."

"Probably he was killed by friendly fire. Sometimes that happens."

"Unfortunately he left his gun on the ground and was running to the rear when he was hit. His entire company was wiped out. The conclusion was that he fled abandoning his comrades. It was Russell's first time in combat, and apparently he wasn't up to such a terrifying experience. So he ran, and probably someone deliberately shot him."

"How do you know?"

"There was a confidential report that was never made public. One day an officer came to the door and handed me an envelope. He was very polite and suggested that I read it in private. It was only three pages long and stated what I just told you. Whoever shot Russell was identified only as an unnamed British infantryman. I kept waiting for the report to be released, dreading the effect it would have on my father. It would have been a terrible blow to him to know that his own son-in-law ran away under fire. He would have felt the entire family had been disgraced."

"Is it possible there could be another explanation?"

"Apparently the inquiry eliminated all other possibilities. After several months, I realized the report had been quietly filed away and would never be released. Probably the matter was handled that way out of deference to my father. Also there might have been the need to bring charges against the individual who shot Russell. It was like they were protecting him and saying that Russell got what he deserved. I never destroyed my copy. I forgot it was in the desk, and one day Karen found it. When I went upstairs, she was staring out the window with the report in her hand. Her eyes were filled with tears. At the time she was only 15. The report doesn't mince words and states explicitly that Russell was guilty of dereliction of duty, deserting his comrades and contributing to the loss of an entire British company. It couldn't be worse than that.

After Karen saw the report, an unmistakable change came over her, and she was never the same. I'm convinced that brief document that I should have thrown away affected her entire life. Also, she was very close to her grandfather, and it troubled her greatly that he was injured so badly during combat and had to spend the rest of his life in a wheelchair. Of course, it bothered me too. He was such a vigorous man when he went to war. A few years later he came back on a stretcher, and when they brought him into the house, I could hardly believe it was him. Suddenly he had aged several years, and his hair had turned gray. It took me a long time to accept with equanimity what happened to him. It was his abiding belief in the value of his sacrifice that influenced me, and eventually I no longer saw him as someone ruined. But for Karen it was different. As far as she was concerned, it was war and its inherent cruelty that disgraced her father and also crippled her grandfather - that in essence ruined both of them."

"I always suspected there was some sort of painful secret she carried with her, that she could never bring herself to tell me," I said, recalling my mother's determined expression as she stared defiantly at the troops in Tiananmen Square. At that moment, she probably felt she was standing up to everything she despised, that in the end proved to be so much stronger than she was. Suddenly many things about her I never understood were clearer, especially her unceasing hostility to anything connected to the military - something that always seemed so odd in view of what her family represented.

"I felt it was important that you know. While Karen was alive, I couldn't say anything. It's our family's unfortunate secret. Most families have one. Now you and I both know the truth. But it must never go beyond this room."

"I'm glad you told me although it's best you waited."

"None of this diminishes what our family stands for, a legacy of which you can be justly proud. Recently I went through

131

some boxes in the attic and found my grandfather's diary from the colonial wars. He fought bravely in all of them. It was men like him that built the British Empire. After grandfather retired, I'll always remember how he gave his old riding boots a good polish every few days. Even now the leather has lost none of its luster. I want you to have the diary. It's a remarkable document, and I know you'll appreciate it. He describes all the campaigns in which he participated, including Kumasi where he served with Garnet Woolsey; the Transvaal against the Boars; and the long struggle in the Sudan with the legendary Kitchener. He led the relief party from Cairo that attempted to rescue his old friend and comrade, Charles Gordon. Unfortunately they were a couple of days late. By then, the entire British garrison, including Gordon, had been killed. It was the greatest disappointment of his life. Until the day he died, he kept a picture of Gordon on the wall. It will mean a lot to me to know that his diary is in your hands. It's appropriate that you have it.

"Although officially an American, you're also British and will always carry with you a tradition of which you can be justly proud. I have no doubt that one day you will acquit yourself well in life and make me proud of you. Perhaps in time you will add something of importance to what our family stands for," she said, the pride evident in her voice. "Unfortunately, my own children don't have it in them."

"They may surprise you," I answered, although I knew what she meant. Ned, her son, was a minor government bureaucrat who would always be content to file reports from behind a cluttered desk. Dorothy, her other daughter, was married to a sheep farmer in northern England. They were very decent people, had four, robust children and also were the most boring people I have ever met. "I hope that one day I will live up to your expectations," I added, knowing how important it was for her to hear that.

132

Just before midnight Lee retired to her room, and feeling restless, I went out for another walk. The night was still warm, and all the houses of the village already dark, the moon casting a dim, soft light over the nearby field where a layer of luminous fog hung motionless. Heading down the road, I tried to imagine the beleaguered British garrison led by the legendary Charles Gordon fighting bravely to the last man at Khartoum. In spite of my mother's attitude towards war, I always felt a strong connection to the members of our family who led such courageous lives, especially my great-great grandfather whose diary would now be one of my prized possessions. Often I wished that I could have lived at a different time instead of the era of Auschwitz, the Russian Gulag and now Tiananmen Square. After the death of romantic nationalism in the lethal trenches of World War I, the modern, totalitarian state with its extraordinary capacity for impersonal brutality made its fateful appearance. Now the human will was dwarfed by such powerful, irrational forces amid a harsh landscape stripped of illusion, and over the years those terrible forces only grew stronger and more menacing.

To her last days my mother never wavered in her belief that somehow the world would eventually become a better, more humane place. Now I couldn't escape the conclusion that her life was nothing but a futile gesture that left behind little but loose ends. Still I will always look back fondly to what I regard as our grand adventure while I was growing up, as if there was nothing the two of us couldn't stand up to as long as we were together. In particular, I often recall the brief years we spent on the island of Ibiza off the Mediterranean coast of Spain.

During the long, lazy afternoons of summer we were usually at the beach, sitting under a bright green umbrella Karen fashioned out of discarded sail cloth. After the sun set, we would head to one of the quaint cafés by the harbor and join her many friends at a table lit by candles that flickered in the warm breeze off the water. Till late at night, they drank wine from large jugs that were passed around while everyone talked endlessly about the vague ideas that supposedly defined who they were - a special group whose members perceived things of importance about the world that others failed to understand. The intensity with which they spoke captivated my attention, especially when they talked about their opposition to the Vietnam war. It was the defining event of their lives, although years later I realized they knew little about what really caused it.

At the time the counterculture, that briefly dominated America, was fading rapidly away, becoming little more than a curiosity associated with quaint images of hippies and flower children. For several, exciting years, however, it fascinated the public, attracting all kinds of people to its ranks. Briefly they attached themselves to what seemed a charming, even quaint adventure, although it was really much more than that. For most, however, it remained only a fashionable sojourn while in college, and eventually they moved on to other pursuits, some later viewing their involvement with embarrassment. Others like my mother and her friends never abandoned the movement, even long after the events ceased that brought them together in the first place. Eventually I realized they considered themselves to be the upholders of a vision, and to maintain its purity, many drifted away to places like Ibiza or islands off the coast of India, trying to preserve a way of life that eventually became little more than a fantasy.

On Ibiza, we lived in a small, stone house at the edge of a field that overlooked the sea. It was a long walk to get there, and at night the distant water of the Mediterranean looked like bright silver in the intense moonlight. Sometimes we were accompanied by a man Karen was going with at the time, who was usually young and good-looking. I don't remember any of their names or where they came from, and after a few months they always moved on.

134

The house had been a storage building on a small farm, and the second year we were there, Karen spent much of her time trying to write a novel about the anti-war movement. There were always scraps of her writing lying around. At night, she would wake up and work by candlelight because the house had no electricity. How animated she grew when she thought the novel was going well. For a time she put so much of herself into those pieces of paper covered with hurried writing that supposedly would bring her fame. However, the little book on which she expended so much effort was never published. An acquaintance knew a printer who ran off a few hundred copies, and her friends took up a collection to pay for the ink and paper. Over the years she gradually gave all of the copies away as if doling out a treasure. Finally only a lone copy was left that one day she handed to me without a word. I realized that from then on I was the sole custodian of her creation.

To my mother can also be traced my interest in literature. As a result I studied English in college, developing an abiding fondness for the world's fictional heroes such as the indomitable Ishmael, who recorded the mythic struggle with the great, symbolic whale; Gatsby who yearned fatefully for the romantic dream embodied in the magical green light flickering seductively at the end of Daisy's boat dock; and poetic Stephen Daedalus who reenacted in modern Dublin Odysseus' grand quest in form of the daily life of an ordinary, modern man. Eventually I turned my attention to my mother's little book into which she put so much of herself, realizing that here and there it showed some promise that was never developed. Instead the writing remained hasty and didn't come together. Through the poorly developed characters, she tried to reach into the hearts of the people she knew in the counterculture and portray their poignant desire for a perfect world - the youthful idyll of love and peace to which she clung till the very end. But in spite of the long months of hard work, her pitiful, little book never managed to capture the powerful message she felt

135

so strongly. Being close to her, I knew what it was. For an outsider the book came across as lacking focus and trailing off into lost hope and confusion, which is ultimately what happened to her and her friends. In that respect the book in its failure symbolized what she wanted so much to tell the world. Perhaps if she devoted more time and study to her writing, she might have succeeded. Like the rest of her life, she soon moved on to other pursuits. Finally she stopped writing altogether and never spoke about it again.

In the winter it was always cold in the tiny, stone house, the chill wind off the sea blowing through cracks around the windows and doors that Karen stuffed with rags. We rarely had enough money to buy more than a small amount of firewood that was used on only the coldest days. But at night we usually had lots of company, her friends trudging out there on a long, meandering path bringing wine and a canvas bag containing chunks of coal. In a flimsy stove made from a metal barrel, the coal burned with an acrid smell, briefly replacing the winter cold with a refreshing warmth. Usually one of our guests read something they had written, and then everyone danced to guitar music while a jug of wine was passed around.

Eventually we left Ibiza living on a couple of Greek islands and then other places increasingly remote, briefly ending up in Nepal. It seemed as if we were fleeing from the world itself. By then, many of Karen's friends had declined into the oblivion of drugs and some were already dead. One day we got up at dawn and started our long trek back to Europe. I don't remember exactly how we got there because it took months, and more than a few times we slept outdoors. Fortunately it was summertime.

After that, we lived in Paris before returning to New York. Over the years Karen worked for various, avant-garde magazines that were critical of modern society, earning just enough to keep us going. Now and then, we went back to Ibiza, and it was like she was returning there for sustenance. But each time the island had changed a little more. Most of the charming cafés by the harbor that I remembered fondly had become tourist traps with expensive menus. We heard about suicides and overdoses among old acquaintances, and I could hardly believe that those still on the island were the people we knew before, most of them having aged cruelly. Later I came to realize that as much as anything, it was the effect of watching helplessly as the world moved on its way leaving them far behind and forgotten. But regardless of how the world changed, Karen never wavered in the belief that one day their pacifist vision would somehow be vindicated. Her ill-defined quest went on and on until it seemed to have no direction. And now it finally ended with her body riddled with bullets, her life snuffed out by the violence she despised. Sadly the world hadn't become the better place she hoped for but instead was far more dangerous than ever before. In fact, I soon realized that it had entered a fateful period when humanity would be imperiled by violence on a scale never thought possible.

10

André Sergeivich Nicoliev, was one of the finest people I have ever known. Now I have to live with the sad fact that I am responsible for the untimely death of a man who was probably the closest friend I have ever had. Of course, he isn't the only person I cared about whom I injured while in China squandering my best years. During the period that Andrei and I knew each other, we shared many pleasant times, which included long discussions about literature, especially Russia's great authors. I found myself fascinated by his fine mind and have no doubt that if circumstances were different, he might have been a scholar at an important university. In many respects he was the type of man I would have liked for a father. While growing up, I often picked out an older man and tried to imagine what it would be like if he was my father. I selected only those in some way unique and supposedly worthy of being the father I never knew. Eventually it was something I stopped thinking about.

Only once did my mother say much about my real father. It was on the beach in Ibiza late one afternoon as she watched the sun set slowly over the water, the breeze playing fanciful tricks with her radiant, red hair that in those days she wore very long. It was like she was talking to herself and I was listening to a private dialogue taking place within her. In those few, fleeting moments, she told me the only details about him that I will ever know. It was apparent that after all those years she still loved and even admired him. Apparently he was from a prominent, New York family and quite good looking. They met at some sort of political demonstration, and immediately she was drawn to this man with an indefinable charm that captured her heart and afterwards would never let her go. Always I tried to imagine what he was really like - this handsome, ghostlike figure cloaked in the lingering mystery of my mother's youthful desires. I got the impression their relationship was a brief, passionate infatuation. It happened during her last year in college, and I suspect that my father didn't love her much, at least not the way she loved him. I never understood why she wouldn't tell me more including his name. Probably she knew that I would try to find him, and it was her way of repaying his rejection because he would never know his own son. After that brief interval, she never said another word about him, always changing the subject when I inquired further. And finally I realized how painful the subject was for her and never brought it up again.

Some might say that I was always searching for a substitute father that for a brief time I found in Andre. We met at the racquet club and immediately liked each other. In spite of his age, he was still a powerfully-built man with thick, dark hair that to the end showed only faint traces of gray. He had recently celebrated his 65th birthday by swimming almost the entire length of Hong Kong Island. He was also an excellent tennis player, and usually I found it difficult to beat him. Perhaps I felt an affinity for him because we both worked in espionage. Like so many in Russia, he believed for a while in Marxism and thought that his actions on behalf of the Soviet state would somehow improve the world. Eventually he saw the true nature of the communist system, turned against it and for a time ended up in prison. Because of the demands of his espionage work, he never married and left the service with little except some memories. It was apparent how deeply he regretted giving most of his life to a cause that in the end proved worthless.

I am certain that he had no idea that I am an American spy. He never asked any personal questions and just let me tell him what I wanted about myself. On occasion, I was tempted to explain what I was really doing in China. However, it was the unfortunate reality of the situation that I couldn't confide in the one person that at the time I considered my only close friend. Occasionally I wondered if he might have figured out the truth on his own. He had an uncanny ability to spot revealing details in people's behavior. Nonetheless,

139

he never gave the slightest indication he suspected anything. In contrast, he told me his entire life's history, and probably I am the only person to whom he unburdened himself so completely.

He lived in a small apartment in a quiet area on the south shore of Hong Kong island, and a few days after he was back in town, I drove over there to have dinner. When I arrived, he was cooking a steak on his little porch that overlooked the bay, and after pouring a glass of vodka, I joined him.

"How was your trip?" I asked as we touched glasses, and immediately I noticed how tired he looked.

"The world is hungry for anything connected to petroleum. It's fortunate Russia has so much crude. It helps to compensate for the country's many deficiencies, including the fact the KGB is back in power. Who thought that would happen? So what have you been up to?" he asked finally venturing a smile.

"The usual," I said and sat down.

"I have a new butcher. He wants to impress me. Supposedly this steak comes all the way from Australia," he said flipping over the piece of meat that smelled delicious in the fresh sea air. "And your charming lady friend?"

"The situation with Lily has gotten serious. Recently she introduced me to her mother."

"That's serious all right. Women don't introduce a man to their mother without a good reason. Sounds like you're the one."

"As you know, her father is a prominent general in the Chinese military and adamantly opposed to our relationship. He will never accept me."

"If you really care about this woman, don't let the father or anyone else come between you."

"He may not see it that way. He has considerable influence and may decide to get unpleasant about the matter. I'm surprised he hasn't done something already."

"Still, a person doesn't have many chances at happiness.

Perhaps you'll never find another woman whom you really care about, and you don't want to spend the rest of your life thinking about all the wonderful things the two of you might have done together. Take that from the voice of experience. Don't you think it's time I met Lily? After all, you've told me so much I feel like I already know her. The three of us should go sailing some afternoon. Do you think she'd enjoy that?"

"Yes," I said, certain the two of them would like each other.

"And business?"

"American companies are still pouring through the door convinced that no price is too big to pay for even a small foothold in the Chinese market. The onerous conditions of doing business here, including the loss of their intellectual property, don't seem to bother them. Of course, few will ever make any money. Naturally I don't go out of my way to tell them. Otherwise I'd never earn another commission."

"When I was with the GRU, we had to work so hard to get hold of America's latest technology, and frequently we didn't succeed. Now your corporations hand everything over to the Chinese on a silver platter, including to many companies connected to their military. And in the name of so-called free trade, your government is determined to facilitate the process by approving all those transfers of sensitive technology that have helped the Chinese military to modernize so rapidly. It's not fair. Your people should have been more generous so we didn't have to put in such long hours.

"My favorite example is the sale of Magnequench. When I told my friends in Moscow about that one, they could hardly believe it. The only company in the entire US that produced the rare earth metals that are essential to the pentagon's smart weaponry, including cruise missiles and smart bombs. Now it is controlled by an entity owned by the relatives of Deng Xiaoping,

141

the former Chinese premier. Not surprising, the factories with all that invaluable technology and tooling are in China under the direct control of the military. Of course, we Russians are just as stupid and keep selling them our most advanced equipment, including some of the latest fighter jets and anti-missile systems that took a generation to develop. I have few doubts that eventually all of this will come back to haunt us."

"Yes," I agreed but didn't continue.

Soon the steak was ready, and André and I ate at the little, metal table on the cramped porch. The one-bedroom apartment was small, and his furniture modest. He didn't have much to show for the many years of devoted service to his country in which he repeatedly risked his life. As we ate, he remained subdued, and I knew something was bothering him. It was rare that he wasn't in an enthusiastic mood, which was one of the things about him that I liked. Usually after a couple of drinks he was joking a lot, and I couldn't remember a dull time when we were together. But now I had to keep pushing the conversation, and for a while he didn't speak at all. The little candle on the table burned down and finally went out as he stared thoughtfully at the bay, still not saying anything. Several minutes passed, and I remained silent not wanting to interrupt his thoughts.

"What's wrong, André? Tell me about it," I finally asked. "As soon as I walked in, I could tell there's something."

"It's difficult to explain. Let's just say that at a certain point in life a person has to take an inventory and see how things add up. For a long time I put it off, and now I can't avoid the unfortunate conclusion that in the overall scheme of things my life doesn't amount to much. I started off with such high hopes. To be accepted into the highest levels of red army intelligence, you had to meet the most rigorous criteria. I really believed that I would accomplish important things that would help the Russian people as well as humanity. As a result I tolerated the long hours and constant need of sacrifice. And in the back of my mind, there was always the grandiose image I had of myself. Such notions can be very seductive.

"One of the unfortunate aspects of the situation is that I never found a woman with whom I could share my life. Probably that's what I regret the most - the loss of intimacy with another human being whom I could consider my partner in life. But my superiors in the GRU discouraged emotional entanglements, viewing them as a distraction that diminished performance. Over the years I saw lesser men find the type of happiness I envied. Now I look back and feel the need of a neat explanation for how things turned out, and it isn't there," he continued, and in the dim light his rugged features looked old as if suddenly he aged several years. "One can reach too high, or maybe I just pursued the wrong goal. And now my life is winding down rapidly, and I can't change anything that's happened. Perhaps the only consolation is that I managed to survive all those dangerous years so I can live out my remaining time in peace. In comparison, many of my former colleagues didn't make it.

"The other day it occurred to me that I don't even have many, happy memories to give me comfort when I awaken late at night. In a way this modest apartment sums the whole thing up. It's something a moderately successful clerk would own. As a young man, I was convinced that something really important awaited me down the road, and at the time I had no doubt that I would achieve it. But in the end the Soviet Union was a colossal lie and its security services complicit in that lie. I was a fool for being taken in for such a long time, and when I learned the truth, it was too late. I tried a number of times to leave the service, but they wouldn't let me go. Finally they became convinced I was a double agent and put me in prison. That was the most difficult period of my life. As a result of my unselfish efforts, I had been reduced to the status of a mere convict. When the Soviet Union ceased to

143

exist, I was finally set free so I can peddle mundane petroleum products around the Far East. At least, I have a product to sell that everyone wants."

"Your motives were noble."

"If you and Lily have a chance at happiness, don't let anything get in the way," he added, and as I stared at his weary face in the dim light, I realized I could be looking at myself several years in the future.

Although it was getting late, I knew he didn't want me to leave and suggested we play chess. But his concentration was off, and he kept making inept moves that were unlike him. For a while we watched a movie on TV. When I finally left and drove back across the island, the first light of day was spreading across the sky. At my apartment there were a couple of messages from Lily on the answering machine, and while replaying them, I kept thinking what a pretty voice she had.

Andre had no way of knowing how much our conversation hit home. For a long time I had been thinking something similar. In spite of the many years I risked my life in China, I hadn't accomplished much. Perhaps I was unrealistic about what one man could do to influence events on the world stage that for years kept moving in such an ominous direction. The chorus of orchestrated, public opinion favorable to China had been too effective. In the interest of profits for a small number of large corporations and lots of cheap goods produced by exploited workers, the American public had been sold the illusion of a supposedly peaceful China evolving into a democracy - something that after nearly a quarter-century hadn't happened and never would.

Also I could no longer disregard the similarity of my situation with my own mother, who devoted her entire life to an ill-defined ideal that over the years only grew more illusive. While vowing not to repeat her mistakes, I too had squandered my best years on what at this point was little more than a misguided adventure. Now as never before, I was in danger of being exposed as a spy and treated accordingly. For any agent, the moment always comes when the game is up, and prudence dictates a quick retreat. I had heard of numerous agents who overstayed their welcome and as a result paid the ultimate price. I was determined that wouldn't happen to me.

Unfortunately Lily wasn't ready yet to leave her country, and I couldn't walk out on her, especially after she endured so much criticism on my behalf. It wasn't easy leaving unfinished what I tried so hard to achieve. If somehow I could expose the regime's plans to launch a major war, it would vindicate all my efforts and demonstrate unequivocally what a danger China represented to the world. Still it was almost impossible to get any hard information on the subject. The well-connected officials I approached expressed skepticism, and some thought I was joking. It was obvious that only the people at the very top knew what was really going on, and they were concealing the whole thing as long as possible. In the past I rarely encountered so many problems getting hold of the information I sought. Nonetheless, there had to be a way of uncovering the truth. Against my better judgment, I decided to stay in China a little while longer and do what was necessary to accomplish what I now considered my ultimate mission. As a result I would experience more than a few, sleepless nights.

11

As I look back now, that final summer in Hong Kong contrasts vividly with the dark tragedy about to engulf China as well as the rest of the world. On one of the most tranquil days of all, Lily and I went sailing with André to the charming Out Islands. At the time I had no way of knowing that afternoon was really a bittersweet farewell, and afterwards I would never see him again.

Like most things to which he applied himself, André was a skilled sailor. Although his boat was 35 feet long with a large sail area, he had no difficulty operating it by himself. Just after noon, we departed from the yacht club and after crossing the West Lamma Channel, stopped first at the scenic island called Cheung Chau, or "old China." It is a real fishing port, its tiny harbor filled with junks and sand pans. During lunch at a restaurant by the harbor, Andrei entertained us with stories of his youth in rural Russia a few hundred miles outside Moscow. Although he knew that I once worked in Moscow, he had no idea that I was familiar with the general locale, having visited it with Vera. I will always cherish my brief stay in the tiny, rustic village where she grew up.

After lunch the three of us strolled through the narrow, dusty streets near the harbor and then returned to the boat. Next we sailed to Lamma Island with its lovely green hills that rise right out of the sea. Near the south end the breeze suddenly died out, and we proceeded by motor into Picnic Bay, mooring at Sok Kwu Wan, the capital that's located at the end of a narrow inlet. The harbor is a popular destination for local yachtsman, and many sailboats were there. The largest belonged to one of Andre's friends, who sent a boat over so we could join them for cocktails. The sun was just setting when we returned to the channel, passing Stanley Bay and the old fort. Near Cape D'Agular a strong breeze came up, and the sea that had been calm all day turned choppy. While heading up the eastern shore, we were buffeted by waves that threw up a refreshing spray. It was just getting dark when we arrived back at the club exhilarated by the long day on the water. It was obvious that Andrei and Lily liked each other, and I was delighted that the two people most important to me hit it off so well. When Lily and I got married, I wanted Andre to be my best man.

After we got off the boat, he shook my hand warmly and continued to hold it, giving me a little wink as if to tell me how much he approved of Lily. He wasn't a person who often shook hands, and at the time it seemed odd that he did so with so much feeling. And then I watched him walk down the dock and disappear into the shadows as if he suddenly ceased to exist. It's my final memory of that fine man.

That evening Lily and I had dinner at a restaurant where I was sure we wouldn't encounter any of her friends. Hardly a night passed that Lily and I didn't go somewhere in town with at least a few members of her ever-loyal gang in tow. If she didn't show up, I knew that they would wonder where she was. From now on, however, it would be only the two of us most of the time because there was no longer a need to have anyone else around.

As we left the restaurant, I noticed the small, dark car that for weeks had been following me around town, always remaining a discrete distance away. Whoever was in it had gotten sloppy, and of late it was easier to spot them. While entering Lily's building, I noted where the car parked. After going up to the apartment, I waited several minutes and then went downstairs exiting by a side door. Reaching the end of the street, I cautiously approached the car from behind, being careful to stay in the shadows so I wouldn't be noticed.

It had been years since I felt the need of a weapon and lately had been carrying a small Beretta. Ducking between two cars, I approached the rest of the way on the driver's side. After taking out the gun, I crawled on all fours the last, several feet. The safety clip was off, and if necessary, I was prepared to use the gun and worry later about the consequences. Reaching up, I pulled the door open, the man inside reaching quickly for the glove compartment.

"Keep your hands on the steering wheel. I have a gun. Don't make me do something we'll both regret," I said nervously, and although not eager to shoot anyone, I was determined to find out what I wanted to know.

"Take the car. You're welcome to it," he said, his hands still on the steering wheel.

"Who are you?" I asked, touching the cold gun barrel to the back of his neck. "And why have you been following me?"

"I don't know what you're talking about."

"Of course you do."

"What's the problem?"

"The problem is that you can't mind your business. With your left hand take out your wallet," I said, and slowly he handed it to me. To my surprise, the license identified him as Chen Song, a detective with the internal police. Threatening someone like him was a very serious matter. Most people would have been intimidated and immediately apologized.

"Is your curiosity satisfied?" he asked and put out his hand for the wallet.

"No, it isn't."

"I don't want to take you to the station unless it's necessary."

"Don't start that stuff with me. You have no right to annoy a prominent American businessman who is a good friend of the regime. I've earned a little respect from people like you," I said, trying to sound as if I didn't consider him important, and looked again at his identification. And then I noticed something familiar about his face. "Where did you live - I mean, when you were young?"

"Near Beijing."

"Did you have a brother named Lui?"

"Yes."

"Don't you remember?" I asked, hardly able to believe it could be the same person.

"What do you mean?" he said and looked at me curiously, a hint of alarm on his face.

"Tiananmen Square. Karen's son," I said lowering the gun as we continued to stare at each other through the dim light from the street lamp.

"I can't believe it… You're so different now. Also I never knew your last name. All these weeks I've been following you and never made the connection."

"Who would have thought we'd ever see each other again, especially under these circumstances? But you, a detective with the internal police. How is that possible? Is the identification a fake?"

"No. I'm a senior detective. They didn't want to assign a junior person to the task of following someone like you. The matter is considered too important. General Chan put in an official request through channels asking that we find out as much as possible about you. For now he only wants some information although soon that will probably change."

"How could you be working for the government? I don't get it."

"Sometime I'll explain," he said moving uneasily, and it was apparent my question made him uncomfortable. There was no subject about which the regime was more sensitive than Tiananmen Square, and if it was ever known that one of their own security operatives was connected with the people who organized it, he would have been promptly executed.

"This isn't the right place to talk," I said putting the gun away. "Tomorrow come to my apartment around two o'clock. You know where I live. We'll talk then."

"All right," he agreed, and handing back the wallet, I saw

149

the perspiration glistening on his face.

While walking down the street, I wondered again how Chen could be a detective, especially with the dreaded internal police. He was one of the most idealistic of all the young men I met at the safe house outside Beijing after the massacre. He spoke with a deep hatred of the regime that had just killed thousands of defenseless, young Chinese, including his own brother. It was rare for someone like him to go over to the other side, and I was baffled how he could be associated in any way with the police.

From what he said, it was obvious that Lily's father was determined to get rid of me, and probably it wouldn't be much longer before he took the necessary steps. He had contacted the police to come up with an excuse, which meant, as far as he was concerned, I was living on borrowed time. My relationship with Lily was about to prove fatal, although I was sure she had no idea what her father was planning. Once some sort of phony grounds was created for eliminating someone, the system would move ahead with brutal efficiency. On the chosen day I would be only one of countless others who disappeared without a trace from the streets of China. It happened constantly all across that huge nation, and only a few on the inside ever knew the truth.

High-ranking party officials had that type of life and death power. It was an envied prerogative of their station: unchecked power to eliminate anyone who displeased them. However, the situation was more complicated with someone like me. I was too well-connected to be done away with on a flimsy pretext. Something significant had to be found that would justify the action taken, and at this point I didn't know what the police might know. At the same time I no longer had any doubts that the general would do whatever was necessary, even if it meant fabricating a reason to get me permanently out of the way.

When I entered the apartment, Lily was watching a corny, "Ballywood" romance from India - a genre that to my annoyance

150

she always enjoyed.

"Does your father know that I was at their house?" I asked and sat beside her.

"Mother told him. She never hides anything from him. That's an important part of their relationship. People who really care about each other should never hide things," she went on, her attention focused on the movie.

"I suppose so," I agreed, wondering what her reaction would be if she knew I was an American spy. "How did your father react?"

"He felt your visit was an affront to his dignity," she said and finally looked at me. "He made mother promise that she would never allow you to come there again."

"What did he say to you?"

"Do we have to talk about this?"

"He obviously doesn't like me. We can't get around that fact."

"I'm sure we'll figure out something. Maybe in time he'll change his mind. Although he can be very stubborn, I've seen that happen."

"Did you ever consider the fact that soon he might do something drastic to prevent us from seeing each other?"

"What do you mean?"

"Use your imagination. Someone in his position has unlimited influence. If he wants to use it in the wrong way, he could have me arrested and sent away or even worse."

"That's ridiculous. My father would never do such a thing. Maybe some low-level functionary, who has no discipline, but not my father. People like him at the top of the party have a sense of responsibility. He believes strongly in his principles. They mean everything to him. I know for certain he would never cause anything improper to happen, especially to someone I care about."

"I hope you're right," I said and wondered if Lily could

151

ever face the truth about the regime of which her father was an essential part. While she wanted the two of us to be completely honest with each other, it wasn't possible to talk to her about what was taking place every day in her own country - and often in plain view. "We could never get married in Hong Kong. You realize that? Who would come to the ceremony except a few of our friends from the clubs, and maybe they wouldn't show up. Everyone else would be afraid and stay away. We would be outcasts and never invited anywhere. We would have to get married outside of the country," I added.

"I've always wanted a big wedding with all of the city's important people there and lots of flowers," she said finally switching off the movie, and for a while neither of us said anything.

"Have you ever thought of what it would be like to live in the States?"

"Don't worry, Lawrence. Everything will work out. You'll see. Stay with me tonight. I don't want to be alone," she said and moved closer, putting her head on my shoulder. For Lily, that's the way it had always been. Somehow things "worked out" as if a fairy godmother was there to waive a magic wand at just the right moment. But it was only because of her family's connections, and I knew that this time it could be very different, which would come as a big surprise for her.

The following afternoon Chen was late for the meeting at my apartment. While waiting, I kept thinking about that cruel, faraway night in Tiananmen Square and all those desperate millions, who for a few, fleeting days really believed that their tragic country would finally be set free. I first saw Chen in the kitchen of the small house outside the city where I stayed after fleeing the Square. Some of the wounded were brought there because they couldn't go to the hospitals. The mere fact that someone had been shot was considered proof of subversive activities.

On the kitchen floor two, young students, who were still

bleeding, lay on towels spread out to absorb the blood. A girl bent over them trying desperately to remove the bullets lodged in their bodies. All she had to work with was a knife sterilized over a flame and some high proof liquor to clean the wound. There was no anesthetic. She managed to extract a bullet from the shoulder of one of them, but the other was wounded far worse and bleeding heavily. As the knife went into his stomach, he began to shake violently and ceased to breathe. The girl didn't want to believe he was dead and kept trying to revive him, pleading with him not to give up. And then she realized how futile the whole thing was and just knelt there motionless as if paralyzed.

I remember vividly the parade of young people who crowded into the small room and stared in disbelief at the boy's thin, lifeless body, the odor of congealed blood almost overpowering. It must have seemed incomprehensible to them that all their bright hopes for democracy could have ended this way. The dead boy looked so pitiful and wasted, the raised palms of his pale hands open as if he was waiting for someone to hand him a gift. Later I learned he was only 18 and had helped to build the statue of the Guan Yin that looked so much like the Statue of Liberty. To create the replica, he and the others copied a photograph from a book, and he kept telling his friends that one day he would travel to the States and see the real statue. He was from a farm family that had grown high quality wheat for generations. None of them had any education, and he was there on a scholarship to study painting, his artistic talents so unique that teachers across the province had signed a petition to get him into the prestigious Central Arts Academy. His abilities were immediately apparent, once again demonstrating how unpredictable is the rare appearance of genuine talent. At the Academy he was soon nicknamed the Chinese Michelangelo, although now it would never be known what his unique abilities might have produced. Later his blood-soaked body was wrapped

153

in a soiled blanket and taken into the countryside where it was buried in an anonymous grave, the only marker a beautiful old tree similar to one in a sketch he once made.

Finally the doorbell rang, and I went to answer it. The night before I couldn't see Chen very well, and as he entered the apartment, it occurred to me how little he had changed. Now after so many years we were meeting again, and since Tiananmen Square the regime had only hardened its iron grip on the nation. After shaking hands warmly, we went into the living room. There was so much to talk about, and I didn't know where to begin.

"I was just thinking about that boy - the one who died on the kitchen floor. I mean after..." I said and paused.

"Yes, sometimes I think of him too. I watched them fashion the Guan Yin with only a few, crude tools, lavishing so much care on it. At times it seemed as if they were caressing the plaster with their hands. Like the rest of us, he believed in what the statue was supposed to represent. We were so foolish and naïve, and looking back, I can't believe that we thought a bunch of university students could stand up to a regime that has murdered countless millions," he said grimly.

"My mother believed the way you did and really thought the student movement would bring a democratic way of life to China. That's why she wanted me to come over from the States so I could experience firsthand the spirit of hope that all of you embodied. I will always be glad that briefly I was a part of something so fine even though it ended tragically."

"We loved Karen because she was willing to share the danger in order to support what we were trying to accomplish. How terrible that she should have died that way. Nothing troubled me so much as her sacrifice."

"She would have never regretted giving her life for something so important."

"After you left, all of us wondered if you would be able to

cope with such a terrible loss."

"That's the reason I'm back here. But how could you be a member of the internal police? You know only too well what they do to people."

"Most of the time I work in the administrative area and am able to avoid participating in anything violent. My position enables me to gather lots of non-public information. In recent years many opposed to the regime have gradually gained influence on the inside. It's difficult and has taken a long time. I thought that if there were enough of us, we might eventually succeed in changing things. But of late we've lost many, key people. It's the effect of the technology obtained from abroad that has enabled the regime to spy on much of the nation, including through the internet as well as internal communications. This has been a disaster for us. Now it's almost impossible to communicate without being spotted.

"Also this new technology has helped the regime to find the many people who recently are being rounded up. Across China there's been a dragnet, and no one knows the reason, not even the police higher-ups. We were given lists, and after the people were found, they were quickly shipped away although not to the regular camps. These are special facilities designed for imprisoning large numbers like the places where the Falun Gong are kept until it's time to kill them."

"Who are these people?"

"Mostly intellectuals and academics. For some reason the regime suddenly wants them out of the way. And with all of this new technology, they've had no difficulty locating them, even those who for a long time have been in hiding. But now it's almost impossible to avoid being tracked down. A few, foreign companies have even trained the internal police on how to utilize the technology in the most effective ways. Also the regime has nearly completed an all-inclusive, nationwide surveillance system under the control of the Ministry of Public Security. It includes a massive, computerized databank with files on nearly the entire population. It takes only about 12 minutes to review the available information on almost everyone in the entire country and less than four minutes to check the status of all driver's licenses. While avoiding any unwanted publicity, the system has been carefully refined over a period of about a decade. It's the most advanced anywhere in the world and also includes a vast network of security cameras in all cities of any importance throughout China. For instance, in Shenzhen City there are more than three-quarters of a million cameras. That's at least one for every 14 people. Linked to this massive, interconnected system of visual surveillance is a facial recognition program connected to individual records. And all of this is also connected to the system that monitors the internet, including web traffic, social networking sites and the military's program of monitoring phone calls. Over time the regime will only make the system even more effective so eventually it will be impossible to do anything without being observed and recorded and every action analyzed for the purposes of total control."

"Incredible. I've heard about all of this but never realized how far it has gone."

"On their own the Chinese never could have developed so quickly such a sophisticated system. These foreign, high-tech companies have enabled them to leapfrog at least a generation, and, of course, they're being appropriately rewarded. It pays for the international, business community to ignore genocide. After Tiananmen Square, I expected a strong reaction from the outside world. Instead Deng Xiaoping opened the economic doors, and quickly forgetting all the people who had been murdered in the streets of Beijing, overseas businessmen, especially from America, eagerly rushed in to make as much money as possible. I still don't understand how that's possible. America is the world's great democracy, and yet many of its businessmen are eager to cozy up in any way they can with the most bloodthirsty regime in history.

We students were convinced that America was our great hope. Sadly it worked out very differently," Chen said, the sorrow evident in his voice, and for a while both of us were silent.

"I know," I finally answered but didn't go on, aware there wasn't a plausible explanation that I could give him.

"About a month ago I planted a listening device in your apartment. I'll remove it before I leave."

"Did you record anything?"

"Yes, and all of it is very incriminating. Last night I destroyed the tapes. It's fortunate that in time I learned your true identity."

"I used to check regularly for listening devices."

"From what I've learned, you're a very clever spy. If your mother knew what you're doing, I'm sure she would be proud. Perhaps in some way we can help you, although you will never meet any of the other people in our organization. We compartmentalize everything as much as possible so hardly anyone knows the identity of more than one or two people. That way, the authorities can get only a few names at a time. Also we always carry a small cyanide pill. If things look really bad, it's our means of escaping before the torture starts. The Chinese are the true masters of torture, and they can get anything they want out of a prisoner. It's not humanly possible to resist them for long. Two of our best people were recently traced through text messages, and both had to take the cyanide to avoid giving up anyone. I wonder how long it will be before our entire organization is wiped out and all those years of effort lost," he said, his face turning pale.

"What are you going to say in your report?"

"That you're a great friend of the government. It's the established view around Hong Kong. You've developed an excellent cover for yourself. No one would suspect you're really an espionage agent. It was fortunate that I was assigned to your case. Otherwise you would have been arrested weeks ago and promptly

157

executed. In the basement of our jail there's a small room that's completely sound proof, and a couple of people are always there to apply electric shock and other stimuli so the necessary information can be obtained as quickly as possible. Then the prisoner is dispatched with an injection. It's all done with maximum efficiency. Occasionally I have to watch although most of the time I find an excuse to leave the room. Once a day a nondescript vehicle that looks like an ordinary delivery van visits the various police stations around the city. After making the rounds, it heads for the crematorium where all the bodies wrapped in plain, brown paper are incinerated. That way, no trace is left. At the station we keep no records, only a numerical designation that a few of us understand. There's nothing about the person's name, background or who they were in life. In this swift, impersonal way all that was a living, breathing human being is effectively done away with, and they cease to exist as if they never walked the face of the earth."

"How much longer are you supposed to follow me?"

"About a week, and then my report is due. In it I will also mention all the important people in Hong Kong who are your friends. It's quite a list. Even the general will have to show some restraint. The higher ups always pay attention to connections. That's the way the system works. Everyone is afraid of stepping on any big toes, which might produce repercussions. In a dictatorship the pecking order always has to be respected."

Before Chen left the apartment, he removed the listening device that was the latest design, and I was amazed at its sophistication. All the technology obtained from foreign, high-tech companies was being put to good use, or at least the regime would think so. We shook hands and hugged each other. I will always remember how slender Chen felt and wondered what would ultimately happen to him. In the shadow of that vast police state, a small number like this courageous, little man were trying valiantly

158

to do the impossible. Although they knew the odds, it didn't prevent them from trying. Eventually, when my real identity was uncovered, questions would be asked about why he didn't learn the truth about me. Now I fear that he may have ended up in the basement of one of those deadly police stations where every day so many, anonymous lives end suddenly.

I was intrigued by the information that of late large numbers had been rounded up and wondered if somehow it was connected to the regime's military plans. Perhaps the authorities were taking control of as many as possible who might cause problems at such a difficult time. With that phase completed, it meant that time was running out even faster than I realized. If I was going to learn what they intended to do, I had to move faster. Still none of my sources had come up with anything tangible, only more, vague rumors. As a result I decided to do something I always avoided and pressure some of the people high up who were indebted to me. I knew they wouldn't appreciate the tactic. It was risky and would alienate many whom I counted on. Under the circumstances, however, there was no choice. After this last attempt to find out what I could, I planned to leave once and for all and hopefully could convince Lily to come with me.

I went over to my desk and took out a copy of a confidential memo that I obtained only a few weeks before after it circulated among members of the Politburo. It confirmed everything Chen told me, especially about the importance of the surveillance technology provided by foreign high-tech companies. I realized that even sooner than anyone imagined, this crucial, technology *would soon enable the regime to make the country's enormous population ,totally and absolutely subservient. In essence, China's murderous government was on the doorstep of achieving the ultimate "1984" state.* On their own the communists never could have achieved such a quantum leap forward in the repression being inflicted on the Chinese people. When George Orwell's novel first appeared, it shocked the world by depicting the monstrous possibilities implicit in the modern, totalitarian state. But Orwell never imagined the extraordinary capabilities that advanced technology would one day afford such governments. In the interest of large, financial gains, the tragic lessons of Tiananmen Square had been disregarded more completely than I ever imagined. The ability to disseminate the truth electronically represented the last chance for democratic change in China, and soon it would be lost forever. In essence, *"Big Brother" in China was about to achieve a form of control that to the end continued to elude Hitler and Stalin, and the regime had the West to thank for this ominous and fatal gift.*

According to the memo:

"We owe a big debt of gratitude to our foreign, corporate friends, who have provided us with invaluable technology and training for the control of information throughout China. This technology has enabled us rapidly to take back supervision of the internet and prevent undesirables from using it to spread dangerous thoughts. Previously the situation regarding the internet was turning into a crisis that potentially could have undermined the regime. Although our scientists and technicians had made considerable progress understanding the necessary technology, our ability to control the flow of information was being overwhelmed. All sorts of propaganda contrary to the interests of the party kept circulating and causing difficulties. Fortunately we are now controlling the internet more skillfully along with other avenues of communication including cell phones so they can never be used again to threaten our interests.

"Additionally, many of these same corporate friends have provided us with technology that enables us to track directly troublesome individuals, who are determined to oppose the party's goals. This includes surveillance equipment and software that permits both facial and fingerprint recognition and is being installed at key locations throughout the country. As a result we are able to follow and monitor more effectively any subversive citizen who comes to our attention.

"Eventually all police organizations around the country will be fully coordinated. In the past it has been a problem that some groups were not fully aware of the activities of others, and therefore much duplication and confusion occurred. That is changing. Our internal police apparatus using this latest technology will soon function in a real-time network so all, law-enforcement efforts can be coordinated to the maximum degree. It is hoped that eventually any undesirable or foolish dissident can be monitored 24 hours a day. Furthermore, we have developed a comprehensive, nationwide database that contains every citizen's documents including medical and work history, financial data and soon how they spend their money. This last feature is particularly significant. The possibilities offered by such an enormous database connected to a nationwide system of surveillance cameras are limitless, especially since every police unit in the country will be able to tap at will into this valuable resource of comprehensive data.

"It is reassuring that what represented a dire threat to the regime is being transformed into a most effective tool for control so the populace can be guided with sufficient firmness. Without the help of these foreign corporations, such rapid progress would not have been possible. As a result they are being rewarded with substantial and very profitable contracts and other incentives, and they assure us their commitment to our interests is ongoing.

"It will be recalled that years ago, there was a hearing in the US House of Representatives (Commission on International Relations, Subcommittee on Global Human Rights and International Operations). Many grandiose statements were made for public consumption that were entirely unnecessary. For instance, a reference was made to a young lady named Miss Ann Frank, who was supposedly executed by the Nazis. A congressman,

161

who was determined to posture, posed the question of whether some of our American corporate friends would have willingly helped the Nazis track down such an individual. This statement was highly offensive, and the comparison inappropriate. Obviously, it was only made for partisan, political advantage.

"It should be pointed out that dissidents, who spread poisonous information, are only monitored and sometimes detained because they have made themselves "class enemies." After the hearings in the House of Representatives, nothing of consequence happened that the government of China should be concerned about. Furthermore, the Western news media typically provides only marginal coverage of such issues. Obviously the periodic statements by American officials concerning alleged human rights violations in China represent nothing more than an attempt to pick up extra votes at the polls. We should expect that now and then someone in either the administration or Congress will voice such criticism. Our corporate friends assure us that nothing will be allowed to harm future cooperation that benefits our mutual interests. The Chinese government has much in common with these foreign companies and their executives. Needless to say, we fully understand each other. They are here to increase their profits and support fully our objectives to develop China economically. Troublesome elements must be prevented from spreading disharmony that thwarts progress beneficial to the global society and brings all of its nations closer together."

The memo provided other information that was equally troubling, including the fact *much of the financing required to underwrite and modernize China's vast, internal security system had come from the West*, especially American groups and hedge funds. The market connected to China's internal police is estimated to be worth at least $50 billion (US) a sizeable profit source that apparently many have been unable to resist. In only one year American hedge funds invested an estimated $150 million (US) in Chinese companies that provide surveillance equipment, facial recognition software and other key enhancements to the country's internal police. This includes China Public Security Technology and China Security and Surveillance, whose chief executive is the technical director of the infamous Ministry of Public Security, one of the centers of repression within China. The finances of China Security and Surveillance were enhanced considerably by a "private" placement of stock with an estimated 17 American institutional investors. Eventually China Security became the parent company which controls most of the Chinese companies that provide surveillance equipment to the police. In addition, China Security purchased a Delaware shell corporation, in effect becoming its own parent (reverse takeover), and through such a bookkeeping slight of hand, was listed on the New York Stock Exchange. *Thus the unavoidable conclusion is that the communists have cleverly made a portion of the outside corporate and investment community a party to repression of the worst sort. In addition the average American citizen has been provided with the opportunity to profit directly from the cruel efforts of the greatest totalitarian state in history to track down and imprison dissidents, crush freedom of thought and murder the helpless Falun Gong.* Either there are a lot of very naïve and poorly informed people currently throwing around large amounts of money, especially in the United States, or these individuals simply don't care what is done with that money as long as it yields a sufficiently handsome return.

12

For a couple of days I couldn't reach Lily, and it was the first time in months we didn't speak at least once a day. Realizing that something was seriously wrong, I suspected that her father had finally taken matters into his own hands. And then Gao came by my apartment to tell me what happened.

"Lily and father had a terrible argument. He locked her in her room and wouldn't let her out until she promised not to see you again. He's never acted like this before. I don't understand what's gotten into him. He's impossible to talk to. Lily keeps appealing to mother, who sides with her, but it doesn't do any good. Father won't relent. Hu supports father, and I side with Lily and mother. The other night we all argued for more than an hour. I never thought anything like this would happen to our family. We've always been so close."

"I'm the cause. I didn't want anything like this."

"Last night, after dinner one of the servants left her door unlocked. Father had gone to his club, and mother was with neighbors so I helped Lily run away. Before anyone noticed, I got her to the ferry. She's on Cheung Chau. She told me the two of you were there the other day with a friend of yours. She thought it would be a perfect place to hide out. No one will guess she's there. She wants you to come over as soon as possible. At seven this evening she'll meet you at the restaurant by the wharf where you had lunch. She said to tell you how much she misses you. This is very difficult for her, Larry. Her life has always been so carefree. Mother and father tried to shelter her so she would never have anything to worry about. Lily is very loyal, and you must never let her down. She really loves you. Because of father's influence, most men would leave her to face the consequences on her own."

"You don't have to worry about that."

"I brought some of her clothes and other things in this

suitcase. I know how happy she'll be to see you. Cheung Chau is very pretty. Occasionally I go there in my boat. It's the perfect place for two people in love to be alone. I envy you. Perhaps one day I'll experience something like you and Lily. It's all that really matters. I know that the women at the clubs don't take me seriously and are only interested in how much money I can spend on them. Underneath many probably think I'm a fool. All these years I've never felt anything meaningful for any of them, and I'm sure they feel the same way," he said sadly. More than a few times I heard the women he dated make cruel jokes about his foppish hairstyle and platform shoes, although I never realized that Gao knew what they said behind his back.

.   "I can't wait to see Lily," I said smelling her perfume as I took her things out of the suitcase and put them in a duffel bag so they would be less conspicuous. "Do your parents realize you helped her get away?"

"No. But they immediately notified the police, and now everyone in Hong Kong is looking for her. They'll leave no stone unturned. I wonder how long she can avoid detection."

"I don't know," I answered, realizing this was the worst thing that could have happened. No doubt, the general would conclude that somehow I was connected to Lily's disappearance. While trying to get my hands on the regime's war plan and escape from the country with Lily, I didn't need the entire Hong Kong police force concerning itself with my every move. Fortunately Chen was in charge of investigating me, and I was sure that I could count on him to distract their attention.

Late that afternoon I slipped out of the building through a side entrance, took a taxi to the ferry dock and rode over to the island. In order to appear inconspicuous, I dressed casually in shorts and a plain shirt like the average, western tourist. Suddenly amid the small crowd on the boat, I spotted Robert Verrelin and quickly turned away, although he already noticed me.

"Larry, such a nice surprise," he said after coming over. "What are you doing here?"

"Just getting away from all the hustle and bustle for a few hours."

"Someone told me how scenic Cheung Chau is so I thought I'd see for myself."

"Good idea."

"Why don't we have lunch?"

"Thanks, but I'm meeting some people. We'll do it another time," I answered and noticed him look curiously at the duffel bag.

The ride from Central takes about an hour, and after getting off at the pier, I said goodbye to Verrelin and then walked down the long promenade that runs along the waterfront. As usual, the harbor was crowded with little, fishing boats, many occupied by the families who live on them full-time and survive from what they catch from the sea. I stopped briefly at the market, which is always a beehive of activity with its many, busy stalls, and then headed back to the restaurant where Lily and I were supposed to meet.

Soon I saw her approach through the crowd. She had on jeans, a plain t-shirt and sunglasses and could have been any attractive, young woman from the city. Without the trappings of her family's important position, she was little different from so many others except she was prettier. For a moment it seemed as if the crowd might swallow her up. And then she spotted me and started to run waving excitedly. As she grasped me tightly in her arms, I realized she was shaking.

"Oh, Lawrence, I was afraid you wouldn't come. How terrible it would have been if I never saw you again," she said and kissed me passionately.

"Gao told me everything. I feel so badly that all of this is happening, especially the effect on your family," I answered and noticed Verrelin, who was nearby in the crowd, watching us

166

intently. It was a bad break that I encountered him. Perhaps he recognized Lily from her picture that was constantly on the TV and would tell the police. After that, it wouldn't take long for them to find us. No doubt, I would be arrested, and it might take weeks or months to regain my freedom. By then, it wouldn't matter.

"Father is determined to have his way. Mother keeps giving in, but I don't have to. I'm not a child anymore and have a right to decide how I'll spend my life," she said with determination as we left the area around the wharf. "Gao is caught in between. He's worried father will cut him off. He has no way to make a living."

"Your father could do the same to you."

"I'll find a way to survive. I can always wait on tables. I'm sure my friends will give me good tips. If they don't, I'll never speak to them again. Over the years they've gotten enough free food and drinks at my apartment. That's the least they can do," she joked and continued to hold my arm tightly as if she would never let go.

"Where are you staying?"

"I found a little apartment in a house near the radio tower. No one will find us there."

"Your father has everyone in Hong Kong searching for you," I said as we headed up the narrow road that leads to the north end.

Cheung Chau is only a few miles long and shaped in the form of an hourglass, the docks, market and commercial buildings crowded together in the narrow strip in the middle. Both ends of the island flare out into hilly masses covered with woods where tiny, colorful houses are scattered about. Since there is no vehicular traffic, the roads are narrow and made only for bicycles and foot traffic. Still holding hands, we continued along the road as it branched off to the right along the shore, finally coming to a dead end near the beach. The house in which Lily was staying was a small, stucco building painted pale orange. It had two floors and was owned by an elderly man who lived there alone since his wife died. For most of his life he had been a fisherman but was too old now to go to sea. The house was an excellent place to hide out, and I was surprised that Lily found it so quickly.

The door was unlocked, and we climbed a steep flight of stairs to a small apartment that had a bedroom the size of a large closet and a second room that served as a kitchen and sitting area. The ceiling was low, and I was taken aback by how modest it was. At the moment Lily seemed to view the situation as some sort of novel adventure, and I doubted she had paused long enough to think the whole thing through and comprehend what she had gotten involved in. I knew she loved me. However, she was risking a complete breach with her family and possibly never seeing her mother again. For the first time in her life she was on her own, and I wondered how long it would be before the full implications of the situation finally dawned on her.

"I brought some of your things. Gao got them at the apartment," I said putting the duffel bag on a small bench. "We forgot to stop at the market."

"I purchased some food this morning. Do you realize I don't have the faintest idea how to cook. I never tried. Someone has always provided my meals whenever I want them, even when I awake late at night and feel hungry. But soon I'll learn, and you'll love what I make for you."

For dinner, we shared some plain salad greens, salted fish and bread that was already getting hard. It wasn't the type of meal that either of us was used to, although at least it satisfied our hunger. Lily arranged her few things in the little cupboard with two shelves that was the only storage area. And then we went outside, walked to the radio tower and over to a nearby beach that's situated in a small cove. Sitting by the water, we watched the darkness settle over the channel. I wanted to believe the police would never find us but knew that an enormous dragnet already reached into every part of the country. If Lily remained on the island, it wouldn't be long before she was caught.

After we returned to the house, she switched on a small lamp that was the only source of light in the shabby apartment that at night looked even smaller. Suddenly she began to cry, and I was sure the implications of what she was doing had finally dawned on her, the expression on her face one of total confusion.

"What is it?" I asked and put my arms around her.

"Nothing. I just need time to sort things through."

"You can still go back. I'm sure your parents will be overjoyed to see you."

"I would have to do exactly what father tells me. I'm in my 30s, and my life amounts to little of importance. They want me to marry an older man who's an important party official. He's small and pudgy and smokes the most awful cigars. I can't stand him. And there are others as well who are just as bad," she said and continued to sob. In Hong Kong, there were countless men who would have jumped at the chance to be Lily's suitor. Unfortunately she had chosen one of the few that her father would never accept under any circumstance.

It was obvious how much Lily loved me. But I knew that our only chance for a life together was to escape from China as soon as possible. Because Lily would have to abandon her family, I decided not to say anything until the necessary arrangements had been made. But with so many police looking for her and a big reward posted, it would be difficult to get her out of the country. As a result we couldn't use most of the escape routes that were available. For now, the risk was too great for her to leave the island, and I decided to wait until things settled down.

Later we went for another walk. There was a gentle breeze off the sea, the trees around us murmuring gently in the darkness. I held Lily close as we walked, and suddenly she stopped and looked at me, her pretty face illuminated by the moonlight that just broke through the clouds.

169

"I love you, Lawrence. No matter what happens, I'll always love you. If we ever lose each other, you must keep that thought forever in your heart," she said, a sudden urgency in her voice, and I will always wonder if somehow she had a premonition of what lay ahead.

"Don't worry. Everything will work out," I said repeating the phrase she liked to use, although I knew only too well how much the odds were against us.

Nonetheless, the following week was very happy, and always I will cling to the warm glow of the love we shared during those fleeting days that were such a gift. Ignoring the fact the police all over China were leaving no stone unturned, we tried to pretend as if nothing was wrong, and each day our love for each other grew even stronger. We spent much of the time on the tiny beach at the bottom of the hill, and with hardly anyone there, it became our private world. One afternoon we emerged from a long swim, and while lying close on the warm sand, I decided it was time to find out if she was willing to flee with me to the West.

"Soon we must leave China. There's no other choice. I've reviewed several escape routes, and at the moment one of the best is through Southeast Asia. I know about some smugglers who enter and leave the country that way without being noticed. Also, they don't want any contact with the government so there's little chance they'll betray us. It won't be easy leaving your family behind," I said, aware how difficult it was for her to think about such an irreversible step that would change her life completely.

"I'll go wherever you want, no matter where it is, Lawrence," she said with resignation but didn't look at me.

The next day I returned to the city but was unable to reach the smugglers. It would be expensive to arrange something like that on short notice but was prepared to pay any price. My apartment seemed so empty without Lily, and I realized how difficult it was being away from her for even a brief period. To my surprise,

Robert Verrelin phoned, and hearing his voice at the other end, I expected the worst. After I saw him on the ferry, he left a brief message on my answering machine, but I didn't call him back.

"Larry, how are you?"

"Fine," I answered cautiously.

"I want you to know that you can count on me all the way. I'm referring to the woman you met on Cheung Chau. I saw her picture on the TV and knew right away who she is. But don't worry. I won't tell anyone. Frankly, I envy you. She's a real beauty. If she has any friends, you should introduce me."

"I appreciate the consideration."

"Not at all. We westerners have to stick together. I'm still waiting for that tennis match."

"Soon we'll play."

"And if I can be of help, don't hesitate to ask. And I mean that. You'll find me a good friend when the chips are down. When I like someone, I'm there for them."

"Thanks. You're a decent chap. I'll be in touch, and I think I can help you too," I added and hung up, wondering if it was possible the information from the CIA could be wrong. Verrelin seemed such a nice person, and I realized that I had gotten to like him.

Late the following afternoon I returned to the island eager to see Lily and hold her in my arms. As I hurried up the narrow road, a neighbor intercepted me, and I learned that two detectives showed up early in the morning and took her away along with the old man. I was surprised they found her so quickly. But there were informers in every community throughout the country, and probably one of them spotted her at the market. After that, it wouldn't take long to track her down on such a small island. It was fortunate that I didn't stay another night or they would have me too. However, I realized it was a mistake delaying our escape for even a few days. Now that Lily had been apprehended, it would be almost impossible to find her in the limited time that was left.

A couple of days later, I returned late at night hoping to see the old man and learn what I could from him. I spoke again to the neighbor and found out that he was still being held by the police. He often brought Lily and me little gifts and liked to tell us about his wife and how much the two of them loved each other. Sometimes she accompanied him in his fishing boat. Although quite small, he had been toughened by years in the elements and reminded me of hardened driftwood. I was sure that he was being detained because he didn't want to betray his "young lovers" as he called us. After that, I didn't go back there again and never found out if he ever returned to his little, orange-colored house where Lily and I briefly found refuge.

13

Gao remained my only hope of finding Lily, although supposedly he still didn't know where she had been taken. I began to wonder if he was being honest with me. Aware how rapidly time was slipping away, I feared that I might never see her again. And then the morning after returning for the last time from Cheung Chau, I got an unexpected phone call from Liao Dan. I hadn't seen him since the meeting of the East/West Friendship Society and recently was unable to reach him by phone. Knowing that he was dodging me, I was about to give up on him. In the past he always came through with something useful. But if he couldn't tell me anything about the regime's military plan, I suspected that probably no one would. To my surprise, he wanted to meet that evening.

I suggested Macau, the former Portuguese enclave that's only a short distance away on the other side of the Pearl River Estuary. In contrast to Hong Kong, the great city of unfettered commerce, Macau remains to this day a somewhat shady place where people still go out of their way not to notice things that aren't their business. In recent years some of Macau's opulent casinos have become a major avenue for laundering the enormous sums of money flowing out of China. Fortunately this competition never caused me any loss of business. Of late, however, activity at the casinos had fallen off noticeably, perplexing many on the outside, who wondered about the cause. Many upper-end criminals hang out in the city including top-level smugglers. At one time I lived on the adjacent island of Coloane, not far from the Macau airport, and made some of my best, early contacts at the Jockey Club on Taipa. I will always have a fond spot for Macau. It retains some of its old world, colonial charm, and occasionally I still go there to gamble and pick up whatever information might be floating around. I arrived early and at the Macau Palace quickly lost several hundred at one of the roulette tables. I've never been much of a gambler and always assume that I will lose. I'm rarely disappointed. The meeting with Liao wasn't until midnight, and I moved on to the Mandarin Oriental Casino where I added to my losses. At a nearby table I spotted a couple of well-connected yakuza with whom I've had dealings over the years. It had been quite a while since we spoke, and they greeted me warmly like an old friend. The yakuza are the most effective of all the large-scale, criminal groups in the Orient. Even the Russian mafia with whom they are often at odds pay them a grudging admiration. As someone active in international money laundering, I always found it useful to have contacts with any group that might be helpful in a pinch, which included the yakuza.

We adjourned to the bar, and I learned that recently both of them had been shot during a gun battle in downtown Tokyo when three of their associates were killed. After expressing suitable admiration for what I diplomatically referred to as their exemplary courage, I got a quick update regarding the Tokyo bank owned by their group. Over the years I occasionally used it to launder funds, although I was never comfortable with the arrangement. To move anything through their network, the fees were exorbitant. Also I was never sure when I would be double-crossed. If they decided to keep all the money, there was nothing I could do.

This same yakuza family also has close ties with the North Korean regime. For years North Korea's foreign exchange has been earned almost exclusively through various illegal activities directed through the infamous Bureau 39. North Korea has the unenviable distinction of being the only country on earth that focuses its national energies almost entirely on criminality. This includes counterfeit cigarettes, drugs and fake currencies such as the acclaimed "super notes," an almost perfect duplication of the US $100 bill. Their copies are so good it's difficult for even an expert to tell them from the real thing. They are produced on the same Intaglio printing machine used at the US mint, and the most significant difference is the quality of the paper. Supposedly the North Koreans are having some success overcoming that problem as well. For years, the yakuza have been a major customer for the super notes because they are so easy to pass. What most people don't realize is that some, supposedly legitimate banks in China regularly facilitate the movement of proceeds from the sale of the super notes as well as counterfeit euros and Swiss francs back to North Korea. In fact, this is only one of many ways that over the years the Chinese continued to prop up the puppet regime that is so useful to them. I repeatedly sent to Washington information regarding China's direct involvement with North Korea's illicit activities. Later I also uncovered hard evidence of Chinese banks covertly distributing money from Iran to various terrorist groups on an ongoing basis. This, of course, was just another example of the connection between the Chinese regime and the ongoing turmoil in the Middle East. Nonetheless, for some unfathomable reason Washington continued to seek China's assistance controlling the situation. Needless to say, I stopped providing any further information on that subject as well.

The yakuza have excellent, long-standing contracts with smugglers all over the Orient. I indicated that I was looking for a quick, inconspicuous route out of the country and was surprised they quoted such a low sum for their assistance. Also I learned that during recent months the volume of people being smuggled out of China had risen significantly. They provided me with the details of a route to be taken. I knew they dealt only with top-flight smugglers and at least in this area could be relied on. When the time came, Lily and I would have a reliable, alternate route out of the country in the event we couldn't use the one I already arranged.

I headed next to the casino in the Hotel Lisboa, my favorite gaming spot in the city. Soon it was midnight, and I went out on the terrace to look for Liao Dan, who was standing at the far end smoking a cigarette. Dressed in an elegant, white linen suit with his black hair smoothed back, he looked like one of the high-stakes gamblers that frequent the casinos. He smoked only the strongest Turkish cigarettes, holding his hand upside down in an affected way with only two fingers delicately gripping the cigarette. As I approached, he kept exhaling little, perfect circles of smoke. Although in the past he was always reliable, I hadn't expected him to show up for the meeting.

"Perhaps a month or two or even a little longer, and it will be very big," he said as I stopped beside him. "I wasn't sure they would go ahead with anything like this. No doubt, many will die," he added, his bland voice devoid of emotion. "Although it's inconvenient having to leave the country at this particular time, I don't intend to hang around and experience firsthand what will probably turn into a catastrophe. It's unfortunate - the timing, I mean. The well-connected members of the party have had such a marvelous run. The prerogatives we enjoyed were extraordinary. I'll miss them, although it's time to move on. Fortunately, like many others, I've already made the necessary arrangements. As you know, a large number of party members hold foreign passports and over the years have stashed substantial sums overseas in preferred locations. Also they've bought western real estate and even valuable art. Of course, many have you to thank. Recently increasing numbers have gone abroad. Perhaps they sense that something terrible might happen soon. You've probably noticed that the regime hasn't done much to halt the exodus among lower level functionaries. As far as I can determine, they want to know who can be trusted at this time and who is weak and eager to jump ship. Probably it's also the reason they're allowing significant sums to leave the country through legitimate channels, especially where emigration is involved. Previously the regime never would have permitted anything like that. However, all of this enables them to know exactly what's going on and whether a particular person has any permanent commitment.

176

"No doubt, you've also noticed the recent purges of high level party officials for alleged corruption - the catch-all term that's always invoked when someone is being pushed aside. Actually the regime is merely shaking up its ranks and getting rid of those who have become too powerful for their own good. For a long time it's been apparent that one day there would be a major crisis that would imperil the regime. In fact, to me it seemed the inevitable consequence of our hegemony over the people, whom we have exploited mercilessly to suit our needs. On the other hand we've provided strong leadership and once again made China a great country to be feared. Unfortunately things are unraveling quickly, and if the regime goes down, the retribution will be terrible. Fortunately that won't be my concern, and I must say, Lawrence, you've served my family well. At first, I was skeptical. However, you always did what you promised. It's not surprising that you have numerous supporters. Some don't even regard you as an American. That's because we all think alike - kindred spirits. Isn't that the term used in your country?"

"Yes. Actually I've come to regard China as my true country. I suppose that surprises you," I said diplomatically, although it was the last thing I believed.

"Not really. The Chinese are a fascinating people with a remarkable culture. Unfortunately history has cheated us, and foreign nations were always eager to exploit our weakness," he answered, exhaling more, perfectly shaped circles of smoke.

"Is it going to be Taiwan, or perhaps a conveniently trumped-up confrontation over an island in the South China Sea?"

"I only know that it will utilize most of our huge, military forces. This is the first time during my many years in the government that I couldn't find out what I wanted to know."

"Well, I suppose that tells me something," I answered, disappointed that he couldn't give me more.

"I'm leaving in a couple of days with my wife on a

diplomatic trip to Australia from which I won't return. Unfortunately I can't take anyone else. It would attract too much attention," he said, his voice still flat and bland. On the side Liao was quite the playboy, and I knew he was referring to his many, beautiful mistresses that he would leave behind. "At least I have a nice nest egg to support myself in appropriate style. Perhaps the change will do me good. And so, Lawrence, I don't think the two of us will see each other any time soon. As I said, my family greatly appreciates your dependability. I've always felt a certain contempt for American businessmen. They're such hypocrites mouthing platitudes while providing us with goods and services that undermine the interests of their own country. But like us, you're a true pragmatist with no failed illusions behind which you try to hide and justify yourself.

"Since you never let me down, I'm going to pass along something that probably I shouldn't tell anyone from the outside. But you always came through for me, at times not asking for much, and I want to show my appreciation. Apparently few, even at the highest levels, know about this. I never told you that at one time I held an important position in intelligence and still have many friends in the service. Not long ago one of them mentioned something quite interesting. Perhaps it's only supposition on his part, although he's convinced there's more to it than that. As a result you shouldn't dismiss too quickly what I'm about to explain," he added, moving uneasily as if having second thoughts about what he was going to say. "As a prelude to the war, the regime is planning to deliver a surprise blow directly against America that will pave the way for everything that follows."

"I don't understand."

"According to my friend, an ordinary, commercial airliner will be employed to detonate a nuclear weapon over Washington DC. In that way America's capital along with the Pentagon and the country's spy agency, the NSA, will be destroyed. In an instant the entire national government and its leaders will disappear."

"Are you certain?" I quickly answered.

"As I said, perhaps all of this is merely supposition, although I doubt it. Of course, such an operation will be handled with the utmost discretion so it appears to be another attack by terrorists using a commercial plane. The scheme will accomplish something quite complex in a quick, economical way. For a protracted period America will be unable to function as a modern nation. Needless to say, the country won't be in a position to interfere with what the Chinese military is planning."

"The plane could be traced."

"I'm sure you recall Malaysian Flight 370 that disappeared back in 2014. At the time many realized that it was a high-jacking, although nothing was ever proved. It was one of our operations, and you must admit a clever one. No transparency at all."

"Also the plane would have to start out anonymously from a remote location and fly a very long distance."

"From the standpoint of fuel that isn't a problem for one of the up-to-date models that can fly nearly eight thousand miles without refueling. Along the way the plane can easily assume the appearance of a legitimate, commercial flight. Since Washington is located near the coast, it would only need to penetrate American airspace for a short distance. The element of surprise will be complete. Who would expect something like that?"

"Yes, who would expect it," I agreed, feeling vaguely ill as I pondered the implications of what I just heard. "But wouldn't a nuclear bomb tip off everyone that China is involved and invite a devastating retaliation?"

"These days such a weapon could come from a number of sources, including Iran. Of course, China's ability to launch this deadly, surprise attack has been greatly facilitated by the fact an American citizen was thoughtful enough to remove so many, top-level secrets about cyber-capabilities from the computers of the

NSA. Then this treasure-trove of information was made available to his country's most dangerous foe. It's interesting that the disappearance of Flight 370 about seven months later is the approximate amount of time that would be needed to evaluate this data. I suspect that China's experts were shocked when they learned about the NSA's ability to penetrate their computers.

"Frankly I find it incomprehensible that anyone would willingly inflict such enormous damage on their own country. Apparently this misguided individual is now viewed by some as an ideological hero who stood up for democracy. I don't believe that such people pay much attention to what's happening in the real world. How fortunate for China that at this crucial time something so priceless would be handed over on a silver platter. As a result of this remarkably irresponsible act, America's prime means of protecting itself has been thrown away," he said, and I knew how right he was. After perpetrating this audacious theft, Mr. Edward Snowden immediately fled to Hong Kong where he disappeared for almost two weeks. He has never been willing to disclose his true whereabouts during this important timeframe. Later he admitted that this priceless data, that took decades to develop, was given to so-called "reporters." What was passed out in Hong Kong has nothing to do with the NSA's surveillance of American citizens – Tier I and II data (about 200,000 files), which is only a small part of the overall theft. Instead this cache of more than a million files concerns America's most important counter-espionage capabilities as well as military strategy and weapons technology. Such information would be useful only to America's avowed enemies – China, Russia, North Korea an Iran, the greatest threats on the planet to democracy and human liberty.

In Hong Kong Snowden initially stayed at the home of a contact that apparently he made in Hawaii, likely a Chinese national. Also there is reason to believe that after getting to know this individual, he soon switched jobs and went to work at Booz

Allen, where the Tier III information was rapidly acquired through various subterfuges. Apparently this was his sole reason for seeking the job. Decades before, far-left ideologues on a self-declared mission of their own eagerly acquired for the brutal Stalinist regime the atomic secrets of the Manhattan project. As a result a dangerous cold war was precipitated that threatened the survival of humanity for more than a half-century. Now something similar had happened again, although this time the consequences could be far more tragic.

"At any rate, Lawrence, you now have all the information at my disposal. I'm convinced that my friend is correct. When you look at the overall picture, everything is coming together quite nicely - at least as far as China and its military is concerned. Hopefully you appreciate the perilous nature of your own situation. What do you intend to do?"

"I was thinking about returning briefly to the States for personal reasons. Instead, perhaps I'll take a nice trip to the South Seas and spend some time relaxing on a sunny and very isolated beach," I answered, trying to appear indifferent like him."

"A wise decision, although don't wait too long. Incidentally I've arranged for a friend of mine, Li Zhou, to contact you in a few days. He will probably be able to provide some of the information that I couldn't access. He's an associate of a top Politburo member, who's connected directly to someone in the Standing Committee. I told him about you. In exchange for his help, perhaps you can get him and his family along with a large sum of money out of the country on short notice."

"I'll do my best."

"Well, good luck. Fortunately none of this is going to be my concern," he added and casually tossed his cigarette.

It was obvious he couldn't have cared less that soon many of his countrymen would die. Apparently the only thing that really bothered him was the inconvenience of abandoning his charming mistresses. Like so many in the regime, he never had any real loyalty to his country. With lots of embezzled money stashed overseas, however, he wouldn't have any difficulty continuing his privileged existence elsewhere. And wherever he went, no doubt, he would find plenty of new mistresses to replace the ones left behind, who at the moment were living on borrowed time along with everyone else in China. After he checked his watch, we shook hands again, and as he hurried away, I hoped never to see him again. I realized now how urgent it was that I locate Lily, inform the Embassy about what I learned and then escape. Soon as the word got around, large numbers would try to flee, the borders quickly slamming shut so no one could get out.

I returned to the bar for another drink and to my surprise, encountered Gregor Korrelin, a Russian gangster whom I know from my Moscow days. There was a rumor that recently he was in Vladivostok smuggling stolen gems into Japan. Since I last saw him, he had aged a lot and acquired an ugly knife scar across one of his cheeks. I soon learned that of late he was busy stealing valuable Chinese porcelains that were easily sold to western collectors, including many, supposedly reputable galleries. These days outsiders were willing to pay top dollar for China's treasures, even if the accompanying papers were obviously fake. Occasionally now he worked with some Vietnamese gangs, a group the Russian mafia once considered the dregs of the Orient. Aware that I might spend some time in Vietnam, I asked for a few contacts, and he provided me with one of his elegant business cards on which he obligingly scribbled a couple of names and phone numbers.

We were soon joined by his girl, Ludmilla, whom I also knew in Moscow. During the peak time at the casinos, she was always one of the most stunning of all the women along with my girlfriend Vera. When a member of a rival crime gang tried to force Ludmilla to become a high-priced call girl, Gregor promptly shot him in the face along with one of his associates outside the Cherry

Casino. After that, no one dared to go anywhere near her. I was glad to see that the two of them were together after all these years and still seemed genuinely fond of each other.

Ludmilla looked quite alluring with her long, auburn hair and terrific figure, and I was genuinely touched that the two of them were pleased to see me. They had heard that supposedly I was run over by a car in Paris, a rumor that briefly circulated around Moscow. I always wondered who started it.

"You never found Vera?" Ludmilla asked.

"Not a trace."

"How sad she disappeared just when you were about to marry."

"I followed her trail down through the Caucuses as far as Turkey. Here and there I got a small lead, but nothing panned out. After more than a year, I had to give up and never learned who kidnapped her. Supposedly she was sold at least a couple of times. Often I still wonder if she's alive, and if so, where she could be."

"I'm sure you know how much she cared about you. We often talked about it. She was so worried that you'd get interested in someone else... Hopefully she didn't end up in one of those horrible brothels in Turkey. It's like a death sentence," Ludmilla commented, and briefly none of us said anything.

"It still baffles me that I couldn't find out anything no matter how much I was willing to pay. For a big enough sum, nearly anyone can be bought back. But not this time. Eventually I had to admit defeat but learned later that she may have been taken east, perhaps to Afghanistan. Unfortunately the Taliban were in power so I couldn't go there."

"Vera would have made such a beautiful bride. She promised to let me help her pick out the dress."

"Probably she's dead," Gregor said patting me on the back.

"You know about...?" Ludmilla started to say.

"What?"

"I guess you don't. Vera wanted it to be a surprise...." she added and hesitated. "She was going to say something when the two of you visited her little village again."

"What do you mean about whether I know"?

"She was pregnant and so happy about it. For several months there was no intimacy with Guydor. When I heard that she was missing, I feared the worst."

"She was going to have a child?" I repeated, the news almost taking my breath away. All those years I never suspected.

Not wanting to talk anymore, I took my drink to the terrace and sat there staring at the water. Because of what happened to Vera, Lily seemed even more precious, although it appeared that I may have lost her too. I wondered if it was possible that Vera had the child and could still be alive. I almost wished that Ludmilla hadn't told me. What good did it do? If I'd known beforehand, I probably would have never stopped searching for her, probing ever deeper into the wretched realm of white slavery that in recent years preyed so viciously on the women of Russia and Eastern Europe. Although slavery was supposedly abolished long ago, it's still very much alive around the world and often in an even more insidious form. At one point I had the misfortune in northern Serbia of seeing an outdoor market where young women stripped naked were sold like cattle to rich pimps bidding for ownership of their young flesh that would be quickly used up in the brothels of the Middle East. But finally I had to abandon my search, realizing that eventually I would have been gunned down in some bleak corner of that cruel world - shot in the back by one of the cheap thugs who surrounded the pimps.

Now and then I still think about the night in the upstairs disco of the Cherry Casino when I first saw Vera among the many, beautiful women on the dance floor. I couldn't take my eyes off of her and knew immediately that we had to meet. Gradually she came closer until I could see her clearly amid the pulsing lights. She was wearing a low-cut, black dress, her white arms and shoulders bare and her long blonde piled up loosely on her head. I envied her companion, who was handsome in a tough way. Soon she was only a few feet from where I was standing, and for a brief moment I could have reached out and touched that perfect, white shoulder. And then she looked at me, her eyes bright and intense as she briefly held my gaze. Her lips seemed to part as if she wanted to say something. And then the moment was gone, and she faded back into the crowd. At the time I was still trying to decide whether to return to New York, and I know now that she was one of the reasons I stayed on and got drawn into Moscow's depraved world.

After I returned to the bar downstairs, she left with her companion, and I learned that he was Guydor Basayev, one of the big car dealers allied to the Chechens. At the time importing expensive, western cars was one of the preferred ways in Moscow to get rich very quick. But there was also lots of competition, and after several bombings it wasn't surprising that the number of people interested in the business dropped off. When I asked Rolfe about Guydor, he warned me to stay away if I valued my life. But in spite of how dangerous the situation was, I didn't and still suspect that it was Guydor who sold Vera into the slave trade.

We started meeting on the side, and she implored me to take her away from him, describing how badly she was treated. It was apparent that Guydor fit in well with the violent Chechens, and I knew that I might be signing my own death warrant. Nonetheless, I couldn't resist becoming Vera's white knight, which is one of the more foolhardy things I've ever done. In Moscow's fast lane it was a major affront to take away another man's woman, and when it happened, violence was inevitable. I was no match for someone tied to the Chechens and making millions from overpriced, luxury cars. When Rolfe was killed, I thought at first it might be Guydor's handiwork, who sent one of his people to shoot up the palace, assuming that as usual I would be there. A few weeks

185

after Vera disappeared, Guydor's dealership burned down late one night with him inside. Probably it saved my life.

Soon after Vera left him, we departed from Moscow for a few weeks to be alone, at one point driving a couple of hundred miles to the tiny village where she grew up. In recent years it had gradually been abandoned like so many, rustic towns across provincial Russia. A way of life that flourished for centuries was slowly dying out as the young moved to the cities. Occasionally Vera went back to visit the old people who stayed on, unwilling to abandon the place they considered their home. Finally all of them had passed away except one, old man with a flowing white beard called Uncle Ivan. He spent his lonely days tending a plot of potatoes and beets and trying to repair the village's crumbling buildings, including the tiny church. Its interior was filled with the most exquisite carvings I've ever seen - the creation of generations of local craftsmen working patiently with their crude tools.

In spite of Uncle Ivan's determined efforts, the village continued to crumble away, and many of the abandoned houses had collapsed completely. Somehow he managed recently to repair the church's roof, although the aging glass kept breaking so most of the windows were boarded up to keep out the elements. We spent a couple of days helping him repair the door that was badly warped. It seemed an act of such futility, although the old man was determined to fulfill his self-appointed mission. Nonetheless, the weeds and saplings in the nearby fields continued their inexorable march forward, having already consumed much of the narrow road so that soon it would be impossible to reach the village by car. Nature was reclaiming what it considered its own, the old man having been granted a few more years at the most to keep up his pointless struggle to halt the inevitable.

The day after we arrived, Vera found a traditional costume in her family's abandoned house and wore it for me, her white-blond hair tied in braids. The transformation was remarkable, and

186

I thought how attractive she looked, even prettier than in the revealing dresses she wore at the discoes so lots of men would desire her. As the afternoon heat faded away, we went for a long walk in a nearby field fragrant with wild flowers, the warm air buzzing with the sound of tiny bees gathering rich nectar. How peaceful it was in this tiny corner of the eternal land of traditional Russia, the type of place that nurtured the beautiful women who went to Moscow to be lusted after and often stolen off the streets to be used up in filthy brothels.

The final afternoon we sat in the church before the hand-carved altar that contained a silver crucifix - for generations the prized possession of the little village. Briefly the sun slanted in one of the few windows that wasn't boarded up, illuminating the exquisite carvings of saints on the walls. I tried to imagine the long-dead craftsman patiently laboring there to create something so beautiful. A little bird flew in the open door and serenaded us. Without speaking, I handed her my mother's rings that she placed on the altar in front of the crucifix. Ever so briefly I experienced a sense of peace and unity that I've always sought in life.

A few days later we returned to Moscow, and I rented an expensive apartment a few blocks from where I had been living. The following week Vera disappeared early one evening on a dim side street, where a witness saw her dragged into a car that quickly sped away. Probably someone spotted her at one of the fashionable stores and told Guydor, who had her abducted and sold to the slavers. Like the Chechens, he was big on revenge and no doubt determined to pay her back for leaving him. And so began my long and desperate search that lead into the Caucasus and beyond. Following the breakup of the Soviet Union, the area was beset with political chaos. With many thousands living in makeshift refugee camps, it was almost impossible to trace anyone.

After returning to Moscow, I decided to visit Vera's village once again. On a warm, summer afternoon I drove there along

187

endless miles of dusty roads, at one point passing the unearthly sight of a white-washed monastery looming in the distance, its golden, onion-shaped domes glistening brilliantly. I reached the village just as the sun set in a copse of nearby trees. The tiny road had gotten narrower so it was barely wider than a large footpath. Leaving the car, I walked the rest of the way on foot, noticing how quiet it was. Repeatedly I called to Uncle Ivan, although there was no answer. Finally I went to his tiny house where the front door was wide open. There were animal droppings all over the floor, and in the next room the old man lay motionless on his bed. He had been dead for months, the flesh on his face having already decayed so large patches of his skull showed through. It was a dreadful sight, especially since I had grown so fond of him.

At long last the vibrant existence of that peaceful, little village and all the lives and hopes it nourished for so many generations had come to an end. The following morning I dug a grave next to the church and lay the prized, silver crucifix on the old man's chest before shoveling back the fragrant dirt. Afterwards I read aloud a couple of passages from the village's aged bible, my voice sounding small and insignificant amid the vast silence of that splendid, summer day. And then I sat in the church where so many of the long-departed were baptized, married and had fervent prayers read for their souls after their earthy journey came to an end. Suddenly on the altar I noticed my mother's silver rings sparkling like tiny stars in the sunlight coming from a nearby window. When we hurried back to Moscow, Vera forgot that they were there, and now like the rest of the decaying village they were nearly covered by the dust slowly drifting over everything. I recalled the fragile peace I experienced the last day as the two of us walked together through the warm fields and then held hands in the old church. Over the years I would try to reclaim that special feeling, although it never returned except briefly with Lily on Cheung Chau.

14

After the meeting with Liao Dan, I waited impatiently to hear from the person he called Li Zhou, although I couldn't be sure that was his real name. When first contacting me, many people preferred to use an alias. A few days later he finally called regarding an "important personal matter" - a phrase I've heard countless times before, and we arranged to meet the following afternoon. Little did I know that the nervous voice at the other end would become the most important intelligence source I ever located or, perhaps I should say, located me.

Usually I preferred to meet with a potential "client" at a bar in one of the more sleazy areas of Shanghai where the prostitutes hang out. That way it wasn't likely that anyone of consequence would spot us. Also it provided an opportunity for both parties to size up the other before doing anything incriminating. A higher-up in the regime always had to be concerned that a political rival might discover that they were siphoning off a fat chunk of the peoples' money and take maximum advantage of that embarrassing fact in order to displace them and grab the money for themselves. Typically this involved informing the Discipline Inspection Commission that was then obliged to enforce laws that under normal circumstances few paid attention to. Of course, if the person doing the stealing still had the right connections and was in favor with one of the top people, nothing would happen. Everything in China always went back to connections and the money going to the right people.

Because of the sensitivity of the situation, I could never be completely sure beforehand how much risk was involved. It was a concern I always had to deal with during my long stay in China, and I knew that at any time I might inadvertently be caught up in someone's unfortunate decline. In essence, there was simply no way to protect myself completely. Nonetheless, I had developed certain methods of proceeding that were quite effective. The initial meeting was particularly important because it enabled me to formulate a firsthand opinion of the individual involved and also find out whether they were in such disfavor that I should avoid them completely. Of course, if they had access to information of real significance, I sometimes overlooked even that unfortunate detail.

Through the years various, investigative bureaus had shown a fleeting interest in my activities, caused as much as anything by their inherent dislike of foreigners. Also, as a prominent American businessman in China, I presented a convenient target for any enterprising detective eager for a quick promotion. Because I regularly brought so much foreign investment into China, it was to be expected that I would be involved in the movement of large sums of money in and out of the country. This always provided me with a convenient excuse in the event something went wrong. After all, misunderstandings happen all the time in China whenever money is involved. Eventually I developed considerable skill identifying police detectives intent on making a nuisance of themselves and using me as a stepping stone. Fortunately most of them weren't as smart as they thought they were. When I spotted one, I always utilized the opportunity to give them a stern lecture on how much I respected the regime and at all times observed my duty to further its corrupt interests. If I was feeling really good and had a couple of stiff drinks under my belt, I could keep my tirade going almost indefinitely like a jazz musician exploring numerous variations on a theme. At the same time I knew that my long-winded dissertation, that would bore even a party fanatic, would soon be played back at the local security office putting everyone to sleep so they never wanted to hear about me again.

After the phone call, I checked around and learned that a Li Zhou was the assistant of one of the Politburo's most important officials. If that was my prospect, he probably had the combination to some file cabinets where a lot of very important secrets were stored. Hopefully that included detailed information about what the Chinese military was planning. What I couldn't be sure of was how much I could get my hands on in exchange for helping him escape along with a nice nest egg that guaranteed a comfortable life abroad.

In the addition to my impressive, main office on a top floor of one of Hong Kong's most prestigious buildings, I also maintained another office in Shanghai that hardly anyone knew about. Its purpose was to provide an inconspicuous place to meet with party big shots eager to hide their ill-gotten gains. Over the years I regularly moved this second office so it wouldn't be discovered - the most recent location in a less than fashionable section above a noisy restaurant and part-time dancehall. The furnishings included a well-worn desk, plain metal file cabinet, two plastic chairs and a floor lamp, all of which had been purchased second or probably third-hand. Also, the file cabinet was stuffed with officially approved brochures and government propaganda in the event someone got in there and snooped around. If they did, they would have never guessed that so much top-level information about China's corrupt government had changed hands in such a modest setting.

After arriving at the Shanghai airport, I took a taxi to a restaurant a few blocks from the office, had lunch and walked the rest of the way. As usual, I entered the building from an alleyway that I reached through a nearby bar and then went up the back stairs. The office hadn't been used in a couple of weeks, and when I went inside, it smelled strongly of the cheap food served in the restaurant downstairs. I opened the window to let in some fresh air and looked cautiously at the crowded street below, detecting

191

nothing unusual. Almost an hour passed, and I kept going to the window, wondering if my prospect got cold feet. It happened occasionally, although not often. Usually I was the one who called things off.

Finally there was a soft knock at the door that opened slowly, and a small, neat man cautiously entered the room removing his sunglasses. He had the clean, well-scrubbed look characteristic of high-ranking, party officials. Instead of an expensively tailored suit, he was dressed in plain, khaki pants and a white shirt with no tie. His fine quality shoes polished to a high sheen were the only indication that he was a person with money. It was obvious he had chosen the outfit carefully. He could have passed for a clerk in one of the city's innumerable, overcrowded offices, and anybody in the street wouldn't have given him a second thought.

He greeted me politely, and as we shook hands, I noticed the apprehension in his eyes. He was obviously afraid, and motioning for him to sit down, I was already sure this was no setup. If Li Zhou was acting, he was doing a very good job. A couple of times after first coming to China, I was almost caught up in some, very messy situations because of my lack of appreciation of party protocol. Since then I learned a lot and never again committed the type of stupid mistakes that almost ended my espionage career before it began.

"Have any problem getting here?" I asked, trying to sound friendly in order to put him at ease.

"I'm vaguely familiar with the area, although I've never actually been here," he responded, making clear that he didn't spend time in neighborhoods like this.

"Do you have any identification?"

"Yes, of course," he answered and handed me a couple of documents that confirmed his identity, including his official pass at party headquarters.

"I made a few inquiries. You have an important position."

"I've served the regime well for many years," he answered, the pride briefly evident in his voice "Liao has a high opinion of you. I mean the way you handled things for him and his family," he added finally looking at me. "He and I went to school together."

"I try to do things efficiently for clients. Of course, there's always the unexpected so any plan needs to be flexible so it can be adjusted to changing circumstances. It's a mistake to be tied to one scenario when moving around lots of money. Tell me what you have in mind."

"I can't continue the same way. China has become an enormous tragedy," he blurted out, his voice filled with emotion.

He tried to remain seated but grew so agitated he went to the window. Silhouetted against the daylight, he stared silently for several minutes into the street. It was obvious that I wasn't dealing with the usual, run-of-the-mill, greedy higher-up like Dan and countless others I've known through the years. Every day they keep stealing as much as they can grab from the public till, some fleeing the country to places unknown after liberally greasing enough palms so their indiscretions are overlooked long enough to get away. In contrast, there was something sensitive about Li Zhou, and I had a hunch that I just encountered a man with a conscience, a rarity for someone connected to the Chinese communist regime.

"Tell me about it," I said reassuringly.

"It's been so difficult trying to act as if nothing is wrong. Months ago, I started thinking about leaving the country. And now with the possibility of a war, there's no reason to wait any longer. Apparently for many years a major war has been the centerpiece of their strategy, although only a few know the truth about what they're really planning. I'm referring, of course, to the select group that operates in the shadows behind the Standing Committee, the repository of the real power in China. Observers on the outside fail to realize that the exalted Standing Committee is merely an administrative figurehead. It's amazing when you think about it - a country with more than a billion and a half people controlled by such a small, mysterious group that no one can observe. Some call them the "elders." That's as good a name as any. What we do know is that all of them are fanatically nationalistic. I suspect they've been planning this war since the days of Deng Xiaoping, or at least that's what my boss thinks. He's quite shaken by what he's heard. He knows the dire consequences of a major war, especially the large number of fatalities that could result. Nonetheless, the regime is apparently convinced it is in the people's long-term interests and supposedly they're the only ones who can successfully serve those interests. What an irony when you consider the terrible damage that for years the communists have inflicted on the nation.

"Eventually someone will notice that things aren't right with me. Even high-ranking officials are under constant scrutiny and expected to conform to the same iron-clad standard of behavior that governs everyone. In essence, we're both the beneficiaries and prisoners of a system erected on lies. You can never show any real feelings and must always maintain the expected image of efficiency and dedication to the party. That way no one feels threatened. As a result, all of us do the things necessary to maintain our position in the hierarchy while also keeping the regime in power. The one, overriding concern is the party's authority. From that you derive your share of the spoils. For most of my life I've been a loyal operative and prospered accordingly. It became my whole existence as well as a substitute for everything else, including my love of China, its culture and people.

"Perhaps you're asking yourself why I didn't try to change things for the better. Briefly I did, although I soon learned that in a system like this it isn't possible to reform anything. Nonetheless, on occasion, I did criticize some things, especially about the environment. But I was warned that I could be subject to discipline and lose my position. Anyone who persists in raising subjects that conflict with the official line can be sent for reeducation or worse. As far as the regime is concerned, anyone, who is overly critical of the approved status quo, is a troubled person and must be dealt with accordingly. Unless you've grown up under a system like this, you can't imagine what it's like, especially how rigidly everything is controlled. And of late it keeps getting worse," he said, his voice quivering noticeably as he continued to stare into the street.

Having just walked into the room, he was unburdening himself to a person he didn't even know, and I suspected there was no one in whom he could confide. Probably he was unable to say much to his own family. In China it's engrained in people from their earliest days to inform on those around them, even children on their own parents. Only minutes before the two of us were complete strangers. Now by default, I had become his reluctant confidant.

"I'll be glad to help in any way I can. Are you sure you want to go through with this?" I asked, concerned that perhaps I couldn't help him.

"There's no other option except to get out as soon as possible".

"So they're going to initiate some sort of large, military action. What specifically do you know?" I asked, getting back to what I really wanted to talk about. I didn't like for a meeting such as this to drag on too long, especially when I was unfamiliar with the other party. Also I still wasn't sure that Li Zhou had access to anything of real value.

"As I said, this isn't something they just thought up. Apparently for decades they've been making preparations with the utmost care. Now they've decided it's time to move, although probably they would have preferred to wait until the capabilities of the military reached an even higher level. But with the internal situation continuing to worsen, the regime has to do something or eventually lose power. That would involve the most severe

195

consequences for party members, who would finally have to answer for their misdeeds. For years, the annual riots have numbered in the tens of thousands, and at times it's only with the most violent methods that the Peoples Armed Police have been able to keep order.

"Recently the situation has grown worse because economic conditions around the world are deteriorating rapidly. China is dragging down the global economy and vice versa. Furthermore, in the interest of rapid industrialization our environment has been totally destroyed, while hundreds of millions live a hand-to-mouth existence in polluted conditions that are ruining their health. Add to all of that the brutal, ongoing persecution of the Falun Gong and dissenters of any kind.

"For decades, the people's vast savings, one of the great treasures on earth, have been systematically looted. This includes the bad loans that funded inefficient, state-owned enterprises along with the lavish lifestyles of party members. When the people discover that most of what they patiently saved is gone, the nation will literally explode. It's one of the main reasons that so many officials have overseas passports. Of course, I'm sure you know all of this - I mean, being in the business. At this point launching a war is the solution to all of the regime's problems. Those at the very top (the truly dedicated) will see things through to the bitter end and have no intention of running away. No doubt, they will claim that all the stolen money was supposedly used for a war intended to make China great. They know that in a time of crisis the country will unite behind them and our ultra-nationalistic military that is so eager to assert its strength."

"Liao wasn't sure about the details, including when all of this will take place."

"It appears that they have some sort of important, new weapon, or at least that's what I've heard. No one seems to know what it is, although apparently they're counting on it," he said, which really peeked my interest.

"What else do you know?"

"At the moment nothing. In a few days I should have something more specific. A top secret report will be released to select members of the Politburo. This will include my boss so I should be able to get you a copy"

"I understand that you want to leave the country with your family."

"Yes. There's my wife, our child and my mother. We have about $50 million (US) that was acquired on the side. My former father-in-law was a top party official in Shanghai, who died several months ago. Over the years he received large payments to facilitate various projects and passed the money on to us."

"Where do you want to go?"

"Hawaii."

"That shouldn't be difficult. Also the amount isn't overly large. However, everything must be done without attracting attention at such a sensitive time. Otherwise questions will be asked, especially about the fact that you're traveling with your entire family. Understandably at a time like this the regime doesn't want people, who might know what's going on, to leave the country. Lower level functionaries, that's different. Instead of traveling directly to Hawaii, I suggest a brief stay at an intermediate location before you move on to your final destination. A lot will depend on how quickly your funds can be transferred. Lately the key personnel at certain banks has changed, although there shouldn't be any problem as long as everyone is paid off. The most important thing is that nothing is done to alert the authorities that you're leaving with your family. I'll need documentation from the accounts in which the funds are located. Is your wife in full agreement?"

"Yes. We've discussed the matter at length. She wants to

leave as much as I do, especially because of our child."

"I assume that she can be trusted. I know of situations where the wife gave the whole thing away. Of late, the authorities have become increasingly observant. I'll speed up my end as much as I can. In exchange I'll expect detailed information about the war. Otherwise, from my standpoint the project wouldn't be worthwhile. I dislike having to state the point so explicitly, but it's important that we understand each other. I arrange deals all over China and need as much information as possible about what's going on. That way I can react accordingly on behalf of my clients. Of course, you understand that anything you provide will remain completely confidential so your role is never known."

"This report should fulfill your needs. I'll have it soon. I suspect that what's going to happen will be terrible. You see, the leadership of the party doesn't really care about the people. Having exploited them all these years for their own purposes, they view them as expendable and aren't concerned that many could die."

"I only want a copy of original documents, not some sort of typed synopsis. After reviewing what you provide, I'll destroy it so nothing can be traced back. That's for your protection and mine."

"I feel like a traitor," Zhou suddenly said which surprised me.

"You're sure the information will be available in a few days? I can't wait any longer. You say they have a new weapon?"

"That's what I heard from my boss, and apparently it's something quite extraordinary," he added, and although intrigued, I knew that there was no point pressing him further. It was never wise to keep after a prospect too much, especially if they're about to come across with something really big. It appeared that in a few days Li Zhou would hand me the mother lode of secret information I always sought that is so damning that even China's highly paid apologists in Washington couldn't explain it away.

15

The following afternoon I called Gao, once again urging him to find out where Lily had been taken. Even their mother refused to tell him, and it was obvious that he was frightened about getting involved in such a difficult situation. Without his help, however, I didn't have a chance of finding her. When I finally learned where she was located, I intended to rescue her no matter how great the risk. Having lost Vera, I wasn't going to let the same thing happen with Lily, even if it cost my life.

After returning from the meeting with Li Zhou, I made my usual, weekly drive past the American Consulate and spotted the fake plant in the second-floor window - the prearranged signal that Kress wanted me to contact him. Usually I employed a cell phone that couldn't be traced. It was rarely necessary for us to meet in person, and when we did, it was at night and always in a different location. Almost four months had passed since we last had any direct contact, and at the moment I didn't want to see him.

When I phoned, he asked to meet as soon as possible concerning the information I left at the Consulate a few weeks before. It was an excerpt from a report that originated in the International Liaison Department and concerned China's long history of proliferating dangerous weaponry including missile technology. In fact, China had for decades been one of the forces behind the ongoing spread of violence, especially in the Middle East.

Among the objectives served by this covertly executed campaign, the report made clear that the transfers were intended to dilute American military power by creating as many threats to western interests as possible. Such activities were a highly sensitive subject throughout the international community. Although China was a signatory to many prominent agreements, including the

Nuclear Nonproliferation Treaty and others, it was well known that its government continued covertly to export dangerous technologies in violation of these same agreements. The proof on occasion had been strong enough to warrant sanctions against several Chinese companies such as the military-owned Northern Industrial Corporation, China Great Wall and even the Chinese National Airline that at times transported illegal goods. In other words, in retaliation the US government sanctioned an entity controlled by the Chinese government while downplaying the fact the government itself was really responsible.

The report from the International Liaison Department was significant because it provided a detailed list of China's proliferation activities going back more than two decades. In some instances, it even contained dates and specific amounts of prohibited materials. As far as I know, no such list had ever been obtained. It finally provided proof positive of what everyone already knew. For years, China had deliberately signed various international agreements of importance while intending to violate these agreements in order to further its perverse interests.

Two, long pages of the report were devoted to items with a military application that had been supplied to various entities in the Middle East. Before passing along any stolen intelligence, I usually waited a sufficient amount of time in the event the person, who was my source, planned to leave the country. Because of such precautions, none of them had ever been caught. This also protected me and meant that other officials were more likely to cooperate. In essence, I had a long-established track record indicating that I knew what I was doing and could be trusted. After obtaining something of interest, I deposited the documents late at night in the Consulate's mail drop, using a plain envelope with a prearranged number written on the outside. Kress was supposed to forward everything to Washington with a copy also going to Ben Cramer. This had been the arrangement since Kress took over a couple of years ago, and I always checked with Ben to make sure that he had been properly informed. Recently, however, Kress hadn't sent anything to Washington. For some reason he was sitting on valuable intelligence and not doing anything with it. I knew that something was wrong.

Rarely was Kress in a hurry to meet, and I assumed that probably he wanted additional data on China's proliferation activities. At the moment I wasn't prepared to give him anything more since he had been holding back what I already provided. He suggested meeting at a location we used several months before on the peninsula of reclaimed land that juts into Victoria Harbor. Afterwards I realized how easy it would be to get trapped there and decided never to use it again. Instead I suggested the park beside Gloucester Road, which afforded me several escape routes in the event any problems arose. Also, Kress wanted to meet in the afternoon, which raised even more red flags. I always considered a nighttime meeting essential to preserving my anonymity. Realizing that I wasn't going to change my mind about that detail, he finally agreed to meet the following night about ten o'clock.

After many years in espionage, one develops a sixth sense regarding potential danger, and I considered not showing up. I will always wish that I hadn't. Shortly after dark I parked on the other side of the Bizarre and walked up Causeway Road, entering the park south of the row of benches where we were supposed to meet. All day I had been uneasy about the meeting. My instincts kept warning me to stay away, and while proceeding along the dimly-lit path, I kept pausing to look around. But nothing seemed out of the ordinary, and finally I went over to where Kress was sitting. He always shook hands formally as if we were meeting for the first time and as usual was wearing a conservative business suit. I'd never seen him dress casually. With his shoe he crushed a cigar on the ground and motioned for me to sit beside him.

"The information about China's transfers is interesting.

Are you sure it's accurate? Among other things, it makes clear that China often signs international agreements it doesn't intend to keep," he commented.

"It's accurate. And does that surprise you? After becoming a member of the World Trade Organization, they're still producing most of the world's counterfeit goods while continually violating copyrights and stealing much of the world's intellectual property."

"A lot of people would take exception to such an all-inclusive statement, although I suppose it's basically true. But sometimes in international affairs you have to be flexible and look at the long term as well as both sides of an issue," he said, almost sounding as if he was reading from a script. In the past he was usually quite critical of China regarding trade, but suddenly his attitude had changed completely.

"What's so urgent that we had to see each other right away?"

"I want you to meet someone," he said, and for a moment I thought that I hadn't heard him correctly.

"What?"

"He's a friend. I think the two of you can help each other."

"Are you nuts?" I said, noticing a man walking towards us along the path. As he passed under a light, I realized it was Robert Verrelin. My suspicions about the meeting being a set-up were correct. Even in the dim light Verrelin recognized me and waved. As I got up to leave, Kress grabbed my arm.

"Keep your cool. This is important. We'll make it worth your while," he added, holding on tightly.

"Larry, wait! I want to talk," Verrelin called, but finally I pulled away and started to run toward Gloucester Road. Glancing back, I saw that Verrelin had pulled out a gun.

"No, don't," Kress yelled as the two of them struggled. And then the gun went off, and Kress fell to the ground. Verrelin started to follow as I reached the road and crossing to the other side, was almost hit by a car. Continuing up Great George Street, I knew that I couldn't use my gun in such a crowded area, which meant that I had to find some other means of getting away. Soon I reached Percival and headed towards the Bay. Looking back again, I saw that Verrelin was staying with me.

It was obvious that I couldn't outrun him, and not sure what else to do, I decided to hide in André's boat. At the tunnel approach the traffic was heavy. Finally a small gap opened among the cars, and I darted across. Just before I reached the other side, a small sports car appeared from nowhere. I could see the shocked face of the driver, who was about to run me over. At the last moment I jumped up rolling over the car's hood and fell hard on the ground. Fortunately I received only a glancing blow, and feeling momentarily dazed, I got up, stumbled a little and ran the rest of the way to the yacht club.

Fortunately Verrelin's view was blocked by the traffic giving me a chance to reach the boat. After letting myself into the cabin, I quickly closed the small door and waited in the darkness, my heart pounding as if it would burst. I was sure he didn't see me and with relief sat down, realizing how lucky I was to get away. I decided to spend the night there and not risk being spotted again. Now and then I looked out one of the portholes but didn't detect anything unusual. Later I made some soup in the small gallery and after a last look outside went to sleep.

In the morning I made breakfast, and to be sure that things were all right, stayed there a few more hours. Assuming the coast was clear, I finally left the boat and headed across Gloucester Road to my car. Along the way I stopped at a couple of stores in order to confirm that no one was following me. I was still baffled that Kress was willing to blow the cover of America's most important agent in China. Somehow he had been talked into doing something incredibly stupid. Also I wondered how he and Verrelin could know each other.

The following day the local newspaper contained a brief item stating that an employee of the American Consulate had been shot to death in Victoria Park. Kress's name wasn't mentioned, and the police requested the public's assistance. Over the years I've had many close calls like the proverbial cat with nine lives. Once again my luck held, although I knew that I couldn't expect to be so fortunate again. Of late, my nerves were getting frayed, and I wasn't making smart decisions. There was no question that Verrelin intended to kill me. The information about him from Cramer was correct. He was a paid assassin dispatched there to insinuate himself into Hong Kong society and find out who was obtaining so much information embarrassing to the regime. With my cover blown, I now had another, excellent reason for leaving Hong Kong immediately.

All day I stayed in my apartment. From the living room window there's a good view of the street, and as far as I could determine, no one had the building under surveillance. Nonetheless, I was sure it wouldn't be long before Verrelin made his next move. He had to eliminate me quickly because I knew he killed Kress and could report him to the police.

That night the situation took an unexpected turn. On the TV news it was announced that late in the afternoon a sailboat moored at the Hong Kong yacht club blew up killing the single occupant. Although it might be only a coincidence, I feared the worst and kept trying to reach André. But there was no answer at his apartment, and I knew that I would never see him again. Somehow Verrelin must have spotted me boarding the boat, or more likely he stayed there all night until I left in the morning. He could have easily planted the bomb, and when André switched on the boat's ignition, the result was instantaneous. It was one of the oldest and most effective ways of eliminating someone. Because of the violence of the explosion, the person who died hadn't been identified yet, which gave me a brief reprieve before Verrelin learned he got the wrong person.

A few days later my worst suspicions were confirmed. The newspaper carried a short piece naming André as the one who died in the explosion, his identity established through dental records. I was stunned by the news, realizing that I caused the death of my best friend. In the newspaper there was a brief obituary released by the Russian company he represented. It mentioned his place of birth and educational background, which included an engineering degree from Moscow University. But there was nothing about his long years of dedicated service in the GRU. It was the mundane, paid obituary of an ordinary, undistinguished businessman rather than someone many Russians would view as a hero.

With the information about André out in public, the clock was ticking down rapidly. Aware that I wasn't killed in the explosion, Verrelin wouldn't wait long to react. I had only two choices. Either I left Hong Kong right away, or I eliminated him. A skilled, international killer would do what was necessary to fulfill a contract. It was a matter of perverse pride to maintain his reputation, and even if I left the city, it probably wouldn't do any good. One night on a lonely street in some faraway place I would suddenly be shot from behind, not knowing what hit me. I decided to take the initiative. During all my years in espionage, I never killed anyone and wasn't sure if I could do such an awful thing. But regardless of how distasteful it might be, I had to go through with it and the sooner the better. Killing someone in cold blood wasn't the type of unseemly conclusion to my espionage career that I hoped for.

In the evening I phoned the hotel where Verrelin had been staying, and the operator was generous enough to give me his room number. It was fortunate that he hadn't moved to different quarters, which would have complicated matters. However, he wouldn't stay idle for long. I had to act quickly but couldn't make up my mind how to kill him. Finally I drove to the hotel and went

205

up to the fifth floor where his room was located. After a brief look around, I returned to my apartment and stayed up till morning formulating a plan. Fortunately I still had the silencer for my gun that I kept for years and now would put to good use. I was a mediocre shot, which meant I would have to get close to be certain that I killed him.

The following morning I went to a costume store looking for an outfit similar to those worn by the hotel's service personnel. Although I couldn't find an exact match, I put together something fairly close. That evening, I returned to the hotel with my face disguised with makeup and a mustache so any witnesses couldn't identify me. All day I was unable to eat and still wasn't sure that I could shoot him, especially at close quarters. I knew, however, that Verrelin would have no compunction about doing the same to me and didn't intend to waste the opportunity to act first. Once again I used the service stairs so I wouldn't be spotted on the elevator. While I walked cautiously down the hall to his room, my hand trembled as I grasped the gun in my pocket. I felt like I was sleepwalking. Pausing at his door, I almost turned to leave but finally pushed the bell. There was a long delay, and I wondered if he was there. Suddenly the door opened, and the two of us looked directly at each other. I could see the color in his bright blue eyes and the faint stubble of beard on his handsome face. It occurred to me that he resembled a model in an ad for men's shirts that I saw recently in a magazine. Also I realized that in a way I had gotten to like him.

"Well, Larry, what a nice surprise. I was hoping we'd have a chance to talk so we could work things out and avoid anything unpleasant," he said with a smile, but I quickly pulled out the gun and fired twice right into the middle of his chest.

A huge, red spot spread over the front of his shirt, an expression of shock and then pain appearing on his face as he toppled backwards. With my foot I pushed him aside and quickly closed the door. Fortunately no one was in the hallway, and because of the silencer the gun made hardly any noise. In only a couple of minutes I was out of the hotel and down the street where I threw the gun into a storm drain. I couldn't believe how easy the whole thing had been. It seemed absurd that taking a human life required barely more effort than swatting a fly. I had just stepped over a fateful line that I never wanted to cross. And then it occurred to me what an appealing person Verrelin was. However, it wasn't the first time during my long career in espionage that I encountered someone whose appearance belied who they really are.

With Verrelin eliminated, I still wasn't out of danger and suspected that after learning that I was the infamous "Sergei," he immediately passed the information along to whoever hired him. It would be only a matter of time before a replacement was dispatched to finish the job. Also I knew that at any time Lily's father might decide to make sure that I was no longer a problem for him. I felt like I was holding a time bomb that at any moment might explode, my every instinct telling me to get out of Hong Kong on the next flight.

Back at the apartment, I phoned Gao and once again got his answering machine. No doubt, he was out at the clubs flirting with the girls instead of trying to find Lily. I left an angry message, and just before dawn he finally called back apologizing profusely. He still didn't know where she was being kept. But after I expressed my annoyance in the strongest terms, he promised to find out something definite from their mother. Once again I wondered if I could trust him. Unfortunately I had no other way of finding her. Although at this point I was little more than a sitting duck, I decided to wait and keep hoping that he learned something.

The following day I received a call from Mr. Ming, a solicitor at one of the large, Hong Kong law firms. He was in charge of André's will and informed me that I was the sole beneficiary. We arranged an appointment, and late that afternoon I went to his office that was located in Central not far from City Hall. Ming was a meticulous-looking, little man, and from the modest size of his office it was obvious he wasn't an important member of the firm. When I walked in, he remained seated behind his cluttered desk and seemed in a hurry to conclude the matter. Having just caused the death of my best friend, I was now the beneficiary of his will. The irony of the situation couldn't have been worse. Slumping in a chair, I realized this brief meeting in a cramped law office was the concluding act of Andre's life. For years he was one of Russia's top espionage people in Europe, who played a significant role in the cold war. Nonetheless, he merited only brief public mention in a cursory obituary that described a mundane existence little different from countless others. Now all that remained was to dispose of his meager possessions to the man responsible for his death.

"It's a short will," Ming said speaking matter of factly. "Mr. Nicolai left you all his assets. A schedule is attached to the back. I will give you a copy. It's a modest bequest. Also, there's a letter. Apparently he felt strongly about your relationship. Did you know him long?"

"A few years. He was a fine man," I answered, tears momentarily filling my eyes. Ming didn't respond to the comment and continued to rummage among the papers covering his desk. I suspected he dealt with wills all day long, and no doubt to him this one was no different from all the others.

"I assume the two of you were not related."

"Correct."

"The letter is very personal. Do you want me to read it, or would you prefer to examine it in private?"

"Go ahead."

"It reads as follows:

"My boy, I hope you don't mind if I call you that. When we were together, I was reluctant to address you in this fashion, not sure how you would react. But now I'm gone, and it's important that you understand my feelings. During the last, few years our friendship has brightened my life, and I always looked forward to the two of us being together. After a while I began to think of you as the son I always wanted. The thought made me happy. Often I said to myself: I wonder how my boy is doing today, and when you called, I was always interested to hear about your activities. Occasionally I tried to give you advice hoping that in some way my experience might be helpful. At times I do think you appreciated what I said.

"Well, my boy, it's all over. Otherwise, you wouldn't be reading this letter. You're the only one who knows the details of my past that I shared with you. I believe that in some ways my life was unique, and now you are its sole custodian. Also, in this will I leave you my few, tangible possessions. There is a bank account, a small amount of stock, my car and the sailboat that I know you will put to good use. Compared to many others, this isn't a lot to show for a lifetime of effort. Nonetheless, it's all that I have, and I'm glad to give it to you. Whenever you go out in the boat, think now and then of your old friend, André, who loved you as a son. I hope that in some way you will find much happiness in the coming years. Good luck. Your devoted friend who loves you. Andrei."

"That concludes the will," Mr. Ming said, glancing at his watch, and handed me the letter along with some other papers. However, my eyes were filled with tears I couldn't control, and I barely saw what he gave me.

"Thanks," I said and placed the papers in a small briefcase.

"He was a nice man," he added noticing my distress.

"Yes, a nice man. I wish I had known how deeply he felt so I could have responded appropriately."

"Often we don't find out important things like that until it's too late," he said, the gentleness in his voice surprising me as I tried to wipe away the tears. "There are certain matters to be worked out such as the stock. It's only a small amount. My secretary will be in touch with you."

"Thanks," I said and left the room feeling overwhelmed. The situation was so sad. I realized that Andre viewed me as his son just as I liked to think of him as the father I never knew. Nonetheless, neither was able to tell the other how they really felt. I wondered how he would have reacted if he knew that inadvertently I caused his death. Probably he would have accepted it stoically the way he did everything else. His death served no purpose at all and in the dark realm of espionage was merely one more, unfortunate episode among countless others. I have often thought that we humans are ill-suited for such a cruel game, and perhaps it's inevitable the fates play tricks on those foolhardy enough to indulge in it.

A couple of days later I finally reached Ben Cramer through a special phone line routed through a local number in Tokyo. He informed me that the day before I met Kress in the park, he resigned from the CIA in order to work for a trade association that represented several corporations with large manufacturing plants in China. Without all that cheap, exploited labor, the bottom lines of these companies wouldn't look so good. Someone guessed correctly that Kress could identify Sergei, the source of so much damning information that leaked out to the West, and had dispatched Verrelin to take care of the problem. Supposedly Kress received a six-figure signing bonus to accept his new position. Plain and simple, he sold out and as a result was willing to compromise an invaluable intelligence source. His act of betrayal wasn't the first I'd seen in connection with the illusive bonanza of riches in China, and I knew it wouldn't be the last.

16

After the meeting at the lawyer's office, I was very depressed and almost overlooked the message on my cell phone from Li Zhou. He already had the information that he promised, and the following morning I returned to Shanghai. It appeared that finally I was going to learn the specifics of the regime's plan to start what I was certain now would be World War III. Hopefully the information would also include the specifics of their new weapon - the most intriguing detail of all. After taking the usual precautions, I arrived early at the office. In the restaurant downstairs the juke box was loud as ever. To my surprise, Li was already waiting in the dimly lit hallway, and without a word he removed an envelope secreted in a newspaper.

We went inside, and sitting at the desk, I took out several typewritten papers, all of them stamped "Top Secret - Not To Be Copied." In my hands was the document recently circulated among select members of China's Politburo. At the bottom were the names of members of the Central Military Commission, Standing Committee of the Politburo, and three, key military figures including Lily's father. The unauthorized possession of such a document was cause for immediate execution.

"This should take care of my end," he commented, his voice quivering noticeably. "How long will it take to complete the arrangements for my family to get out of the country?"

"Because there's little time, you'll leave from an airfield in Guangxi province. It's a route that's worked well in the past, especially on short notice. You'll fly in a small, private plane. They easily avoid radar, make little noise, and no one pays attention to them. I brought a map that shows the exact location of the airfield. The way to get there is highlighted. Memorize it and destroy the map. Tomorrow I'll provide you with a departure time. Don't forget to destroy the map."

"I won't. But are you sure this will work?"

"Don't worry. In a few days you and your family will start a new life abroad. Also, by tomorrow I should have your funds out of the country," I said after examining the records of the accounts that contained his money.

"When I first learned that the regime might start a war, I hoped it would be something modest so the casualties would be limited. But as you'll see, they're planning a major conflict in order to seize vast amounts of new territory. It's madness. Of course, that shouldn't surprise anyone. I know the grandiose way they think. Years ago, statements by key members of the military became public regarding their intention of one day initiating a major, expansionist war. But no one paid attention. It sounded so senseless," he said, and I knew exactly what he was referring to. The provocative speeches made by various members of China's high command included those by Zhu Chenghi and Chi Haotian, who at the time was the country's most important military theorist. Because the statements indicated a willingness to employ the most dangerous weapons, most observers dismissed them as so much rhetoric. To some, however, they had the familiar ring of truth, mirroring almost exactly the genocidal thinking in Hitler's *Mein Kampf*. In particular, emphasis was placed on the need to seize a large amount of new "living space" for the Chinese people. It appeared that soon history would repeat itself, although once again humanity had been given a fair warning that it chose to ignore.

"I could only get the first section. There's a second part that contains the actual details of what they're planning to do. Without the other part, it is impossible to know exactly where the attack will occur or what form it will take."

"Is there any way you can get the rest? Otherwise it's all guesswork," I said with disappointment.

"It wasn't possible to get any more, especially information

212

about the new weapon," he said shaking his head.

"What can it be? Is it a biological agent? Something like that could spread around the globe and kill everyone, including the Chinese.

"I don't know, although apparently it's very destructive."

"Do you know anything about a place called "X?" I asked, convinced that mysterious place was pivotal to what they were planning.

"Over the years I've heard the term although nothing specific was ever said. But it sounded important. That's why I remembered. What does it mean?"

"I was hoping your information would tell me," I answered, aware that the crucial, missing section of the war memorandum contained the answers I sought. What at the moment was the most important document in all of China and perhaps the entire world was probably in General Chan's desk along with the other papers I'd already seen there. If I was going to discover the truth about the nightmare about to descend on the world, I somehow had to return to the Chan's apartment and steal what I needed from the general's desk. But trying to get into such a well-protected residence was nothing short of suicide. I could never do it on my own. I needed help, and only Lily could provide it.

While returning to Hong Kong, I thought of Li Zhou's earlier comments about all the harm that had been inflicted by the communists on the Chinese people - a cruel spectacle that was about to evolve into a total disaster. Through the years I'd seen how the impressive, showcase cities of the "gold coast" were used to hide the truth about what was really happening throughout China. All the cleverly orchestrated propaganda directed at the West was used to keep alive for outsiders the illusion that China was supposedly becoming more progressive and humane. As proof, appealing photographs kept turning up on American television that showed successful and happy, young Chinese climbing the ladder of western-style success. In essence, the country was supposedly developing an educated middle class inclined to democracy. The truth is that only a small portion of the population received any real benefits from the ruinous rush to industrialize and build up the military, and they had little political freedom. *All along it was the hidden agenda of the party leadership to keep the masses of the Chinese people mired down in poverty so they could be controlled and exploited in the most effective way.*

Meanwhile the supposedly objective, western press continued to ignore the true China far removed from all the glitz of the gold coast - a vast, impoverished area that few in America would ever hear about. To the north of Hong Kong, the hills of the New Territories were on most days barely visible behind an acrid fog emitted by the countless factories and plants burning sulfur-laden coal. Every week another large, coal-fired plant opened somewhere in the country, and currently China burned at least one-half of all the coal consumed around the world. Meanwhile more than a billion, uneducated "peasants" in the interior provinces stoically scraped out a meager, pitiful existence in the badly polluted environment. Many could barely survive after being dispossessed from their land to make way for the wasteful projects that profited the politically powerful. Some had virtually no identifiable source of income.

It is an astonishing fact that the bulk of the wealth in China was held by barely .02 % of the population, almost all of those people connected in some way to the all-powerful, communist party. While those who consider themselves farmers comprise most of the population, their collective wealth was at best only about 5 - 10% of the national total. In other words, the vast majority of people were little more than pathetic paupers. At the same time over a million lost their meager parcels of land each year while receiving little or no compensation. As a result the average income of the country's one billion "peasants" was only about $2 US per day - that is, if they had any income at all.

Meanwhile the number of unemployed kept growing so an endless stream of the desperate and vulnerable kept drifting into the sweat shops of the "economic zones." Often they worked seven days a week for a pittance. It wasn't surprising that each year so many demonstrations and riots took place throughout China. Some involved violent, pitched battles between the outraged populace and the heavily armed police (PAP), who were actually internal, combat troops.

The true reality of what had been happening in China was recently brought to my attention by a confidential memorandum I obtained that concerned the country's devastated environment. In essence, the core of the sugar-coated, "communist" apple was even more rotten than I imagined. The memorandum had circulated among the members of the powerful Central Committee, which elects the Politburo. Over the years I came across other documents from the Central Committee, and they were always highly informative. For a long time it was known that because of rapid economic development, China was experiencing an environmental crisis of unprecedented proportions. Not surprising, it had become increasingly difficult to obtain accurate information on the subject.

The signs of environmental degradation were everywhere one traveled. Those rivers and lakes that hadn't dried up completely were often an odd, putrid color. Unexpectedly along some highway I often encountered a noisome smog that burned the eyes while reducing visibility to practically nothing. In addition, there was the ever-present threat of being trapped in an unyielding pocket of warm, stagnant air that smelled like it just blew out of the overly large toilet of some communist fat cat.

The environment in China had deteriorated to such a degree that probably nothing could halt this incredibly destructive process. In essence, the unique land the world had long associated with traditional China was completely gone, destroyed by pollution and industrial waste on a monumental scale. This tragic fact is demonstrated most vividly by the wanton destruction of the country's lakes and rivers including the legendary "Yellow River." The heartland of Han people, the river is in a pitiable state and in some places has almost ceased to exist. I realized now that the regime's willingness to tolerate such environmental ruin had an element of premeditation. At some point the decision was made to sacrifice the land for a larger purpose - to win a monumental war of conquest for new territory of vast proportions.

While China is a large country with an overall land mass equal to that of the continental United States, one-third of its territory has always been unsuitable for habitation on any significant scale. Under communist rule the land usable by people has shrunk steadily from over six million square kilometers (2.4 million square miles) to only about three million. At the same time the nation's population more than doubled, squeezing this ever-growing mass of people into an ever-smaller area, much of it badly polluted. Particularly hard hit is the limited area used for farming and grazing - 90% of all natural grasslands degraded significantly. The situation is especially bad for key crop growing areas such as the invaluable North China and East China Plains. Because of the rapid over-extraction of ground water beneath the North China Plain, a depression covering 50,000 square kilometers has developed as the land continues to sink. As a result some superstitious farmers fear that one day the land will collapse completely, and anyone working in the fields will fall deep into the earth. Where too much ground water has been removed, it's often replaced in the aquifer by polluted wastes and even salt water, an irreversible process rapidly overtaking both the East China Plain and other important areas. Thus an extraordinarily destructive sequence of events has been set in motion that eventually will make additional hundreds of millions of Chinese homeless and unable to feed themselves.

In all of history such an environmental calamity has never been visited upon a society. Gradually the powerless masses of China have been poisoned and their health ruined solely for economic and political expediency. To illustrate the point, an important Chinese academy concluded that Beijing, the country's prestigious capital, is the second most polluted major city on the entire planet. This report also indicated was that an environmental catastrophe was rapidly overwhelming the entire country, escalating the incidence of disease and premature deaths. In fact, this destructive process was so far-reaching it had begun to undermine the climate of the entire planet. The party big shots in their scented penthouses along the coast could no longer ignore such extraordinary, environmental ruin. Because of enforced secrecy, however, I suspected that some of them didn't know how bad the situation really is - that is, if they cared to find out. After reading the memo, I knew that such a situation couldn't continue much longer, and it was only a matter of time before there was a total collapse of Chinese society.

"This memorandum will inform the members of the Committee about the nation's rapidly escalating, environmental crisis. It is important that everyone in a position of authority is able to minimize or deny that such problems exist. Otherwise, they could undermine the party's interests even more than has already occurred. The number of riots in response to land seizures and environmental contamination continues to grow. However, the People's Armed Police has demonstrated an admirable record of suppressing such unforgivable lawlessness.

"To review the more prominent aspects of the situation, it is necessary first to take note of the current condition of the country's water resources. At the present time nearly one-half of the people in China have access on a daily basis only to polluted drinking water. The groundwater under 90% of the nation's cities is polluted and probably beyond reclamation. This unfortunate problem is compounded by the fact that about 80% of the nation's rivers are also polluted - degraded for the most part to level 4 or 5 (undrinkable). An example, for significant periods of the year the Yellow River hardly exists. Diverting a portion of this limited, polluted resource to Beijing has not solved the capital's severe water crisis. During the last half-century more than 1,000 valuable freshwater lakes across the country have been lost completely, and over 75% of the remaining 20,000 lakes of various sizes are polluted. *Some rivers are so polluted by chemicals they can be set on fire with a match.* Furthermore, the water in some locations is dangerous even to "touch."

"At this point it is inevitable that the environmental situation will continue to deteriorate and cause a further rise in serious health problems including widespread hepatitis, liver and intestinal tract cancers and even male impotency. (For instance, almost 150,000,000 Chinese are currently estimated to be infected with the hepatitis virus.) Environmental difficulties are, of course, the unfortunate by-product of rapid industrialization. All societies that change from a farm-oriented regimen to one based on manufacturing experience regrettable, environmental consequences. Therefore, the current problems in China should not be considered novel. The important consideration is that disclosures of such information are strictly limited. Any open discussion will only cause panic and limit needlessly further progress developing the economy. Nothing must be allowed to thwart the exemplary achievements that have already been made.

"A variety of solutions for the water problem are currently being worked on. These include our intention one day to take most of the water from the Tibetan highlands and move it east and north across China. These highlands are the source of nine of the world's most important rivers such as the Brahmaputra in India and the

Mekong that nourishes much of South East Asia. It is not known what the impact will be on the many nations that depend on this water, although the migration of significant portions of their populations could occur.

"Regarding the overall status of the environment, the following, additional statistics can be noted. Because of the ongoing need to suppress disclosures of specific data, only those already public are used here. However, it should be realized that in some instances the current situation is more serious:

- 60% of the nation's 350 large and medium-sized cities are significantly polluted. Over 400 million people in urban areas regularly breathe badly polluted air. *One of our prestigious academies concluded that at times Beijing is barely suitable for human habitation.* Harbin often experiences air pollution 40 times the internationally accepted level, and on occasion the air can be considered almost lethal.

- The Bohai Sea, the important maritime hub near Beijing, that was known traditionally as the "fish warehouse," is essentially a dead sea. At one time more than a dozen varieties of valuable fish were harvested there. The spawning areas for these fish are now 100% polluted.

- 80% of the 600 large cities in China suffer water shortages on a regular basis, including such important metropolitan centers as Beijing and Tianjin.

- Lake Baiyangdian, the large freshwater lake essential to the ecology of the crop-growing North China Plain, is polluted. Known traditionally as the "Pearl of the North," the lake is still used for fish farming.

- The Yangtze, China's longest and most important river is rapidly turning "cancerous," three-fourths of all maritime species in the river having perished years ago. Of the 400 cities situated along the Yangtze, half utilize the river as their source of drinking water. This includes the delta area, which is the nation's economic powerhouse, and the cities of Shanghai, Chongqing, Wuhan and Nanjing. Each year more than 30,000,000,000 tons of industrial and human waste are deposited in the river, at least 80 percent untreated in any way. The enormously expensive construction of the much-heralded Three Gorges Dam has unfortunately greatly reduced the river's rate of flow and hence the ability to cleanse itself. This has caused a massive accumulation of algae that's accelerating the destructive process.

- Because the Yangtze is one of the principal sources of drinking water for Shanghai, the country's economic showplace, it has been necessary to pump water in ever-larger quantities from the aquifer beneath the city. This has caused significant, soil settlement along with infiltration of salt water into the aquifer. Eventually the accelerating rate of settlement could impact the city's numerous skyscrapers.

- Acid rain now falls regularly on more than 50% of China's cities (63% in southern part of the country).

- The spread of deserts has caused the loss of more than a quarter of China's limited, arable land. One-third of the country is now essentially a vast desert. The continued growth of these deserts is occurring at a rate 18 times the world average, and sandstorms are now 20 times more frequent than in the 1960s. Desertification currently threatens 400,000,000 people in 471 counties in eighteen provinces and regions.

- A massive desert continues to spread eastward across the North China plain, where much of the country's wheat is grown. It is rapidly nearing Beijing and one day will engulf Shenyang, the industrial center of 40 million people with consequences it is difficult to predict. Several times a year, massive sandstorms sweep over Beijing depositing more than 1,000,000 tons of dust and sand on the city.

- For years, grain production has been falling at an alarming rate so the country can no longer feed itself adequately. One-quarter of farmland is now polluted, which includes the widespread presence of such dangerous substances as toxic, heavy metals. A survey found that half of the restaurants in Guangzhou were serving rice seriously contaminated with cadmium. This substance is highly damaging to the human body, including the kidneys and also the skeletal bones where it tends to concentrate with regrettable consequences...."

And so under the leadership of the dedicated communists, it had become the cruel fate of the storied land of ancient China to decline inexorably into a terrible destruction. But always in the world's consciousness will linger familiar images of water-covered, rice fields - glasslike expanses tinged with the pale green of tender plants beneath the red ball of an eternal sun floating in the balmy mists of the tropical south. In this peaceful, ordered place peasants inseparable from the land had labored patiently for centuries to feed the rich cities of the Orient. Now all of that splendid largesse had been corrupted and brought to ruin in only a few, mad and wasteful decades.

In *Revelations*, "water" is often employed as a symbol for renewal and spiritual nourishment, a corollary of its essential role in nature itself - "a pure river of water of life, clear as crystal." (22:1). The Biblical text also speaks of these invaluable waters being perversely transformed into "the blood of a *dead man*...the rivers and fountains of waters; and they became as blood." (16:3-4) Of late, in China there were repeated episodes when expanses of important rivers, including the giant Yangtze, suddenly turned a menacing red color from pollution. One morning an estimated fifteen thousand, rotting pig carcasses turned up in one of the rivers that provides drinking water for Shanghai with its big-spending tourists. In essence, much of China's water resources were no longer life-giving at all but instead had been transformed into a lethal medium to be feared - in some places reported to be *"black"* as death itself.

According to China's own experts, substantial portions of the nation's forests (that once included some of the most beautiful stands of exotic trees) had over the years been destroyed by air pollution or deliberately cut down for various ignoble purposes. This included satisfying the world's insatiable need for cheap, disposable *chopsticks*. Near the end of the memorandum was a particularly gruesome example of China's escalating, environmental collapse - the insidious plague of rats. In many areas, including Hunan Province not far from Hong Kong, it has been reported that at times <u>billions</u> of rats are breeding uncontrollably. This nightmarish situation goes far beyond anything in the most outlandish horror novel. In some locales, such as scenic Dongting Lake, China's second largest freshwater lake, the rats have known to form a vast, grey carpet of tiny, squirming bodies. Moving inexorably over the land, they devour everything in the way. The intrepid farmers fight back valiantly and sometimes kill several tons of rats in a week. According to reliable sources, truckloads of the dead carcasses are sold regularly to fancy restaurants along the coast. The rodent meat, that can be diseased, is prepared in a variety of highly inventive ways. It is then served by waiters with impeccable manners on fine china and linen to the discriminating diners, who pay for the privilege with their high-limit credit cards. I have been told that with the right combination of spices and fancy garnishments, choice cuts of rat meat, including from those that inhabit sewers, can be quite succulent and pleasing to the eye. It is not uncommon for the chef to be praised by the appreciative diners for his exemplary efforts to please them.

17

I began to think that only a few weeks remained before the great war finally began. This left me with hardly any time to locate Lily, remove whatever information I could from the general's desk, and get the two of us out of the country. After returning from Shanghai, I spoke again with Gao, who learned from his mother that Lily was at a house belonging to their aunt. It's on the coast south of Hong Kong. He knows it well and was able to give me a detailed description. The house has four bedrooms, three of which are on the second floor and include the one where Lily usually stayed. It's on the corner, has a small balcony and can be reached from the ground. He was sure that armed guards would be there to thwart any attempt to rescue her.

I quickly came up with a plan on which I would risk everything. Fortunately I had André's boat that included the latest electronic equipment, including GPS. It was just what I needed to pull off the rescue, although it was obvious how difficult that was going to be. Probably I would have to overpower some guards, and if we got away, a manhunt would be unleashed immediately throughout China. Although the odds against me were enormous, this was my only chance, and I couldn't delay even a single day. The plan was to arrive late at night when everyone was asleep. With a rope I would climb up to her room on the second floor, take down the guards, and escape with her in the boat. Stealth and speed were essential. If I was lucky to have everything go as planned, Lily wouldn't be missed until later, and by then we would be far at sea. While it sounded simple enough, numerous things could go wrong, and at best it was a long shot.

After stocking the boat with supplies, I finalized the arrangements for Li Zhou and his family to leave the country. This included routing his money through a Moscow bank that in the past always provided excellent service in exchange for an exorbitant fee. Also I chartered a plane at the small airport that was little more than a dirt landing strip. It belonged to a well-connected smuggler, who regularly paid protection to the local authorities so he was free to do what he wanted. The Zhous' initial destination would be another, private airport in the Philippines. A flight across the South China Sea takes only a few hours, and from there, the rest would be easy.

That evening I destroyed all incriminating documents in both my office and apartment and sailed out of the harbor. About a mile offshore, the wind strengthened, and I put up the sails. The boat was controlled more easily than I expected, and soon I was making excellent time down the coast. My only concern was that at night I wouldn't be able to locate the right house. It was like finding a needle in an enormous haystack. Supposedly there was a buoy about a half-mile offshore almost directly in front of the house as well as a dock with a red light at the end.

To occupy the extra time, I read the memo obtained by Li Zhou, and what it told me was even more shocking than I expected.

"My dear comrades, the hour is fast approaching when our people will finally fulfill their long-awaited, historical destiny - a momentous event for which the most exacting preparations have been made over many years. At last China will break the shackles imposed for centuries by the outside world and respond to the command to make the great "move outward." Never again will our people be held in check by other nations more powerful than we are. Whether it was the Europeans, Americans or Japanese, they all exploited our weakness and took maximum advantage of our long-suffering people. During that time we were viewed as easily manipulated. However, history belongs to the most determined and ingenious of peoples, and we, Chinese, will demonstrate now our inherent superiority over other races and nations. Our unique

224

qualities will enable us to subjugate them, especially those that persecuted us. Thus we will finally assume our rightful place of dominance in the world.

"It is appropriate at this time to quote from the comments of our great, military thinker Chi Haotian, who helped to fashion many of the ideas that motivate us. These were expressed in speeches given several years ago by this prominent member of the Central Military Planning Commission and others.

As comrade Chi stated eloquently:

"The Chinese are different from other races on earth. We did not originate in Africa. Instead *we originated independently in the land of China.* The project of searching for the origins of the Chinese civilization, currently undertaken in our country, is aimed at a more comprehensive and systematic research on the origin, process and development of the ancient Chinese civilization....We can assert that we are the product of cultural roots of more than a million years, civilization and progress of more than 10,000 years, an ancient nation of 5000 years and a single Chinese entity of 2000 years.... Hitler's Germany once bragged that the German race was the most superior race on earth, but the fact is, our nation is far superior to the Germans.

"We all know that on account of our national superiority during the thriving and prosperous Tang Dynasty, our civilization was at the peak of the world. We were the center of world civilization, and no other civilization in the world was comparable to ours... Later on, because of our complacency, narrow-mindedness, and the self-enclosure of our own country, we were surpassed by Western civilization, and the center of the world shifted to the west... Comrade He Xin put it in his report to the Central Committee in 1988: it's the fact that the center of leadership of the world was located in Europe as of the 18th century, and later shifted to the United States in the mid-20th century, and then in the 21st century the center of leadership of the world will shift to the east of our planet. And the east, of course, mainly refers to China....therefore, if we refer to the 19th century as the British century, and the 20th century as the American Century, then the 21st century will be the Chinese century.

"To understand conscientiously this historical law and be prepared to greet the advent of the Chinese century is the historical mission of our party. As we all know, at the end of the last century we built the altar to the Chinese century in Beijing. At the very moment of the arrival of the new millennium, the collective leadership of the party's Central Committee gathered there for a rally, upholding the torches of Zhoukoudian, to pledge themselves to get ready to greet the arrival of the Chinese century. We are doing this to follow the historical law and setting the realization of the Chinese century as the goal of our party's endeavors.

"Germany was defeated in utter shame along with its ally, Japan. Why? We reached some conclusions at the study meetings of the Politburo, in which we were searching for the laws that govern the vicissitudes of the great powers and trying to analyze Germany's and Japan's rapid growth. When we decided to revitalize China based on the German model, we must not repeat the mistakes they made. Specifically, the following are the fundamental causes for their defeat: first, they had too many enemies all at once, as they did not adhere to the principle of eliminating enemies one at a time; second, they were too impetuous, lacking the patience and perseverance required for great accomplishments; third, when the time came for them to be ruthless, they turned out to be too soft, therefore leaving troubles that surfaced later on...So the fundamental reason for the defeat of Germany and Japan is that history did not arrange them to be the "lords of the earth," for they are, after all, not the most superior race.

"Ostensibly, in comparison, today's China is alarmingly

226

similar to Germany back then. Both of them regard themselves as the most superior races; both of them have a history of being exploited by foreign powers and are therefore vindictive; both of them have the tradition of worshiping their own authorities; both of them feel they have seriously insufficient living space.... Our Chinese people are wiser than the Germans because, fundamentally, our race is superior to theirs. As a result, we have a longer history, more people and larger land area. On this basis, our ancestors left us with the two, most essential heritages, which are atheism and great unity....What makes us different from Germany is that *we are complete atheists*....Maybe you have now come to understand why we recently decided to further promulgate atheism. If we let theology from the West into China and empty us from the inside, if we let all Chinese people listen to God and follow God, who will obediently listen to us and follow us?....Germany's dream to be "Lord of the Earth" failed, because ultimately, history did not bestow this great mission upon them. But the three lessons Germany learned from experience are what we ought to remember as we complete our historic mission and revitalize our race. The three lessons are: firmly grasp the country's living space; firmly grasp the party's control over the nation; and firmly grasp the general direction towards becoming the "Lord of the earth."

"*The first issue is living space.* This is the biggest focus of the revitalization of the Chinese race. In my last speech, I said that the fight over basic living resources (including land and ocean) is the source of the vast majority of wars in history...But the term "living space" is too closely related to Nazi Germany. The reason we don't want to discuss this too openly is to avoid the West's association of us with Nazi Germany, which could in turn reinforce the view that China is a threat. Therefore, in our emphasis on He Xin's new theory, "Human rights are just living rights," we only talk about "living" but not "space," so as to avoid using the term "living space." From the perspective of history the reason that China is faced with the issue of living space is because Western countries have developed ahead of Eastern countries. Western countries established colonies all the world, therefore giving themselves an advantage on the issue of living space. To solve this problem, *we must lead the Chinese people out of China, so they can develop outside of China.*

"The second issue is our focus on the leadership capacity of the ruling party....whether we can lead the Chinese people out of China is the most important determinant of the CCP's leadership position....After the June 4 riot (Tiananmen Square) was suppressed, we have been thinking about how to prevent China from peaceful evolution and how to maintain the Communist Party's leadership. We thought it over and over but did not come up with any good ideas. If we do not have good ideas, China will inevitably change peacefully, and we will all become criminals in history. After some deep pondering, we finally came to this conclusion: *Only by turning our developed national strength into the force of a fist striking outward - only by leading our people to go out - can we win forever the Chinese people's support and love of the Communist Party.* Our party will then stand on invincible ground, and the Chinese people will have to depend on the Communist Party... Therefore, the June 4 riot made us realize that we must combine economic development with preparation for war and leading the people to go out! Therefore, since then, our national defense policy has taken a 180 degree turn and we have since emphasized more and more "combining peace and war." *Our economic development is all about preparing for the need of war!* Publicly we still emphasize economic development as our center, but in reality, economic development has war at its center! We have made a tremendous effort to construct "the great Wall Project" to build up, along our coastal and land frontiers as well as around large and medium-sized cities, a solid *underground "great wall"* that can *withstand a nuclear war.* We are also storing all necessary war materials. Therefore, we will not hesitate to fight a Third World War so as to lead the people to go out and to ensure the party's leadership position. In any event, we, the CCP, will never step down from the stage of history! *We'd rather have the whole world, or even the entire globe, share life and death with us than step down from the stage of history!* Isn't there a 'nuclear bondage' theory? It means that since nuclear weapons have bound the security of the entire world, *all will die together if death is inevitable.* In my view, there is another kind of bondage, and that is the fate of our Party is tied up with that of the whole world. If we, the CCP, are finished, China will be finished, and the world will be finished.

"Comrade He Xin put forward a very fundamental judgment that is very reasonable. He asserted in his report to the Party Central Committee: the renaissance of China is in fundamental conflict with the western strategic interest, and therefore will inevitably be obstructed by the western countries doing everything they can. So, only by breaking the blockade formed by the Western countries headed by the United States can China grow and move towards the world! Would the United States allow us to go out to gain new living space? First, if the United States is firm in blocking us, it is hard for us to do anything significant to Taiwan and some other countries! Second, even if we could snatch some land from Taiwan, Vietnam, India, or even Japan, how much more living space can we get? Very trivial!

"We must also never forget what Comrade Deng Xiaoping emphasized: *"refrain from revealing the ambitions and put others off the track."* The hidden message is: we must put up with America; we must conceal our ultimate goals, hide our capabilities and await the opportunity. In this way, our mind is clear…. To resolve the issue of America we must be able to transcend conventions and restrictions. In history, when a country defeated another country or occupied another country, it could not kill all the people in the conquered land, because back then you could not kill people effectively with sabers or long spears, or even with rifles or

229

machine guns. Therefore, it was impossible to gain a stretch of land without keeping the people on that land... When Comrade Deng Xiaoping was still with us, the *Party's Central Committee had the perspicacity to make the right decision not to develop aircraft carrier groups and focus instead on developing lethal weapons that can eliminate mass populations of the enemy country*....This yellow land has reached the limits of its capacity. One day, who knows how soon it will come, the great collapse will occur at any time and more than half of the population will have to go.... The population, even if more than half dies, can be reproduced. But if the party falls, everything is gone, and forever gone! In Chinese history, in the replacement of dynasties, the ruthless have always won and the benevolent always failed....History has proved that any social turmoil is likely to involve many deaths. Maybe we can put it this way: *death is the engine that moves history forward*... Of course, a few people under the western influence have objected to shooting of prisoners of war and women and children. Some of them said, "It is shocking and scary to witness how many people approved of shooting women and children. Is everybody crazy?" Some others said, "the Chinese love to label themselves a peace-loving people, but actually they are the most ruthless people. The comments resonant of killing and murdering sends chills to my heart." Although there are not too many people holding this kind of viewpoint and they will not affect the overall situation in any significant way, we still need to strengthen the propaganda to respond to this kind of argument....

"Certainly, in spreading Comrade He Xin's views, we cannot publish the article in the party newspapers, in order to avoid raising the enemy's vigilance. He Xin's conversation (with Hong Kong businessmen) may remind the enemy that *we have grasped the modern science and technology, including "clean" nuclear technology, gene weapons technology as well as biological weapons technology, and we can use powerful measures to eliminate their populations on a large-scale.*

"The last problem I want to talk about is firmly seizing the preparation for military battle. Currently, we are at the crossroad of moving forward or backward. Some comrades saw problems flooding everywhere in our country - the corruption problem, the state-owned enterprise problem, the bank's bad accounts problem, environmental problems, society security problem, education problems, the AIDS problem, even the riots problem. These comrades vacillated in the determination to prepare for the military battle.... Marxism pointed out that violence is the midwife for the birth of the new society. *Therefore war is the midwife for the birth of the China century. As war approaches I'm full of hope for our next generation...*"

"Thus did our distinguished comrade state in eloquent terms the formidable task facing the Chinese people. Subsequently our inspired, former leader, Jiang Zemin cited certain, key steps that must be implemented before we are fully prepared for the upcoming battle to secure the new living space so our people can finally realize their historical destiny as the world's dominant power.

"These steps include a vigorous campaign to arouse the nationalistic feelings of the Chinese people. A key component was the Olympic games of 2008. In addition, the party membership has been carefully scrutinized for dependability and loyalty, and any member, who might oppose military action, moved aside. Over the years we have expanded rapidly the capabilities of the People's Armed Police in order to suppress the riots that now occur constantly across the country. Well-trained and heavily armed PAP are currently located in 156 cities and have shown themselves to be a very effective means of inflicting highly punitive action whenever necessary. Undoubtedly they will be able to deal with any potential uprising that might inhibit the war effort. Also, at this time troublesome, dissident elements are being rounded up and dealt with in an expeditious manner so they cannot cause problems.

"Immediately after hostilities commence, an Emergency

231

Act will be passed that confiscates all private property in China, including the peoples' savings and the assets of foreign businesses. The era of courting American business interests in order to gain access to their capital and technology is over. Fortunately, as we expected, they eagerly responded to our blandishments, hoping to make large profits from the Chinese market. This prospect blinded them to all, other considerations. As a result we were able in record time to overcome the substantial technological deficit in key areas so the nation could successfully modernize our military forces and with confidence go to war. Fortunately, the substantial cost is subsidized by the generous trade surplus based on a favorable currency relationship and also large amounts of investment funds, most of them from America. At this point, our technological expertise has reached a level that we no longer need to tolerate the presence of outsiders within our industries. Most of the employees in the companies controlled by these outsiders are Chinese, and they are more than capable of running the operations when they are seized. After the war commences, all foreign nationals will be rounded up and promptly deported. We anticipate a backlash in the outside business community regarding the seizure of property. However, this should not be viewed as a matter of concern since such a measure is a legitimate step in connection with any nation's war effort.

"Previously the CCP amended the Constitution to protect private property so outsiders would be encouraged to invest in China. However, this was done in a way that does not foreclose the government's ability to seize property in the event of war. The right to private property was referred to only as "inviolable." The key word "sacred" was removed, which permits confiscation in the event of a national emergency or war for the "sacred" purpose of protecting the nation.

"It should not be forgotten that for years we permitted almost unlimited access by foreign corporations, especially

232

American, to inexpensive Chinese labor. This enabled them to produce products very cheaply. In this way they made enormous sums of money. At the same time we tolerated extensive damage to the environment. All of this was, of course, done deliberately and with a wider purpose in mind. This includes both the rapid expansion of our industrial base and also to make foreigners dependent on our labor and the profligate use of our resources. Thus their own industrial capabilities were weakened significantly while key, industrial sectors were transferred to our shores.

"The plan of opening up our country to the outsiders so we could dominate important parts of the world economy has worked better than we anticipated. One aspect of the situation that deserves note is our acquisition of significant influence in America's corporations and financial institutions so we had access to the important information they possessed. This is especially true of certain Wall Street firms that have always been eager to please us. Over the years, under the guise of so-called engagement, we also placed large numbers of spies within America's academic circles and industrial base. Our ancient mentor, Sun Tzu, emphasized the invaluable contribution of spies. As he stated: 'what enables the wise sovereign and the good general to strike and conquer...is foreknowledge...Knowledge of the enemy's dispositions can only be obtained from other men...the dispositions of the enemy are ascertained through spies and spies alone.'

"What would Sun Tzu have said if he knew that we have been able to cloak the spy in the guise of the diligent investor or conscientious, corporate executive working comfortably beside those he seeks to destroy. It is obvious the West is not capable of understanding our capacity for long-range planning, in which an emphasis has been placed on cleverly misleading those we seek to dominate. This has been caused to a large extent by the West's prideful attitude and their belief in the superiority of their culture.

233

The expectation they would be able to influence us politically through trade and economic interaction was a naïve assumption on their part that caused them to overlook what was really taking place in plain view.

"Eventually the foreigners became so dependent on our largesse that they were reluctant to criticize the internal methods we used to control the citizenry and also our subversive activities in the worldwide community. Because of the size of the financial rewards, we knew it was a tradeoff they couldn't resist. For the Americans, the profit motive is at times all-consuming. Thus they even tolerated our program to eradicate the Falun Gong. Some in the West even did us the favor of denying repeatedly that such a program exists, questioning why the Chinese government would direct such strongly punitive methods against an apparently innocuous organization. However, the number adhering to this pacifist discipline began to outnumber those in the communist party. *It was feared correctly that eventually the Falun Gong ideology could have a significant, enervating impact on the nation's militaristic spirit* and the ability to successfully prosecute a large scale war. As a result, our former head of state, Jiang Zemin, wisely instituted the 610 office and the highly effective program to crush decisively the Falun Gong.

"In conclusion, the escalating internal problems that plague the nation, including the deteriorating environment and the perilous state of the nation's finances, demand decisive action. Unfortunately we underestimated the unpredictability of the world economy including the financial markets so beloved to the capitalists. As a result we did not comprehend the adverse impact these markets could produce on our own internal situation. The reversals that we continue to experience have caused us to depart from our original plan and accelerate the timetable for prosecuting the war. We cannot delay much longer or risk being overwhelmed by the problems confronting us. The numbers of riots, especially

234

those caused by large scale unemployment, continue to endanger the nation as well as the survival of the party. Through the decisive step of going to war, the ever-worsening internal situation will be quickly neutralized. In addition, the nation's historical destiny will finally be realized through the party's leadership as we create the vast, new living space for our people. Fortunately, both Western corporations and the Russians have generously shared their technology, providing us with the means to wage this great struggle. As a result we can proceed with confidence in the eventual outcome when China will finally assume its rightful place in the world.

"In regard to the specific details of this complex undertaking, nothing further will be provided in writing. All future communications on the subject will at the appropriate time be done verbally during private meetings. This will avoid the possibility of any unauthorized disclosures of vital information on the subject, especially regarding how and where the devastating blows will be delivered against our foes. In recent years, large amounts of highly confidential information have somehow been lost from the innermost recesses of the government that we could not stop. How this happened we have been unable to determine, although it appears to be the work of a very clever spy that we could never identify. If we did, he would have been dealt with in the harshest way possible. As a result, the concluding portion of the memorandum will be provided to only a select group that will conduct the required briefings. This additional section includes the specifics of the strategy and forces to be used. In conclusion, let us all be heartened that the hour to fulfill our nation's long-awaited destiny has finally arrived."

For several minutes I sat there staring at the papers clutched in my hands, hardly able to believe what I just read. It was madness on an epic scale, reflecting to the fullest the grand deviousness of the regime. In the speeches by leaders of China's military that reached the West, war was emphasized repeatedly, including reliance on the most destructive weapons. It was apparent that these individuals meant exactly what they stated in unmistakable terms. I realized now that soon the mythical horsemen of *Revelations* would ride forth again, and this time they would bring destruction to the earth like never before.

They appear out of the mist like the dead
coming to life in a night graveyard -
silhouettes, gaunt and black, etched by lightning.
Why are such creatures here now
led by the rider on the pale horse
whose companion is Hell,
their power to kill with sword and hunger
and with the ravenous beasts of the earth?
Who with evil incantations
has summoned these grotesque mutations
that live on in a decaying chrysalis, never to die?
Under the hoods of ragged capes
are those faces or only the flash of disembodied eyes
terrible with an unquenchable fire -
minds that are furnaces.
In awe and fear we gaze at them
perplexed by tales of history's distant fields
when the horsemen were magnificent
under colored banners,
silver and gold armor brilliant in the sunlight.
With the beating of great drums that shake the earth,
they thunder out of the mist
aflame with breastplates of fire,
the heads of their horses the flaming heads of lions.
Soon all is engulfed in chaos and terror
until exhaustion and death take hold.
And when the fiery pulse throbbing against the sky

is finally gone beyond the horizon,
there is only an eerie silence
and time to wait for morning.
But the sun returns to warm only blackened land
and the skeletons of unrecognizable things
as if the earth in all its splendor
had been plucked bare by giant, ravenous crows.
And for those still living,
there is no sustenance or shelter -
witnesses to history's cruel, oft-repeated tale
that leaves only desolation and orphans,
who wonder pitifully
if the songbird will ever be heard again
or lovers seen beside the softly-running brook,
knowing that the horsemen will always return -
until one last, long and terrible night…

18

Early in the morning I reached the coastline where the GPS coordinates indicated that the house belonging to Lily's family should be located. After finding what I thought was the correct buoy, I took down the sails and proceeded by motor. With nighttime binoculars I scanned the shoreline, wondering what I would do if this wasn't the right place. In the darkness all of the houses looked similar. Staying a couple of hundred feet from the shore, I finally spotted a dock with a dim, red light at the end. Slowing down, I moved towards it cautiously trying to make as little noise as possible. With relief, I realized this was the right location and could hardly believe my good luck.

Instead of mooring at the dock, I dropped anchor offshore where the boat wouldn't be noticed and rowed the rest of the way in a dinghy. By the time I was on the lawn in front of the house, it was almost four a.m.. There were lights on the first floor, although it appeared that as yet no one was awake. Cautiously I moved nearer, hoping there wasn't a dog that would wake up everyone. The sliding door to the small, corner balcony on the second floor was open, although there was no light inside. Hopefully that was the room where Lily was staying. If someone else was there, it would be a disaster. As I moved closer, every sound seemed magnified, and I was sure that at any moment I would be discovered. After several attempts I secured a rope to the railing of the balcony and climbed up there. Slipping into the room, I saw Lily asleep in a large, double bed. Cautiously I approached not wanting to startle her. A few more steps, and I was beside the bed. Reaching down, I put my hand gently over her mouth, and with a start she tried to sit up.

"It's me, Lawrence. Everything's all right," I whispered and taking my hand away, held her tightly for a moment.

"I knew that somehow you'd find me," she said, feeling so

warm and tender in my arms. "The guard's just outside the door. He drinks heavily at night and probably is asleep."

She got out of the bed and dressed quickly. From the balcony I lowered her to the ground and then jumped down beside her. Holding hands, we ran to the dock and climbed into the dinghy. The house was still quiet, and I realized the plan had worked perfectly. I didn't have to use my gun, and fortunately we would get away undetected. As I rowed back to the boat, the first light of day appeared in the distance. Many people in China get up early, and if I had arrived later, we never would have made it. I put up all the sails to catch as much wind as possible, and by the time it was completely light, we were already out of sight. For the first time since leaving Hong Kong I was able to relax. I noticed how drawn and pale Lily looked and assumed it was from being cooped up inside.

"I never would have believed such a thing is possible," she suddenly said and bursting into tears, put her face in her hands.

"Everything will be fine. Don't worry. We're going to leave China and go to the States. You'll love it there, and just think how much Gao will enjoy visiting us," I said and briefly held her again.

"I saw the pictures, and you can't imagine how awful she looked," Lily said and continued to cry.

"What are you talking about?"

"Topsy," she answered referring to the beautiful, teenage girl who was the daughter of her aunt's cook. Occasionally Topsy came to Lily's apartment where I met her, and a few times we all had lunch together. The two of them had become very close, and Lily often took her to Hong Kong's best stores to buy the latest clothes. Recently she decided to pay for the girl's university education that was supposed to start in the fall. "Topsy was like my little sister. I had no idea she had become a Falun Gong practitioner. She was arrested by the police while handing out brochures in a park. She refused to renounce her beliefs and was sent off to one of the detention camps for re-education. As you've probably heard, if someone persists in their beliefs, they are imprisoned and even killed, the younger, healthy ones murdered for their organs. Until now, I didn't want to believe the rumors that something so terrible was really happening in China. While I was at the house, cook told me all about it. I wondered why I hadn't heard anything from Topsy for weeks. I thought she'd gone on a trip. After she was arrested, cook implored my aunt to help free her. After all, poor Topsy hadn't done anything. Aunt spoke to father who refused to intervene. He said that she was being detained according to the official state policy being implemented by the 6-10 office. I can't believe that my own father could be so cruel. He even wanted aunt to fire the old woman who has worked loyally for the family all these years.

"People from their village went to the camp and tried to bribe the officials to let Topsy go. However, she had already received the required, medical examinations and her organs listed officially with the hospital system. If she wasn't available when required, everyone running the camp would be subject to discipline. It was only a matter of time before they came for her. The organs of people her age are in great demand. What makes the whole thing even worse is that this terrible atrocity is ultimately for the benefit of the military," she rambled on, and briefly the parallel to Hitler's militaristic SS and their death camps came to mind. "Afterwards, in exchange for a big bribe the villagers were allowed to view the body before it was thrown into an incinerator to destroy the evidence. Some pictures were taken secretly, and cook showed me one of them. For a couple of days I felt ill. You remember how pretty Topsy was. Instead she had been turned into a hollowed-out shell with crude incisions all over her body. Most of her internal organs were gone as well as her eyes. As long as I live, I'll never forget what she looked like. It was horrible! How could any Chinese citizen be treated in such a barbaric fashion?" she asked and continued to sob.

At last, Lily could no longer ignore the atrocities that for years had been perpetrated throughout her country and also the connection to the military and her own father. I knew what a terrible shock it must be for her. The situation was particularly reprehensible because many of the stolen organs were purchased by foreigners, who willingly flocked in large numbers to China and paid handsomely for transplants. It was as if tourists had lined up at the gates of Auschwitz and Dachau to purchase for personal use some of the body parts removed from the helpless victims of the Holocaust. Although for years, compelling evidence of the deliberate campaign of murder for profit conducted in China's military hospitals and other, medical facilities continued to reach the West, the information received hardly any attention in the media.

"To think my own father wouldn't lift a hand to help Topsy. He has great influence and could have easily gotten the poor girl released so she'd still be alive. But he didn't want to act contrary to official policy. He once had such a great love of the Chinese people and wanted so much to protect the nation. That's one of the reasons he became a soldier. But somehow along the way he became separated from the people so he no longer feels anything for them and what they are being forced to endure.

"I don't understand how he could have become so callous. But now I realize that another side of him has taken over that I was never aware of. Although he knows how much I love you, he's adamant in his opposition to our being together. He acts like he hates you, and it's only because you're an American. It doesn't matter to him that he's breaking my heart. Even mother is unable to influence him. Apparently he's concerned that our relationship makes him look bad among his associates. Now that takes precedence even over his own daughter's happiness. When he finds out that I got away, he'll be furious. He's used to making

241

people do whatever he wants, and now for the first time he hasn't succeeded. I intend never to see him again. It would have been so easy for him to prevent Topsy from being butchered. How can doctors, who are sworn to be healers, do something so horrible to such a wonderful person?"

"Try not to think about it, although I know that's difficult. Ahead is our new life together, and you'll never have to worry about such terrible things again," I said, certain that a wonderful future awaited us in America. Unfortunately there remained one, last hurdle to be completed before we escaped, and at last I could put behind me all those dark years that I thought would never end.

"I didn't have any doubts that you'd rescue me," she said, although I remained silent, unable to stop thinking about that poor girl murdered for merely being a pacifist. In a vivid way the persecution of the Falun Gong was a deliberate attempt by the regime to mock humanitarian values and demonstrate its superiority. Unfortunately poor Topsy was no different from countless others who had experienced the same, cruel fate. How awful to endure such misery, knowing that you have fallen into the hands of the truly heartless and all is lost. For years this thought troubled me constantly, and now I gazed at the tranquil sea, trying to imagine what it would be like to experience such utter hopelessness.

> *Gone forever* - *sunlit clouds above the salty sea*
> *drifting away into the glory of days end,*
> *the birds completely free soaring with grace.*
> *In the windowless room*
> *a fetid smell lingers in the damp air,*
> *bare lights peering down on those below,*
> *who listen with dread*
> *to distant, muffled voices and*
> *the rattle of the metal carts —*
> *the production line.*

Nothing more - night and day after day.
Their blood has been drawn to match the type,
and now there is only time to wait,
always cold with fear,
knowing that soon the strangers will come.
Time to wait and dream
about sweet moments lost forever -
the scent of roses in a walled garden,
the touch of a kind hand, soft, parted lips...
One night or perhaps morning,
they finally came with masks over their faces
like bandits on a dark road.
She was strapped to a cart
and moved swiftly down silent corridors
to a small, hot room,
her heart pounding as if it would burst
and send blood into her eyes.
And then the terrible pain,
her mind fleeing into the blinding light above -
a tiny bird impaled on a sharp, steel rod.
She never saw the flaming square of the furnace,
her end to be thrown into fire,
in time followed by unknown millions
as if suddenly the whole world
plunged into a white-hot sun
dispatched there by the anonymous, little men
attending the furnace door.

19

On my cell phone I finally reached Gao, who was overjoyed to learn that Lily was free. He wanted to hear all the details of how we pulled off her escape and agreed to meet us at the yacht club. On the way up the coast I debated with myself whether to go to the Chans' apartment in order to find the other documents. I needed only a few minutes and was sure they would be there. I didn't want to take the risk, especially since Lily and I were free now to leave the country. Nonetheless, I couldn't disregard the fact that something of such enormous consequence to America as well as the entire world was involved. Her parents always went out in the morning for a few hours. If they weren't there, I could get into the apartment with Lily's key and quickly take what I wanted from the general's desk. If I was caught, it would be the end.

As we approached the yacht club, I saw Gao on the dock. Lily jumped up and waved, and he waved back eagerly. I realized how much I had gotten to like him. My original assessment of Gao as a shallow Hong Kong playboy was totally wrong. Finally we reached the dock, and Lily ran over and hugged him.

"You made it. What a relief," he said happily.

"Your directions were perfect. The light on the dock really helped. Fortunately I got there just before dawn when everyone was asleep. It went like clockwork."

"I'll bet the guard was furious when he discovered that I was no longer there. He was always so mean," Lily said proudly.

"Phone your parents' house and see if they're gone," I said to Gao.

"What for?"

"I'll explain some other time," I said as Lily looked at me with alarm.

The servant who answered confirmed that the Chans just

left. There was no time to waste. I had to get over there immediately, and then Lily and I would be on our way to our new life abroad.

"Why do you want to go to my parent's house? It's too dangerous. Everyone is looking for me," Lily asked, her eyes filled with apprehension. "What are you after?"

"There's something I have to find. It's important and could save many lives. I have to do this."

"But how could you know what's there?" she said, probably realizing that I was involved in matters she never suspected.

"Believe me it's worth it. Just trust me," I said, briefly holding her hand, and will always wish I never uttered those words. "I need your key. I'll go by myself while you wait in the car. If I'm not back in ten minutes, take the car and leave."

"I won't let you go in there by yourself."

"No."

"I don't care. From now on, I'm going wherever you go," she insisted while we hurried to the car.

As we drove through the tunnel, Lily kept looking at me nervously.

"I have to know why we're going to the house?" she insisted.

"There's going to be..." I answered but paused. "A war, a great and terrible war."

"When?"

"That's what I have to find out."

"But how could you know such a thing?"

"I have confidential sources. Your father is involved in the planning. Countless lives could be lost," I answered, aware of the effect my words were having on her. She started to say something but instead merely slumped down as if crushed.

In Kowloon we parked a short distance from the Chans'

building. There's a back entrance used mostly by servants, and while riding up in the elevator, I realized I never felt more nervous in my entire life. With Lily's key I opened the back door, and leaving her in the kitchen with the two servants preparing lunch, I hurried down the hall to the general's study. Reaching his desk, I carefully opened the drawers worried I might not find anything. Fortunately the folder containing the seal of the Chinese government was still there, and in it the papers I'd already seen. And then beneath them I spotted a folder with an additional document and realized it was the one I was looking for - the invaluable, last section of the war memorandum. I could hardly contain myself. In spite of all the efforts to protect this priceless document, it was now in the hands of an American agent and would soon be on its way to Washington. Quickly I looked through the other drawers to see what else I could find and spotted a folder marked with a large red "X" on the front. I suspected it contained their biggest secret of all that few, even in the government, knew about. Stuffing all of papers in a large envelope, I glanced nervously at my watch and hurried from the room. I had been there less than two minutes.

"Stop!" a voice called sharply as I started down the hallway. I froze and turned slowly, seeing a man in a military uniform who stood in the living room with a gun pointed right at my chest. I didn't have a chance.

"Go away. You're interfering with us. I will report you to my father. He will have you arrested," Lily called as she ran from the kitchen and stepped in front of me, making herself a shield. I tried to push her out of the way. But at that moment the guard fired, and she staggered and fell on her back. I quickly pulled out my gun and emptied it at the guard, who went down discharging his gun into the ceiling. Kneeling beside Lily, I saw the excruciating pain in her eyes and then the blood coming from her chest.

"I didn't want him to harm you," she said struggling to

breathe. "So many have been hurt - so many, and no one can stop it."

"Oh Lily, dear Lily," I said unable to hold back the tears. And then her head rolled to the side, her eyes taking on the hard, lifeless stare of death. "Please, no," I gasped as her blood spread over the floor. I kept shaking her limp arm and calling to her, but there was no response. Realizing that all her youthful promise was lost forever, I placed her arms across her chest and gently kissed her cheek. There was nothing that I could do. I had to leave but for a while couldn't move. Minutes dragged by ominously. The servants came from the kitchen to stare in horror. I continued to hold Lily's hand that already was turning cold. Seeing my mother's rings on her fingers, I took them off and kissed her cheek again. Standing up, I staggered and then ran to the kitchen and out the door.

I felt like I was living a nightmare. Having just lost Andrei, I now had lost Lily too. Knowing how dangerous it was to go to the Chan's apartment, I never should have allowed her to accompany me. Nonetheless, without her I would be dead. The guard had me in his sights and was about to fire when she intervened, sacrificing herself to save the person she loved. We could have left immediately in the boat and enjoyed years of happiness in the West. Instead I had to push my luck one time too many. Life had handed me a priceless treasure that carelessly I threw away, and I couldn't stop thinking of the horrible stare in her once-beautiful eyes.

Somehow I had to keep from falling apart. All that remained was to get the documents to the Consulate and then escape in the boat. While driving back through the tunnel, I recalled her words filled with pain and bewilderment - "so many have been hurt, and no one can stop it." Yes, so many, unknown and wretched creatures hidden away in China's vast system of desolate camps, legions of the tormented known only to God. And now the world would soon pay the ultimate price for all these years their cruel fate had been ignored.

Back on the island, I stopped at the yacht club and in the boat copied all the documents. I then drove to the Consulate and deposited the envelope in the mail drop. While returning to the club, I tried to drive in a manner that wouldn't attract attention, expecting at any moment to be pursued by a police car with its lights flashing. Fortunately I reached the boat without incident and then left the harbor, realizing that I was going to get away. On the radio there was a news bulletin that included my description given by a doorman who saw me running down the street. It would be a while before it was determined that I was the same person and also that I stole the war plan. I wondered what the reaction would be among the high command when they realized the details of their ingenious scheme were known in the West. Perhaps they would call everything off, although after so many years of careful preparation, the situation had gone too far. The regime had no choice except to proceed, hoping that no one believed that in this advanced, modern era anyone would be crazy enough to start another major war, especially one involving nuclear weapons.

20

As night descended, I continued to sea in the direction of the Philippines, passing several, enormous container ships on their way to the Chinese coast. Because of the heavy ship traffic, I would have to stay up all night to avoid a collision. Slowly the sun set gloriously. Darkness settled over the ocean, and with only the jib, I was able to capture the moderate breeze. Locking the steering wheel, I went down to the cabin, turned on the overhead light, and eagerly examined my copy of the papers taken from the general's desk.

I soon realized the war was something that no one, including myself, had expected. Instead of an attack against Taiwan, Japan or even the United States, the Chinese military was about to launch a massive land invasion in the opposite direction in order to conquer the enormous, Siberian land mass east of the Ural Mountains. The emphasis on Taiwan and the recent provocations regarding islands and drilling rights in the South China Sea were merely a convenient distraction intended to throw everyone off. This includes the Russians, who of late were so determined to alienate themselves from the West while working with the Chinese on many, important projects, including those involving natural resources. In essence, they had systematically increased their vulnerability to the nation that in reality was their worst enemy.

As I reviewed those crucial documents, the plan in its various aspects seemed so logical, and I wondered why something like this had been overlooked. It was a classic case of misdirection. For a couple of decades everyone was focused on Taiwan and never considered another possibility. Attacking Russia made far more sense. The vast, sparsely populated Siberian land mass was the answer to all of China's overwhelming problems, especially the need for unspoiled living space as well as lots of fresh, arable land.

The parallel was obvious to the fascists of Nazi Germany and Imperial Japan, both of whom had coveted Asia's enormous landmass.

"My dear comrades, our great. long-awaited adventure to establish China as the world's preeminent country is about to commence. Afterwards history will never be the same, the mighty Chinese people having finally taken the crucial steps that will enable our nation to attain its rightful position of dominance. For more than a generation we have focused attention on the Taiwan issue and various grievances with Japan and the United States. This was intentional and effectively distracted everyone's attention from our true objective.

"The land of traditional China is exhausted and no longer capable of sustaining its huge population. It will take generations to repair the damage to the environment from rapid industrialization, and in some areas the damage is irreparable, especially to the water supply. We came to the conclusion that the only viable solution is to acquire large amounts of new, unspoiled living space. In prior, policy statements over the years that were allowed to become public, emphasis was placed on conquering areas other than our real objective. These include America, Canada and Australia. However, for colonization purposes it would be impossible to move large numbers of people to these faraway locations.

"To the immediate north of China is a huge, open area that is sparsely populated and rich in resources, including petroleum, coal and natural gas for our ever-increasing energy needs. Also, much of this land is adaptable to large-scale farming. As you know, in recent years China has steadily lost arable land and can no longer grow sufficient crops. This unfortunate situation can only worsen until in the near future we become dependent entirely on foreign nations, including America, to feed our population. This is totally unacceptable.

"Over centuries much of the Siberian landmass was seized unfairly from the Chinese people by the rapacious Russians. Utilizing their overwhelming strength, they imposed on us punitive treaties that established an unjust status quo. It is only right and fair that our people reclaim this stolen prize and utilize it productively. While China struggles against ever-worsening environmental problems of pollution, desertification and overcrowding, this vast territory is hardly used. It represents an inequitable situation that we intend to correct. The acquisition of this area will more than double China's territory, relieve the pressure of our ever-expanding population, and allow us to grow to a sufficient size that our nation will represent at least half of the world's population. It will not be our intention to conquer all of Russia but only the territory east of the Ural Mountains. This will leave Russia with more than adequate territory to support its dwindling population. We do not seek the destruction of the Russian nation but only the reduction of its territory to an appropriate size. While we are a nation on the ascendancy, they like so many others are a declining people.

"The Russians do not have the military capability to defend the enormous area they currently occupy. Their Far East district is more than 2500 miles from the Urals. The logistics of waging a protracted war so far from their main base will be insurmountable. In contrast, most of this territory is immediately accessible from China's northern border, and we will not face any difficulties quickly moving troops and war materials into the contested area. Historical necessity dictates that the Russians should not be permitted to hold on to this underutilized resource that we can rightly put to more productive use. It will be Russia's choice whether the upcoming conflict turns into a brief struggle over territory or one for survival between our two societies. Either way, it is obvious that China will prevail. It is not anticipated that Russia will attempt a war of attrition they cannot win. Our population is more than ten times larger, and such a war would not work in their favor. At this time we have sufficient weapons to destroy Russia completely. It would be suicidal for them to oppose us.

"Their only hope of thwarting a land invasion was the technological advantage that at one time they enjoyed over us. However, that advantage disappeared long ago. Important in that regard has been the ongoing sale to China of their military equipment. The motivation was apparently rooted in their hatred of America and the desire to form a counter alliance. It is a credit to our carefully executed policies that they overlooked completely the real threat to them. The fact they willingly strengthened our capabilities demonstrates the skill with which we managed the campaign of disinformation.

"For many years, large amounts of military hardware and supplies have been stored in the tunnel system in the northern part of our country. As you know, these were excavated after the Korean War in anticipation of a possible conflict with the United States that would have involved massive, aerial bombing similar to what devastated the Korean peninsula. These supplies will be more than adequate to support the upcoming war effort. In addition, we have recently excavated additional, large, underground areas beneath 35 of our major cities. These massive shelters average 200,000 square meters and can each accommodate 100,000 to 200,000 people. The area beneath Beijing is over 20,000,000 square meters and particularly important because it interconnects with the main tunnel network. There is also the 1,000,000 square meter shelter beneath Shenyang. These facilities, that include electricity, water, foodstuffs and hospital supplies, will afford protection in the event there is an exchange of nuclear weapons with Russia. The shelters are only for select party members, their families, government officials and essential personnel. They are not for the general populace. In addition, there are the many new, unoccupied

252

cities that were constructed recently across the country. The foreigners refer to them in a cavalier fashion as "ghost cities," never guessing that they are intended to provide immediate replacements for any of our current cities that are destroyed during the war.

"Our military plan is for a surprise land attack in which the primary objective will be to trap and quickly exterminate Russia's limited military resources in the Far East. This can be done quite easily. At this time our overall land forces outnumber the Russians by a factor of at least six to one. At the same time we only need to deploy and supply our much larger force in a limited area. In comparison, the logistical problems facing the Russians are insurmountable. Although we anticipate some losses, the Russians will be rapidly exhausted and forced to capitulate to our demands.

"Based on reasonable estimates, they cannot replace more than a small portion of their available force. In contrast, our reserves are virtually unlimited, numbering in the tens of millions. Because of the fervent nationalism of the Chinese people, it will not be difficult to enlist this vast, human resource to overwhelm the enemy. Ultimately it is anticipated that as many as *"200 million"* of our people will be sent across the border- most of them for the purpose of colonizing the conquered land.

"The initial phase of the military operation will involve only a limited portion of our land army heading north near the Khingan Mountain Range - the objective to quickly isolate the Far Eastern district. Thus the entire area will immediately be placed in an indefensible position. At the same time the Trans-Siberian Railroad, that runs near the Chinese border, will be severed so the Russians will be unable to use it. This 2500 mile logistical pathway cannot be defended effectively against air attack.

"It is our intention to confine most of the campaign to the area that is attacked initially, where we enjoy an advantage in every respect. Based on their actions in response to our prior activities

253

along the border, we expect that the Russians will quickly commit most of their available forces in the hope of achieving a quick victory. We will encourage them to take such a self-defeating step, holding back most of our soldiers who will remain hidden in the tunnel system. At all times the full extent of our strength will be obscured, creating the illusion that we can be easily defeated. In addition, the Russian troops will at all times be fully exposed and face the added disadvantage of engaging in combat after traveling such a long distance. The battle will be conducted in a manner that holds out the illusion the Russians are winning, in this way encouraging them to squander quickly their limited resources. No doubt, they will be unable to resist taking the "bait." When it is concluded that a sufficiently large number of their troops is involved, we will quickly eliminate the entire force with our new super-weapon.

"At that point a second wave of Chinese troops will emerge and move north utilizing a route west of the Altai Mountains onto the southern Siberian plain preventing reinforcements, especially by rail. This will complete the disposition of our forces, most of which will be held in reserve in order to deal with any unforeseen contingencies. No doubt, the Russians will also try to oppose this second group, although whatever resources are still available to them will not be sufficient to impede our progress. As a result the campaign should come to a prompt conclusion with only limited Chinese casualties. In contrast, the Russian losses will be enormous and produce a devastating effect on their morale.

"Attached is a schedule of troops and equipment and how they will be utilized and in what sequence. This document cannot be copied. All units and supporting, civilian personnel will be funneled through the tunnel system. They will be concealed and protected until the last moment from air attack and the element of surprise preserved.

"As stated, our intention is to confine the conflict to the

Far Eastern area where we can easily re-supply our forces and prevent them from being overextended. The remaining land east of the Urals will be added at a later time. We fully anticipate that with its limited resources, Russia will soon be forced to accept the new status quo. It will be to their advantage to do so once they understand that the Chinese forces do not intend to invade European Russia or impair its ability to survive as a country.

"A key component of the campaign is our new weapon that will be employed as necessary in order to guarantee success. This remarkable tool of war will astonish the world community. Also it will help convince everyone, including the Russians, that is futile to oppose our ambitions. They have no idea that in a cavern beneath a mountain in northern China, we have for years manufactured and stored large amounts of this ingenious device. After acquiring the technology on which it is based, we promptly finalized our war plan knowing that this extraordinary device could be relied on to assure complete success. In essence, we have the capacity now *to annihilate quickly and efficiently as many Russians as necessary as well as anyone else who opposes us, including all undesirables in the conquered area that we intend to colonize.*

"Recently the world's attention has been distracted by other events, including the widespread violence in the Middle East that covertly we have encouraged. Furthermore we believe that in the preparation of our war plan all eventualities have been considered, and we will quickly achieve complete success. A great day for both the party and the country is now upon us, and the first, crucial step about to be taken that will enable China to fulfill its long-awaited, historic role as the world's dominant people ascendant above all others."

Finally I knew the details of their diabolical scheme and thought how clever it was, especially the reliance on the vast tunnel system developed during Mao Zedong's reign. Located in the northern part of the country, it is estimated to extend hundreds of miles. Supposedly some of these enormous caverns, excavated at considerable human cost, are large enough to hold a significant portion of the nation's war materials and personnel. For years, I was aware that large, additional underground facilities were being created all over the country that also include hidden, submarine bases along the coast. For some reason few in the West bothered to question why the Chinese would embark on such a costly project, adding so much, additional space to a system that supposedly they would never use - that is, unless, they intended one day to initiate a major war that ultimately might involve nuclear weapons.

Also the construction of so many, unoccupied "ghost" cities appeared to be merely a profligate waste of resources to inflate GDP statistics. However, like everything done by the regime, those cities (in the aggregate almost a small nation in itself) was an integral part of their overall plan. The ones that survived in tact would provide invaluable living accommodations for many of those displaced from the areas devastated by the coming war.

It is generally not known that Russia never ended its own preparations for a potential nuclear conflict in spite of the fact the cold war supposedly ceased long ago. In the Urals 3000 feet beneath Yamantau Mountain in the Beloretsk area, they have for decades continued to build a giant, underground city estimated to cover over 400 square miles. It contains sufficient room for tens of thousands (perhaps as many as 60,000 people) and even has an underground railroad system. A similar but smaller site exists in the Kovinsky Mountains. In addition, hundreds of emergency bomb shelters are rumored to have been constructed in and around Moscow as much as 15 meters underground. Supposedly some are large enough to hold upwards of 1000 people. Recently Russia also constructed a major, underground command center that includes a supercomputer for data processing. Thus it is apparent that neither

China or Russia ever abandoned completely the insane notion that nuclear war is a viable strategy of state policy.

I also realized how closely the Chinese war plan embodied the principles espoused in Sun Tzu's "Art of War," the great treatise of their military thinking. In essence, it emphasizes two, key concepts: "All warfare is based on *deception*" and the systematic use of "*spies.*" Thus, "Let your plans be dark and impenetrable as night..."

Years ago, I carefully read "The Art of War." It is a remarkable document, and immediately several, key points came to mind:

- " The general who is skilled in defense *hides in the most secret recesses of the earth*, making it impossible for the enemy to estimate his whereabouts. This being so, the places that he shall hold are precisely those that the enemy cannot attack."

-"Rapidity is the essence of war. Take advantage of the enemy's unreadiness."

- "Move only if there is a real advantage to be gained."

- "He will win who knows when to fight and when not to fight."

- "*Whoever is second in the field and has to hasten to battle will arrive exhausted...* entice him with a bait."

- "The best thing of all is to *take the enemy's country whole and in tact*, to shatter and destroy is no good."

- "What enables the good general to strike and conquer... is *foreknowledge*... Knowledge of the enemy's dispositions can only be obtained from other men... *Spies are a most important element in war...*"

While China's ambitious plan of conquest was rooted in Sun Tzu's thinking, the West out of naivete and at times blind greed had greatly facilitated the process, especially in regard to espionage. In fact, at times the governments of the West seemed incapable of grasping what should have been obvious. Fortunately the documents detailing China's strategy were at the Consulate and would soon be headed to Washington. Hopefully America wouldn't be caught again by surprise, although I couldn't be sure that assumption was correct. Unfortunately over the years most of the top secret documents that I obtained at great, personal risk had been largely ignored. Now I faced the disheartening prospect that all the sacrifice to acquire their war plan might be in vain, including the agonizing fact that my beloved Lily was dead.

I wondered about the reaction in the outside world when the cruel deeds of the communist regime were finally known in all their gruesome details. Probably it will never be possible to uncover the full extent of the crimes committed in China's vast system of detention camps and psychiatric hospitals. Nonetheless, I am sure that after awakening from a prolonged state of denial, the world community will try belatedly to justify itself. At the same time all sorts of journalists and intellectuals will no doubt seek research grants and book contracts while expressing an appropriate revulsion. Thus a whole new industry of indignation will flower after the fact as the recently enlightened eagerly vie with one another to demonstrate an appropriate concern for the fate of man. Also comparisons will probably be made to Auschwitz, the Soviet Gulag, the killing fields of Cambodia and other dark places of mass cruelty during our supposedly enlightened era. Of course, the question can be raised about where all these indignant individuals were for so many years when large numbers of well-documented atrocities of the worst sort were committed in China, especially to peace-loving groups such as the Falun Gong. However, as everyone knows, at any time there are always lots of things to be offended about on humanitarian grounds, and it's wise to time one's indignation correctly for maximum advantage.

With trepidation I opened the file marked ominously with a large red "X" and learned the final detail of their monstrous scheme. In a cavern beneath an obscure mountain in northern

China, the PLA had been manufacturing and storing large quantities of "neutron bombs," the super-weapon they were relying on to eliminate quickly anyone who opposes them. In essence, a regime, that was the greatest mass murderer in history, possessed the most lethal, killing machine ever devised by the human mind. And now the magical power at the very heart of creation would be perverted in order to inflict death and destruction on a truly epic scale.

Years ago, I read a scientific article that reviewed the publicly available information about the "neutron bomb," a compact, hydrogen bomb developed in the West for use on the battlefield. In contrast to other forms of nuclear weapons that devastate a large geographical area, *this "enhanced radiation device" mainly kills living entities while causing only limited, physical damage.* The blast effects are confined to a relatively small area around the epicenter while the lethal radiation extends out as much as 1.5 miles or more depending on the payload. Thus, a few, neutron bombs can quickly eliminate an entire, modern army or all the occupants in a city, while leaving largely intact much of the area occupied by those people. Immediately I recalled Sun Tzu's emphasis on the importance of taking "the enemy's territory whole and intact." Also, as he stated, "no country [ever] benefited from prolonged warfare." In essence, the neutron bomb amounted to a priceless gift enabling the Chinese military to achieve a quick, total success.

Any attempt to protect against the radiation emitted by such a bomb is difficult because of the thickness and density of the materials required. Modern, armored vehicles, including tanks, afford limited protection and in some respects only intensify the deadly radiation. In comparison to chemical and biological weapons, a neutron bomb is a far more effective means of eliminating large numbers of people, especially if the objective is colonization. With chemical or biological weapons, the contested area can be contaminated for decades or even longer. Similarly, the lingering radioactivity from a standard atomic or hydrogen bomb only compounds the problem of the widespread, initial destruction.

Exposure to a neutron bomb causes death quickly or over a few days at the most. In essence, an army subject to such an attack would perish rapidly while being unable to protect itself, the destructive results irreversible for both a defending army and/or the indigenous population. The long-term effects of neutron bombs on a biologically diverse, geographical area have never been accurately determined. Although all genes and their chromosomes are susceptible to rapid mutation because of radiation, different forms of life do not respond in an identical fashion. In areas where the dosage is not high enough to be fatal, highly unusual genetic consequences can be anticipated. Thus a *significant alteration of existing life forms would likely occur in the ecosystem* under such an attack and in time produce highly bizarre and even monstrous mutations.

It was thought that no nation would ever deploy the neutron bomb on a large scale. I realized this assumption had proven to be completely naïve. In comparison, the extermination methods employed in Auschwitz, the Russian Gulag and the killing fields of Cambodia are primitive at best. In essence, the nightmare of "Armageddon" would soon take place because humanity was privileged to access the extraordinary secrets that lie at the heart of creation, and there are those willing to misuse this precious knowledge in the worst possible way.

The implications of such a weapon for anyone opposing China militarily were obvious. This includes America's aircraft carrier fleets that in recent years have been so important to projecting the nation's power. A few neutron bombs exploding in proximity to a carrier group would quickly neutralize much of the force. Most of the people on board would be killed almost immediately, while those ships, that weren't destroyed, would be left to wander like a ghost armada over the oceans of the world.

21

Another, uneventful day on my island refuge while I continue to wait for the greatest war of the ages to begin - one that will eclipse even the epic struggle when the devil's "horsemen" of the Mongols thundered out of the East devastating much of the civilized world of the 14th century. Still I wonder if this horrific spectacle will really take place, and the cruel, age-old drama of warfare played out to its ultimate and most violent conclusion. If it does happen, will the conflict be confined to the vast grasslands and deserts of East Asia, or will it spread to Europe and elsewhere, quickly escalating beyond anyone's control? Only time will tell.

I have moored the sailboat in an inlet on one side of the island, affording it protection from the waves coming from the sea. How fortunate I am to have found such a perfect hideaway where I can await the outcome of the horrific events that now seem inevitable. The radio is my only link to the outside world, although occasionally I see a distant ship passing like a phantom on its way to China's coast. The limited amount of food I brought lasted only a few weeks. Now I depend entirely on the bountiful ocean and fortunately have enjoyed considerable success learning to fish. A few days ago, on the reef surrounding most of the island I caught a large fish that provided me with several, excellent meals. I continue to discover new species of marine life that inhabit these warm waters and with my limited equipment may eventually become a skilled fisherman. In addition, I gather seaweed and the tasty berries that grow here in abundance. It's reassuring to know that I will never want for food. Considering the brief time I've been here, I'm doing well and already feel at home. As a boy I was fascinated by the story of Robinson Caruso, the 18th century seaman stranded on a remote island. In a way you could say that I'm a modern Robinson Caruso; at least I'd like to think so.

At night I often build a driftwood fire on the beach and sitting alone in the flickering light, think of my beloved Lily, who sacrificed herself to save me. I would give anything if she was here. What an idyllic place for two lovers to share. Last night she appeared in my sleep and told me she's alright. How beautiful she looked. I often feel her presence and know that in spirit she will always be with me whether here or anywhere else. I try not to imagine her lying on the floor, her eyes horrible in death - an image that can never be erased from my mind. Also I will never be free of the realization that I am responsible for both her death and Andre's, the two people I truly loved.

A couple of times each day I scan the radio for news the war has finally begun. Usually the reception is good, and I'm able to get stations from all over the world, including many from the States. Without the radio the loneliness would be unbearable. Most of the time I listen to stations from China, although of late there's been nothing unusual in any of the news reports. I'm sure that by now the Chinese authorities know that I'm the one who stole the documents in General Chan's desk, and every policeman in the country is searching for me with orders to shoot on sight.

I can well imagine the astonished reaction of many, communist officials when they learn my true identity. I suspect they will have difficulty accepting the fact that the obsequious opportunist they knew so well, who for the right price was always eager to be of service, was really an espionage agent. After all, on the surface I appeared to be so much like them, and, of course, that was the reason they accepted me. At the office I left behind lots of the propaganda materials that I frequently used to demonstrate my unwavering commitment to the regime. This included an article I wrote for a prominent journal that extolled in glowing terms the close economic cooperation between China and America. Like most scholarly articles published in China, it was nothing but rank propaganda, and the flunky academic, who edits the journal, couldn't praise it enough.

Fortunately all that dissembling is finally over, and I can put behind me those long and troubled years I thought would never end. Always I worried that I would be found out and shipped off to one of the dim hospital wards where brainwashing drugs are administered to those considered a threat or merely undesirable. Most of all I feared being under the total control of the party's henchmen while my mind was systematically erased. It is an insidious process Chinese doctors have brought to perfection, their methods going far beyond anything the Soviets achieved in their own perverted, "psychiatric" hospitals. During my stay in China, I often awakened late at night to ponder what such a fate would be like. Now for the first time in years, I'm able to sleep soundly, the balmy sea air blowing gently in the porthole by my bunk. I had almost forgotten what it was like to be at peace, that never-ending threat finally removed like an enormous weight always about to crush me.

While awaiting further developments in the outside world, I often recall my final meeting with Professor Chesley and still wonder if it's possible that the *Book of Revelations* could have predicted events so far in the future. I have to admit that at first I was skeptical. Nonetheless, based on what I know now, *it appears the sacred text written almost 2000 years ago does in fact accurately describe what will soon take place in the early 21st century.* For instance, John emphasized that the lethal process leading to "Armageddon" would *commence in the Middle East*, when the *"four* angels [of violence] which are bound in the great river Euphrates ...were loosed" (9:14). In fact, this is exactly what has occurred in the "four" nations in proximity to the river, where of late there has been so much violence rooted in religious ideology that supposedly justifies such deeds in the name of God. What could represent more vividly the perversion of human belief that has occurred in various ways during the modern era. John also states that the violence would then spread elsewhere, finally coming to fruition in China and Russia, after "the way of the kings of the *east*... [had been] prepared." (16:12)). And finally there's the location similar in appearance to ancient Megiddo that John saw in his ominous vision - an innocuous looking mountain containing a small town in northern China that all along was the focal point of the regime's grand scheme to wage the most destructive war in history.

I have also pondered the significance of the pivotal number "666" that is emphasized throughout *Revelations*. A particularly revealing passage occurs when the "sixth" seal is opened at Chapter **6**, verse 12 (**6+6**) = "**666**." From the standpoint of numerology this is most significant, and on that basis this brief passage can be regarded as one of the key locations in the entire document: "And lo there was a great *earthquake*; and the *sun* became black as a sackcloth of hair, and the moon became as blood..."

For months I tried to figure out what John could be describing in this powerful vignette, and after speaking with Liao Dan in Macau, I went to various libraries looking for relevant information. It appears that the image contained in Chapter **6**, verse 12 fits exactly the appearance of a nuclear bomb exploding high in the atmosphere Initially it produces a brilliant, white-hot sphere of light resembling the sun that rapidly turns "black as a sackcloth of hair." Then there can follow a red afterglow, and if the event occurs at night, it would briefly color the moon so it appears" as blood." To date, I have been unable to find a more reasonable explanation that fits closely what is described in that pivotal section of *Revelations*.

Such an explosion can be employed to initiate what is known as an "electromagnetic pulse" attack. To produce this result, an EMP explosion emits gamma rays that cause large amounts of electrons to be released that are captured by the earth's magnetic field and directed downward with a devastating effect. A massive release of "radiation" is exactly what a neutron bomb accomplishes regardless of the elevation at which the explosion occurs, and it does so in a far more damaging way than a conventional nuclear bomb. In essence, the image described in *Revelations* (**6**:12) is nothing less than a vivid illustration of history's most deadly weapon that will be the focus of World War III (Biblical Armageddon), causing suffering and a loss of life on an epic scale.

In addition, it appears that this pivotal number ("666") provides invaluable insights into the lethal agenda pursued by the forces of evil throughout history's long expanse. Some might conclude that what follows is mere coincidence. Those who one day read this account will have to decide that for themselves. As Professor Chesley emphasized, the 14th century was the last, historical period when the forces of chaos and violence became so strong that it was thought to be the end of the world. At that time the exploitative activities of a small number of overly powerful, financial institutions gradually crippled the world's fragile, economic system. For more than a century the rapacious banks of northern Italy gained a near-total control of global commerce through monopolistic practices on a grand scale. Entire kingdoms and their means of production were ensnared. Eventually the collapse of these banks caused by their own greed undermined civilized society.

The failure of the "*Black* Guelph" banks commenced in the year <u>1342</u>. Count forward by exactly <u>666</u> years and you come to <u>2008</u> when a comparable, near-total collapse occurred in the modern world's financial system. Once again highly leveraged "banks" and allied groups and institutions engaging in destructive speculation wreaked havoc with the established order. The only thing that of late prevented a total collapse of the global economy is the existence of modern nations and their institutions. In the 14th century there were as yet no such nation-states. Unfortunately after 2008 the pace of large-scale speculation only accelerated.

The precipitous decline of the economic system of the 14th century worsened greatly the destructive effects of the genocidal invasion of the brutal Mongols *out of the east*. Their vicious, mounted hoards destroyed virtually everything they touched. Whole cities were razed to the ground and their populations murdered or enslaved. It is for this reason that in method and appearance the Mongols are often compared to the dreaded Horsemen depicted in *Revelations*. In addition, the Mongols brought with them the insidious plague known as the "*Black* Death," at times even utilizing the plague as the means of facilitating their murderous conquests. This was biological warfare in a primitive sense and the first use in history of what amounts to a weapon of mass destruction. If the parallel with the 14th century is correct, it is reasonable to expect that this latest invasion out of the "east" will also involve some sort of terrible weapon capable of inflicting death on a massive scale.

I also realized that the relevance of "666" can be noted in relationship to other, recent events of significance that are less widely known. This includes the theft of the vital nuclear technology the Chinese are relying on to guarantee victory. In the mid-1990s it was concluded that virtually all of the atomic research information at the Los Alamos Laboratory and other, top-secret American nuclear facilities had been stolen by Chinese agents posing as scientists. This invaluable information, that was pilfered so easily, represents the crown jewels of Western theoretical physics with a military application. Among others, it includes the design of key warheads. The theft of the neutron bomb technology (W-70 warhead) is estimated to have occurred in the late-1970s with the missing details acquired shortly thereafter. From the time of Mao Zedong the Chinese had carefully implemented a multi-generational program intended to displace the United States as the world's dominant power. Emphasis was placed on systematically siphoning off capital and technology by various, devious means.

266

After the mid-1980s and the acquisition of the most lethal, nuclear technology, the character of the program changed drastically, becoming far more sinister. In effect, what had been little more than a vague aspiration among China's hardliners evolved into the plan to wage a massive war of conquest - World War III.

The most recent National Congress of the Communist Party (18th) took place in 2012. *Eighteen is the sum of* "**666**." At the **sixth** Congress in 1928, the PLA (People's Liberation Army) was created to serve the party's objectives that emphasize now the waging World War III. At the 12th Congress (**6+6**) in 1982, the decision was likely made to commit the resources to develop the recently stolen neutron bomb technology - the initial phase of that process completed around 1985. And finally, not long after the 18th Congress in 2012, the fateful decision was finalized to move ahead to war and utilize the neutron bomb and other advanced weaponry to implement the regime's master plan for world domination.

As noted, the genocidal Mongols introduced the first weapon of mass destruction in <u>1347</u>. This occurred at the Genoese possession of Caffa in the Crimea. During the siege of the city, the corpses of those who died of the plague were used as projectiles catapulted over the city's walls. The objective was to infect the inhabitants and thereby defeat the city's impregnable fortifications. Following this and related events, the *Black* Death spread rapidly into Europe killing at least a *third of its inhabitants*. Counting forward by 666, one arrives at the year <u>2013,</u> the year immediately following the 18th National Congress. At that time a new Standing Committee of the Politburo took over under the control of the shadowy, behind-the-scenes group often referred to as the "Elders." *This small cabal of aging fanatics (three from the party, three from the PLA and a seventh swing vote from a leading party member – the one most committed) holds the real power in China. Thus each hand-chosen member of the Standing Committee represents one of these individuals and does their bidding.* The overall party structure merely functions as a privileged, administrative machine that carries out the rigid directives that ultimately come from this unseen group. Contrary to accepted wisdom on the outside, the exalted Standing Committee is nothing more than a carefully controlled tool and glorified figurehead. This deception puts a more benign face on those who really run the country while also concealing the extent of the PLA's influence. The similarity between the so-called "Elders" and the ancient, Chinese emperors hidden away and all-powerful in the Imperial City is unmistakable. Even in high-levels of the party, few know who has gained the right to sit among the Elders and possess such power. *During the 20th century the world was repeatedly thrown into chaos by a small group devoted to a fanatical cause. Now this will happen again with the most fateful consequences, although this time the perpetrators will bring their cruel agenda to its fateful conclusion while remaining unobserved and unknown by a world they could possibly destroy.*

One of the most intriguing disclosures in *Revelations* concerns the fact that three, key, political leaders would play a decisive role causing the events that ultimately lead to the climactic violence perpetrated by the modern, totalitarian state. Thus John refers to "three unclean spirits [who will] come out of the mouth of the *dragon*, and out of the mouth of the *beast* and out of the mouth of the *false prophet*. For they are the *spirits of devils, working miracles*, which go forth unto the kings of the earth and the whole world to gather them to the battle of that great day of God Almighty." (16:13-14).

Professor Chesley explained this statement as follows: "According to Christian theology, the bountiful Trinity (the three personages that comprise God), functions as a unit that creates and nourishes life. In contrast, the three, greatest angels, who rose to oppose God, are embodied in the forms of the "dragon," the "beast" and the "false prophet" – in essence, the tangible counterparties of the Trinity. (It is perhaps no coincidence that "**666**" is a three-part number, each digit the symbolic number "**6**").

"Throughout history these primordial figures have manifested themselves repeatedly in earthly leaders characterized respectively by their reliance on "cruelty," "terror" and "deceit" (or the perversion of belief) - the three, diabolical traits linked together that give power to the modern, totalitarian state. The terminology "out of the mouth" demonstrates John of Patmos' considerable knowledge of Scripture, paralleling a prominent statement in one of the sapiental books regarding Jesus: "I came out of the mouth of the Most High, the first born before all creatures..." *Ecclesiasticus* 24:5. John also speaks of the "miracles" or extraordinary events that these demonic spirits will cause - the term "miracles" indicating amazement at the power yielded by this trinity of evil. Through their chosen, human surrogates, they have repeatedly perverted the course of history and caused catastrophic events."

Upon further reflection, I realized that this is especially true of the modern era that has been influenced in such a malevolent way by three, pivotal leaders: Hitler, Stalin and China's Jiang Zemin, each of whom embodies vividly one of these dark forces. Within China, one can also observe another trinity dedicated to domination in the forms of Mao Zedong, Deng Xiaoping, and also culminating in Jiang Zemin, the cruel leader who among his many, malevolent deeds engineered the systematic destruction of dissidents and peace-loving groups such as the Falun Gong.

John of Patmos tells us that he actually saw the three primordial creatures, who led the celestial rebellion, as they ride forth in flaming glory out of the depths of hell on their mission to inflict on humanity the desolation of history's greatest war: "And I saw the horses in the vision, and them that sat on them, having breastplates of fire, and of jacinth, and brimstone, and the heads of the horses were as the heads of lions and out of their mouths issued fire and smoke and brimstone..." (9:17)

In fiery triumph they emerge
from their distant, burning realm
obscured forever by the vapor of death -
flaming princes who forfeited beauty
to become fire and chaos,
its substance and agents:-
terror, cruelty and the deceit of the false prophet
who inspires the lie, proving
there is no reason for reverence.
We know well their enticing presence
With perverse "miracles" they enthrall us,
bringing fear and cruelty that is beautiful to some
irresistibly seducing the lusting heart.
During the season of the "misshapen,"
they lure us again and again
to despicable places we long to forget,
where human skeletons
wander helplessly through torchlight
and the cries of the desperate are unheard
behind walls of sharpened wire -
the bleak domain of humanity's intimate <u>companions</u>
in our most horrific deeds.

In their wake follows the "fourth beast," the way prepared for the one that brings destruction and is destruction. And now with history's greatest war he will emerge again in all his perverse glory. This fourth beast is described vividly in Chapter 7 of *Daniel*, the Old Testament counterpart of the *Book of Revelation*: "dreadful and terrible, and strong exceedingly…with teeth of iron and nails of brass, which devoured, brake in pieces and stamped the residue with his feet…shall devour the whole earth and tread it down in pieces… till [one day] his body [will be] destroyed and given to the *burning flame.*"

At times I have wondered if it's possible the regime would be successful executing its grand, malevolent scheme. They appear

270

to have thought of everything. This includes not only their clever military strategy but also the way they "enticed" the naïve foreigners into providing the technology and resources that enabled such a corrupt regime to survive and grow ever stronger. I knew, however, that the Chinese leadership had overlooked one, key detail. The destructive forces they planned to unleash are too powerful for any human to control. Once again the inevitable and destructive consequences of prideful hubris or overreaching would intervene to determine the course of history - the profound lesson that humanity has never been able to learn.

How often during the long sweep of recorded time have we seen an age of man commence with enthusiasm, evolve into infallible belief and end in ruin. Although the ancient Greeks repeatedly emphasized this troubling phenomenon in their pioneering drama, they nonetheless succumbed repeatedly to what they condemned so eloquently. One of the most vivid examples is the grand tragedy of the Trojan war, a prideful, life and death struggle over a beautiful, faithless woman that ultimately brought down Mycenaean civilization. That ruinous war became the central parable of Greek literature, embodying the enduring dilemma those insightful people recognized but could never resolve. Now the tragic reality of hubris at its extreme would soon be expressed through organized warfare in its most terrible form. And like the "fourth beast," those willing to perpetrate the horror of a nuclear war would also be devoured by the "*flame*" of the most terrible of all weapons that they have chosen to inflict on others: "And I beheld when he had opened the **sixth** seal, and lo, there was a *great earthquake*...and the great men, and the rich men, and the chief captains, and the mighty men, and every bondman, and every free man hid themselves in the dens and in the rocks of the mountains (underground shelters); And said to the mountains and rocks, Fall on us, and hide us ...For the great day of his wrath is come; *and who shall be able to stand?*" (**6**:12 (**6**+**6**)-17).

22

After a couple of weeks my routine is established, and it almost seems as if I've always lived here. Still no word about the war. Fervently I continue to hope that the Chinese regime under the control of that tiny cabal of determined fanatics won't proceed with their insane scheme. Perhaps at the last moment they will come to their senses. I suspect, however, that too many preparations have been made to change things now. For better or worse, the die has been cast, and regardless of the consequences events will soon be set in motion that no one believed would ever take place.

I feel like a marathon runner who has suddenly stopped and somewhat bewildered, looks back at the blur of what has gone before. Even now, I don't understand fully everything that I've experienced. Eventually I got around to examining the papers hurriedly stuffed in a briefcase when I departed from my apartment for the last time. In a haphazard way these assorted documents form a tangible record of my many years in China - a sequence of convoluted events extending back to that cruel night in Tiananmen Square when my dear mother was murdered.

Near the bottom of the briefcase is an envelope containing an article written by Professor Chesley that he handed me at the conclusion of our meeting. It concerns *"Fatima"* and the events that transpired there in the pivotal year - 1917. At that time certain predictions (the "Three Secrets") were disclosed by a figure believed to be of heavenly origin Although deemed "worthy of belief" by theologians, debate about what they really mean continues to the present. Like many others I paid little attention to the subject, assuming that it involved nothing more than three, impressionable children from a religious background, who naively thought they experienced a spiritual vision. After reading Chesley's article, however, I realized that I greatly underestimated the situation. In fact, Fatima represents nothing less than an episode of profound historical significance, whose importance cannot be overstated. Essentially *this extraordinary episode has a vital relationship to the "Book of Revelations," in essence clarifying with specifics what was predicted almost 2000 years ago.*

In mid-1916, while tending sheep near their home village in central Portugal, three children reported encountering an angel on three, separate occasions. Subsequently on May 13, 1917, they reported something more dramatic: "[seeing a lady who was] *brighter than the sun, shedding rays of light clearer and stronger than a crystal goblet filled with the most sparkling water and pierced by the burning rays of the sun...*" The children believed this mysterious figure was the Virgin Mary, the mother of Jesus Christ. Additional encounters took place on June 13 and finally July 13 when the beautiful lady conveyed to the children the "Three Secrets." In 1941, at the behest of the Bishop of Leiria-Fatima, Secrets One and Two were revealed by the eldest and only surviving child, Lucia dos Santos. (The two, younger children died during the flu pandemic of 1918-1920.) The third and most controversial secret was written down but not made public until 2000, when it was finally revealed by Pope John Paul. Lucia, who became a nun, died in 2005 at the age of 97. Over the years she reported other contacts with the beautiful lady first encountered in the fields near Fatima. Lucia is the source of information about what transpired there, including the written version of the Three Secrets. These cryptic messages ignited a controversy that probably will never be resolved completely.

When word of the visitations became known, the children were ridiculed, and briefly a local official had them jailed for disrupting social order. In general, however, they received strong support by people in the area, and soon thousands of the curious were visiting Fatima. Convinced that skeptics would never believe them, the children asked the lady to perform a miracle that would provide indisputable proof of her visit. As a result on October 13, 1917, an event occurred that became known as the "Miracle of the Sun." It was witnessed by an estimated 100,000 people that included representatives of prominent news organizations. The various accounts of what took place are consistent, and almost everyone who was there reported seeing the appearance of the sun change in highly unusual ways that cannot be explained.

Rain fell most of the day, and after the sky finally cleared, the sun could be seen rotating and changing colors rapidly, some referring to the "sun's dance." A reporter from *O Seculo*, Portugal's most important newspaper, stated that "the sun trembled, made sudden, incredible movements outside all comic law: the sun "danced" according to the typical expression of the people." In the Lisbon daily, *O Dia*, it was reported: "the silver sun, enveloped in the same gauzy purple light, was seen to whirl and turn in the circle of broken clouds... *The light turned a beautiful blue, as if it had come through the stained-glass windows of a cathedral...*"

Outside the immediate area of Fatima, no such, unusual changes in the sun's appearance were seen. As Professor Chesley points out in his article, "there are only two alternatives to be considered. Either tens of thousands of rational people over an area extending about 25 miles, experienced a sudden, mass hysteria; or a vivid, physical phenomenon beyond human understanding occurred that day in the sky over Fatima."

After disclosing the first two Secrets in 1941, Lucia refused to reveal the third, believing the time wasn't right. Two years later, the final Secret was written down. It has proven to be particularly controversial and as a result given the most emphasis. In fact, the most significant secret is actually the Second. As Professor Chesley notes, "unfortunately the full import of that Secret has not been adequately appreciated as well as the close connection of the Fatima episode to the momentous events in Russia that also occurred in 1917.

"In essence, the Second Secret takes the form of Mary's explicit statement, quoted by Lucia, that includes her predictions regarding humanity's immediate future. In contrast, the First and Third Secrets constitute vivid, symbolic descriptions of key aspects of what is conveyed in the Second Secret. Specifically the Second refers to the sudden rise to power of the Bolsheviks and atheistic communism (Marxist Leninism) in Russia, an event that irrevocably changed the course of history. In that pivotal year the great, totalitarian state of the modern era first arose in all its perverse glory and implemented an agenda that emphasizes mass cruelty as well as a virulent hatred of religion. It was the official position of the communists emanating from Lenin that religion was the "opium of the people" and an obstacle to progress. As a result religious belief had to be eliminated by whatever means necessary. Soon a dark night of persecution swept over a vast country that previously was one of the most religious on the globe. Church lands were confiscated; the number of churches reduced from approximately 30,000 to less than 500 in remote, rural areas; and at least 100,000 priests summarily executed. In essence, a religious establishment beloved by the people for centuries was quickly decimated. Other religious groups were also treated harshly including the Jews, who were always persecuted in Russia. Along with a reliance on extreme violence, the communists' antipathy to religion, or in the alternative a willingness to pervert true religion, is characteristic of all modern, totalitarian states. The reason is that a belief in a benevolent God impedes the ability of the state to dominate the citizenry so they can used to further its cruel agenda."

As Chesley explained the interaction of the Three Secrets, "in the Second Lucia quotes what <u>Mary specifically stated</u> about the future. In the other secrets <u>Lucia describes what she saw</u> in the two, accompanying visions that are both vivid and highly symbolic. The Second Secret contains the following, detailed statement:

"...The war (World War I) is going to end; but if the people do not cease offending God, a worse one will break out during the Pontificate of Pope Pius XI (World War II). When you see a night illumined by an unknown light, know that this is the great sign given you by God that he is about to punish the world for its crimes, by means of war, famine and persecutions of the Church...If... Russia will be converted, there will be will be peace; if not, *she will spread her errors throughout the world, causing wars and persecutions of the Church. The good will be martyred... various nations will be ANNIHILATED...*"

"In this way Mary states that if Russia did not return to its spiritual roots, communism would spread elsewhere resulting in catastrophic events of a global nature. Already this has happened. Additional "wars" (plural) subsequent to the First World War were predicted, indicating that this violence on a grand scale would not end with the Second World War. Furthermore, while reference is made to "persecutions of the Church," the term is used generically. Thus religious belief of many kinds would be undermined, an interpretation verified by subsequent events.

"In March 8-12, 1917 (new style or Georgian calendar), the Russian Revolution commenced - the event that gave birth to the modern, totalitarian state in all its perversity. The Czar formally abdicated on March 15, and on April 16 Lenin returned from Europe to Petrograd, the center of the Revolution. On July 1, 500,000 Bolsheviks demonstrated, an unsuccessful coup attempted two weeks later. Finally on November 7, Petrograd was seized and the next day the Winter Palace, a key symbol of the monarchy. These events effectively gave power to the Bolsheviks and are often referred to as the "October Revolution" according to the old style or Julian calendar in effect in Russia at that time.

"These events, that would have such a far-reaching impact

276

on history, occurred in the same timeframe as the visitations at Fatima. The chorological parallels are very close, and the linkage unmistakable. The one (Fatima) is a response to the other, warning humanity in vivid terms of what could lie ahead. The first contact between the children and Mary (May 13) occurred shortly after the turmoil in Petrograd began to escalate. The Three Secrets (the Second of which specifically refers to the events in Russia) were conveyed on July 13 or only a couple of days after the first attempt at a coup. At that time the success of the revolution was already apparent. The miracle of the sun, that was intended to demonstrate the validity of the Secrets, occurred only a few weeks before the Bolsheviks finally gained power. Unfortunately, the Russian nation did not return to its religious roots and instead communism ("her errors") spread elsewhere - "causing wars and persecutions…"

"The Second World War followed - "a worse one [than the First World War].… during the Pontificate of Pope Pius XI." Furthermore, it was predicted that the advent of this second, major war would be preceded by "a great sign given to you by God." On January 25, 1938, there was massive, solar flare activity that disputed radio transmissions over a large portion of the globe. Manifesting itself by multi-colored aurora borealis seen atypically as far south as northern Africa., this solar activity was the most powerful in over 100 years. Some have concluded that it was the so-called "sign" referred to in the Second Secret.

"Because the statement is made that there would be additional "wars," *we can conclude that there will be another, major conflict beyond the Second World War. It will be global and involve unprecedented violence because at that time* "***various nations will be annihilated.***" The terminology employed here is very important, emphasizing two, key words: "various" and "annihilated." Reference is not made to several or numerous nations but instead "various" nations. The word "various" means nations of "many different kinds," implying that they will cover a wide, geographical area.

Furthermore these "various nations" will be "ANNIHILATED." This word is probably the most important in all of the Three Secrets. Thus the subject nations will not merely be ruined or destroyed. "Annihilation" is something quite different. It is the strongest term that could be used. It means "reduced to nothing." Usually warfare merely damages or incapacitates a defeated nation. Rarely is that nation reduced to virtually nothing. During the Second World War several nations were severely damaged. Even after incessant aerial bombing, substantial portions of the targeted cities remained. In only two locations did true annihilation occur - Hiroshima and Nagasaki after they were struck by atomic bombs. Pictures of those tragic cities portray annihilation in the true sense of the term and the nothingness implied. However, *the "annihilation" predicted by Mary will engulf entire "nations" and not merely a few cities. Therefore, it can be reasonably concluded that at some point in the future a war will occur that will be monumental in scope and employ nuclear weapons (World War III) - one in which a number of nations over a significant geographical area will be reduced to nothing. In that regard the ruinous descriptions contained in the Book of Revelations come readily to mind."*

According to Professor Chesley, "the First and Third Secrets serve the purpose of making Mary's explicit words in the Second Secret come alive in a tangible (visual) sense. Thus, in the First Secret Lucia states:

"...Our lady showed us a great sea of fire...Plunged in this fire were demons and souls in human form, like transparent burning *embers*, all *blackened* and *burnished bronze*, floating about in the conflagration, now raised into the air by the *flames*... now falling back like *sparks in a huge fire*, without weight or equilibrium...the demons... all *black and transparent*. The vision lasted but an instant..."

"Mary later comments at the start of the Second Secret that

278

"you have seen hell where the souls of *poor* sinners go." Most scholars have concluded that she is referring to the mythical "hell" of the afterlife, where it is believed that all evil is consigned. However, Mary does not refer to "the" hell but rather hell in a generalized sense as a state of torment engulfing those described as "poor" sinners - a generic term often applied to humanity in the aggregate. Furthermore, the word "poor" implies individuals who are pathetic, deprived and even victimized by circumstances. This is very different from evildoers receiving their just dues for deliberately harmful acts. Mary's message in the Second Secret is not about personal atonement for moral culpability but instead illustrates vividly the catastrophic nature of the events during the final, great conflict set in motion by the rise of modern totalitarianism.

"Many medieval saints had visions of the traditional hell, and while emphasizing visible fire in connection to what amounts to a state of intense, spiritual pain, they differ in key respects from what Lucia describes in the First Secret. What is portrayed in that Secret is likely the "hell" visited upon the "poor" citizens of those nations that will be "annihilated" during the predicted, major war still to come. In fact, many of the descriptive terms that appear in Lucia's account are very similar to those given by witnesses at Hiroshima and Nagasaki - humans turned into "transparent burning embers;" "burnished bronze;" "sparks in a huge fire;" or creatures "black and transparent." Only nuclear weapons can produce this type of grotesque carnage. In sum, the powerful imagery in the First Secret illustrates nothing less than the use of nuclear weapons on a civilian population – the ultimate form of the mass murder that has repeatedly characterized the modern totalitarian state.

In the Third Secret, that is also highly symbolic, the following appears:

"...And we saw in an immense light....a Bishop *dressed in White* 'we had the impression that it was the Holy Father.' Other Bishops, Priests, men and women religious going up a steep mountain, at the top of which there was a big cross of rough-hewn trunks as of a cork-tree with the bark; before reaching there the Holy Father passed through a big city half in ruins, and half trembling with halting step...he prayed for the souls of the corpses he met on his way; having reached the top of the mountain, on his knees at the foot of the big Cross he was killed by a group of soldiers who fired bullets and arrows at him, and in the same way there died one after another the other Bishops, Priests, men and women religious, and various lay people of different ranks and positions..."

"The focal point of this powerful image is the figure in "white." Lucia makes clear that she is uncertain about the specific identity of this individual, although she and the other children "had the impression" it was the "Holy Father" or Pope. The three children came from a nation that is overwhelmingly Roman Catholic. Thus they viewed religious belief in that context. However, the message from Mary concerns "various nations" that would likely include those with differing religions. As a result we can conclude that the figure in white stands for a generic man of holiness representative of the earth's many systems of belief that have been under attack during the modern era. Furthermore, this figure is clothed in *"white," a color often employed in the Book of Revelations to represent Truth.* As stated there: "...arrayed in fine linen, clean and white; for the fine linen is the righteousness of saints...And I saw heaven opened, and behold a white horse; and he that sat upon him was called Faithful and True... and the armies which were in heaven followed him upon *white horses, clothed in fine linen, white and clean...*" (19: 8 - 14).

"In Lucia's vision the figure in white is followed by many,

who accompany him through a "big city half in ruins," where discarded "corpses" of the dead litter the urban landscape - a cruel, desolate place deprived of life. The processional proceeds stoically "with halting step" to a nearby mountain, where the man in white is slain on his knees in the shadow of the great Cross primeval in its character that appears to arise out of the essence of nature itself – formed "of rough-hewn trunks as of a Cork tree." The figure in white and his followers are then "killed" by a squadron of soldiers who fire both bullets and "arrows" at them. Soldiers have not employed "arrows" for many centuries, their use along with bullets indicating that the destruction of truth by violent means is not confined to modern times.

"Through the symbolic images contained in Secrets One and Three, the essence of Mary's pronouncements about the future course of history in Secret Two come vividly alive. Thus it can be concluded that arising out of events commencing in Russia in 1917, the world will experience additional "persecutions" and "wars" - the tragic legacy bequeathed to humanity by the rise of the modern totalitarian state with its contempt for religion and reliance on cruelty. And one day the results of this tragic process will be expressed to the ultimate degree in the greatest war of the ages, a global conflict that will employ the limitless power at the heart of creation to exterminate human life on a truly monstrous scale.

"Finally it should be noted that all of the key events connected to Mary's visitations at Fatima (four) occur on the 13th of the month, especially July 13th (disclosure of the Secrets) and October 13th (miracle of the sun). Thirteen is the sum of seven and six – the key numbers representing God and the realm of evil that structure the inner meaning of *Revelations*. Mary's appearance at Fatima and the disclosures she made about the future occurred at the exact time when the modern totalitarian state arose in all its malevolent glory. She made clear exactly what that momentous event would mean for humanity. This emphasis on the number

281

"13" indicates that what is to come will form the climactic resolution (a violent synthesis) of the two, spiritual forces that have opposed each other through human warfare during the long and cruel reign of the "Four Horsemen." Thus the connection to *Revelations* is readily apparent and also the fact that the predicted upheaval will embody the catastrophic events and great suffering first described by John of Patmos almost two-thousand years ago. And this will happen now because our privileged knowledge of nature's wondrous, inner design will be perverted to cause desolation and suffering beyond imagining that few will escape.

At dawn the earth born anew,
nature's great lantern in the East
that warms the earth and the heart,
bringing the gift of beauty, a summer day.
On a dark, bitter night this gentle radiance
transformed by our own hand
into a fiery globe of radiant death --
the fate of man to be exiled
for the cruelest time to a lifeless shore,
and in the fading light over a desolate sea
witness the comely form broken,
the rose crushed,
while all become the prey
of mutants from the heart of darkness
and gaunt creatures never imagined,
set free to lay waste to the magical land of flowers
and the radiant, rainbow humming bird.

23

One night as darkness settled over the island, I walked by the water wondering if the record I have created of this tragic period will ever be read. Will Professor Chelsey be vindicated, who labored all those years in his study trying to unravel the great conundrum of human history, including the meaning conveyed in *Revelations*? And what will people think of me, the reckless adventurer, who ended up on this tiny island in the middle of nowhere and every day feels himself grow older with little to show for so many years of troubled effort?

The words I have carefully put on paper often seem so inadequate, although it's the best that I could do. Perhaps the subject is so vast and troubling there is no way to capture it completely. In the extraordinary document left by John of Patmos for future generations, he speaks of various "books," including the greatest book of all "held in the right hand of him that sat on the throne, a book…sealed with seven seals." And "I saw the dead, small and great, stand before God, and the books were opened, and another book was opened, which is the book of life…" What is history but humanity's great book or collective tale that records the long and difficult journey through which the meaning of "existence" is gradually determined by our own perilous deeds. Meanwhile each human, who briefly walks the earth, writes his or her personal book that embodies their private quest, in a small but essential way influencing humanity's collective passage. This manuscript written under such unfortunate circumstances represents what I have witnessed - a slender volume that I bequeath now to those who hopefully will read it one day and understand what I have tried to tell them.

The moonlit sea is becalmed with hardly a ripple on its glistening surface. What an exquisite evening. I returned to the boat and lay on the deck staring with wonder at the vast, star-filled sky filled with the twinkling lights of millions and billions of stars and distant worlds. How awe-inspiring. Finally I go to sleep, my heart overflowing with a deep sense of peace because of the beauty of the exquisite order I just witnessed, knowing that somehow I am a part of it.

The following afternoon I turned on the radio again. It is fortunate that I have it - one, lonely man amid the boundless sea, who might perish at any moment and not be missed by another human. The atmosphere is very clear, and the reception excellent, so many stations coming in they almost crowd each other out. After arriving on the island, I made a list of the most important stations around the world and stop at several of them. Suddenly there is intense static. I can pick up only a few stations and wonder if the radio is broken. Later I learn that Washington D.C. has been struck by an atomic bomb that leveled the entire city, killing the national leadership. America is in chaos, and it's uncertain who is in charge of the country. It appears that the bomb was dropped from a commercial airliner, and as far as can be determined, the "death plane," as it is being called, came from the direction of Africa. With its transponders turned off, the plane was almost invisible at night as it came in low over the ocean. Traveling at over 500 miles an hour, it was impossible to intercept. At this point its place of origin cannot be determined.

Throughout the eastern United States the electrical grid has shut down completely along with air traffic control facilities, causing chaos in the skies. As a result a number of collisions occurred in the air resulting in a total loss of life among those on board. With one, modest-size bomb, the mightiest nation on earth has been brought to its knees. My worst fears have been realized. World War III and the inevitable destruction that will result has commenced. God help all of us! Unfortunately the attack is mistakenly attributed to an unidentified, terrorist group that somehow acquired the weapon. It appears to be primitive in design and could have originated from a number of sources. The destructive yield is estimated at three to four times the Hiroshima bomb. Immediately I wonder if the documents left at the embassy ever reached Washington. If so, what was done with them?

Several weeks have passed, and the news on the radio grows increasingly grave. It's apparent how much the United States has been impaired by the attack. This includes the loss of vast amounts of electronic information essential to the government and economy. The daily workings of society are being conducted at the state level, while a substitute national government composed of high-ranking military officers is attempting with difficulty to provide leadership.

One night on the radio I hear a raspy voice speaking Russian that repeats the message that an invasion of the country's Far Eastern territory is in progress. I'm not sure where the station is located. Soon news of the invasion is reported elsewhere. Although many of the satellites passing over the area are blinded by ground-based lasers, it's determined that the invading force is comprised of several columns of infantry and armor emanating from northern China - this large force having literally appeared from nowhere. The reaction of the world community is one of shock and disbelief, everyone astonished that in this advanced age such an invasion could have occurred without being detected beforehand.

For many days no further news as the world drifts into a state of suspended animation. Filled with trepidation I await the next move in this lethal chess match that will determine humanity's fate. Conditions in America continue to deteriorate. In some urban areas the violent are using the opportunity to loot. Still no response from Russia that faces insurmountable problems trying to defend such a large, remote area. Not surprising, the limited Russian force on hand is quickly overwhelmed. Reinforcements are rushed in, and the battle continues. Knowing the details of China's clever strategy, I realize the Russians are being drawn into an enormous trap - the classic, military "cauldron," where they can be encircled and destroyed by a larger force, much of it still lurking unobserved in the tunnel system of northern China. Then even worse news. It's reported that a couple of violent explosions have reduced the Russian army to a mass of lifeless corpses scattered over the battlefield. At the same time their equipment, including tanks, remains in tact. While the dead are left to rot in the sun, the world awakens to the chilling realization that the Chinese invaders possess the neutron bomb and are willing to use it indiscriminately to achieve their objectives.

To get my mind off these terrible events, I explore another area of the reef, where I catch a couple of fish with a new device I have fashioned. A few nights later there's a report that the Russians have struck the invading army with battlefield nuclear weapons. In addition, a furious barrage of nuclear bombs is unleashed on the entranceways of the tunnel system. This pivotal area, that includes the neutron bomb storehouse, has for now become the focal point of the conflict. The vast amount of destructive energy that is released alters the terrain. Based on satellite photographs, the area is described as an apocalyptic scene of destruction beyond imagining. In connection with the site referred to in *Revelations* as "Har Megiddo," John of Patmos observed with amazement that there were "thunders and lightnings; and there was a *great earthquake, such as was not since men were upon the earth* so mighty an earthquake and so great... and the mountains were not found..." (**16**:18-20). "*...the heaven departed as a scroll* when it is rolled together; and every island and mountain were moved out of their places..." (**6**:14-15). Soon the gruesome downward spiral into chaos accelerates. There is news that all of European Russia has been hit with neutron bombs, some of which cause a pervasive, electronic pulse that paralyzes the entire nation. Russia has gone completely dark, and there is a question about how many could still be alive.

During the coming weeks the available news grows even more tragic. It's difficult to sleep, and when daylight appears through the porthole near my head, I'm usually awake. The Russians have attacked heavily populated areas in Herbei province including Beijing and Shenyang that are almost completely destroyed. No doubt the huge, underground bomb shelters recently built beneath China's major cities provide only limited protection: "And the great men, and the rich men, and the chief captains…and every free man, hid themselves in the dens and in the rocks of the mountains…" (6:15). A few days later the Chinese respond by striking every key Russian city with neutron bombs. No doubt, many millions on both sides have perished with additional millions soon to follow.

I sit on the deck, the moonlit ocean becalmed with hardly a ripple on its glass-like surface. A seabird calls from a nearby dune, and suddenly I hear a faint, dull noise like something heavy dropping on a hollow floor followed by a quivering roar. A series of brilliant flashes reverberate through the sky like summer lightning. I know immediately what caused such a menacing sound. A large nuclear bomb has struck one of China's southern-most provinces (that once-lovely tropical region), obliterating many of the people who lived there. In seconds countless, additional souls have disappeared from the face of the earth, vaporized by such a powerful weapon. Wondering how something so terrible could have happened during the advanced 21st century, I know only too well that in recent years supposedly civilized, modern humans have demonstrated repeatedly their capacity for monstrous cruelty. Now

287

this tragedy has happened again on an even greater scale, leaving the survival of much of humanity in doubt.

It's apparent that these suicidal exchanges between Russia and China are only the beginning of a prolonged drama of suffering as radiation spreads and the world plunges ever deeper into chaos. Many cities are dying, and in some nations, especially in central Asia, it appears that much of the indigenous population has perished. Probably the true horror experienced in many places will never be known. This includes areas hit directly by explosions so powerful that afterwards the land cannot be recognized. Russia is littered with dead that far exceed anything experienced during World War II. In China nuclear fallout continues the inexorable process killing additional millions. Around the globe the biggest problem is the lack of food. Countries that still have agricultural reserves attempt to rush supplies to damaged areas, although some are contaminated so badly by radiation it's impossible to enter them.

> Amid the dimming light millions of the lost
> stare with fear at the pulsing, blood-red sky
> above a world that is burning,
> the hot blast of the wind unceasing
> over blackened lands parched and burning.
> The nights and days echo with
> the roar of great waves
> against the cliffs of the land.
> The dirt-filled rains bring no relief,
> oozing over broken window glass
> and the soiled faces of the lost and starving,
> falling in torrents that wash away fields
> and dying towns and the countless dead
> yet to be found, as if nature will weep forever
> for what has been brought to ruin
> by its most wondrous creation of all.

The dust emitted by such massive explosions has risen intothe atmosphere where it drifts around the globe, in places falling to earth in the form of radioactive rain. Crops and livestock are contaminated, and the world's diminished food resources depleted further. Because of the release of so much dust into the atmosphere, the global climate is cooling rapidly, inhibiting the growth of crops needed to replace the exhausted reserves. On the few radio stations that I am able to find, there are gloomy predictions that decades will pass before the world can return to a state of normalcy - that is, if something like that is still possible.

For months not a single ship has passed the island, and without the radio I would have thought that I was the last person on earth. Most of the stations I listened to before the war haven't returned. The sun continues to dim, soon becoming a faint, glowing ball obscured by a perpetual mist suspended over the ocean that has turned a soiled, brown color. The oddly luminous moon barely rises above the horizon and finally not at all. And then *the frightening reality of a world descending into the perpetual night that prevails forever in the cruel realm of the great serpent and his legions of lost angels.* An unrelieved chill has enveloped the earth, and at times the wind off the ocean is so cold I huddle for days inside the boat. The world's climate is in chaos, and I fear the exquisite, natural order, that we humans foolishly took for granted, will never return. There is news of continued lawlessness in many of the world's great cities. Fortunately, with its enormous resources America is beginning to recover.

One night in a troubled dream I see the ruined mansions in the privileged enclaves across America, the once-grand houses built during the recent period of speculative euphoria and self-indulgence. Once coveted and eagerly competed for, these grand structures stand empty now and devoid of life. Illuminated by a ghostly light, they are open to the elements, their opulent interiors and delicate furnishings rotting under a coating of rain and ice. There are far too many to count, thousands and thousands with no one left to claim them for a pittance – a vivid illustration of the sad tale of pride and excess repeated throughout the ages with the rise and fall of great nations. Now I am left to wonder if soon humanity itself, and all that we were privileged to create, will cease forever to exist...

After several, long and agonizing months, the darkness has muted somewhat, becoming a dimly luminous gloom. And then one day what I can only call a true miracle! While I walk by the water, the sun unexpectedly breaks through the mist, and I feel its life-giving warmth on my weathered face. What a wondrous sight, the most beautiful I have ever seen. Immediately I know what this means for the long-suffering world. Gradually conditions around the globe begin to improve, and it appears that humanity's long nightmare will soon come to an end. Even the sea returns to a semblance of normalcy, although while diving on the reef, I discover there are far fewer fish. I have no idea where all the others could have gone.

When arriving on the island, I hoped that somehow this monumental catastrophe would never take place, and at the last moment reason would intervene to prevent such folly. Now large areas of Asia lie in ruin with many locations uninhabitable for generations, perhaps forever. Millions around the world have died from the effects of radiation. Probably it will never be known for certain how many have perished, their tragic end obscured by meaningless statistics that no one can agree on. I try not to think of the irreparable harm done to nature, including the area around the little village where Vera and I walked hand in hand on those perfect, summer days. No doubt, all the beauty that flourished there has perished, replaced by a lifeless realm that soon will be inhabited by grotesque creatures spawned by so much radiation.

In China, chaos continues to prevail in many locations, some of which are still too dangerous to enter. Several of the country's major cities have been destroyed completely, especially in the north. Guangzhou, the old Canton, and Shanghai are also badly damaged. Because so much of China's territory is contaminated, the movement of its desperate citizens northward has become a torrent flowing onto the Siberian landmass emptied of its original population. Ironically the objective for launching the war has to some extent been achieved. However, the cost is so monstrous that it can hardly be viewed as a victory for anyone.

While this tragic spectacle continued to play itself out, I remained on the island for two, additional years, waiting for the situation in the outside world to stabilize. During that interminable period I survived on food provided by the bountiful sea while writing this account of humanity's greatest act of folly. I am reluctant to abandon the safety of my tiny island that has afforded me precious refuge during these horrific years. Eventually, however, I realize it's time to leave. While sailing away, I look back fondly at what becomes only a speck of land that finally disappears far across the water. I know that I won't return. Nonetheless, I will never forget that special place, including the abundant sea life that nourished me and the beautiful birds that flourish there sustained by a faithful adherence to nature's perfect order. At last I will see for myself the tragic land of ancient China where so much torment has been unleashed by the hubris of fools. I'm sure that no one I knew is still alive. At the same time few of them would recognize me, my face weathered from long exposure to the elements. In many ways I'm a very different man.

Finally I sail into Hong Kong harbor and can hardly believe how it looks. The bustling port from which I hurriedly escaped years before is completely empty. Along the shore all the buildings scarred by fire look drab and pitiful with their windows broken. Not a single automobile or person is in sight, although I hear repeated gunshots. The acrid smell of smoke from fires burning endlessly fills the air, the city transformed into an enormous ghost town inhabited by the violent. Like Babylon of long ago that is described in *Revelations*, once grand Hong Kong has become the "hold of every foul spirit and a cage of every unclean and hateful bird…"

As I approach the yacht club, a bullet ricochets off the deck, and I quickly head back to the middle of the harbor, knowing that if I go near the shore again, I won't have the boat for long. Gradually night descends, and a dim moon rises over this desolate place - not a single light anywhere, including in the once-luxurious high-rises of Kowloon. With aching heart, I recall the vibrant metropolis ablaze with countless lights that I saw from Lily's terrace on the night of her last party, everyone drinking sweet, champagne cocktails as string music played softly among the lush shrubs adorning her garden in the sky. At that perfect moment one might have thought that such a magnificent city would last forever, defying time itself.

How I loved that great metropolis of wealth and modern commerce, although at its core it was a heartless place where money could buy anything, even the innocent. Nonetheless, it was grand and exciting, and briefly Lily and I were happy there. But unlike the celestial city John of Patmos glimpsed among the radiant mists of eternity - a *"city that was pure gold like unto glass…[that] had no need of the sun… for there shall be no night there,"* all the fleeting abundance that briefly captured my heart had vanished completely. Once again I recalled John's prophetic words as he gazed upon the desolation caused by Armageddon and reflected on the inevitable decline of all of humanity's great cities amid history's long expanse - the spectacle of fleeting triumph and ruin rooted in mankind's flawed nature. And sadly now that included the forlorn sight that lay before me illuminated by a dim, lifeless moon that seemed hardly real ---

"Babylon, that mighty city... And the merchants of those things, which were made rich by her, shall stand afar off... saying, alas, alas, that great city Babylon, that mighty city for in one hour is thy judgement come. And the merchants of the earth shall weep and mourn over her for no man buyeth their merchandise any more. The merchandise of gold, and silver, and precious stones, and of pearls and fine linen, and purple, and silk, and scarlet...For in one hour so great riches is come to naught. And every shipmaster, and all the company in ships, and sailors, and as many as trade by sea, stood afar off and cried when they saw the smoke of her burning, saying, what city is like unto this great city!... for in one hour is she made desolate...and the voice of harpers, and musicians, and of pipers, and trumpeters, shall be heard no more at all in thee...and the light of a candle shall shine no more at all in thee...**for thy merchants were the great men of the earth; for by thy sorceries were all nations deceived...**" *Book of Revelations* Chapter 18 (**6+6+6**).